A Cruel Courtship

A Cruel Courtship

Candace Robb

WILLIAM HEINEMANN: LONDON

First published in the United Kingdom in 2005 by William Heinemann

1 3 5 7 9 10 8 6 4 2

William Heinemann
The Random House Group Limited
20 Vauxhall Bridge Road, London, SW1V 2SA

Random House Australia (Pty) Limited
20 Alfred Street, Milsons Point, Sydney,
New South Wales 2061, Australia

Random House New Zealand Limited
18 Poland Road, Glenfield,
Auckland 10, New Zealand

Random House (Pty) Limited
Endulini, 5a Jubilee Road, Parktown, 2193, South Africa

The Random House Group Limited Reg. No. 954009
www.randomhouse.co.uk

A CIP catalogue record for this book is available from the British Library

Papers used by Random House are natural, recyclable products made from wood grown in
sustainable forests. The manufacturing processes conform to the environmental regulations
of the country of origin

ISBN 0 434 00912 1

Typeset in Caslon 540 by SX Composing DTP, Rayleigh, Essex
Printed and bound in the United Kingdom by
Mackays of Chatham plc, Chatham, Kent

Contents

In Memory of

Hilde Bial Neurath

ACKNOWLEDGEMENTS

I wish to thank Elizabeth Ewan for sharing with me her research in Scottish women and Scottish history, as well as for reading and critiquing a draft of this book; Kimm Perkins for her research in medieval Scottish nunneries; David Bowler of the Scottish Urban Archaeological Trust for pointing me towards detailed maps of Stirling; Kate Elton, Joyce Gibb, Georgina Hawtrey-Woore and Evan Marshall for careful readings and critiques of the manuscript; and Charlie Robb for photos, maps, and tender loving care on our travels and at home.

Last but certainly not least, I want to thank Peter Neurath for inspiring some aspects of Peter Fitzsimon – his physique, his good looks, and the idea that he posed to me that a great warrior might have fear as the sole motivation for honing his fighting skills. Peter donated a generous sum of money to the Washington State Alzheimer's Association to appear in one of my books and what do I do, I make him an unsavoury character! But he'd given me carte blanche with good humour. Peter's generous gift to this non-profit organisation, which provides much-needed support for those caring for Alzheimer victims, was in memory of his mother, Hilde Bial Neurath, and I in turn dedicate this book to her. In her willingness to open her house to Margaret at a dangerous time,

Ada is a kindred spirit to Hilde, whom Peter described as loving to match people with the perfect house, being a terrific hostess, and enjoying good conversation.

Glossary

barded   adj. caparisoned, protected with armour

carse   n. marsh

cockered   adj. pampered

cruisie   n. an oil lamp with a rush wick

gey   adv. very

Holy Rude   n. 'rude' is dialect for 'rood', or cross; the name of the kirk (not to be confused with Holyrood Abbey in Canongate) is still spelled this way

pows   n. marshy area south of the Forth River, named for all the streams, or pols (becoming 'pows'), that drain it.

spital   n. hospital

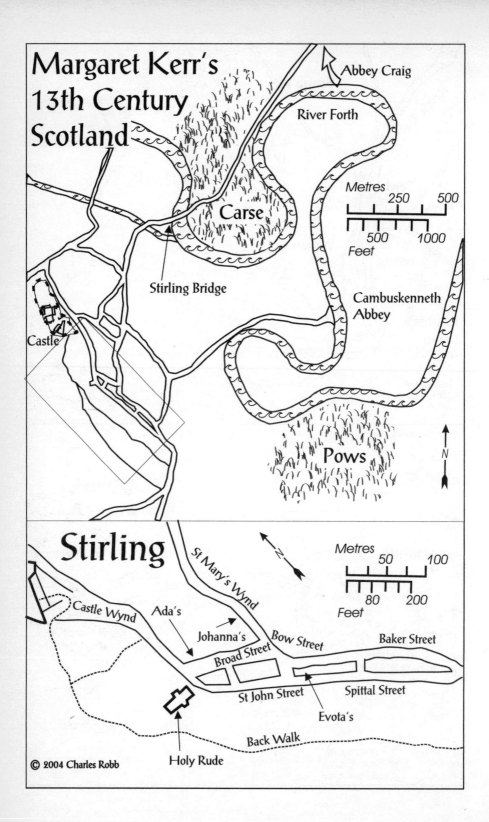

Margaret Kerr's
13th Century
Scotland

Abbey Craig

River Forth

Carse

Metres
250   500

500   1000
Feet

Stirling Bridge

Cambuskenneth
Abbey

Castle

Pows

N

Stirling

St Mary's Wynd

N

Metres
50   100

80   200
Feet

Castle Wynd   Ada's

Johanna's   Bow Street   Baker Street

Broad Street   Spittal Street

St John Street

Evota's

Back Walk

© 2004 Charles Robb

Holy Rude

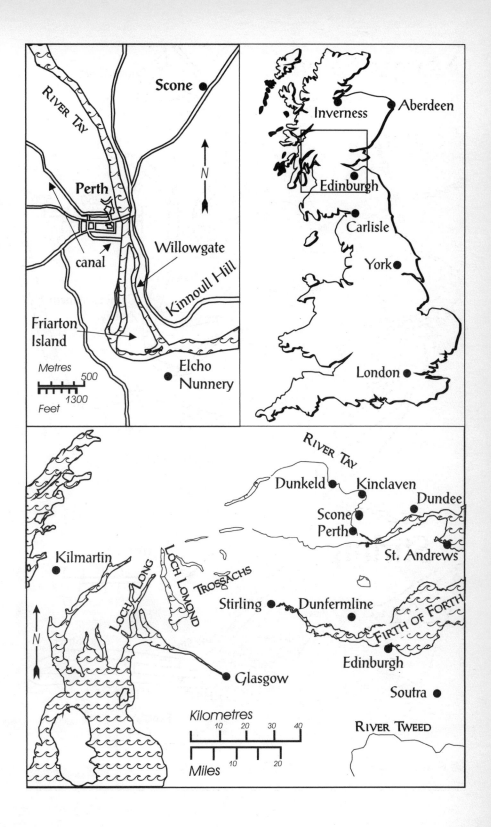

EPIGRAPHS

'Was ever woman in this humour wooed?
Was ever woman in this humour won?
I'll have her, but I will not keep her long.'
Richard III, Act I, scene ii, ll. 228–230

'. . . oftentimes, to win us to our harm,
The instruments of darkness tell us truths,
Win us with honest trifles, to betray's
In deepest consequence.'
Macbeth, Act I, scene iii, ll. 123–126.

PROLOGUE

For this execution the gallows in the bailey of Stirling Castle would not suffice; a special one was set up in the market square so that the townsfolk would find it difficult to avoid. Huchon Allan was a traitor. He'd been caught about to ford the River Forth with more weapons than one man could reasonably use – William Wallace and Andrew Murray were gathering their Scottish rabble on the far side of the river and the English accused Huchon of intending to take the weapons to them. His hanging would serve as a warning to the Scots of Stirling that King Edward of England would not turn the other cheek.

Johanna had never known such fear as she suffered now, nor such a debilitating guilt. She did not doubt the righteousness of her cause, to return King John Balliol to the throne that King Edward of England had stolen, but the danger for her and for her lover, Rob, had never been so real, so clear. She knew from Rob, a soldier at the castle and her unwitting informant, that the English were furious about the raiding of Inverness and Dundee by Murray and Wallace, and that they were expecting rein-forcements soon. They were abandoning their earlier efforts to keep peace in the town, convinced that their generosity had simply bred rebellion.

Johanna had much to tell Archie, the lad who carried the information she coaxed from Rob down to someone in the valley who passed it on to Murray's and Wallace's men. But she'd not seen the lad in days. When she'd first heard that a traitor had been caught she'd feared for Archie, or for Rob, and had been giddy with relief that it was Huchon. But her relief had not lasted, for she knew and liked Huchon and his family, and his capture brought home to her the mortal danger in which she was placing Rob. She worried even more about Archie and what kept him away of late. She'd found it difficult to trust him; in fact she'd urged Father Piers to find someone else to carry the messages. The priest had argued that there was no one else foolhardy enough to take the risk, and they needed someone small and known to be a forager, a lad folks were accustomed to seeing everywhere.

For two days Johanna had been unable to keep anything down, so real had the danger of her activity become to her. Yet on the day of the hanging she could not stay away from the square. She arrived just in time to see Huchon's parents, Ranald and Lilias, led from their house by soldiers. The expressions on the Allans's faces broke Johanna's heart. Only when they were in their designated position at the head of the small group facing the galley was their son led from the kirk at the top of the street and down towards them, paced by a mournful drumming.

'His betrothed has been sent away to kin in the highlands,' said the woman beside Johanna. 'She should have been here.'

'Hush, Mary, she's too young to witness such a thing,' said another woman.

Johanna had not known Huchon was betrothed, but she did not ask to whom, trusting no one now. She said a prayer for the young woman, pitying her for such a horrible end to her betrothal.

Peter, a young, handsome, well-spoken English soldier, read the accusations against Huchon. His manner chilled Johanna, for he read Huchon's death sentence with indifference, as if it meant nothing to those watching.

Suddenly several things happened at once. As the soldiers tied Huchon's hands behind his back and covered his eyes, his mother lunged towards Peter and grabbed his hand screaming, 'What right have you to wear that? Thief!'

Her husband grabbed Lilias at almost the moment that Huchon dropped, his body doing a ghastly jig, his face darkening.

Johanna fell to her knees, hiding her own face in her hands. *Dear God, may he rest in peace*, she whispered over and over to shut out the horrible screams of Lilias Allan.

❧ 1 ❧

Owls

Perth, end of August, 1297

As the summer wore on the presence of King Edward of England's army in Perth began to fray the tempers of the towns-folk. Women increasingly complained of the rude behaviour of the soldiers, and theft was rampant, the thieves aware of the backlog of more serious crimes to be presented at gaol delivery sessions than their small felonies. The walls that the army had reinforced and extended now surrounded the town on three sides, cutting off the merchants' access to their warehouses from the ships in the canal. The English might have compensated for some of the inconvenience by allowing general access along the riverfront on the east – it would have quieted tempers and cost them little in security. Instead they restricted access from the River Tay, allowing only one ship per day to offload. Now ships might idly sit at anchor in the river for days, impeding traffic and slowing trade to almost a standstill. Even though the fighting in Dundee at the mouth of the Tay made shipmen hesitant to sail upriver, some still did, and to the townsfolk the restrictions were symbolic of the potential loss of freedom if Edward Longshanks was not defeated.

For several mornings now the English soldiers had found

breaches in the town walls, small areas where stones had been taken away. Though it was a minor rebellion they were now questioning all who lingered on the riverfront, so that the towns-folk were fearful of going abroad.

James Comyn had watched an interrogation turn ugly the previous day – a man who loudly protested at having his person searched had been thrown to the ground and brutally beaten. That was enough to convince James that he should depart Perth while he could. As a member of the powerful Comyn clan and kinsman of the Scottish king deposed by Edward Longshanks, James was ever wary. He'd intended to leave soon in any case, for he'd been summoned to a meeting with William Wallace and Andrew Murray, the leaders of the Scots who were presently at Dundee trying to force the English troops west towards the highlands where, fearful of being lost in the mist-shrouded valleys, the English would predictably turn south.

As he packed a few possessions an ache in his left shoulder reminded James of the night several weeks past when he had escorted Margaret Kerr to Elcho Nunnery. He'd caught an arrow in his shoulder as he stealthily rowed past Perth – apparently he'd not been stealthy enough. The ache was nothing compared with the pain he'd experienced when the arrowhead had first struck into the muscle. At the time he'd been grateful that the invisible archer on the riverbank had hit him and not his companion in the boat, the fair Margaret Kerr. He still felt the same.

She had been much on his mind the past few weeks, ever since she'd walked away from her husband Roger, who'd been injured by the men guarding the nunnery as he tried to break in. It was not the first time the lovely young Margaret had confounded James's expectations, but this time he was suspicious of his own feelings, of the relief he felt. He'd thought it was because he needed Margaret to continue her work in support of his kinsman, John Balliol, the deposed king. This work was one of the issues that had come between husband and wife, for Roger supported

Robert Bruce for the crown of Scotland. But James found himself seeking Margaret's companionship more and more often – how strange that he'd connived to keep her occupied without understanding he was falling in love with her.

He wished he might ignore the summons from Wallace and Murray – he knew what his assignments were. He'd prefer to begin another journey that was critical to the cause, escorting Margaret and her friend Ada de la Haye to Stirling. He'd agreed to give Margaret a real mission. He hoped he wouldn't curse himself for telling her that the messenger who'd been carrying information from Stirling to the farm of James's comrades down in the valley below Stirling had grown unreliable.

'In fact they've not seen him in a few weeks. I need someone to find out what has happened.'

'You're leaving for Stirling?' she'd asked.

He shook his head. 'I can't go. I'm known to too many of the English and the Scots in the town.'

'I'll do it,' she said, fixing her eyes on his.

'Maggie, that is not why I mentioned it. You can't go.'

'Why not?'

'With the English holding Stirling Castle and town it's a dangerous place. I would not risk you there.'

'As a young woman unknown to anyone in Stirling I would be scrutinised no more than the other townsfolk.'

'But all *are* scrutinised.'

'That is also so in Perth.'

James could not deny that.

By the following day Margaret had recruited her friend Ada de la Haye, also keen to help the cause, as part of the scheme. Ada had a town house in Stirling where they might lodge. Both women were ready to depart at a day's notice.

But now James must delay. What stayed him from disobedience was the possibility that Wallace and Murray might have changed their plans and he might be following discarded orders. So be it. Margaret must wait. He had, at least, presented her with a gift. A Welsh archer had arrived in town after escaping from the Hospital of the Trinity at Soutra Hill, an Augustinian establishment that stood on the main road from the border between England and Scotland. The English were using it as an infirmary and camp for the soldiers. The archer had news of Margaret's brother, Father Andrew, who had been sent to Soutra as a confessor to the English. Margaret had seemed comforted to hear he was well.

Whence comes the knowledge of dreaming when one is dreaming – for a fleeting moment Margaret wondered that, but her sleepy, thoughtful mood quickly turned to dread as she recognised the dream space in which she stood, behind a once unfamiliar kirk, familiar now that she'd dreamt of it so often. It sat on a rocky plateau beneath a great castle that stretched high above on an outcrop. Here below, the kirk was dark except for a lantern over the east door that was for her but a twinkle in the distance; the castle was lit by many torches that danced in the wind of the heights, making the stone walls shimmer against the heavens. At the edge of the kirk yard her husband, Roger, stood atop a huge, scrub-covered rock that rose four times Margaret's height, looking up at the castle. She stood far beneath him in the rock's shadow, terrified because she knew what was to come. *I pray you, Lord, let this time be different. Spare him, my Lord God.* But the cry came, and then Roger came falling, falling, his head hitting the uneven, stony ground with a terrible sound. Margaret knelt to him . . .

An owl's screech rent the fabric of Margaret's dream, letting the true night reach through and waken her. Rubbing her eyes, she rolled over to find her maid, Celia, sitting bolt upright with her hands to her ears, staring into the darkness of the curtained bed in Margaret's chamber. Shivering, Margaret asked her if she'd shared her nightmare.

'It was the shriek of an owl that woke us,' Celia whispered, as if fearful the bird might hear her. 'My ma always said such a visitation was a forewarning that the master of the house is to die.' She crossed herself. 'Master Roger is in danger.'

Holy Mary, Mother of God, keep him in your care, Margaret prayed.

'What should we do, Mistress?' asked Celia.

Waking a little more, Margaret realised that Celia had not shared her dream, but was speaking of the owl on the roof. It seemed a silly worry compared to her nightmare. 'Visitation? Owls hunt at night, Celia, and I'm sure they often alight on roofs. Surely they cannot always mean to warn someone.' Margaret spoke loudly to drown out the chilling rustling of the bird's talons in the thatch.

'This one shrieked and woke us, Dame Margaret.'

When she was a little girl, Margaret recalled, she, her father, and her brothers Andrew and Fergus were out late one night in the water meadows downriver from Perth. A shadow gliding across the moon had frightened her, and she'd screamed as it disturbed the air above her head. Her father had picked her up, and she'd buried her face in his neck. *It was but an owl*, he had said, *and already far away. It is but a bird, Maggie, a bird of the night*.

So, too, might be the owl this night. 'If God means to warn me, I should think He would send a clearer message,' said Margaret. Such as her dream? 'Roger is safe in the infirmary at Elcho Nunnery – the same guards who injured him will do so to any others who arrive unannounced.' She prayed that was true. Turning away from Celia, Margaret settled back into her pillow with a loud sigh that she hoped would silence her maid.

'Can the Sight come to you as an owl?' Celia asked.

Could she not be still? 'In faith, I know not,' said Margaret, 'and I am too weary to wonder about that now.' Second Sight – several of the MacFarlane clan, her mother's kin, were afflicted with it; her mother had nearly been destroyed by it. All her life Margaret had resented the suffering it brought to her family and for years had been thankful that she had not been so cursed. But that had changed of late. 'Go to sleep, Celia. You can conjure more worries in the morn.'

But the damage had been done, for Celia had touched on a subject of much concern to Margaret of late. She shivered as her thoughts turned to the possibility that her mind was opening to the Sight. Celia must be cold, too, because as she rolled and tossed seeking a comfortable position she brushed Margaret with an icy foot. The jolt of cold was like the chill Margaret felt when her surroundings grew strange and time past and future fused with the present. Of late, she might be kneeling in the garden tending the beds when without warning the earth seemed to drop away from her and she would gasp for breath, suddenly somewhere else and possessing frightening powers – hovering over people as she listened to their thoughts. They were often strangers and yet she knew them.

'Shall we light a cruisie and talk?' Margaret said to Celia's back, suddenly wanting the reassurance of her pragmatic company.

'It's still night,' Celia murmured, 'time for sleep.'

She had a talent for sleep – the blessing of an untroubled soul, Uncle Murdoch would have said. Troubled or untroubled, that did not seem to matter for Celia.

Margaret both resented and envied Celia's slumber as she herself lay in the dark weighing the possibility of God's moving one of His most unsettling creatures to cry the darksome warning that her estranged husband was marked for death. His injuries had not seemed mortal, but wounds could so easily fester and then so quickly kill that even the most skilled healer might lose a patient. Indeed, Margaret had based her confidence in Elcho's infirmarian on little information. But the recurring dream of Roger falling to his death made her question her judgment.

She lay in the dark full of remorse for neglecting him. He was her husband in the eyes of God regardless of their estrangement. She did not wish him harm.

The difficulty was that she had promised James that she would wait for him in Perth and then ride with him to Stirling. He had a mission for her, one that she had begged him to entrust to her, and he had particularly asked that she not involve herself in anything that might prevent her from leaving Perth when the time came. James's opinion of her meant a great deal of late. If something were to come of their relationship over and above their work for his kinsman, she wanted James to have the memory of her courage in successfully completing a mission so that he would never look upon her as Roger had done, as a woman to be installed in his household and then largely ignored, never to be a confidante.

That she was thinking of James in a romantic way would puzzle her Uncle Murdoch, who had introduced them in Edinburgh. They had not seemed destined for friendship, let alone anything deeper, in the beginning; in fact, James had threatened her and she had suspected him of being a sadistic murderer. Even now she tried not to think of the events that had led her to believe that of him. She understood that war changed the rules. She tossed in bed, uncomfortable with her acceptance of that. Losing her heart to someone other than her husband embarrassed her here in the dark of the bed she'd shared with Roger. Eager to be of some use, she had vowed to do all in her power to help James in the effort to restore his kinsman John Balliol to the throne of Scotland. Desiring James had not been part of her plan.

She trained her thoughts on the owl's visitation, returning to the question of whether Roger was safe at the nunnery. It was not a small thing, to go to him there. With the English, who held Perth, closely watching the countryside around the town and considering no wanderer innocent, she had little room to manoeuvre. She prayed that her mother might also have premonitions of Roger's danger and warn him. It was because her mother bided in Elcho Nunnery that both Roger and her father were there. Her mother had retired to the nunnery when Margaret was wed. Her father had been pleased for her to do so at the time, but he'd recently returned from abroad determined to coax her back into living as man and wife. Roger had accompanied her father to the nunnery, apparently hoping to convince her mother to give him details of a vision she'd had of Margaret standing with her husband and child watching the King of Scotland arrive in Edinburgh. Roger's chosen lord, Robert Bruce, was understandably keen to know whether he was that king. James, too, was keen, but hoped the king was his kinsman. That they had all arrived at Elcho on the same evening had been an unfortunate coincidence – two boats stealthily arriving on the riverbank had thrown the guards into a panic that resulted in injuries to Roger, his companion Aylmer, and her father.

Although the English soldiers left Elcho Nunnery in peace as a favour to her mother, who had to her shame done them an inadvertent service, Margaret feared she might not be included in her mother's protected circle. It was possible the English knew of her connection to James Comyn, and thus to William Wallace and Andrew Murray, who were fighting to return the throne to John Balliol. She should not risk the possibility that the English might be waiting for her to leave the town and the protection of her neighbours so that they might take her for questioning without raising an alarm. But she had agreed to help James, and so she must wait for his escort.

Margaret's resolution unfortunately did nothing to help her sleep, for she had a wealth of worries awaiting her attention. The owl's visit was only the most recent one. She had hoped to enjoy some quiet after the storm of familial troubles that had brought her back to Perth from Edinburgh. She must have been mad to think there would be any peace for her when all her family were involved in the struggle between the Scots and King Edward of England. The immediate danger was a fresh English army approaching the southern border. Margaret had thought the summer's end would be relatively peaceful because King Edward was in the Low Countries, but apparently his presence was not necessary for an attack. Worst of all, the army would be marching across Soutra Hill, the site of the spital where her brother Andrew was confessor to the English soldiers. His assignment there was a condemnation, for as he was a Scot he would never be released now that he had heard the confessions of the enemy – which is precisely why his abbot had sent him there.

Worries upon worries, cares upon cares. Yet despite it all Margaret must have drifted off because suddenly the dawn shone softly through the bed curtains that Celia had parted as she slipped out.

'I must go below,' said Celia, noticing that Margaret stirred.

'Tom can see to the kitchen fire,' Margaret assured her.

'He can't manage everything,' Celia said. 'If we overwork him we'll lose him.'

The new servant was a young man with whom Margaret was mostly delighted; he was efficient and energetic, though she did wonder why he had not chosen a side in the struggles and gone to fight. Celia believed that a man might be just as reluctant to fight as any sensible woman would be. Indeed Celia worried that Margaret's hovering might frighten him off when there were so few young men to help with the heavier work.

Falling back on the pillow, Margaret immediately resumed her inner debate about whether Celia had been right about the owl and she should go to warn Roger. But she had no idea what to warn him about. It had been his choice to risk his life and his property, knowing full well that as Robert the Bruce's man he would be considered a traitor by the English. And the owl might simply have been hunting.

Margaret spent the day in her garden, arguing with herself about her responsibilities while cutting down the spent plants, weeding, hoeing composted leaves from the previous year into the soil. It was good work for anger, and she had the garden to herself while Celia was at the river with the laundry.

This was not a time to put her own feelings first, especially since she had coaxed James into allowing her to take on this mission. Wallace and Murray needed news from Stirling Castle and the lad who'd been providing it had been failing them. News from the castle was critical because in order to regain control of their country the Scots must control the crossing of the River Forth, which was guarded by Stirling Castle – now in the hands of the English. Therefore they must wrest control of Stirling and its castle from Longshanks's army.

She'd wondered why they'd left it so long. It had seemed foolhardy for them to focus so much of the summer's fighting at Dundee when holding the bridge over the River Forth was so crucial to the protection of the north. She imagined that merchants concerned about their shipping were buying some of Wallace's and Murray's wits, pressuring them to keep the port open. Now, with English forces approaching, the two needed as much information about the English plans as possible, and as soon as possible. Margaret could not allow her concerns about Roger to distract her. She could not jeopardise the mission she'd fought for by rushing off to Elcho.

Certainly Roger had not put aside his work for Robert Bruce in order to pay attention to her. And therein lay the crux of their marriage's failure. Roger had disappeared the previous autumn, promising to return by Yuletide, but he had not returned until early August, lying his way back into their conjugal bed by swearing that he'd not meant to desert her, but rather he'd been caught up in the struggle against Edward Longshanks and then judged it dangerous to communicate with her. Margaret had been cautiously happy for a time, particularly with the bed sport, but once she'd learned the extent of Roger's lies she could no longer trust him; nor could she see how they could peaceably bide together while supporting competitors for the Scottish crown. She wished he might have come round to her way of thinking.

Margaret did not understand how Roger could believe that the Bruce, who had until very recently supported the invader, King

Edward Longshanks of England, cared a whit for the people of Scotland. Two powerful Scots families had made claim for the empty throne, and Longshanks, invited to advise, had chosen the Comyn claimant, John Balliol. Now Robert Bruce, the young heir to the other claimant, was gathering supporters. Roger argued that Robert Bruce was the country's only hope against Longshanks, that he'd proved steadfast in his defence of Ayr against the English troops in weeks past. That he had not surrendered despite being overpowered was proof of his loyalty to his people. As punishment for his rebellion Bruce was to deliver his daughter to the English as a hostage. Margaret had said a prayer for the daughter, but she'd reminded Roger that Robert Bruce had been defending *his* lands, which was no more than his duty. When Roger further argued that John Balliol had failed his people and would never regain their confidence or even more importantly that of the nobles, his argument had fallen on deaf ears, for Margaret was convinced of the opposite, that the nobles, including Robert Bruce, had failed Balliol, their king.

Their warring loyalties and Roger's lies had created such a rift in their marriage that Margaret had finally suggested to Roger that he use whatever influence and wealth he had to annul their marriage. But it seemed he'd belatedly decided their marriage was salvageable.

She slept poorly again that night despite all the tiring work in the garden, plaguing Celia with her tossing, eventually falling into a brief, exhausted sleep at dawn. Waking with the indecision still gnawing at her, Margaret pushed back the covers and pulled aside the bed curtains. Sunlight streamed in the open windows and filled the room with a delicious heat. She was grateful for the warmth of the floor as she slid out of bed. She might think it a glorious day had there been no owl a night past. But it had kindled a sense of guilt she'd struggled to ignore, and now she thought that because she'd been anxious to escape Roger she'd not questioned the level of care he would receive at Elcho if she were not there to supervise.

She struggled into her simplest gown, impatient with her awkwardness. She'd become too accustomed to Celia's assistance in dressing. She was muttering to herself when a darksome thought stopped her in mid-motion: Celia believed the owl portended the death of the head of the household – not a possibility, but a fact. There was nothing she could do to avert his fate. Nothing . . . She rejected that idea as she slipped on her shoes and went off in search of Celia. Margaret could not think that God would be so cruel as to warn her if she was powerless to prevent her husband's death. God was good. God was love. God was at least reasonable or mankind was doomed.

But should she not at the very least tell Roger of her fears? In the eyes of the Kirk she should honour her marital vow above her vow to James Comyn. She should go to Roger at Elcho Nunnery. It was only a short distance downriver. Besides, James was away, somewhere between Perth and Dundee conferring with Wallace and Murray – he might be away for a long while. She would leave a message with one of his men still in town asking that James meet her at the nunnery and continue to Stirling from there.

In the kitchen, drawing Celia away from the capable Tom, Margaret proposed her plan – the woman was not only her maid, but her trusted confidante, although she had told her nothing of the visions or the recurring nightmare.

Celia listened, hands on hips, never one to let her small stature give the impression of timidity. As soon as Margaret had presented her case, Celia rejected it with a shake of her head, her straight dark brows joined in a forbidding frown. 'I fear you're thinking with your heart, not your wits, Mistress. Master James instructed you to bide here until he returns, and you did promise.'

Margaret threw up her hands. 'Then what am I to do about the owl that so frighted you the other night? It's not like you to defend James – you do not trust him.'

'But neither do I trust Master Roger.'

'So I'm to say nothing to my husband?'

'Perhaps a messenger could be sent?'

Margaret imagined asking someone to risk their life to tell Roger that a bird had warned her that he was marked for death, and it made her wonder at her own wits for having given it any thought at all. Still, it had forced her to face her unease about his welfare.

'Dame Margaret?' Celia awaited a response, her brows knit in concern. 'Are you unwell?'

'No, uncertain what to do. I need advice from someone less caught up in these matters of the heart, but there are few I trust in Perth since the English arrived. Folk are too eager to prove themselves friends of the English in order to protect their property.'

'I'm sorry I've given you a new worry.'

'Not a new one. You merely made me face myself.' There *was* one woman she trusted. 'We'll consult Dame Ada.'

Ada de la Haye was not only Margaret's old friend but she also happened to be an integral part of James's plan, for she was to provide lodgings for Margaret in Stirling and a plausible reason for her presence, as well as being a travelling companion.

Celia nodded her approval.

By the time they crossed North Gate the sun beat down unmercifully. What faint breeze came from the river did little to relieve the heat. Margaret and Celia mingled with townspeople listlessly going about their errands. Fortunately Ada de la Haye's house was not far along the main street, and the two women were soon welcomed in to the cool shade of Ada's hall. From without it was a modest house, disguising the wealth of the inhabitant and the richness of the furnishings within.

The de la Haye family were well connected leaders in the community, but Ada's station and wealth had to do with her kin's ambition, not their generosity. She'd been an orphaned niece who was given the choice of being a pawn for the family's gain or being married off to either a very elderly man or a younger son. Having set her mind to wealth, and already fond of men, Ada had chosen to be a mistress to the powerful and thus aid her family's influence in politics. Marriage had sounded boring to her.

For many years her beauty and grace had held the devotion of her lover. Simon Montagu, an Englishman who had won King Edward Longshanks's favour in combat and diplomacy, had been generous to her, and now in her mature years she enjoyed a comfortable life. After returning to Perth from the English manor on which Simon had kept her, Ada had in turn been generous to St John's Kirk and had thus earned the respect of the community on her own terms. She was an educated woman and despite her unmarried state she was as influential as any de la Haye. In short, she was a force to be reckoned with. Margaret admired her above all women and most men. In her childhood she had often fantasised about life as Ada's daughter, particularly when her mother Christiana was lying abed, exhausted after having a vision.

Now Ada, elegant in her silks, her white hair caught up in a fussy cap that emphasised her still slender ivory neck, listened with growing concern to Margaret's account of the owl, and her indecision. Margaret relaxed as she spoke, imagining that Ada was already devising a plan, but was disappointed by her friend's initial comment.

'This is too unlike you, Maggie. All this confusion because an owl lit on your rooftop two nights ago? Are you unwell?'

Perhaps she was – it was the second time someone had asked that this morning.

'I upset her with my ma's tale of the owl,' said Celia.

'She woke me to my responsibility,' Margaret said.

Ada sat back a little, gazing at the ceiling. 'I tried hunting with owls when I lived in the south. I loved their silent flight and their feather weight – despite their huge wingspans, long claws and noble beaks they weigh so little.' She tilted her head and smiled as if admiring one on the blank ceiling. After a pause, she drew her attention back to Celia. 'They are fierce birds; one would be unwise to trust them. It seems perverse to cast them as messengers.'

Celia shrugged.

'But I hear something else in your words, Maggie,' Ada continued. 'You will be no good to James Comyn while you fret about Roger. Perhaps it would be best to begin our journey to Stirling by visiting Elcho. My menservants can escort us. My household has made the journey before, though, I grant you, we haven't for a long while.'

Celia gave a little cry. 'But Master James–'

'Needs your mistress calm, Celia. What he is asking of her requires that she have all her wits about her.'

Ada was right, Margaret thought, and she wished only that she had expressed herself more rationally. It frustrated her to have stopped short of reasoning through her worries so that she might have simply said that until she was satisfied that Roger was receiving the care he needed she would not be able to concentrate on her work for James.

'How soon might we depart?' she asked Ada. She was sorry to see Celia's stony expression, which clearly conveyed her regret about having said anything about the owl. If stopped by the English Margaret might explain her own travel to Elcho – both her parents and her husband were biding there. 'But how can I explain a company of not only my maid but you and your servants, Ada? The English here in Perth have no doubt heard of your former connection to Simon Montagu, but the mere act of leaving the town seems to make one suspect.'

'I pray you, one question at a time is only fair,' said Ada. 'Why not leave tomorrow? We'll manage, Maggie, just as we planned to with James escorting us.' Ada cradled one of Margaret's hands in both of hers. 'Do not be fearful of God's intention. I do believe He means for you to thrive.'

'I am doubting,' Margaret admitted, dismayed by how quickly she'd slipped back into doubt. If she was to be of service she must trust that it was God's will.

Ada pressed Margaret's hand, then let go as she rose. 'Come, let us prepare.' She smoothed down her skirts, ready for action. 'A few of the household will ride straight to Stirling with enough silver to bribe any soldiers on the way. I want my bedding to be there on my arrival.' She broke out in an impish grin.

Margaret had only recently discovered Ada's penchant for intrigue; but she'd learned to expect the unexpected from her friend.

'I'll leave a message for James, and I'll also tell Tom where we'll be, in case James comes first to my house,' said Margaret.

She often wondered what unnatural powers Ada wielded that fed her confidence, for on the following day they were miraculously spared the need to explain their journey to anyone. Indeed they travelled through a quiet countryside to the nunnery with no encounters with soldiers.

Elcho Nunnery sat on the south bank of the River Tay just beyond where it turned east from Perth towards the sea, across from the high promontory of Kinnoull Hill. The whitewashed nunnery buildings were primly clustered on a gentle mound that rose from the water meadows, like a swan atop her nest. Prioress Agnes de Arroch delighted in beautiful surroundings, so the grounds flowered cheerfully in late summer and all was ordered and pleasant. The prioress's kinsmen guarded the dozen nuns and their servants, the chaplain and the staff. The armed men of either side in the struggle for the throne might find a convent a tempting place to loot.

The guards recognised Margaret at once and escorted her small party safely to the nunnery. Her father, Malcolm, napping in the guest-house hall, woke with a start as Dame Katrina, the hostelleress, welcomed them.

He was paler than when Margaret had last seen him, the eyes beneath his bushy brows dull and shadowed, and his belly had shrunk. She was surprised that he'd stayed so long at the nunnery;

he must truly be determined to win back her mother. While their maids arranged their belongings, Margaret and Ada took some refreshment with him.

'What brings you to Elcho, Maggie?'

'My husband. How is he, Da?'

'Fairly mended. But here I thought you a clever lass to choose your time so cunningly, for you've just missed him. He left a few days ago.'

'No!' Margaret cried.

Ada slipped a protective arm around Margaret.

'Dear Lord, watch over him,' Margaret prayed as she crossed herself. It had never occurred to her that Roger might no longer be at the nunnery. 'Did he say where he was going, Da?'

'You're as changeable as your ma,' Malcolm exclaimed. 'You hated him a fortnight past.' He shook his head and winked at Ada. 'I feared she'd forget his neglect and go running to him.'

'She has forgotten nothing,' Ada said, 'but the other night–' she stopped as Margaret nudged her foot. 'She wished to consult him about business.'

Margaret was grateful for Ada's quick wit, having no intention of telling her father about the owl.

'Did he leave with Aylmer?' she asked. The man had been Roger's travelling companion, a kinsman of Robert Bruce. Margaret loathed and distrusted him, with good reason, but at least he might watch out for Roger.

'Aye, they left together. Don't tell me you're worried about Roger?'

'As Ada said, I needed advice on a business matter.'

'Humph. Well, I could help you with that,' said Malcolm.

'And you, Da? How are you faring? You don't look well.'

'It's your ma.' He launched into an account of her mother's extreme repentance, how her condition was breaking his heart.

Margaret knew why her mother undertook such extreme

penance; through the use of Second Sight Christiana had unintentionally caused the death of five of her countrymen at the hands of the English invaders on Kinnoull Hill. Although she had been coerced by the prioress and her kinsman to fabricate a vision that would lead the English away from the nunnery, it had touched off a true vision over which Christiana had no control. Once in its grip she'd been unaware of what she said or did. Yet she insisted that the blame fell squarely on her shoulders because she had ignored her misgivings about playing at a vision. All her life Margaret had witnessed in her mother the suffering brought on by Second Sight, and this was why she so feared it. But the tragedy on Kinnoull Hill had left Christiana more shattered than ever before.

Despite all his years of complaining about his wife's behaviour and his original enthusiasm for her withdrawing to Elcho Nunnery, Malcolm obviously loved her and belatedly regretted their separation. Eyes glistening with tears, he described his attempts to convince Christiana that God did not require her penance, and surely nothing so severe as what she had undertaken.

'She'll not listen to me. But you might reach her, Maggie,' he said with a spark of hope.

Margaret climbed the stairs to the gallery and approached her mother's chamber dreading what she would find. She would have preferred to go to the kirk and pray for Roger, sick at heart that he'd departed the nunnery on the day after the owl had presaged his death. She was frightened that her dream of his death was a foretelling.

Marion, Christiana's handmaid, welcomed Margaret into the room with her customary apologies.

'I have done my best to convince her to eat . . . I have not been able to console her . . . I have not the gift . . .'

'Bless you for all you do,' Margaret said, taking in the chaos of a chamber stuffed with the contents of several much larger rooms.

Her mother had found it impossible to part with all of her things when she had retired to Elcho and the room was filled with tapestries, cushions, chairs, small tables, all exquisite gifts brought back by Malcolm from his travels.

'Dame Christiana spoke of your arrival yesterday,' Marion continued. 'She hopes you will untangle the tablets for the border she has been weaving while the two of you talk.'

'She knew yesterday that I would come?'

Marion nodded.

Margaret wondered whether the owl had brought this news to her mother. Such a messenger, such messages unasked for, these were not changes she welcomed. *Dear God, I humbly pray you, relieve me of the Sight. I am not worthy. I haven't the wisdom to use it for the good.* As she stepped around the carved screen that shielded her mother's bed she found Christiana lying with eyes closed, though it was mid afternoon. Stepping back, Margaret whispered to Marion, 'My father thought she might be awake, but I see–'

'Do you speak only to my maid, daughter?' Christiana called out in a voice that was scratchy, as if little used.

'I thought you were asleep.'

Marion shook her head in sympathy. 'She drinks little water. Her throat is ever dry,' she whispered.

Returning to her mother, Margaret knelt and kissed Christiana's parchment cheek. Despite the mounds of bedclothes her skin was dry and cold. A month ago she had still been lovely, indeed had seemed more vigorous than in recent years. Now her eyes were shadowed, her hair greyer.

'How is Ada?' Christiana asked.

Margaret wondered whether her mother had been told about her arrival or whether she had foreseen her visit. She did not ask. 'Ada is well, Ma. And you? Are you eating? Resting?'

Christiana stopped the questions with a cold finger to Margaret's lips. 'I am as you see me, as the Lord hath made me.' She fumbled about. Marion hastened over to hand her the basket of tablet weaving. 'Can you untangle this, Maggie? It's snarled and needs your patient hands.'

Glad for the distraction from her mother's condition, Margaret took the basket and sat down on a high-backed chair that Marion had placed close to the bed. The work was far more skilled than anything Margaret could recall her mother doing. The pattern puzzled her for a moment, but after some study she recognised the outstretched wings and the large, round heads. 'Owls,' she whispered with a shiver of dread.

'The work helped me stop thinking about the men who died,' said Christiana. 'But one night the head on which I worked became a man's and I saw that he was tumbling from Kinnoull Hill – one of the men I betrayed.' She gave a sob and turned away from Margaret. 'I could not bear to hold it.'

The Sight was a curse. Her mother had received no joy from it, her marriage had been ruined by it, her children had suffered. A cold panic numbed Margaret's fingers. *Dear Lord, not me.*

'Marion,' Christiana called out, 'I would sit up in my chair now.'

Margaret glanced up from her work and involuntarily winced as she witnessed how Christiana clutched Marion's arm and struggled to rise from the rumpled bed. Beneath the wool tippet her mother's thin gown hung loosely. Her hands were claw-like in their fleshlessness.

'How long have you been fasting?' Margaret's voice cracked with emotion.

'You know when my penance began,' Christiana said. 'You tire me with such questions.'

Marion held firmly to her too-slender mistress, helping her shuffle to the cushioned chair near the bed. Christiana held Marion's hand as she turned and sank down, and then the maid quickly tucked a lap rug about her. All was done with practised efficiency. Such quick deterioration bespoke a severe fast. As Marion straightened she gave Margaret an apologetic look and shook her head. Margaret did not blame the maid. Her mother would be far worse if she were not in Marion's loving hands.

Christiana studied Margaret with fevered eyes. 'Did Malcolm send for you?' Her voice was surprisingly stronger now that she was sitting up.

'No, Da did not summon me. I came here to see how Roger was healing before I go on to Ada's house in Stirling, but I've learned he left a few days past.'

Closing her eyes, Christiana slowly nodded, and tears began to fall. Bowing her head, she crossed herself.

Margaret's heart skipped a beat. 'Ma, what is it?'

'I fear for him,' Christiana whispered.

'What have you seen?'

Christiana shook her head. 'I did not need the Sight to ken his condition. He has not recovered enough to travel. He limps so, he will be unbalanced in the fight.'

'What fight?' Margaret asked. 'You must have had a vision.' Not to mention that it was not her mother's wont to be concerned about the consequences of another's affliction.

Christiana's pained expression suggested an affection of which Margaret had not been aware.

'What have you seen, Ma?'

'I told you, I saw how he limps.' Christiana looked at the tangled yarn and tablets in Margaret's lap. 'Oh, put that aside, Maggie. I haven't the strength to work on it anyway.'

Margaret persisted, finding the painstaking unravelling calming. 'Did you see Roger often?'

'I asked after him daily. When he was able to walk along the gallery he came to see me at least once a day. He is a good man, Maggie, a kind man. He told me you spoke of annulling your marriage. Did you?'

Margaret was confused by her mother's sudden approval of Roger, whom she usually disliked. 'You know of our troubles,' she said. 'Some things cannot be mended.'

'But you came now to see him?'

'I loved him once,' Margaret said. 'We are still man and wife in the eyes of the Kirk.'

'Indeed you are, and he means to keep it so. Pity. You are only nineteen and so pretty – we might have found you a more worthy husband.'

'But you just said he is a good man.'

'Did I?' Her mother looked at her with an expression so blank Margaret thought it must be sincere.

'Ma, do you know where was he going?'

Christiana averted her eyes, but not before Margaret saw a shadow fall across them. 'He did not say.' She shifted in her chair and fussed with her sleeves. 'Why are you for Stirling? What is there for you?' Her voice trembled.

Margaret could not confide in her mother; in her state she could not be trusted to practise discretion. 'I have been lonely. Ada has invited me to her home in Stirling for a while. There is nothing holding me in Perth, so I am accompanying her.'

'If only you'd had children. They give a woman purpose.'

Margaret agreed. But God had not yet granted her children.

'Would that you had the Sight,' Christiana murmured, then shook her head fiercely. 'No, no I did not mean to curse you with this wretchedness.'

This wretchedness. Margaret shivered. 'Why did you choose to weave a border of owls, Ma?'

'Aunt Euphemia said owls had the wisdom of women and lived in the moon's cycles, as we do. I feel the need of the owl's strength.'

'Celia told me that her ma believed that when an owl alights on a roof and wakes the household the master is marked for death. Have you ever heard that?'

'I recall something like that. There are no roofs in this border.'

Not wishing her mother to read anything in her eyes, Margaret kept them lowered and tried to focus on the matter of her mission to Stirling.

But what came to mind was David, the Welsh archer James had brought to her in Perth, the man who'd deserted the English army at Soutra, intent on finding William Wallace and fighting for him. He'd brought news of her brother Andrew.

She remembered how shocked she'd been by the archer's condition. 'But you should be abed,' she'd said to David, looking askance at James. It was inhuman to push this man to speak to her when he was so ill. He was sweating and obviously weak with fever, and his hands and face were disfigured with a crimson rash. Margaret tried to keep her gaze from it after expressing her sympathy that the brothers at the spital had been unable to ease it.

David had lifted his hands, turned them over to reveal oozing scabs on his palms, and shaken his head. 'It was not for this I was at the spital, Dame Margaret. It is the price I paid for my freedom. I escaped by crawling out of the infirmary drain, which carries away the blood and offal.' He gave a little shrug. 'Freedom to choose for whom I fight – that is not so easily won. When I heard that you were Father Andrew's sister I asked to come to see you.'

Celia brought cushions for the one chair with back and armrests and Margaret invited David to sit. She took a seat on a bench, James beside her.

'Andrew is well?' Margaret asked.

'He is,' said David, 'and respected by all the men. All trust him and find comfort in his presence, which is as it should be with a priest, I'm thinking.'

'All the men,' Margaret said softly, 'even the commanders? The master of the spital?'

David nodded. 'It is plain to all that Father Andrew was called by God to be a confessor to men. He chooses no sides.'

Celia brought ale and they were quiet as she poured.

'He spoke of you, Dame Margaret,' said David after a good long drink. 'He said if I made it, and if by some blessed chance I saw you, that I should tell you he is glad he went to the castle.' The man kept his eyes on his cup as he spoke the words, as if he did not wish to know how they were received.

Margaret crossed herself. 'Bless him,' she said softly. Andrew's subtle message was that he did not blame her for being sent to Soutra. Ah, but she still blamed herself. She had asked Andrew to go to the English sheriff at Edinburgh Castle, the father of an acquaintance from his time at Oxford, to inquire about her husband. Andrew had disobeyed his abbot in granting her wish. It was this defiance that had sealed his fate.

'Father Andrew knew of your plans to desert?' James asked, half rising to reach for more ale.

'I had much on my mind, and Father Andrew listened. He sometimes talked about God's kingdom on earth, how men should all join together in community, and how it's our greed and jealousy and fear that divide us. He is a holy man, Father Andrew is,' David said, nodding down at his cup.

For a moment, no one spoke. Margaret was moved and not a little surprised by the man's description of her brother. She had never doubted Andrew's vocation, but she had never heard anything so profound and all-encompassing from his mouth. 'How do the other priests regard him?'

'He and Father Obert seem easy with one another. I think Father Obert worries that he will lose Father Andrew to a more important post.'

'In truth?' Margaret murmured, glad that Andrew had a friend in his fellow priest. At least he had that companionship, and perhaps protection.

'It is men like Father Andrew who helped me see the evil in King Edward's ambition.'

'I should have thought a Welshman would have learned to hate Longshanks while in swaddling clothes,' said James.

Something in James's tone caught Margaret's attention, and she realised how restless he was, playing with his cup, shifting on the bench. James was not easy about David. Neither was

Margaret. She did not believe his last statement.

'My da said that Scots fought with Longshanks against us, so it was fair to return the favour,' David said, ducking his head. 'But Father Andrew helped me see it differently.'

'Did he encourage your desertion?' Margaret asked, anxious about her brother's trust of this man.

'He – no,' David shook his head. 'He made sure I understood the danger. Not that he knew how I meant to sneak away. He forbade me to tell him that.'

'You said he is well. Does he seem – content there?' Margaret asked.

'Not when he talks of home. And how nothing is as it might have been. But as I said, he is respected and the soldiers are grateful for his readiness to hear confession at any time.'

Later, Margaret learned that James was indeed uncertain whether to trust the Welshman, so he was keeping David in a shed in the backlands with a midwife to attend him.

'He'll not fight with the Wallace?' Margaret asked.

'I would not risk it,' said James. 'He escaped too easily for my comfort.'

'The rash, Jamie, and the fever – his escape brought him great hardship.'

'It smells wrong to me, Maggie.'

'Except for his suffering, I'm uneasy about him too, Jamie.' Margaret admitted. She wondered whether there were different degrees of the Sight.

The thought brought her out of her reverie and back to her mother's quiet, stifling room. The tablets were in order now. She handed the basket to her mother.

Christiana waved it away. 'I'll tell you this, Maggie. I've had no visions since the one that sent those men to their deaths.'

'But you knew I was coming.'

Christiana shrugged. 'Perhaps the Sight has been taken from me. I pray that it is so.'

Margaret knew it was not so, but that her mother wanted to believe it. 'And you did not have a vision of Roger's danger?'

Christiana shook her head. 'I told you I'd had no need. I could see with my mortal eyes his unsteady gait.'

'What did Great-Aunt Euphemia teach you about the Sight?'

Christiana idly poked at the tablets in the basket. 'I pray that I have the strength to complete this soon.' She sat back and gazed past Margaret's shoulder. 'She told me to discipline myself with meditation and long stretches of solitude to provoke the Sight and thus learn how it comes and how I might make use of it.' She sighed and dropped the basket on to the floor beside her. 'I have not the patience. Even the holy Dame Bethag despairs of me – though she never says so.'

'Ma, your fasting is going to provoke visions. Hasn't Dame Bethag told you that?'

Christiana shrugged, picking at a thread on a cushion.

Margaret said nothing of the fact that Christiana had at long last discovered to her sorrow another way to provoke the Sight – by *pretending* to have a vision. The Sight was a dangerous gift, requiring careful training, else it was as treacherous as a bird of prey in the hands of an inexperienced master.

❦ 2 ❦

ANDREW'S MISSION

Hearing of the English force moving north towards the border, Father Andrew crossed himself and prayed for God's help in finding a way to get word to William Wallace. His disgust with himself for blindly obeying his abbot's orders in support of Edward Longshanks had led to his defiant act of going to Edinburgh Castle on behalf of his sister Maggie, and thus to his abbot's condemning him to the post as confessor to the English troops that camped at Soutra on their arrival in Scotland. As a Scotsman hearing the confessions of the enemy he would never be allowed to escape, nor would his own countrymen trust him if he managed to do so. But he kept despair at bay by telling himself God had a purpose in bringing him to this English camp, and he believed it was for this – to pass information about the strength of the companies to Wallace.

It felt as if it had been long ago that Andrew and his servant Matthew had arrived at Soutra, but in fact they'd made the journey but four months earlier. They had approached the gate of the spital to the sound of their horses' breath, the clop of their hooves on the stony road. The wind had funnelled beneath Andrew's mantle as if urging him to fly. He remembered the bitter cold.

In the spital's forecourt the soldiers had hovered close to a crackling fire. Though the high walls created a windbreak, it was still very cold on the height. Several large tents took up most of the courtyard. Andrew was taken aback, wondering how many English resided here that the guest house and infirmary were not enough.

'I had not expected so great a company,' he'd said to his servant.

'Where will we sleep?' Matthew asked.

'I'll propose that we sleep in the canons' dormitory.' Andrew was determined to keep the lad with him, for Matthew had volunteered to accompany him into this exile. 'They would not bed soldiers there.'

The dormitory – Andrew wanted nothing more than to go straight there to lie down, but a servant greeted them with the news that the master of the spital wished to meet with Andrew at once.

'Go with the groom,' he told Matthew. 'See that the horses are well rubbed down and then have him show you to the kitchen.'

The servant led Andrew past the soldiers' tents, the infirmary, and the kirk, to a half-timbered house of imposing size. A clerk greeted him at the door and led him through a hall in which several men lounged, all with the presence and expensive clothing of nobles, and on into a windowless chamber monopolised by a large table with intricately carved legs. A leather-backed chair stood behind it, a hide-covered bench before it. Three oil lamps illuminated the table, the doorway and the chairs. Andrew settled on the bench. Presently a servant arrived with wine, a bowl of fragrant soup and a chunk of brown bread.

'Master Thomas invites you to take some nourishment and assures you he will not come so hastily that you need hurry.'

Andrew was not acquainted with Master Thomas. He wondered whether he should be pleased by the courtesy or whether he should prepare himself for a long delay. It irked him that he might have taken some rest in the dormitory after all. But the soup warmed him, the bread filled him, and the wine soothed him.

He would like to know the lie of the land before speaking with Master Thomas. According to Abbot Adam, Master Thomas had been vague about precisely why he required an additional priest, particularly one well versed in diplomacy. It was to be assumed that King Edward trusted Master Thomas or he would have replaced him; therefore he would share Abbot Adam's rather than Andrew's political affinity, at least officially. Andrew must trust to his own skill at divining the man's heart, a difficult task with a stranger. He bowed his head and prayed for God's guidance.

Approaching voices brought him to his feet. The door opened and a large man in a dark gown quite tight about the middle paused, his head turned away, still summarising orders to a clerk. When he dismissed the clerk, he closed the door behind him and leaned against it, bringing short-fingered, dimpled hands to rest on his belly.

'Father Andrew Kerr, at last.' The voice was nasal despite a hawk-like nose that should have provided sufficient breath for more resonance. Master Thomas had deep-set eyes, heavy brows, fleshy lips, several chins and ears with oddly elongated lobes. His grey hair was clipped short about his tonsure and oiled.

Andrew thought him an exceedingly ugly man. '*Benedicite*, Master Thomas.'

The master sniffed. 'We expected you a week ago. I pray it was not misfortune that delayed you.'

'I am surprised that my coming was so long in the planning as you imply. I learned of it but a few days before departing.'

Thomas's expression was unreadable as he motioned Andrew to sit. Moving around the table to the chair behind, he walked heavily and with a pronounced limp.

As he took his seat Thomas frowned and shook his head, jiggling his many chins. 'I find myself in a parlous position, Father

Andrew. I have gathered all my wits about me and keep them well honed.'

Andrew thought this an odd beginning.

Thomas blotted his flushed, sweaty face with a cloth. 'I am not a doubter by nature, so I blunder.' He leaned forward, elbows on the table, stubby hands folded. 'War kills courtesy. So I ask you frankly, where is your heart in this matter of the king of Scots?'

Although surprised by the man's abruptness, Andrew had prepared for this question. 'My mission is to serve God and to obey my master. Whether I hear the confession of an Englishman or a Scotsman, I keep the sanctity of the confessional.'

'I inquired about your heart, not your head.'

'I do not think about it.'

'You still answer with your head. You are a man, you must feel one way or another.'

'I mean no disrespect, but you are wrong that a man must take sides in this. My ultimate Master is God, the Pope his mortal representative, and he is neither an Englishman nor a Scotsman.' Andrew bowed his head, praying that the man would be satisfied.

Thomas sighed and fidgeted with his ring, the blue stone catching the light. He rose with effort and stood for a moment with his back to Andrew. 'No doubt you wonder why I insist on your answer. The brethren here have begun to bicker among themselves. Some are supporters of John Balliol, others think Robert Bruce would have taken a firmer stand against the English, a few see good coming of King Edward's interest, some pray only for peace. What were once irritations now grow to arguments, feuds.'

'Surely not among those who wish for peace?'

Thomas did not answer at once, but tilted his head, as if considering what to say. 'Is that your wish? For peace?' he said at last.

Andrew was startled into saying simply, 'It is.'

Thomas turned to him. 'Then you are welcome here. I assure

you I am most grateful you have arrived. I need another confessor for the English soldiers, and a man who takes no interest in the conflict is the ideal man for that task.'

Or one who supports the English. Andrew wondered what Master Thomas knew about why Abbot Adam had chosen him to come. 'They have no confessor?'

'Father Obert is their confessor, but with so many men, and so many fearful of dying without confession, he is exhausted. He is no longer young and needs assistance.'

'Surely there are others here who might have shared the burden with–' Andrew stopped.

Thomas was shaking his head. 'Abbot Adam told me that you were a man whom I might trust not to reveal anything you heard in confession.'

'No priest may break the seal of confession.'

'Few are tested as you might be, Father Andrew.'

'I understand.'

'It was good of you to agree to come.'

In keeping with his stance of neutrality, Andrew did not contradict Thomas. He had not expected to be able to pretend he had agreed to come; he had expected Abbot Adam to have made him doubly damned by revealing that he knew this was a severe punishment and cursed the abbot for it.

'You will be my guest in this house,' Thomas said.

Doubt teased Andrew with this news. He wondered whether this invitation was a gesture of trust, or a way to watch him closely. But he must not appear uneasy. 'I thank you for that. I'll of course require my servant to bide here with me.'

Thomas spread his hands. 'Of course. And now I bid you goodnight. You are weary. A servant will show you the way. Go to your rest and sleep as long as you wish tomorrow.'

Thinking back to that first night Andrew remembered how he had despaired about being able to sleep, and yet had fallen almost at once into a deep, exhausted slumber.

On Andrew's second day at Soutra he had been summoned to Master Thomas's chamber to meet Father Obert. He'd expected a doddering, milky-eyed priest. He found a small man sitting at Master Thomas's table, long-fingered and delicate hands steepled before him. He was bald of pate, although his sharp eyes were crowned by long and wild white eyebrows.

'Father Obert?' Andrew said.

The priest inclined his head. '*Benedicite*, Father Andrew. I thought we should talk before we dine with the English captains.' He lisped, as he was missing a number of teeth. 'They are uneasy regarding your being their confessor, of course. Anyone might be an enemy, even a priest.'

'They are wise to be cautious,' said Andrew. 'How did you gain their trust?'

'I was born and raised in York. They take comfort that my family still resides in the country about that fair city.' He flattened his hands before him, as if getting down to the point. 'Tell me about yourself. You were born in Perth?' Obert cocked his head, but his eyes remained on Andrew's.

'Melrose. But I was brought up in Perth.'

'I understand you are the eldest son of a merchant. Why did you take vows?'

'It is what God wished, Father Obert.' Andrew fought to keep his gaze steady and his body still despite his impatience with this questioning.

Obert responded with a quizzical lift of the brows.

God's blood but the man was nosy. 'I was called.' Andrew immediately regretted how his words snapped with irritation. More softly he added, 'I cannot remember when I did not know that God called me to serve Him in the Kirk.'

Obert's smile seemed guileless. 'It is good when a priest has a sincere vocation.' He adjusted his sleeve, a fussy gesture. 'Abbot Adam sent you here as someone Master Thomas could trust in this circumstance – the English using this as their camp and spital.

Do you favour King Edward's claim over John Balliol's?'

'I strive to be indifferent.'

'You say that as if it is virtuous.'

'You would counsel me to represent myself as devoted to King Edward?'

'I would counsel you to tell the truth.' Obert's gaze held Andrew with such intensity he felt like wood.

Yet who was Obert to speak to him in such wise? 'Abbot Adam and Master Thomas have chosen me to assist you. Do you question their choice?' Andrew spoke quietly.

Obert sat back with a play of horror. 'I see I have touched a wound. Or at least a tender scar. But I meant my comment as advice.' He rose, revealing a crooked back, and reached for a stick to assist his walk. 'It is time for introductions in the hall.'

Andrew reached out to halt the old priest. 'Why do you distrust me?'

Father Obert did not raise his head at once. He seemed to consider his reply. Then his sharp eyes met Andrew's. 'You are Abbot Adam's secretary, the one he trusted to gather the treasures of this country from the abbeys and kirks. Tell me I am being unjust and I shall believe you.'

Andrew had done so, turning his head when the soldiers accompanying him beat those courageous enough to defy them in the name of their king, John Balliol. His cowardice in that time would haunt him to the grave. The old man had thrust right into Andrew's deepest wound, baring his terrible shame. He could not trust his voice.

Obert rested both hands on his stick and straightened a little. 'What is this? Remorse?' His mouth was pinched, from irritation or pain, Andrew could not guess.

'Might we talk?' Andrew managed, though he did not know what he would say.

Obert inclined his head. 'Later. There will be time to speak of many things.'

'Now, I pray you,' Andrew said, inexplicably desperate to explain himself, wanting Father Obert to believe in his decency.

Obert shook his head. 'Master Thomas awaits us.'

The elderly priest led the way to the master's hall. Master Thomas and several of the men Andrew had noted in the hall the previous day rose to greet them as they entered the room. They rose not for Andrew, but for Father Obert. All greeted him with respect. Then Master Thomas introduced Andrew.

Sensing this to be a significant gathering, Andrew worked to set aside his irritation with Obert so that he might concentrate on memorising each name. Sir Francis seemed uncomfortable in his finery, as would be St Francis of Assisi. Sir Marmaduke – the name was Irish, servant of Madoc – though the man's accent was like Father Obert's, that of Yorkshire. But he also dressed more simply than the others – servant, Marmaduke. And thirdly Sir Simon Montagu – this name was familiar.

'Perth, did you say?' Sir Simon studied Andrew closely as if he, in turn, thought he should remember him.

As Andrew's memory found the connection, he tried to cover any sign of recognition with a simple, 'A fine trading port, Sir Simon. I've always thought it deserved a cathedral – and an archbishop.'

The English made polite but amused noises. Scotsmen were always complaining of their lack of an archbishop.

Andrew tried not to stare at the thick-necked, broadly built man who had been the lover of Ada de la Haye. This was the man whose wealth had bought Margaret's friend a house in Perth as well as some property in the west. Her family had arranged for her to meet him when he was an influential emissary between King Edward and the much mourned King Alexander of Scotland, whose untimely death without a male heir had led to the present troubles. Andrew did not need memory tricks to remember Sir Simon.

Indeed he knew his instinct had been correct that these were all important men and he doubted he would forget meeting any of them. It made him even more fearful for his life and he cursed Master Thomas for inviting him to sup with them. Fortunately, they did not need him to carry the conversation at the table.

But after dinner the Englishmen gathered round him to ask what he had seen on his journey. A hard rain as they'd departed Holyrood Abbey had forced Andrew to keep his hood up, blocking his peripheral vision, and he'd been so closely watched by his English escort that he'd noticed little once they rode out of the storm. But even with so little to report, by the time Andrew had broken free of them Father Obert had departed.

Again that night he'd surrendered to a deep sleep despite his unease. But in the months following he'd spent the bulk of his nights pacing back and forth in his room until his body insisted on rest.

Father Obert had suggested the pacing as an aid to sleep. 'I prefer brandywine, but that is in such short supply it is not even given to those lying bleeding in the infirmary – only the landed nobility are its beneficiaries – and Master Thomas, of course.' As always, his sarcasm was softened by a mischievous grin, but Andrew knew the words trumped the genial mask.

Determined to continue his interview with Obert, convinced that the priest had hinted at a disaffection with the English that might make him an unlooked-for ally, Andrew had hounded him for a few days, shadowing his pale, halting presence, until the elderly priest invited him to dine in his chamber.

'I see that you'll accomplish nothing until we clear your mind,' said Obert after the servant had withdrawn. 'I begin to imagine that Abbot Adam was glad to be rid of you if this is how you behaved with him.'

'I avoided him,' said Andrew. 'Our parting lacked affection.'

'That is interesting,' said Obert as he thrust his knife into a piece of meat. He sat back, chewing it thoughtfully.

Andrew fell to the food. The meat was tough, overcooked, but the stew of vegetables was well seasoned and tasty, and good for softening the brown bread. He'd noticed the absence of oatcakes on the first night – in deference to the English, he supposed.

'So there is a rift between the abbot and his secretary?' Obert asked, breaking into Andrew's reverie.

Andrew grabbed his cup and washed down a mouthful of bread and vegetables.

Obert chuckled. 'There is no need to hasten through your meal. I'll not send you off before you are satisfied.' He was smiling when Andrew met his eyes. 'Faith, I am most curious to hear what you are so driven to tell me.' The pale eyebrows joined briefly, then separated as the old priest smoothed his brow and smiled genially.

Now that he held Obert's attention Andrew found himself choked with doubt. Suddenly it seemed absurd that this venerable priest would wish to hear of his remorse and his resolve to help his people. Indeed, Andrew questioned the wisdom in confiding in Obert, doubting the perception that had drawn him to desire to do so.

Apparently sensing Andrew's confusion, Obert busied himself with some food and ale.

Andrew was relieved that Abbot Adam apparently had not told Master Thomas of Andrew's disobedience. It permitted him some dignity and made it possible for him to be accepted as a trustworthy confessor, which might eventually allow him to help his people with information. But that hope would be dashed if he was wrong about trusting Father Obert. Yet as he considered the pale old man Andrew sensed God shining through Obert, and the more he watched him, the more convinced he became.

Obert sat back in his seat, patting his belly, his hunger apparently satisfied. 'Well? Have you found your voice, Father Andrew?'

He thought he'd found the courage, but now Andrew felt

emotion welling up within to challenge his ability to speak intelligibly. 'You were right about my blind obedience to Abbot Adam in his service to King Edward. What you do not know is how I have since cursed myself–' As tears rose, Andrew looked away and breathed deeply. Obert did not comment. When Andrew could again breathe evenly, he continued. 'I have since disobeyed the abbot, defied him in a matter concerning my family, and he no longer trusts me. That is why he sent me here. He knows that a Scotsman who has heard the confessions of English troops will never again be welcome among his people, nor will he be trusted to leave the English camp. This is my penance and my condemnation.'

Obert pursed his mouth and frowned, his gaze fixed on the air beyond Andrew. 'I wondered about his wisdom in sending someone from Perth. I know there are canons born in my shire and others south of the border residing at Holyrood.' The old priest sighed, shook his head slowly, and then gestured towards the food. 'Satisfy yourself, my friend. I am glad to know your heart.'

'What of you, Father Obert? Forgive my saying this, but I was surprised that the English commanders would bring such a venerable priest on campaign.'

Obert's face lit up as he laughed in surprise. 'Oh, bless you, but you are right, no commander would trust I'd survive such a journey. I have served here at Soutra for many years. First the Scots, now the English.'

This made no sense to Andrew. 'You served my countrymen and yet the English trust and respect you. How can this be?'

Bowing his head, Obert muttered something to himself.

Andrew thought it a prayer. He helped himself to more of the food, some ale, and was beginning to think the old man had no intention of responding when Obert lifted his head.

'*They* know that *I* know I'm too old to do anything rash.' Obert smiled with his mouth, but not his eyes.

They had bonded that evening, and were now like father and son; Andrew enjoyed working with Obert. He had also been surprised by Master Thomas's character. Abbot Adam had lately written to warn Thomas of the reason he'd sent Andrew to Soutra, advising him to keep a close watch on him. Andrew had wondered at Thomas's reading the letter to him, until he heard the anger in the Master's voice.

'He insults me with this letter,' Thomas growled, tossing it away from him. Then he'd looked at Andrew long and hard. 'So you lied to me about your impartiality, eh?' He wagged his head, his chins dancing, and then he shrugged. 'To save your hide. I would have done the same. I have no complaints about you, Father Andrew. I believe you to be an honourable man of God. Abbot Adam is perhaps not the man of God he should be.'

So Andrew grew comfortable at the spital. But he did not forget his conviction that God's purpose in bringing him to Soutra was so that he might provide information to William Wallace, and to do that he must escape. This it was that kept him pacing at night.

Escape. He had thought himself close to an attempt at escape, hesitating only because a Welsh archer he'd befriended had disappeared the previous week and every room and all the grounds were being searched. This morning Obert said that it was believed the Welshman had escaped out the infirmary drain, or sewer.

'God help David. Who could survive such a journey through hell?' Obert had said with an unreadable expression.

Andrew could not spit out the curse that came to his tongue on hearing of David's escape route. Andrew had not told Father Obert he was plotting to escape and get word to William Wallace of all he'd learned at Soutra. He could not be certain how Obert would react to the plan. But the news was maddening. Andrew had intended to use the infirmary drain, certain that no other human would be so desperate, that only a man who had forfeited his soul would attempt such an escape. Now the drain would be guarded. In the same breath he both cursed David and prayed for his safe journey.

❧ 3 ❧

MYSTICAL GIFTS

The afternoon sun was softened by a humid haze rising up from the river. Margaret stepped from her mother's chamber and stood leaning out over the rail that bordered the gallery hoping for a brisk wind to cleanse her of fear and sorrow. She was disappointed to find the air still and warm.

There was so much she wanted to ask about the Sight, but her mother, so frail in body and spirit, was not the one to ask. Though her mother felt cursed by the Sight she seemed never to have questioned it or tried to understand it despite her aunt's urging. Margaret regretted not having known her Great-Aunt Euphemia, although she had never wished to learn about the Sight until now.

Margaret did not blame her mother for her incurious way; her heart overflowed with sorrow for her mother's suffering, and she understood her fear.

She bowed her head to pray for her mother's malaise to pass, but her father chose that moment to join her. Margaret tried to hide her tearful eyes but of course he caught her gesture.

He raked his age-spotted hands through what was left of his hair. 'I'm not much of a praying man, Maggie, but I've been on my knees ever since coming to this godforsaken place and to what end, I ask myself, for the Lord has turned deaf ears on me. I cannot think why He's so cursed our family. I've done nothing to deserve such suffering, I'm sure of it. I've offered myself, asked Him to take me and give my Christiana back her wits and her health. And even that He's not accepted. What am I to do? Sacrifice one of my children, as Abraham was told to do?'

'I will speak with Dame Eleanor the infirmarian about Ma,' Margaret offered. 'She might find a way to convince Ma to take a physic for strength.'

'Did your mother say anything to give you hope that she wishes to get well?'

'She said she has suffered no visions since the one for which she performs penance,' Margaret said. 'She seemed grateful for that.' It was not a lie, for her mother claimed it to be so.

Malcolm crossed himself, his expression lightening. 'That is promising.' He hugged her. 'You've given me hope, Maggie.' He glanced at the door to Christiana's room. 'I'll go to see her now.'

Margaret did not want to detain him long, for she yearned to be alone to think – but she felt compelled to ask one question. 'Ma is weaving a border of owls, Da. What do they signify to her?'

'Owls?' He repeated absently, and then he rolled his eyes and threw up his hands. 'That border. Why must she work on such a darksome thing, I ask you? She's weaving it for Euphemia, her aunt.'

'Great-Aunt Euphemia is still alive? But she must be so old. Is it possible?'

Malcolm nodded. 'Like the prophets of the Old Testament she lives and lives. Owls signify the power of the woman and the moon, she says. Blasphemy, I say. But Christiana hopes to honour her aunt with a mantle bordered with those unholy birds of the night. Perhaps she believes Euphemia has caused the Sight to leave her?' He threw up his hands in frustration. 'I do not under-stand Christiana's reasoning.'

Margaret did not know what to make of her mother suddenly

46

wishing to gift Euphemia with a mantle. 'But Euphemia bides far away, doesn't she?'

'Aye, in Kilmartin now, cursed place at the edge of the land. Loch Long is where she belongs, among her kin.'

She remembered her mother's descriptions of a great glen far to the west filled with monuments to the ancestors. 'How is Ma to present her with it?'

Malcolm's momentary buoyancy was gone and he slumped in defeat. 'Your mother does not fret over practical matters, lass.'

When Christiana had first shown signs of having Second Sight her mother sent her to her sister Euphemia for training; although she was not the only living MacFarlane with the gift, Euphemia had embraced it as her purpose in life and had sought out the most respected seers with whom to study, so the family deemed her the most knowledgeable regarding the gift. Margaret had only half listened to her mother's stories of her time with Euphemia because she'd considered her mother's gift a curse. So she had not known that her great aunt held owls in special regard – learning the significance of the bird that had wakened her in the night added to Margaret's already considerable anxiety about that event.

She found herself thinking of Hal, her uncle's groom in Edinburgh, who knew much about animals. She imagined he would know the lore of owls, and he would be so easy to talk to. She missed his companionship, how she could go to him when troubled and know that he would listen without ever judging her, and often surprise her with an insight that helped her see things more clearly. They were close in age and both still wondering what life had in store for them. She'd never guessed for her it would be the Sight.

Taking her leave from her father, Margaret withdrew towards the nunnery kirk, walking slowly in the hazy sunshine, the humid air weighting her steps. She loved her father, but did not much like him. He'd had little to do with them as children, and he'd resented Christiana for the hostility and fear her visions provoked, cursing her for causing rifts with colleagues that took great efforts to close. He'd been relieved when she had suggested retiring to Elcho after Margaret's marriage, and as soon as the troubles with Edward Longshanks began he'd fled to Bruges. In his loyalties he supported what was lucrative for him, most recently dangerously offering his ships to King Edward while cheating him out of mint fees by carrying silver on those same ships to have minted in the Low Countries. His original reason for returning a month ago was to collect more of his wealth while Edward was busy in the Low Countries. Margaret thought his sudden need for Christiana had arisen after his ship had been boarded by the English and he'd realised the danger he was in.

As Margaret approached the kirk she heard a voice lifted in song and was disappointed, having expected to find solitude there at this hour. At the door she hesitated. But the devotion with which the woman sang touched Margaret's heart and the beauty of the sister's voice drew her; on easing open the side door she found Dame Bethag standing alone before the altar with arms outspread, her face lit from an invisible source as she sang. She was not a young woman, yet she looked fresh and untouched by time, her white wimple framing her glowing face and her dark habit graceful and rich with mystery. This sister had befriended Christiana and spent much time in her apartment. Margaret believed it was because many in the community believed her to be a mystic, a seer like Christiana.

The beauty of Bethag's singing brought Margaret to her knees, and lifting her eyes to the nun's radiant face she let the angelic voice fill her heart. From her eyes spilled tears of joy, and her throat tightened with emotion. The chapel brightened and grew comfortingly warm, and hearing the name 'Maria' as Bethag sang, Margaret sensed the Blessed Mother as the source of the warmth as she shone the light of her love on them. She felt as if she knelt on air, and Bethag's song echoed as if she'd been joined by the angelic choir.

Holy Mary, Mother of God, guide me to use myself in your service. If I have been given the Sight, if it is not blasphemy, help me to use it for the good of my people.

She sensed the Virgin Mary smiling down on her and was filled with ease.

But her joy faded, and her mind eventually returned to her worries as tears slipped down her face. She had struggled to accept the travails God sent her way, but they multiplied too quickly, and just as she overcame one she would feel another clutch at her heels, pulling her down into despair. It was sinful to despair, but God gave her no peace. She did not pretend to being an innocent, but surely there were many far worse than she. She stopped herself, realising she was puling like her father and she begged the Blessed Mother's patience.

It was all the worse because she had allowed herself to hope that she might find some joy in James Comyn after the humiliation of her marriage with Roger. James had been attentive and affectionate of late, and she'd found it comforting to have a man concerned for her, gifting her with food in short supply – a little meat, a small barrel of ale – advising her on problems, and praising her accomplishments. They had grown close. He'd brought the Welshman to give her news of her brother – that was the third time James had brought her word of Andrew since Abbot Adam had condemned him. With what seemed immense patience James had worn down her initial distrust of his kindness, and she had come to think that although he might be using her for his own ends as had Roger, he had been a good friend to her. It did not hurt his cause that he also had a face and manner that Margaret found pleasing. Yet now she felt alone again. Her mother was wasting away, Roger was in danger, James was long away at his meeting with Wallace and Murray. She closed her eyes, praying for some good news, and found herself lingering over a memory of their last parting. James had pulled her into his arms and kissed her, a kiss so sweet, so welcome that she thought she might love him.

As she knelt at her devotion she felt the now familiar chill, so unlike the Virgin's warmth, and the floor opened beneath her. She gasped to find herself falling. Dame Bethag's song had slowed and softened, but now it was drowned out by a rushing sound all around Margaret. She fought to open her eyes, frightened by the sensation of freely falling through the air, but her eyes would not open. Her stomach heaved at the weight-lessness.

And then, as suddenly as it had begun her fall ended, and her body was shot through with a pain that left her breathless, her ears assailed by a terrible roar of agony. She thought she screamed, but could not hear herself for the roar. The moment she collapsed, unable to bear any more, the pain and the terrible noise withdrew. She felt her feet touching the ground. She did not trust her legs after her terrifying fall, but she stood without effort and opened her eyes with ease. She was no longer in the kirk but standing at the foot of a rock outcrop, in a dusty pre-dawn light, and someone lay at her feet, his breath rattling piteously. She crouched down and to her dismay found it was Roger. He lay sprawled on the ground with his head at a frightening angle against a stone. The rattling ceased.

'Christ have mercy!' she cried. She attempted to arrange his head and limbs in a more natural order telling herself that he might recover if his humours could flow more easily. But his skin was cold and his body was already stiffening. 'Roger, stay with me, I pray you, breathe!' She felt herself pulled away, lifted off her feet, and she floated away, hand in hand with a warm, shining companion. 'No! I cannot do this – I cannot leave him.'

'Be at peace, Dame Margaret.'

Bethag's voice called her from the dream. Her arm about Margaret's trembling shoulders was warm and reassuring. Bethag gently touched her cheek. Margaret opened her eyes. Bethag's eyes were wells of light.

'What vision did the Lord bring you, young Margaret?'

'I pray that it was no vision, but a dream.' It was her recurring dream, yet different this time, *experiencing* Roger's fall, and seeing him as he lay dying. Margaret crossed herself. 'Your song made me think of those I love, those I am worried about.' If it had been real she would not have abandoned him though dead. She would have sought a way to protect Roger from scavengers.

The nun's focus was turned inward. Excited, she said, as if to herself, 'My song inspired a vision. I have heard of this happening.'

'But your song was joyous and the vision was filled with pain.' Margaret struggled for breath and found it difficult to keep her eyes focused. She was being pulled down into the sleep of exhaustion.

'Rest a while,' Bethag whispered, stroking Margaret's forehead as she drifted off.

Margaret woke with a start, confused by the high ceiling and the rattle of beads near her ear. Moving her head she discovered it was resting in Bethag's lap and the nun was praying, her paternoster beads rattling as she fingered them.

'I must have slept,' said Margaret, her voice cracking a little.

'Are you thirsty?' asked Bethag. She set the beads aside and helped Margaret sit up, then handed her a cup of water.

Only then did Margaret notice the servant kneeling a few paces from them, her expression one of rapt wonder. She was about to ask whether the woman had been there earlier, but Bethag answered the question before she asked.

'Mary came to change the flowers on the altar and found us here. She brought water for you.' Bethag smiled. 'Your colour has returned.'

'How long have I been here?'

Bethag laughed as she stood up and took a few uneven paces,

rubbing her right thigh. 'Long enough for my right leg to lose all feeling, but at my age that does not take so long as it did in my youth.'

It took all Margaret's strength to struggle up on to her feet. She felt shaky, as she often did after falling asleep during the day, but also as if all the light in her life had been smothered.

Dame Bethag saw her anguish. 'Do not be afraid. God spoke through me to you.'

Owls and mystics – Margaret wondered why God would speak to her through others. 'Why do you think God used you?' Margaret asked. 'What did you see while you sang?'

'The Blessed Mother's light of grace.'

'So, too, did I – at first. But afterwards–' Margaret hesitated, glancing at the servant Mary. 'Might we talk privately?'

Dame Bethag nodded to the servant, who shyly rose and departed. The nun withdrew to a bench to one side of the altar. Margaret joined her, still feeling almost as if she were walking in her sleep so tentative did her movements feel to her.

Bethag smoothed Margaret's forehead and then took up one of her hands. 'You are so cold. Tell me what troubles you. As God is my witness I shall not betray your confidences to the other sisters.'

Margaret was loath to call to mind her terrible vision; but she needed guidance, and with the hope that Dame Bethag might be able to help her she described her experience, as well as the recurring dream.

As Margaret spoke, Dame Bethag dropped her head and listened with eyes half-closed. Margaret felt the nun's hand grow as cold as her own.

'Oh my dear,' Bethag said at last, raising a tearful face to Margaret. 'This is indeed a frightening vision. But the Lord must have cause to show this to you. Give thanks to Him and let it be – in prayer it will come clear to you why you have seen your husband's death. It may not speak to his actual death at all. It might not even have been Roger Sinclair whom you saw.'

Margaret shook her head. 'No, I am certain it was my husband.'

'If he suffers such an end, it is God's wish.'

That made it no more palatable for Margaret. 'Have you ever had such a vision of what might come to pass?'

Bethag sighed. 'I have been graced with no such power, young Margaret. My visions are but expressions of the ecstasy I experience when I touch the divine.'

'How do I know that this vision is not the devil's work?'

'You also saw the Virgin Mary's grace,' Bethag said, as if that were all the argument necessary.

She looked so serene and spoke with such confidence that Margaret was tempted to believe her; but Bethag made it all seem too simple. Life was far more complicated.

'I believe you are gifted with both the Sight and divine grace,' said Bethag. 'These are gifts you must honour with prayer and contemplation.'

'I have work to do out in the world.'

Bethag was nodding.

'How do I honour these gifts out in the world, in the midst of the fighting in our land?' *Tell me that*, Margaret thought, but left it a question, not a challenge.

'Do not be frightened. You walk in the light of the Lord. He will show you. You must keep your mind open to His guidance. Come.' Bethag rose and held out her hand. 'I'll walk with you to the guest house.'

Bethag helped Margaret rise, and then gently brushed her fingertips across Margaret's forehead and down one side of her face.

'You lack all joy, young Margaret. Surely God's gifts, the most precious one being that of life, are to be treasured and rejoiced in.' Her expression was one of gentle inquiry as she searched Margaret's eyes.

Margaret thought of all her worries, but was struck by how self-pitying she would sound if she recited them. She could not imagine Bethag complaining about her lot in life – but then she seemed to enjoy a quiet peace here.

'I forget to laugh,' Margaret said, though she had not realised it until she spoke the words. She was embarrassed to have blurted out such a silly worry. 'You must think me a child, fretting about whether or not I laugh.'

'No, Margaret,' said Bethag. 'I see that you have left your childhood far behind.'

They had moved down the aisle and Margaret now stepped forward to hold open the door for Bethag. As she passed, the nun gave her such a beatific smile that Margaret found herself responding – tentatively, but she did manage a smile. It was such a small gesture, but it shifted something within her. Perhaps God *was* speaking to her through Bethag. Margaret crossed herself as she let go the door and joined her companion.

They walked slowly through the convent yard. As they approached the guest house the long shadows of early evening already stretched across the garden.

Margaret asked, 'What did you mean, that I've left my childhood far behind?'

Bethag nodded at the question. 'You carry yourself with a gravity unusual in a young woman. At your age I had been here for almost half my life and my cares were shared by a community of women. With your parents away, and your husband, too, you are responsible for your own well-being. I think I was fortunate in being called to God and to this place where I am not alone.' She gave Margaret an apologetic smile. 'I've never before considered how selfish we sisters might seem to you, how cockered.'

Margaret wondered whether the nun could read her thoughts. 'Without your prayers we would be lost. I imagine all those who are cloistered resenting the rest of us for requiring so much prayer.'

They laughed companionably.

At the guest-hall door Dame Bethag paused and, catching Margaret's smile, mirrored it in her beautiful face. 'A smile is one of God's little miracles, young Margaret. It is good to remember that.' She pressed her hands together and bowed. 'Now I must return to my cell. God go with you.'

'And with you, Dame Bethag.' Margaret wanted to wish her more than that, but she could not think what the woman did not have. She mulled this over as she stepped into the hall, unaware of Ada's presence until she was swept up in her affectionate embrace.

'You have been long away, Maggie,' Ada said as she stood back to hold her at arm's length and study her face. 'I see a hint of a smile. Oh, that is so good to see. Your meeting with Christiana must have pleased you.'

As a cloud sweeping past the sun the memory of her mother's condition swept over Margaret, chilling her. 'No, it was not Ma who made me smile.' Her throat tightened. 'It was Dame Bethag. She was so kind to me.' Her eyes filled with tears as she remembered how little cause she had to smile, a thought that irritated her, seeming so self-pitying.

'What have I done?' Ada steered Margaret towards a chair. 'I've turned your smiles to tears. I pray you, let me make amends. Rest here, and I'll bring you a cup of wine.' Her silks rustled as she fussed about Margaret.

For her part, Margaret felt there could be no better person than Ada for her to be with right now, a practical woman whom she could not imagine suffering visions. Margaret was just sipping at the wine when her father arrived. He was not so welcome.

'Ah, Maggie, I am glad to find you here. What are your plans now? Are you headed straight for Stirling?'

Margaret had said nothing to him of her destination. She glanced with suspicion towards Ada, who had remained in the hall with Malcolm while Margaret was with Christiana. Had she spoken to Malcolm?

Ada shook her head and shrugged.

Then it must have been Christiana who had divulged her destination to Malcolm. It was Margaret's own fault for having mentioned it to her mother.

'Give your daughter some peace,' Ada said. 'Go rest, Malcolm. You look weary.'

Her father's indignant expression and Ada's imperious stance with hands on hips almost made Margaret laugh. But she quickly sobered when Malcolm poured himself a cup of wine and sat down beside her. She knew by his affectionate smile that he wanted something from her.

'Why would you go to Stirling?' he asked. 'You have a fine home in Perth.'

She hoped this was all he was after, to feel informed. 'My home in Perth holds too many memories of my failed marriage, Da.'

Malcolm placed his other hand over hers and looked her in the eyes. 'Ah. Well I ken such pain, Maggie. Would you at least heed some advice?'

She hesitated, wary of promising her father anything. 'What would that be?'

'Stay here, don't return to Perth. James will come here when he doesn't find you at home.'

She tried to withdraw her hand, but her father held it fast. 'I said nothing of James,' she said.

'There was no need, lass. I know you and he have an agreement, and I'm sure it's James who has you scurrying off to Stirling. Bide here until he comes for you, that's all I ask.'

'I'd never planned otherwise, Da,' she said. 'I left word for him to meet me here.'

Celia, Margaret's maid, had been sitting in a quiet corner of the hall listening to the conversation, except for carrying the tray with the wine and cups over after her mistress arrived. She felt comforted that Margaret still intended to wait here for James

Comyn. Her companion, Maus, Ada's maid, had quietly stated her hope that Margaret would decide not to wait for James to escort them, but would carry on to Stirling. She was eager to reach her mistress's comfortable town house. Celia disapproved of Maus, a young woman who thought only of finery. She was also jealous of her – she had been training to be a lady's maid like Maus when her former mistress, Margaret's goodmother, had sent her off with Margaret. Celia loved Margaret now, and was proud of her role in assisting her mistress in her work for James, but she envied Maus her soft hands that did not snag the silk of her mistress's gowns. At the same time Celia enjoyed having Maus's companionship and could see that her mistress was easier with Ada close at hand. Perhaps the time in Stirling would be pleasant, something Celia had not expected, as long as her mistress did not take too many risks in teasing out the reason the person carrying messages for James from Stirling had disappeared.

She wished Master Malcolm would leave and she might ask Margaret about the little smile on her face when she'd arrived just now.

But the old man was nothing if not a talker, and he'd now begun on Margaret's Great-Aunt Euphemia and the cursed mantle her mother was making for the woman. Celia had never met the kinswoman of whom he spoke, but she could see that her mistress found the conversation distressing for she hugged herself as if feeling threatened.

'Are you cold, Mistress?' Celia inquired, and was rewarded by Margaret's expression of gratitude as she rose and, making her excuses, withdrew to their chamber.

'What was so distressing about a mantle for a kinswoman?' Celia asked when they were alone, settled on the bed.

Margaret's face was in shadow, but her hands plucked nervously at her skirt. 'Euphemia MacFarlane is a great seer. My mother was sent by her parents to live with Euphemia to learn about the Sight.'

'She does not bide in Perth?'

'No. She lives far to the west.' Margaret hugged herself. 'Ma's weaving a border for the mantle, a border of owls. They are special to Great-Aunt Euphemia.'

Celia was puzzled. 'You laughed at my fear the other night.'

'I know.'

Celia realised her mistress was shivering and she fetched her favourite plaid.

Margaret pulled it around her shoulders and up around her neck despite the warmth of the evening.

'Ma said she has had no visions since the one of Kinnoull Hill. But while in the chapel – Celia, I *felt* Roger fall to his death. I thought *I* was falling, but then I saw him lying dead at the foot of the rock.' Margaret crossed herself. 'I was so frightened.'

'Heaven have mercy on us.' Celia crossed herself. She had much feared that Margaret was developing the Sight, for she was changing in subtle ways, becoming secretive, praying far more than was her wont. 'But you were smiling when you returned to the hall.'

'Dame Bethag had eased my mind.' Margaret took a deep breath and let it out as a groan. 'She is right, I carry such a weight. I must put my trust in God and believe that He will guide me. I have waited for the time to tell you, Celia – I–'

A knock on the door brought both of them to their feet.

'Tell no one,' Margaret whispered.

'I swear,' said Celia, hurt that her mistress felt the need to command her silence and frustrated by the interruption.

Ada entered the room, breaking the tension with a good-natured chuckle. 'Your father is a difficult man to escape, Maggie. You are blessed with a perceptive handmaid.' Ada gave Celia a warm smile. 'I could see that all his talk of Euphemia and her owls distressed you. Oh that man!'

Celia was relieved to hear her mistress laugh.

'Ada, you do my heart good. And you are right about Celia.'

Margaret shed the plaid. 'Will Da join us for the evening meal?'

Ada shook her head. 'He is apparently in the habit of eating with the prioress's kinsmen and the chaplain. Thanks be to God.'

Andrew no longer cursed David for escaping through the drain. He was grateful that God had spared him and Matthew, for the guards sent through it afterwards were now very ill. He believed Sir Francis and Sir Marmaduke had sent them through to impress upon Longshanks's royal lieutenant John de Warenne, Earl of Surrey, and his treasurer the hated Hugh Cressingham, the seriousness with which they took desertion. It had seemed that David's disappearance had been forgotten – a week had passed since he'd gone missing – when the administrators paused at Soutra for a night on their way to Stirling with their horse and foot soldiers. It was only then that the search had been ordered.

'No one is likely to try the drain again,' said Father Obert after Mass. 'My flesh crawls to recall the suffering of those two when we took communion to them in the infirmary.'

'I pray for them,' said Andrew. The men's faces and hands had been covered with suppurating sores and they were feverish and weak. Had his loyal servant Matthew not been ill with a rheumy cough, he and Andrew would have been the first through the diseased drain. He had been frustrated when he'd realised how ill Matthew was, and how impossible stealth would be with the young man's wet cough. But as it turned out, Andrew thanked God for sparing him and Matthew. 'I doubt David went far before illness felled him.'

'I expected much rejoicing from the commanders about that,' said Obert. 'But they have proven themselves Christians first. One has given money towards Masses for David's soul.'

'I've wondered about his escape. The hue and cry over it was so delayed. And now Masses for his soul? Is it possible that David deceived us? Might he have been a spy and the commanders staged his "escape" to warn others off, then sent the two guards through?' To warn himself off, in fact. Andrew now suspected he'd been noticed lingering around the drain – he'd spent some time gauging its width and memorising all that surrounded the entrance since he'd planned to escape by night.

'I think the commanders are far too busy with battle plans to stage such a ruse. They need only to have posted guards on the entrances to the drain – as they have now.' Taking up his walking stick, Obert made his way to the door. 'I should have thought you would understand how a Welshman might open his eyes to the treatment of the Scots and feel ashamed of his doing unto others . . .' Breathing strength into his back, Obert straightened a little and hobbled from the sacristy.

Andrew believed that the old priest knew he planned to escape.

Margaret sought out Dame Bethag the following day. As she'd lain awake long into the night she'd wondered whether the nun was right, that Margaret's visions were holy visions and not the suffering of an accursed state. She hoped that although Bethag had been sheltered most of her life she might still have some helpful insights into visions and how one lived with them. Margaret was frightened; she needed guidance.

She found the nun sitting in the cloister, eyes closed, head tilted up towards the warm sun. Not wishing to disturb her peaceful moment, Margaret sat down a little way from her and looked at the flowers, the bees going about their business, the birds drinking from a bowl-like depression in the sun-warmed stones. The wind sighed in the grass and moaned now and then through the stonework. This and the humming of the bees created a soothing cocoon of sound interrupted at irregular intervals by birdsong. How peaceful it was here. One could forget that armed guards were needed to protect this community. Certainly the birds, the bees, the flowers, the stones had no knowledge of the troubles out beyond the walls of Elcho. The river still ran past, the rain still fell, sun and moon and stars still defined the day and night, the season turned slowly towards autumn. One might be tempted to dismiss Longshanks's betrayal, for it had changed little here. Except for the guards. And Margaret's presence here, as well as her father's.

'Young Margaret! God has drawn you to a healing spot, has He not?' Dame Bethag's smile seemed to emanate from the beauty of the cloister.

'I did not wish to disturb you.'

'And you did not.' The nun resettled beside Margaret, her face turned towards her as she smoothed out her skirts.

Realising Bethag was studying her, Margaret asked her whether what she had experienced the previous day had been a holy vision or the Sight.

Bethag responded without hesitation, 'Does it matter what you call it?'

Margaret did not reply at once, expecting the nun to continue, but Bethag had turned her attention to the garden, apparently content with her answer.

'How could it not matter?' Margaret said. 'Your visions bring you joy, they are blessings. My mother's visions have caused so much pain and they've destroyed her soul.'

Bethag shook her head. 'Your mother's soul is not destroyed, Margaret. She does not understand, that is all. I understand that you want to know what to call what you've experienced, and I say what we call a thing does not change it.'

'But what if it is a foretelling?' Margaret asked. 'Does that not mean I have a responsibility to *do* something with the knowledge? I must know whether my husband is truly in danger, whether such a terrible end is what shall come to pass and whether God is guiding me to do something to prevent it. What if I'm just not wise enough to understand what He is telling me?'

'Time will show you, young Margaret. More I cannot say. God will show you the way.'

Margaret felt close to tears and could not return the nun's gentle smile.

Bethag turned away for a moment in the direction of the outer courtyard which had come alive with the clatter of horses. 'More travellers arriving?' For once she sounded impatient.

Margaret was glad to see the woman had emotions. 'You must find visitors distracting. We bring news of the world outside, unfamiliar voices.'

Bethag looked askance at Margaret. 'Oh, my dear, distractions are something to celebrate here. We begin to gnaw on the slightest irritations when we have no variety. But I do fear that we might soon be crowded with exiles from the troubles.' She smiled. 'Though I should be delighted if *you* chose to bide here awhile.'

How tempting that would be were Margaret not needed in Stirling, and not worried about Roger – though where he might be, how she might reach him, she did not know.

'Do you ever fear your visions, Dame Bethag?'

'Why should I fear a gift from God?'

'Because you are suddenly swept up in such feeling, unable to temper it, completely in the hands of – God.'

'That is ecstasy, young Margaret.' Bethag had tears in her eyes. 'You will see, in time.'

'You were never frightened?'

Bethag shook her head.

Margaret despaired of learning anything from Bethag. Her attention returned to the sounds in the yard, and she grew curious about the new arrivals.

'I must see – someone might have brought news of my husband.'

'God go with you,' said Bethag, bowing her head.

Margaret almost stumbled over her skirts as she flew from the cloister, suddenly convinced that she would have news of Roger. She arrived at the guest house in time to see James dismount. With him were several other men, but no one she knew. As she hurried forward, her eyes met James's and she read relief in his countenance.

'Dame Margaret.' He made a formal bow for the sake of the others, 'I looked for you in Perth.'

It was not the friendliest of greetings. She wondered whether he'd received the messages she'd left him.

'Tom was to tell you where we had gone.'

'You mean the drunk I found sleeping in your bed? He said not a word.' James looked both angry and disgusted.

'Drunk? Tom? Curse him.' How could he play them so false? 'But I also left word with Gilbert Ruthven that I had come here.'

'I have not seen him,' James said under his breath. 'I specifically asked you to remain quietly in Perth.'

Margaret saw no point in arguing. 'You truly found my servant drunk?'

'I sent him off and closed up the house as best I could.' James nodded to the other men who were watching him for instructions. 'Those of you set to ride out soon, drink little ale, eh? The rest of you can sleep off what you drink, for we'll wait until nightfall to depart.'

'We are to leave so soon?' Margaret said.

'The English are moving more quickly than we had expected.'

As the men moved past, Margaret noticed that one wore some of James's clothes.

'He is dressed as your double?'

James gave a curt nod. 'I am counting on his daylight departure to mislead anyone watching us.' He glanced round. 'I presume Dame Ada is also here?'

'Yes.' Margaret was put on guard by the abrupt change of subject.

James took her by the elbow. 'Where might we speak alone?'

Her heart pounded; she was not yet accustomed to his touch. 'What has happened?'

'Let us walk in the garden.' James steered her in the direction from which she had just come and hastened her towards a bench well out of earshot of the others.

'What is it, Jamie?'

He settled on the bench, but Margaret stood before him so that he could not ignore her.

In a quiet voice he said, 'God's blood, Maggie, I don't know what I would have done had I not found you here.'

She realised now that his anger came from his fear for her. 'I thought I'd left sufficient word that you would not be so worried.' She sat down beside him, hoping that he might touch her again.

He glanced round and, seeing no one near, lifted her hand and kissed it, then leaned forward and kissed her forehead. 'Forgive my temper,' he said, 'I was worried. And then to find that sluggard in your chamber–' he made a noise deep in his throat, much like a growl.

Margaret melted in the warmth of his gaze. 'I am sorry you worried so.'

James leaned forward and kissed her cheek. His breath tickled her and she could not resist turning towards him, letting her lips brush his. He pulled her closer and with his tongue teased open her lips. Margaret loved the taste of him. She was disappointed when he released her.

'I forget where I am,' he said a little breathlessly.

So, too, had Margaret.

They sat quietly for a while.

'I bring news of your brother Fergus,' James said in a brisker tone.

Margaret searched his face. 'Good news, I pray.' Fergus was younger than she, and despite being quite untested by life had accepted a mission to carry a message for Andrew Murray from Perth to Aberdeen.

'I trust you'll think it so. He's come south with Murray and should be with him now on Abbey Craig. I introduced him to our friend Hal from Edinburgh who I think will be a good influence on him.'

At last some good news. 'Fergus is safe. God be praised.'

'Alive and unharmed when last I saw him. I cannot of course promise that all will be well.'

Margaret chose not to dwell on that. 'I am not surprised that soldiering appealed to him more than being a secretary to Uncle Thomas.' Their uncle had a shipyard in Aberdeen and had requested that Fergus come to work for him as his secretary. Her brother had intended to take up the position after delivering the message he'd carried north to Murray. She was glad to hear that he would have her good friend Hal as a companion, dependable, capable Hal. 'Uncle Murdoch must miss Hal sorely.' Once again she realised how much she missed his counsel and company. 'How did you find him amidst all the troops?'

'I brought him with me from Edinburgh.'

'You hadn't told me.'

James shrugged and left Margaret to imagine the scene when Hal had announced his departure. Her uncle was very fond of him.

'Was it your idea or his?'

'Mine. We need men with his skill with horses, and his courage – that most of all.'

Margaret sensed that there was more to it, but James had already changed the subject.

'So Ada is here?' he asked.

'You sound as if that displeases you,' Margaret said, sensing his mood shift.

'I wish to God you had waited in Perth as we'd agreed. I don't know how we'll be rid of her now.'

This was an unexpected turn. 'Rid of her? I'm to stay in her house.'

He looked worried. 'That might no longer be wise.'

'Are you mad? It's part of the plan.'

'It was she who suggested you bide in her house, was it not?'

'Yes and no. When I told her about the mission it was with the thought that she might be of help.'

'What possessed you to involve her?' he snapped.

'Don't talk to me like that. You were delighted that I had. It's not my fault that you've changed your mind.'

'Christ, Maggie, do you realise–' he broke off, looking away with an exasperated sigh.

Margaret saw more than anger in his posture. 'What has happened?'

'She could not have known beforehand.' He spoke as if to himself. 'She would have needed another ruse.'

'She did not trick me, James. It was you who asked me to go to Stirling, not Ada. For pity's sake, tell me what has happened! You're frightening me.'

For the first time she noticed the shadows beneath his blue eyes, the lines about his mouth. He was exhausted and tense. 'Ada's lover Simon Montagu is expected in Stirling – at the castle.' James said it as if blaming her.

'*Former* lover,' Margaret said absently as she strove to comprehend the significance of this news. 'Her English lover,' she whispered. 'Of course I had no idea he would be there. And neither did she.'

'He will join his son – *their* son, Peter Fitzsimon.' James watched her reaction.

Margaret felt her face burning. According to Ada she had not seen Simon in years. But a son? 'I knew nothing of Peter Fitzsimon.'

'He was brought up in England. He's already renowned for his valour.'

But of course he must have been brought up there – Margaret had known Ada all her life, or since she could remember, and there had never been a child in her home. 'This is an unwelcome piece of news.' She bit her lip. 'I see the problem. Our party will attract too much notice – even more so if I play her niece.' Which had been the plan.

'That is not my greatest concern,' said James. 'I worry about their hold on her, where her loyalty will lie once she knows of their presence.'

'Her son's, yes. I doubt she feels much for Montagu – she seldom speaks of him. They did not part friends. I wonder why she did not rear her son here.'

'He's a Montagu,' said James, 'though by blood, not by name. A Comyn would do the same. Perhaps Simon thought one day to legitimise him in the event he had no other sons.'

They stared at one another for a few moments.

Margaret shook her head. 'She will not compromise us.'

'How can you be certain?'

'I can't.' Margaret's heart was pounding. She could not keep the fear from her voice. 'But we need her even more now.' She took a deep breath and said more strongly, 'We must present the facts to her.'

James rose with a curse.

He moved a little away from her, then turned on his heel and paced past her. There was nothing to do but sit and wait for him to walk out his aggravation. It occurred to Margaret that had she remained in Perth it would still have been necessary to find a way to present Ada with a change of plan, and she could not imagine Ada agreeing to stay in Perth without good cause.

'I apologise again,' James said when he'd calmed. 'My temper is too easily kindled of late.'

'I understand, Jamie. These are desperate times.'

He straddled the bench, facing Margaret. 'It is still true that she can provide you with the cover of being a supporter of Longshanks – once her relationship to Montagu is known.' He pressed one of Margaret's hands as he studied her. 'Your life is in her hands if you follow through.'

'I see that, Jamie.'

'You are not wavering in your trust of her?'

'No,' Margaret said without hesitation. 'I understand that Montagu is an added risk, but I think our original plan is the best we can do. What of you?'

'I don't like this complication, but I see no way out of it.' James sighed. 'We are decided then.' He reached out and cupped Margaret's head in his hands.

But noticing someone approaching the steps nearby, Margaret drew away and James dropped his hands. It was one of the guest-house servants carrying pillows.

'Servants are the worst gossips,' said Margaret. She grew uncomfortable under his blue gaze and shifted to face the garden. The midday sun had dried and cracked the soil and the blooms hung limply, the soil too sandy to hold the morning's moisture. 'You said the English are moving quickly?' she asked.

'Yes. I don't like it that a man of Montagu's standing has arrived. And worse, Warenne and Cressingham have left Berwick and are riding west with troops. The English are invading faster than we'd anticipated. We need news from the castle.'

The royal lieutenant and the treasurer – Margaret understood now why James was in haste. 'There is still silence from the castle?'

'Not utter silence, but too little information to be of help. I am almost certain the messenger has been compromised and is being told what to tell us.'

Margaret rose. 'Then come. We must go to Ada.'

Taking advantage of the light from a south window, Ada was absorbed in needlework. No one else was about. James spoke quickly, as if he feared that at any moment they might be interrupted. His manner was so different from that of a few moments before in the garden that Margaret felt uneasy. She'd noticed this ability of his before, shedding one mood for another, and even, when playing a friar or some other character, trading one accent for another, as well as mannerisms. She realised it was the latter that disturbed her the most. He moved as a noble now as he sat with Ada; in the garden he'd been less grand, simpler.

Her attention returned to Ada, who was quite visibly shaken by the news of her lover and son being in Stirling. She sat stiffly, as if afraid to move. 'Peter,' is the only word she'd yet uttered. 'Peter,' she repeated, as if growing accustomed to saying it.

'Are you still willing to take Maggie with you?' James asked.

Ada shook her head slightly and glanced at James, then Margaret, as if she'd just realised their presence. 'My son was not yet walking when they took him from me,' she said softly. 'I doubt Simon's told him that his mother is a de la Haye of Perth.'

Margaret took Ada's hands in hers. 'How hard it must have been for you.'

'My family had warned me that I would not keep my children, though of course I had not understood how terrible it would be, how a mother loves her child.' Ada caught her breath and dropped her chin.

'Shall we leave you for a while?' Margaret asked.

Shaking her head, Ada pressed Margaret's hands and released them to dab at her eyes. She took a deep breath and then faced them both, with chin up despite tears still balanced precariously in the corners of her eyes. 'It will not be the first time my skills as a player are tested.'

James nodded. 'They will be tested. I must also warn both of you that the tempers of the townsfolk are brittle, distrust divides them, and as in Perth some are eager to prove themselves trustworthy to the English by betraying their neighbours. If either of you has any doubt of your ability to carry through with your roles, tell me now. It would be better to stand aside here than to fail us in Stirling.' His eyes searched Margaret's face, then Ada's.

Margaret realised she was holding her breath and clenching her hands.

'When are we to depart?' Ada asked.

'Nightfall,' James said. He turned to Margaret. 'And you, Maggie, are you still with us?'

The magnitude of what she was about struck her afresh. 'I am.' Fear might catch her breath and bring on a sweat, but she would not withdraw. There was no turning back for her.

James nodded to each of them. 'I'll find some refreshment for my men while you prepare for the journey.'

As Margaret rose she found her legs unsteady.

❦ 4 ❧

TRUST

Time and again James was reminded of Margaret's youth. Just now she had sounded strong, and yet as she'd risen she'd almost swooned. She claimed her leg had cramped, but he guessed she was frightened. It was her youthful innocence that he hoped would protect her, but it was a gamble and he was very worried that he'd made the wrong decision to put her in such danger. Her friend Hal would never have wittingly put her in such peril. He loved her too. His disappointment when Roger had returned for Margaret was what had convinced James that the young man needed to leave Edinburgh and apply himself to winning this battle for his country's independence from England. James understood such disappointment – he'd experienced it when the woman he loved had married his cousin. He'd thought he'd never love again. Margaret had changed all that. He reminded himself that he was not sure he knew Margaret's heart. She might in time decide to stay in her marriage to Roger; it was the comfortable thing to do.

With a hand beneath Margaret's elbow, James escorted her and Ada out to the garden and then watched as they parted from him and crossed to the outside stairway. Both were tall, one with red hair, one with white that had in her youth likely been honey gold for her brows were still a dark honey, and both had strong jaws and prominent cheekbones. It was plausible they were kin. He counted on that.

The friendships of women were strange to James, the need they had to know the whole histories of one another, not satisfied with the kinds of things men wished to know of other men – how they fit within the present and in relation to their goals. Margaret had been taken aback and, he thought, quite disturbed to learn of Peter Fitzsimon. Certainly James would have preferred to have known of the man's existence when making the arrangement for Stirling, because he affected the plans. But it seemed to him that Margaret's unease only partly stemmed from that – she seemed equally disturbed to learn that there was someone so dear to Ada about whom she had never spoken to her. James wished he knew whether that was significant; he was not entirely reassured by his conversation with Ada.

'So you're off to Stirling, eh?' said Malcolm Kerr. He stood only a step behind James, hands clasped behind his back, watching the landing though his daughter was now out of view.

Under his breath James cursed whoever had told Malcolm where he was headed. But the damage was done. He nodded. 'We must ride on today.' He expected an argument about Margaret's part in his plans. But he was surprised.

'I'm proud of my daughter, her courage,' Malcolm said. 'I'd not have thought of her as part of all this, but she has chosen, and though I could not bear to lose her, I've no means to keep her safe, not here.'

'In these times no one is safe,' James agreed. Malcolm was less like his brother Murdoch, James's business partner in Edinburgh, than he had realised. Curious about him, he asked, 'Will you join me and my men in some refreshment?' He would find out just what the man knew.

But Malcolm shook his head. 'I was on my way to my wife's chamber. If my daughter leaves without stopping there, will you tell her I'm proud of her?'

'I will. And I'll tell you this, I'll do everything in my power to protect her.'

Malcolm gave a little laugh. 'A Comyn's no more able to do so than I am. Save your boasts for the ladies.'

Malcolm bowed and walked on, leaving James irritated. Perhaps he *was* just like Murdoch. Margaret's parents seemed liabilities James could not afford, not if he was to help his kinsman regain the throne of Scotland. He had not intended to be more than Margaret's compatriot. He had not been looking for love. But his panic when finding only the drunk servant in Margaret's house had revealed his heart to him. She was admirably courageous for such a young, inexperienced woman and intriguingly complex. But such a father – and a mother so fey. He would be glad to leave them behind.

After Margaret had given Celia instructions to prepare for departure and answered her questions as briefly as possible, she looked for Ada. Maus was anxiously packing and did not know where her mistress had gone. From the gallery Margaret soon caught sight of her sitting quietly on the garden bench that James had chosen earlier, her eyes cast down. As Margaret hurried down the stairs Ada lifted a tear-streaked face.

'I am so glad you've come to me.' Ada dabbed at her eyes with a square of linen.

'I thought you might like a companion,' Margaret said. 'You seemed quite shaken by the news.'

'I was.' Ada straightened and took a few deep breaths. 'It is a heartless practice, though common enough among the noble families.'

This was an Ada that Margaret did not know – sorrowful, wounded. 'I thought you were content with your life,' she said.

Lifting her chin, Ada seemed to study the branch above, but she clutched the cloth in her hand and breathed shallowly as if holding back more tears. 'I was far too young to understand the finality of my choice, how unlikely it was that I would one day be settled with my own family round me. Nor had I understood that I would not be choosing my liaisons. In faith, I was fortunate in Simon. By the time he bedded me I knew enough to be ready to do anything he asked if he would only keep me by him, for he was loving and thoughtful in bed.'

'I had not known you had a son.'

'Two sons and three daughters.' Ada nodded at Margaret's expression of surprise. 'And how could you know?' In her voice Margaret heard a weary resignation. 'I've regretted having to give them up to the Montagu family to wed well. I am not complaining about Simon – he has been generous.' She gave a silken shrug. 'Though it would have inconvenienced him little to have been kinder about our children. I thought surely he would relent and let me see them from time to time. But eventually I understood that he would not bend. I returned to Perth, wealthy and alone.' She gave a bitter little laugh. 'My kin did not know what to do about me. They told the impressionable young ones that I was a childless widow.'

'Is Simon the father of all your children?'

'The four living, yes. My third daughter was not so fortunate.' Ada bowed her head for a moment, then rose with a sigh. 'I must see to Maus,' she said with unconvincing energy. 'She can be quite contrary when she does not like her orders.' Ada looked older than usual, tired, defeated.

'I'll take my leave of Ma,' said Margaret. She waited a few moments, allowing Ada her solitude, then made her own way up to the gallery and on towards her mother's chamber, preparing herself for a difficult time. It would be easier simply to depart without a farewell, but she felt it important to take leave of her mother.

From the partially opened door Margaret heard her father bragging about her commitment to King John. She cursed under her breath as he noticed her and waved her into the room, where she was relieved to see that he had been talking to Marion, not her mother. She prayed her mother had not yet heard of her departure – she would prefer to tell her herself.

'Maggie, lass, your mother is praying with the holy sister,' said Malcolm. 'I've been telling Marion about your mission.'

'Da, you must talk of this no more. You'll do naught but harm if you go on so about what should be a secret.'

'I'm not simple, lass,' he snapped.

No, she thought, just a braggart.

'Young Margaret? Is that you?' Bethag stepped out from behind the screen. She smiled when she saw she'd guessed correctly. 'Come, your mother is anxious to speak with you.'

Margaret was glad to escape her father. But it was not truly an escape.

Her mother sat up. Marion had taken more pains dressing Christiana, for a wimple now covered her hair and tucks in the sides of her gown tidied its drape. Yet she looked no less haunted. Her gaunt, ageing face was pinched and puckered by the wimple; her eyes sleepy and focused on air. This was Margaret's mother, and soon herself?

'Is it true, Maggie, did you have a vision?'

Margaret glanced at Dame Bethag with an anger that caused the nun to step back and bow her head.

'I swore I'd say nothing to the sisters, but you need your mother's advice,' the nun said in a timid voice.

'Have you the Sight, Maggie?' For a moment, Christiana met Margaret's gaze and held it.

God help me, but I cannot bear to talk of it again. 'No, and we'll speak of it no more. I came to bid you farewell for a while. My escort to Stirling has arrived and would be away as soon as we are ready.'

Her mother was plainly not listening, her eyes focused beyond Margaret. 'It was Roger you saw, dead at the foot of the cliff, was

it not?' she asked. 'You must have been frightened. Poor Maggie.'
It was sweetly said, but spoken to the air.

'Ma, did you hear me? I am leaving for Stirling.'

'God go with you, Maggie.'

As Margaret bent to kiss her, Christiana suddenly grasped her
chin and looked her in the eyes. 'See to your own safety, Maggie,
you cannot save him.'

'Roger?'

Christiana let go of Margaret and lifted her cheek for a kiss, her
eyes closed. 'He was never right for you.'

'Ma, did you have a vision about Roger?'

Christiana sighed. 'I expect a kiss and receive a shower of
questions. Such a contrary daughter.'

'Tell me about it, I pray you. What did you see? What do you
mean that I cannot save him? From what?'

'You put words in my mouth, Maggie. I've said no such thing.'

'Ma!' Margaret cried in frustration, 'you are toying with me.'

Christiana closed her eyes and pressed her cheeks with the
backs of her hands. 'How can you speak so to me when I'm
burning with fever?'

Margaret pecked her mother's cheek, which *was* hot, and
wished her good health, then departed, grateful to breathe the
fresh air without.

Now and then Master Thomas invited Fathers Andrew and Obert
to dine with him, and this evening was one of those occasions. But
it was quickly obvious to Andrew that this evening was unusual,
for instead of settings for a half dozen or more the trestle table
held only three. Andrew did not like it.

The master of the spital was already seated at the table,
relaxing in his leather-backed chair with a mazer – filled with
wine, Andrew guessed, for he'd never seen the man drink ale.
With his oiled hair, his many chins, the high-backed chair and
elegant gown, Thomas was the picture of prosperity, which

seemed at odds with the war parties assembling daily in his domain. Andrew had noted the master's talent for knowing all that went on around him and yet remaining unmoved by it. In such times it seemed a handy talent.

As had become their habit, Andrew and Obert entered slowly together, the elderly priest using Andrew's arm for balance on one side, his cane on the other. Obert was able to straighten his back more with Andrew's support, which eased the strain of walking.

'*Benedicite*, my brothers,' Thomas cried in his nasal voice.

He always spoke over-loud in the presence of Obert, apparently believing the old priest hard of hearing. *I have never missed a word that he's said, more's the pity, but my response must have been lacking in something several times, which he believes can only be explained by my being deaf*, Obert had told Andrew.

'You two seem comfortable in your partnership,' Thomas noted.

'You need not shout at us,' Obert muttered as he lowered himself on to a chair across from Thomas. 'It turns pleasantries into threats.' He motioned to the servant to pour him some wine, ignoring Thomas's reaction.

But Andrew could not ignore Thomas's angry flush and the narrowing of his eyes. Andrew wished Father Obert would not bait Master Thomas as he did, particularly when he had been looking so smug as they arrived, like a cat who knows that his prey has no escape. Andrew asked the servant for half wine, half water. He wanted his head clear.

'With Sir Simon's departure I became lax in entertaining,' said Thomas as a small salmon was placed before them. 'Sir Marmaduke spends all his time with his war council and I've been free to work well into the evenings. But one must balance all things. So I look forward to a good meal and pleasant conversation.' He looked at his guests as if expecting some response, but an uncomfortable silence ensued.

'And what of Sir Francis?' asked Andrew, embarrassed by how

tight-throated he sounded. 'I had not heard that he had departed.'

Master Thomas had begun to spear himself some fish, but he paused and raised an eyebrow. 'Are you tracking the English commanders?'

God's blood he was difficult this evening. 'No,' said Andrew, 'You implied–'

'Father Andrew dislikes silences, so he was politely filling in conversation,' said Father Obert with affectionate amusement. 'His earnest courtesy can be painful, and often misunderstood.' He wrapped his long, slender fingers round his mazer and smiled over the top at Thomas.

'Do you think so?' asked Thomas, settling back with some food. 'I have heard only praise for Father Andrew.'

'But Thomas, you know that I have little tolerance for courtesy.'

The two men laughed. Andrew was uncertain whether Obert truly did amuse Thomas with his acid tongue, or whether Thomas pretended for the sake of his pride. Andrew liked Obert, and respected Thomas for his steadfast rule of the spital in difficult circumstances. But he trusted no one here except his servant Matthew. He was certain that everyone in the spital was working for one side or the other, or if not, they would freely betray anyone necessary in order to protect themselves. He gazed round the room, remembering other evenings with English commanders. More candles and lamps had been lit on those occasions, and often a canon had played a gittern in the corner.

'You miss the music, Andrew?' Thomas inquired.

'I was remembering it,' said Andrew, vowing to keep his eyes on the table before him for the remainder of the evening, for the master's scrutiny made him feel frighteningly exposed, as if his intention to escape was written in the movement of his eyes.

'They say that David, the Welsh archer who escaped, was an accomplished musician and had a remarkable voice,' said Thomas.

'I regret not having known that while he was here. They say the Welsh have the most beautiful voices.'

'I have heard that said of Italians, but not the Welsh,' Obert countered.

'What say you, Andrew?' Thomas asked.

Andrew prayed that the dimness of the lamplight hid the sweat on his upper lip and forehead, of which he was damnably aware. 'The French have a delicacy of phrasing that is often praised,' he said.

'Do you not wonder what poor David suffers?' said Obert. 'The guards sent in after him are yet in the infirmary. What did he achieve?'

'I should think it would be a great challenge to escape from such a well-guarded place,' said Andrew. 'But so far from his own people, where would he go? How would he eat?' He hoped his voice sounded as normal to them as it did to him.

Thomas was nodding. 'I, too, wondered that.'

'Perhaps he did not escape,' said Obert.

'What?' said Thomas, but then he seemed to see that it was possible and began to smile. 'He is in hiding. Who would notice a little food missing from the kitchen, eh? Yes. It is quite possible.'

Obert, bent over his trencher, glanced at Andrew and shook his head slightly. Andrew took it as a warning not to voice his theory, that David was a spy who merely left, that the story of the drains was to discourage anyone seeking to escape. Andrew still found it difficult to believe the English captains would have sacrificed two of their men to make the story seem real.

As the meal continued, the conversation quieted into domestic issues and innocent gossip. But towards the end of the evening Master Thomas began a unsavoury game of pitting one of them against the other. 'How do you feel, having such a popular assistant, Father Obert?', 'You must find it difficult to obey a man not because he is a better priest but merely because he is older, Father Andrew.' And he watched them squirm.

No, he watched Andrew squirm. Obert seemed mildly amused.

Later, in Obert's chamber, Andrew asked if they might talk before he went to his own bed.

'Help me with these first,' said the elderly priest as he eased himself down on his simple bed and proffered his booted feet. 'In my youth I imagined an old age in a warmer clime where I might wear sandals. Instead I end my service in the windiest spital on earth.' Obert pressed his stomach. 'Oof. I already feel the food burning holes in my flesh. I'll not be lying down for a while. To invite us to dine with him and then create such a strained mood is too cruel. I shan't forgive him for this night.'

'You do inspire him to prick at you.'

'I have cause. Working well into the evening – that man's never worked a whole day, much less into the evening. But do not fret, I have made my honesty into a game that he believes he is enjoying with me.' Obert chuckled, but suddenly bent forward, his hand to his stomach, his face contorted in pain. '*Deus juva me,*' he groaned. 'Fetch me the little bottle on the shelf over there.' He nodded towards the foot of his bed.

Andrew fetched it and pulled out the stopper before handing it to the elderly priest, who drank down its contents and then sat back against the wall with a sigh.

'It will soon work, else I'll take a powder of crowfoot and die laughing.' Obert chuckled weakly. 'Does that not sound pleasant, to die laughing?'

'Were I assured of dying so I should not fear it,' said Andrew, easing down on to a stool near the bed. Obert had closed his eyes. 'What *did* you take?'

'Oh dear, I forgot – the crowfoot works only on an empty belly, and mine is far from empty,' said Obert, tears of laughter streaming down his eyes.

Andrew did not know whether his companion was laughing or crying, or indeed whether or not he had lost his wits. 'Father Obert?'

'I took rue,' the old priest whispered. 'It often works miracles.'

'Are you in much pain?'

Obert eased upright and opened his eyes. They were still quite filled with tears, but he was now smiling. 'Old age is so filled with pain, how might I measure this one alone?' He used his sleeve to blot his tears. 'Oh my, forgive me, I've frightened you. And why not?' He let out a sound between a groan and a sigh and then took a deep breath. 'Better. So. I shall live another night.'

'Can I fetch you anything else?' Living another night did not seem compensation enough for what Obert had seemed to suffer.

But the old priest shook his head. 'I need to be quiet, breathe deeply, from the bottom to the top of my lungs, and it will all calm.' He demonstrated, coughing a little, but after a few rounds the coughing ceased and his expression was much less strained.

'I must remember that,' said Andrew. He thought he should leave the old man to his rest. 'Sleep well,' he said, rising.

'But you wished to talk, eh? You held your own part well this evening. I do not believe Thomas could see how his talk disturbed you.'

That was not reassuring. 'You could.'

Obert, still leaning back against the wall with his eyes half closed, smiled a little. 'I know you far better than he does. Now. What is on your mind?'

'Thomas was looking for something, wasn't he?'

Tilting his head from side to side as if it was not such a terrible thing, Obert said, 'He expects us to spy on one another.'

'But we are priests.'

'We are human, Andrew, just men beneath these gowns, and Thomas never forgets that. I advise you to pay more heed to that. Have I not told you that I betrayed someone to save myself?'

'You've told me little. Even what you just said is more than you've revealed before.'

'Let that satisfy you for tonight. My belly has suffered enough.' He closed his eyes.

'But–'

'Leave me now, I pray you,' said Obert.

Andrew withdrew, wide awake and frightened that if something should happen to Obert he would be responsible for the souls of all in this godforsaken place.

The assemblage of belongings Margaret and her friend presented was far smaller than James had expected. Margaret had more than did Ada, who he had expected would travel with household items as well as clothing.

'Is this all you have brought?' he asked her. 'Are you so confident that your kinsmen's house in Stirling will be in readiness for you? The English have taken over many dwellings.'

'The tenants are skilled in gaining grace with whoever holds power,' Ada said. 'But I also sent my butler and cook on to prepare the house. So I carried only what was necessary for this journey and brought only my lady's maid and the two menservants with me.'

James silently cursed himself for not having anticipated that Ada would send servants ahead. Now Simon Montagu might be forewarned and expecting a de la Haye. But it did not change anything, merely hastened the meeting, for Montagu would have soon discovered Ada's presence anyway, gossip typically being rife in a town under siege; unfortunately the gossip did not pass so easily out of the town to the countryside, and hence his need for Margaret. He noticed that she, however, looked distraught.

'From this moment on I must think of myself as Ada's niece,' she said quietly to him. 'For–'

Ada interrupted.

'I heard you curse beneath your breath, James, but what would you have had me do? I could not expect the tenants to rejoice if they were suddenly consigned to the hut in the backlands.' Her voice was tensely defensive. 'Nor could I be certain they would have cleaned and laundered everything before they withdrew from the house.' She was quite flushed with self-righteousness.

'It is as it is,' James said. 'Come. We must make some distance before we rest tonight.'

Celia remembered an earlier journey made mostly by night, when Roger Sinclair brought Margaret from Edinburgh to Perth. She felt safer in the present company; James Comyn was not new to stealth and he seemed to have armed men at his beck and call. He was also more open about his purpose than Roger Sinclair had been.

But she was not confident about her mistress's mission in Stirling, especially now that Dame Ada's former English lover was there. Margaret had been frank with Celia, as always, about the added danger, and although she understood that both her mistress and James Comyn considered it the best they could do when time was so short, Celia was worried about going on with the original plan. But not even fear would make her desert her mistress.

The land began to rise and the night grew chillier. Celia was grateful for the warmth of the horse beneath her, and for the wimple that just hours earlier she'd resented because of the damp warmth near the river. When not far along the road they turned off into a copse of trees she eagerly watched for light from a hut or a barn. One of the men opened the shutter on a lantern and she saw that they'd come to an earthen mound in a small clearing. She hoped it was a natural hillock and not a burial mound.

As she did not see or hear a stream or see any shelter Celia felt anxious, worried that the men had sensed someone following them and intended to make a stand here, which seemed quite ill-advised near a burial mound. Strange things happened around them, especially at night, and the battle might be fraught with surprises. She hoped she was wrong. Perhaps they were awaiting additional horses here, for with the men walking and leading the horses with the women astride they moved slowly. The man leading hers came around to assist her in dismounting.

'Don't be alarmed,' James was saying to Margaret, 'we will rest here for the remainder of the night and my men and I will change into our disguises. We want to escort you near enough to Stirling that we can be fairly certain you'll safely reach Dame Ada's house, so we must look like farmers.'

'We'll sleep in the open?' Margaret asked.

'No, in the barn.'

Celia had just heard a strange sound, the groan of something large being shifted, and turning to look back watched what she'd thought a section of the mound swing wide. It was a large door camouflaged with sod, part of an earthen barn, and within was a two-wheeled cart such as farmers brought to market.

Lanterns were lit within and soon Margaret and Celia were lying side by side on hay, beneath a blanket and hide.

'I thought this was a burial mound,' Celia whispered.

Margaret shivered. 'So did I. I pray that keeps us safe from attack.'

Celia pulled out her paternoster beads and prayed until she realised she'd fallen asleep and had been dreaming about doors in trees and riverbanks, then turned on her side and slipped back into sleep.

She woke confused by the smell of animals and the murmur of men's voices, but when she remembered the barn and the night journey she settled into her nest and fell into a deep sleep once more. When next she woke the barn door stood slightly ajar and a misty dawn freshened the air. Margaret was already sitting up with a small wooden cup in her hands. When she noticed Celia watching her, she proffered the cup.

'Cider – it is strong, so just sip it.' Her hands trembled.

Celia tasted the cider and sighed with pleasure. 'I like travelling with James Comyn.'

Margaret laughed, but it sounded sadly forced.

'Did you sleep?' Celia asked.

Margaret nodded. 'Not peacefully.'

'You need this more than I do, then,' said Celia, handing back the cup. 'I'll fix your wimple when you are finished.'

'See to your own needs first,' said Margaret. 'There are oatcakes and perhaps more cider near the door.'

As Celia moved out of their little corner she saw that the men now wore undyed tunics and leggings well patched and stained from work in the fields. They were quite believable, and disturbingly quiet and grim-faced. Maus was busy fixing Dame Ada's hair in the opposite corner. Celia wished them good morning and then hurried out to relieve herself, trying not to look at the man who escorted her and stood at a discreet but careful distance with an arrow at the ready.

Back in the barn she took several oatcakes and another small cup of cider to her corner. Margaret had already folded the blanket and put the hide atop it. The oatcake took the edge off Celia's anxiety, and she tried to engage her mistress in talk, but Margaret seemed distracted.

'What troubles you?' Celia asked.

'I'm worried about Roger. Ma felt he was still much too weak to leave the nunnery.'

Celia was relieved that it had to do with Roger and not with this journey. She murmured some inane comfort while combing Margaret's lovely russet hair and then covering it with the wimple and veil.

At last ready, they joined Ada and her servants near the door.

James approached with an odd gait. 'We'll escort your company to Stirling, Dame Ada,' he said in a voice quite unlike his usual one, and no wonder with the odd twist to his back and neck which made him look frail. 'But it will cost ye.'

'I had no doubt of that,' said Ada. Then she laughed and clapped her hands.

Margaret shook her head but Celia saw the admiration in her expression.

'Why are the men so grim?' Celia asked.

'Because the English army is not far behind us,' said Ned, one of Ada's servants, his eyes jumpy with fear.

Andrew had retired to his room after hearing confessions for several hours – a troop of soldiers was preparing to march on and the fear in their voices had been terrible to hear. Abbot Adam would have urged Andrew to lecture the men on the terrible sin of despair, but he could not find it in his heart to do that. To be absolved of their sins was small enough comfort when facing the fear of losing courage, suffering mutilation, dying without the last rites, far from home, for a cause they'd never understood.

He fell on to his bed and tried to free his mind from the morning's work, but he felt as if his ribs were bound by steel too tightly to allow him to breathe. He felt guilty about the soldiers' fears, as if he should be able to reassure them as a mother her children. As if it had been he who had ordered them to invade his country, or perhaps as if he'd taunted them to come and attempt to conquer his people, or as if he'd trained his own people to be far stronger than the English had expected. He amused himself with these variations on his sense of guilt, and gradually his ribs began to expand with his breath.

He ignored a knock on the door. But whoever it was knocked a second time and then entered the room. Andrew recognised Father Obert's shuffling gait, and as the elderly priest had never before intruded, that he was doing so now meant something serious was on his mind.

Andrew sat up.

Father Obert leaned on his cane, his back so crooked that his hips seemed those of an animal that walks on all four legs. 'We are summoned to Master Thomas's chamber,' said Obert in a slightly breathless voice.

Andrew's heart sank. 'I have heard confession all morning and I am weary.'

Obert grimaced sympathetically. 'I know, my friend, but I also know the matter about which Thomas would confer with us and I urge you to put on a pleasant face and come along.' Without waiting for Andrew's reply, Obert turned to withdraw.

'Tell me – what is this about?'

Obert shook his head. 'You will hear soon enough.'

Taking pity on the old priest, Andrew hurried to join him, offering his arm for support to ease Obert's twisted spine. Of course he hoped the priest would trade information for relief. 'It is always of benefit to know something of the reason for a summons.'

'I know nothing for certain,' said Obert.

'You are a stubborn man.'

'I think of it as cautious rather than stubborn.' Obert grinned with mischief.

Andrew found himself incapable of being angry with Obert when he exhibited this lightness of spirit. How the old priest found it possible to smile and tease when trapped in a twisted, pain-wracked body filled Andrew with wonder and he believed it must be a sign of God's grace. It inspired Andrew to seek an uncharacteristic lightness, which felt oddly calming.

'Cautious,' Andrew repeated. 'It does sound less irritating.'

But the flicker of amusement faded quickly as their slow progress through the hall to Thomas's door brought back Andrew's grim exhaustion.

'I feel your weariness,' Obert commented when they paused at the door. 'Laymen are doubtless unaware how they weigh us down with their sins and fears. I've heard them complain that we do little to earn the relative comfort in which we bide. It is not so.' He lifted his hand to knock, but the door swung open, the servant bowing them in.

Master Thomas stood with another visitor, Sir Francis, whose men were to depart on the morrow for the north, taking the land route across Stirling Bridge. As Andrew stepped into the room he had noticed a fleeting, angry expression on Thomas's face, and a frustrated look on Sir Francis's, but they then stepped away from each other as if they'd been interrupted in a private conversation. As he helped Father Obert settle down on a chair it seemed to Andrew that Thomas and Francis regarded him with unease. The room was stuffy. The day was warm and the wind that had seemed never to abate had done so just when it would be appreciated. Sir Francis wore a simple dark tunic and surcoat and fine leather girdle and boots, the picture of simple elegance next to the unlovely Thomas, whose green tunic hung limply on his heavy frame damp with sweat.

After all had exchanged greetings, Sir Francis chose the seat nearest Andrew and nodded to him.

'I am aware that you have heard the confessions of my men all morning, Father Andrew,' he said, 'and I am grateful that even so you have agreed to meet with us.'

If he'd meant to disarm Andrew with his considerate words he'd succeeded. Father Obert nodded as if approving the sentiment.

'He is a hard worker and I have much appreciated his assistance these past months,' said Obert.

Sir Francis did not look pleased by the comment.

'Have you changed your mind, Father Obert?' Master Thomas asked.

'Has he changed his mind about what?' Andrew asked, feeling as if he were being deliberately kept in the dark.

'I told him nothing,' said Obert.

Sir Francis glanced at him in puzzlement. 'Forgive me,' he said to Andrew. 'I'd expected you would have heard about it from Father Obert. I have a problem that must be resolved before we ride in the morning. The chaplain who arrived at long last to travel with my men and Sir Marmaduke's has broken his leg – it is very badly broken. He cannot sit a horse. I cannot in good conscience continue without a man of the Church. You've listened to my men, Father Andrew, you know how frightened they are, hearing awful tales of the Wallace and the bloodthirsty highlanders—'

Andrew smiled without being aware of it, but Francis paused. 'What is amusing?'

'Forgive my discourtesy. The men from the highlands have no cause to join with the Wallace for they are not under siege – nor can I imagine them fighting under a lowlander. Your words painted an unlikely picture, that is all. I am tired, as you so kindly noted.' Andrew felt like a babbling fool.

'Sir Francis is not a Scotsman, Father Andrew,' said Master Thomas. 'He knows not the—'

Sir Francis held up a hand to stop the conversation. 'I thank you for pointing out my error, and see yet another good coming out of Father Guthlac's accident – if you agree to accompany me and my men in the morning, Father Andrew.'

Andrew glanced at Obert, who was gazing at the floor, then at Master Thomas, who looked uncomfortable. Sir Francis had an encouraging expression on his face, as if hoping that by his demeanour he might persuade Andrew to risk his life on the march. But of course Andrew could hardly contain his excitement, could not believe his good fortune, feared that at any moment Master Thomas would cry out that Andrew could not be trusted outside the close confines of Soutra where his Abbot had placed him. For outside the spital he might escape. With Matthew.

'My servant Matthew would accompany me?'

Sir Francis nodded. 'Tell me your requirements and they shall be met if it is in my power. And if Father Obert is still willing to accept Father Guthlac as his assistant.'

Father Obert shifted slightly in his chair, his face unreadable to Andrew. 'As I said earlier, I'll feel the lack of Andrew, for he has been of great help to me. But your men deserve a chaplain, and I am far too old to undertake such a duty. There is no question, Father Andrew is the one to help you.'

'I am in favour but for one significant fact about Father

Andrew,' said Master Thomas, 'that he is a Scot.' He frowned down at Andrew.

Andrew held his breath, expecting Thomas to reveal that he'd been banished to Soutra.

Sir Francis was balanced on the edge of his seat, ready to argue. 'Many of the men fighting for King Edward are Scots. Father Andrew is caring for the souls of the English forces – therefore he is a wise Scot who sees that strong rule is only possible under King Edward.'

As Thomas remained silent, Andrew forced himself to say calmly, 'You will find many wise men among us, and I am grateful for the chance to prove as much to you.' He glanced up at Master Thomas and could clearly see by his expression that he was not happy with the arrangement.

'I should feel better had I the time to send a messenger to Abbot Adam to request your release,' said Thomas.

'But we cannot delay,' said Francis.

Thomas shrugged. 'It is in God's hands. So be it.' He rose. 'I'll leave you to your planning. God go with you, Father Andrew, and thank you for all you have done here.' He bowed formally.

Andrew felt it a pointedly final farewell, as if Thomas was certain they would never meet again.

Father Obert said, 'Such a farewell, Master Thomas. I look forward to Father Andrew's return when Sir Francis marches south.'

'If God so chooses,' said Master Thomas.

'I have been pleased to carry on my work at Soutra,' said Andrew. 'I'll keep all of you in my prayers.'

'God bless you, Thomas,' said Sir Francis. 'I'll not forget this favour.' When Thomas was gone, Sir Francis turned to Andrew, who was weak with relief. 'I do not pretend to know your heart in this matter of the Scots throne,' he said, 'but I have seen you with my men and know you for a holy man. I am much comforted, as will they be, that you have agreed to ride with us.'

Andrew silently applauded Francis on his courteous mani-
pulation of his heart. He had just made it more difficult for
Andrew to simply walk away.

'You spoke of a manservant,' Francis said. 'He shall accompany
you. Now we must discuss what else you will need.'

Father Obert sat back with a small smile on his wizened face.

❦ 5 ❧

Is It Love?

Standing at the foot of the road leading up the gently sloping, wooded side of the crag that was crowned by Stirling Castle, Margaret watched as James and his men departed, the old cart squeaking and thudding, one of the men singing a bawdy song. As soon as the party had come down out of the hills towards Stirling Bridge and Margaret had caught sight of the cliffs below Stirling she had been haunted by the dream of Roger's fall. It possessed her so completely that she rode as if in another world.

But now she was fully here, standing on the road, midges swirling about her, the air close, the sun too warm, and there had been no sign of Roger as they rode – she had thought she was about to encounter what she'd seen only in her dreams and visions.

In her trance state she'd allowed her horse to wander to a burn to drink. She had not regained consciousness until James, with Celia assisting, had lifted her from the saddle and, holding her, splashed water on her face.

'What is it, Maggie?' James had asked, his face close to hers, his expression troubled and even frightened.

Realising that she had no recollection of being brought down from the saddle and no idea where she was, Margaret experienced a fear icier than the burn waters. She shook her head, not knowing how to explain. Nothing like this had ever happened to her.

'Did you fall asleep?' he asked. 'Are you unwell?'

'I did not sleep well last night – faith, what sleep I had was troubled with dreams.' She sat up to dry her face on a cloth Celia proffered her. Glancing around Margaret saw that all in the company were trying to look elsewhere and give her privacy. What must they think of her? 'James, what if I fail you?'

He shook his head. 'You won't. Is that what kept you awake last night?'

'Yes. How do you know that I'll succeed? I don't know that.'

'You are strong, Maggie. And Father Piers will guide you.'

She was terribly aware of the castle crowning the rock above them. 'Someone will note that I'm asking questions.'

'You won't be the only one.'

'I'm frightened.'

He squeezed her hand. 'Of course you are. I'd worry were you not.' He helped her rise.

'You are not making sense, James. You are not listening to me.'

'I am, believe me. It is the nature of danger to make us fearful.'

'What if no one believes I am Ada's niece?'

'Why would they even question it?'

Ada had joined them. 'We look enough alike, Maggie. Simon did not ken all my family, so why would he know of you? We shall be under his protection.'

Perhaps Margaret was making too much of daydreaming on a long ride in the late summer heat. Looking around at the dusty company she noticed how wilted they all looked. 'Of course. The heat and my lack of sleep have confused me. I feel foolish. Forgive me, I pray you. I'll not forget myself again.'

Ada nodded, satisfied, and withdrew to where the rest had settled behind a screen of brush.

'Remember, Maggie, when you've completed your mission, or if you have need to flee Stirling, make your way to Elcho as quickly as you can, and I'll find you there.' James kissed her on the forehead. 'I love you, Maggie. I would have you near me always. I lay awake nights cursing Roger Sinclair.'

Margaret could not think how to respond. He'd never spoken of love to her before. 'Love?' she whispered, searching his eyes, wanting to know whether this was an act meant to bolster her courage or ensure her commitment. His gaze did not waver. 'This is not the time, Jamie.'

He stroked her cheek. 'I agree. Escorting you to spy on the English is a cruel sort of courting. But the heart does not choose the time, and I wanted you to know my heart in the event . . .'

She knew the end of that thought. 'I am honoured by your love, Jamie.' She kissed his cheek.

'And you? Do you think you might love me?'

'When I said it was not the time, I meant for me, Jamie. I'm so filled with remorse over Roger and I feel so guilty about my feelings for you – I can't tell whether or not it's love, but it's sinful, of that I can assure you.' She brushed his lips with hers.

He held her there when she began to move away, and what had been the ghost of a kiss became a long, passionate one that left Margaret breathless and wanting desperately to lie with him, feel his nakedness, his desire.

'What have I done, Maggie?' James whispered. 'I must leave you now and I've made it all the more difficult.'

'We both have.'

But was it love? Margaret turned away and hid her confusion by calling for Celia to assist her with her wimple. God forgive her, she was still a married woman and her feelings for James were doubly sinful. Perhaps that was why she was obsessed with Roger's danger – to appease her conscience. Yet there was a part of her that had felt unmoved by the kiss. Her conscience held her back – that was possible.

Now, as she stood on the Stirling road, she watched James and his men fade from sight and prayed he'd been right to trust that she would be successful in re-establishing communication from the castle. She wanted to live up to his expectations of her. She desperately wanted to see him again.

'Come, Maggie. I am weary and ready for an ale and my bed.' Ada, already mounted with Maus behind her, spoke as if this were the last leg of an ordinary journey. She seemed unconcerned as strangers moved past, casting them curious looks. Alec and Ned, the menservants, impatiently held the reins.

Margaret mounted, then reached down to assist Celia.

'You look no happier than I feel,' Celia said once she had settled.

'Is it so plain?'

'To me, Mistress, and to your aunt, I should think.'

They had practised referring to Ada as Margaret's aunt for days now, and it was beginning to sound convincing. But in her heart Margaret feared she would slip in front of someone. She must bury that fear – James had said that the trick was to convince herself that she was not playing but living the new role.

She wished James were with them, but though he'd passed as a farmer with the soldiers they'd met on the road he reiterated that he would not risk entering the town in daylight, for there were too many in Stirling who knew him. A disguise would be seen through in time, particularly by someone expecting him to appear. *If you see me there, it will be at night and will signal danger*.

Up through the woods they slowly rode, branching off from the high road to follow another that ran lower along a burn.

'The other way leads to the castle,' Ada explained. 'My family's town house is on the market square, across the burn on lower ground.'

'At the market,' Celia said. 'It must be grand.'

'Not grand,' Ada said, 'but pleasant.'

As the number of people sharing the road increased, the women dismounted, Maus and Celia leading the animals while Alec and Ned walked ahead and behind. Ada commented on the number of armed men, and the condition of many of the houses at the edge of town, still in the wooded areas. It was plain that trees had recently been cut for bonfires, the remains of which scarred the landscape, and many of the houses, too, were charred. It took Margaret back to her arrival in Edinburgh in the spring, the houses along the Grassmarket scarred by fire and wreckage everywhere. Here the damage was not so extensive, but none-theless it served as a reminder of the violence of the occupation. The dishevelled but strutting trio who approached them now were another, more visceral reminder – foot soldiers on their own far from home and looking for trouble.

'Fine mounts,' one of them said, his accent that of Flanders. 'You won't be needing them in the town.'

'Whence came you here with them?' asked another.

'From my home in Perth,' said Ada.

Alec and Ned had drawn in towards Ada; as the first speaker reached for one of the horses Ned lunged for him, then drew back his arm with a shout of pain, holding his bleeding hand to his chest.

'You've wounded my servant,' Ada said with a sharpness that Margaret admired though she wondered at its wisdom.

She thought it best to keep moving. As she walked on, Margaret prayed that all the men wanted was the horses. She was frightened, and her fear intensified when the third soldier joined her, too close for comfort, matching her stride and staring so boldly that her face burned and she felt sick to her stomach. A greasy cap did little to hide the hideous scar where his right ear had been, and his clothes smelled of urine.

'Dame Maggie!' Celia called out from behind.

Sweet heaven, Ada had been stopped by the others, and Maus was back there wrapping Ned's bleeding hand. Margaret was now several houses beyond.

'Maggie,' the soldier said with a chuckle. 'A pretty name for a pretty lady.' He dared to touch her shoulder. She reached out to push him away and he caught her hand, squeezing it so tightly that Margaret feared he'd break her bones.

Another soldier suddenly grabbed the man's wrist, and Margaret, her hand released, backed away.

'King Edward expects you to respect the women of Scotland,' her rescuer said to her attacker.

'Bastard,' Margaret hissed as she withdrew, pushing back through the onlookers to join Ada and the others.

'We should have come on foot,' she said to Ada as she rubbed her hand. When she received no answer, she realised that her friend was staring back down the road. Several liveried men now surrounded the other two who had accosted them.

'They wear Simon's livery,' said Ada. 'Perhaps he is in charge of the peace here.' Her eyes brimmed with tears; she must have been as frightened as Margaret had been.

'God bless him,' Margaret said, meaning it with all her heart. Perhaps Simon Montagu would be their salvation after all, though she was not so certain when his men encircled her little party.

'We are to escort you to the castle,' said Margaret's rescuer. 'It is customary for my lord to speak with newcomers.'

'Might we first retire to my home to tidy ourselves?' Ada asked.

'No, Mistress. My orders are clear.'

'So be it,' Ada murmured.

The men led them up Broad Street, the way suddenly much less crowded.

James had warned them that they were likely to be questioned upon entering Stirling, but Margaret had put it from her mind. The steep climb was exhausting after so little sleep and her trance journey, not to mention the fright the disgusting soldier had given her. She wanted only to rest. As they crossed over a sluggish burn and turned into the market square she sighed over the distance yet to go – all uphill.

'There is our house,' Ada said.

Margaret saw Ada's butler John standing in the doorway looking worried. Ada nodded to him.

'I wonder whether he was escorted to the castle when he arrived,' said Margaret.

'You ken his ways, Maggie. John's countenance is ever solemn, even when he's laughing. Do not assume that his grim face means danger. It's more likely a sour stomach.'

Ada's chuckle teased a smile from Margaret.

'The market square isn't much changed since last I was here,' said Ada, 'but I can tell even from down here that the castle walls have been patched and fortified.'

With Ada's commentary distracting Margaret it was not so long after all before they entered the outer bailey of the castle. It was crowded with small, flimsy buildings and tents, wagons, carts, and men everywhere. Margaret wondered at the numbers.

They were led to a wattle and daub building. Within, a well-dressed, grey-haired man stood talking with a few soldiers. He waved them on when he saw Margaret's party in the doorway.

'I understand that these women arrived on fine horses,' the man said.

Margaret's saviour gave a curt bow. 'They did, Sir Simon.'

So this was Ada's long-ago lover. He had an air of command, and the soldiers deferred to him. Margaret tried to imagine him twenty years younger. He had expressive eyes and a jaw line that would have been strong in youth. At present he looked bored.

'What is your business in Stirling?' Sir Simon demanded of them. His expression changed as Ada stepped forward to respond. 'It cannot be,' he said. 'Ada de la Haye?'

Ada gave a graceful bow. 'Yes, Sir Simon. I have brought my niece to stay in my family's town house on the market square.' She met his eyes. 'I hope that you remember me?'

'Dame Ada,' he bowed slightly, 'I remember you well, and with affection. This is your niece?' He met Margaret's open stare with a quick smile.

'This is my niece Maggie,' said Ada.

'Dame Maggie,' said Sir Simon with a polite bob of his head.

'What brings you to Stirling?'

'I am recently widowed, Sir, and would escape the memories that fill my home in Perth.'

He turned back to Ada. 'I can see that you are weary from your journey. You will dine with me here tomorrow, both of you. Until then.' He bowed and dismissed them.

Heaven, thought Celia, could be no more welcoming than the two-storey house on the market square, its paint fresh and the butler John standing solidly beside the doorway to receive them. Wealth was more than pretty clothes, solid furnishings and good food; it was security. She had seen the relief on Dame Ada's face and known that they had been rescued by the liveried soldiers who surrounded the frightening men who'd threatened her mistress, despite their having to report at the castle. Celia had gladly handed Sir Simon's men the reins. She'd had enough of animals for one day, human and otherwise.

The fragrance of fresh herbs in the rushes strewn on the floor took Celia back to her days with Margaret's goodmother, Roger's mother. The house in Dunfermline had not been grand, but it had always been clean, with fresh, fragrant rushes in summer. Neither in Edinburgh nor in Perth had they been able to completely replace the old straw or rushes on the floors because the English commandeered it for their animals. Here was another sign that Dame Ada's kin were important to the powers in this town. Celia hated the English, but at the moment she was glad that they were unaware where her loyalties lay. She prayed that tomorrow her mistress and Dame Ada handled Sir Simon well. She was sorry Margaret would not be spared the occasion. Her odd behaviour on the journey made Celia wonder whether she was in any condition to carry out this mission. Had Margaret merely been dozing she would have responded to Celia's attempts to rouse her, but nothing had reached her until with James's help they'd lifted her from the horse and splashed her with the cold burn water. Celia knew the owl's visitation haunted her mistress, followed so closely by the daydream in the kirk.

With the menservants seeing to their packs Celia had an opportunity to pause and admire the hall. High windows faced the street and the backlands, the shutters opened to catch the upland breeze. The ceiling was high and whitewashed, with painted flowers on the border between ceiling and walls. A table was laid with cheese and bread and large flagons of ale that made her aware of her thirst.

Gradually she also grew aware of a man standing in the shadows watching Margaret and Ada as they discussed the sleeping arrangements. The intensity of his expression and posture alarmed her. He wore almost the same livery as did the men who had led them here. She wondered what right a soldier had to stare so at her mistress and the mistress of this house. Edging closer to Margaret, she caught her eye and nodded in his direction.

Margaret glanced in the direction while Celia poured her a cup of ale.

'What was I to note?' Margaret asked, taking the cup with a sigh of pleasure.

The man was gone.

'I did not like the look of one of the men, but he has gone.'

Her mistress sipped the thick ale and nodded. 'Rest easy. Dame Ada seems welcome here, and we with her. Have a cup of ale.'

'I'll do so if you'll step out into the backlands with me for a breath of air,' said Celia.

They settled on a bench under the eaves of the main house, facing the kitchen. Wattle panels made a mud-free path between the rear door of the hall and the kitchen doorway.

'What happened down there, at the burn, Mistress?'

Margaret closed her eyes and bowed her head for a moment. Celia waited.

'I started to tell you at Elcho, but Ada interrupted us. The dreams about Roger's death, the vision at Elcho, they are part of something that has been changing in me, my friend.'

'It *is* the Sight, isn't it?'

Margaret nodded, turning to look Celia in the eyes. 'I am not mad like my ma, and I won't be. I'll learn how to live with this . . . gift.'

Celia saw how difficult it was for Margaret to speak of this. 'You had a vision on the horse?'

'My dreams of Roger came flooding back and filled my head so that I was not aware of where I was,' said Margaret.

'That sounds frightening.'

'It was. But I won't fail James, nor you, nor Ada.'

'Is there anything I can do to help you?'

'Listen and watch so that I have two sets of eyes and ears,' said Margaret.

Celia nodded. 'Does Dame Ada know?'

'I've told no one else, and that is as it must stay for now.'

Celia was honoured to be her mistress's sole confidante. 'I'll not fail you, Mistress.'

Margaret pressed Celia's hand.

Andrew's dreams were of his family, and when he woke he fell to worrying about Margaret and Fergus. He had heard nothing of his brother in a long while, and when last he'd seen Margaret she was so unhappy in her marriage. Dawn had not yet coloured the small window in Andrew's bedchamber when Obert knocked at the door. Perhaps he'd guessed that Andrew would sleep little, but Matthew still slept soundly at the foot of his pallet, and after his bout of illness he needed rest before the journey ahead. Barefoot, Andrew went to the door and slipped out. In the dimness of the corridor Father Obert waited, bent over his stick with the stiffness that afflicted him in the morning. Without a word, he led Andrew to his own chamber and shut the door. A small lamp smoked by the bed.

'The wick needs trimming,' said Andrew, wanting to break the silence with something ordinary.

Father Obert grunted as he eased himself down on to a stool. 'Time enough for that when you are on your way. I pray you, sit so that I need not crane my neck to see you.' He patted his pallet.

Andrew settled down on it cross-legged, covering his cold feet with the edge of a blanket. He would be uncomfortable enough in the saddle today after months of enforced inactivity. 'I shall miss you, Father Obert.'

'You'll have little time to notice.'

'Do you regret putting me forward for this journey?'

'Do you ask whether I regret I'm not the one about to travel?' Obert chuckled at Andrew's nod. 'No, my friend, I am too old to ride all day, even in summer. My legs are so weak it would be necessary to strap me onto the poor beast, and the cramps I would suffer would have me howling in anguish.' He paused, but as Andrew was about to respond that he, too, foresaw discomfort at first, Obert continued. 'And the captains are pleased with your reputation.'

Surprised by the unexpected comment, Andrew did not respond at once, uncertain what the old priest meant, but when he understood he blushed and bowed his head. 'You mean my work for Abbot Adam.'

'Yes, of course. I advise you to accept this twist of fortune with a prayer of gratitude, Father Andrew. Is it not pleasing to be able to benefit from it? I know you're ashamed of what you did, yet it is allowing you to escape this sentence that your abbot inflicted upon you.'

'Gratitude,' Andrew whispered.

Father Obert nodded, his eyes half-closed. 'I have watched you, I believe you have been aware of that, and I've concluded that you are about God's work.'

'You arranged this as my escape?'

Obert responded with a wag of his head that Andrew inter-

103

preted as maybe, maybe not, which of course meant yes. He wanted to fall on his knees and thank the old priest.

'Was the priest truly injured?'

Obert threw up his hands. 'Heaven kens I am not that devious, Andrew. Father Guthlac had been injured and he feared he would end up a cripple if forced to ride on, so I suggested a solution, that is all.' His expression was one of fondness.

Andrew was still very moved. 'What convinced you that I am doing God's work?'

'The infirmary drain, and your concern for your servant Matthew. Though now that we have seen the cost of crawling through the detritus in that great sewer I imagine you thank God you were so considerate of the lad.'

Andrew would never had guessed that the elderly priest could possibly have noticed all that he had. He despaired of having any talent for cunning deception.

'I pray that you follow your conscience in what you do with this opportunity,' Obert continued. 'I believe that God will guide you.' The old man's beetled brows drew together, and he dropped his head for a moment as if praying.

'God grant you everlasting joy, Father Obert,' said Andrew.

The old priest raised his eyes. 'You might wish to retract that prayer once I tell you a story I would share with you. It is only fair that you know my shame as I know yours.'

Andrew could not imagine what shame the elderly priest could carry, but if it somehow motivated this unexpected act he would hear it. He wished to know whether Obert had arranged this out of trust, faith, defiance, or some other inscrutable motive. 'I pray you, tell me.'

The old priest nodded. 'It is a common sort of tale, an example of the fear in which we hold ourselves prisoners, desperately holding on to a life that is only the beginning of our existence.' Obert glanced away for a moment.

Andrew waited, his feet now warm and his muscles beginning to waken. He realised that he would miss Father Obert, for it was only the constant knowledge that he was imprisoned in Soutra that had made him intent on escape. He'd found his work here fulfilling and his companion warm, profound in his faith, amusingly acerbic in his observations of others. The other Augustinian canons at the spital, those not acting as confessors to the soldiers, went about their own work, neither troubling Andrew and Obert nor including them in their community. Lost in thoughts of the months past, Andrew was startled when Obert resumed speaking.

'Had I told you my story earlier, you would not have trusted me when I found a way to free you from your shackles,' said Obert. 'So now I confess my sin. You were not the first assistant confessor provided by the English. Last year I shared the confessional with a Scot who had been captured in Berwick and brought here to end his days in the service of his enemies. Master Thomas instructed me to spy on him so that at the first sign of an attempt to escape or somehow pervert the mission here he might be punished and by such means convinced to mend his ways.'

'I had judged Master Thomas to be fairer than that.'

'I saw that you did, but recently you witnessed how he tried to play us against one another. His purpose is the same as mine was then, to save his own neck. We become so attached to this fleshly shell.'

'So you betrayed your fellow priest?'

'Don't hurry the tale, Father Andrew. Let me tell it fully, and in my own time.'

'Forgive me.'

'Forgiven. The young are always hastening to their ends, I do remember being so.' Obert rubbed his eyes, as if he were reading the tale. 'I falsely befriended the man, having no intention of keeping his counsel if I judged him unworthy. And when I had observed him long enough to be satisfied that he was an idle, lazy priest with no apparent calling I met with Master Thomas.'

'You played God,' Andrew observed, trying not to sound angry.

Obert closed his eyes and nodded. 'I did.'

'Was there much to tell?'

A tear slipped from one of the old priest's closed eyes. 'Oh my yes. His flesh was weak; he was overly fond of his young servant, a pretty lad who was only too glad to be away from the soldiers. Of course my comrade tried to be discreet, but I do not sleep as soundly as I did in my youth.' Obert dabbed at his eyes. 'Who was I to judge him? The captains here look the other way when their men are too fond, and I cannot imagine what that young servant suffered. No doubt you've heard enough confessions here to know how it is in the camps. And is it worse than a group falling upon the camp followers and coming down upon them until they scream for the pain of it? You've heard those cries. They may be whores, but they are God's children.' The old priest looked up at him. 'You must think me mad, to go on like this.'

'The soldiers have not taken vows,' Andrew said. 'You were right to question the priest's morals.'

'Precisely what I told myself. My assistant needed to be reminded of his duty, of his vows. I told myself that it had never occurred to me he might take his own life. I told myself all this, but it was a lie. I had noticed how he took all imagined slights to heart because he knew he was weak and it tormented him. I knew he would be shattered, and Master Thomas knew that I knew.'

'The priest took his own life?'

'He hanged himself. And then the serving lad did likewise a few nights later.'

Andrew could not think what to say beyond, 'May they rest in peace.' He'd been here for four months and never heard anything about what must have been a very unsettling experience for everyone. 'Were they living here in the master's house?'

Obert shook his head. 'We were then with the canons. Afterward I was removed at their request. Your more comfortable quarters have been thanks to my betrayal.'

'You don't believe that you told Master Thomas out of a sense of duty?'

Obert shook his head. 'I have vowed never to deceive myself again.'

Andrew raised an eyebrow. 'A good intention, but hardly possible to achieve. We seldom fully know our own hearts.'

'Of course. I have the intention. But I am certain that my intention then was to convince Master Thomas that I was trustworthy. That I would choose my own life over that of one of my countrymen.' Obert's voice rasped on the last few words.

'And over one of his also, if it served you.'

Obert shrugged. 'You see why I did not tell you of this before.'

Andrew did indeed. The story had saddened him. He'd come to like Father Obert very much, but it was difficult to forgive such selfishness, such loss of life, especially to push two men to commit the unforgivable sin of taking their own lives. He could only pray that they saved themselves from the fires of hell by last minute repentance.

'Longshanks believes us to be no better than beasts, and if we have not a care we shall become so,' Andrew said as he rose. 'God forgive us both, Obert.'

'Pray for me, Andrew.'

'I'll pray for both of us. I do not think that saving me makes up for those lives.'

'That depends. If you are the man I believe you to be, it will.'

Wallace and Murray needed news from the castle at once with the troop reinforcements arriving from England, and so James had rushed Margaret's company to Stirling – these were Margaret's first thoughts when she woke at dawn. Her heart pounding, she fell to planning how she would approach Father Piers after Mass at Holy Rude Kirk – for he was to be her guide in finding the messenger. She could not linger on concerns beyond that at present, not fret about whether Father Piers would preside at the

Mass or whether the messenger could be or wanted to be found, and once found, whether he was still to be trusted. She had no time to worry, she must act. James had assured her that if the lad had been compromised Father Piers would be able to suggest another messenger. Pray God that wasn't necessary, but if it was, pray God the priest had someone in mind. She woke Celia, who was surprisingly still abed, and then had a time convincing her that she must dress at once.

'It is not a matter of whether I feel fresh enough.' Either the journey or yesterday's confidences must have addled Celia's wits, for she spoke as if this were nothing more important than a polite visit. 'Our commanders need information,' Margaret reminded her. 'The armies are massing. Dress me now.'

A sleepy Celia insisted on accompanying her to Mass but Ada was able to dissuade her by insisting on being Margaret's companion. Margaret was relieved; Ada would be far more helpful than Celia for she knew Father Piers. James had described the priest, but it was comforting to climb the hill with Ada's chatting again about what had changed – some houses had been enlarged, others, particularly near Castle Wynd, had suffered damage.

'I'd not noticed these yesterday in my fear,' she confessed.

Within Holy Rude Kirk they found a crowd of worshippers far greater than Margaret had seen in either Edinburgh or Perth.

'The people of Stirling fear the end is near,' Ada murmured as they paused at the back of the nave. 'Father Piers must be rejoicing at their strengthened piety. Come. We shall kneel beside Isabel Cowie, the goldsmith's wife, and hear some gossip of the town.'

Ada led the way towards a large-boned woman in a fine wool gown – Margaret thought it might be scarlet, the finest wool cloth. She wore a gold fillet over her veil and the paternoster beads moving through her fingers were ivory. Shoulders proudly thrust back, she might have been posing for her figure as pious donor at the base of a stained glass window. As Ada knelt beside her she

whispered something that Margaret could not hear. The woman
lifted her head with a start, and a sorrowful expression turned to a
smile. She was a handsome woman, no longer young but with
large eyes and a smile that lit her face.

'St Columba, I never thought to see you here, Ada.'

'Nor did I, Isabel, but it warms my heart to see you.'

The woman leaned forward to look past Ada to Margaret. 'And
who is this young beauty?' she asked, eyeing her up and down.

'My niece Maggie,' said Ada.

Margaret nodded to Isabel.

'She is as bonny as you were in youth. But fie on you for
bringing her here now. You expose her at the worst time, with the
English king's felons lying about. You've risked all bringing her
here. And yourself.'

'There's nowhere except the highlands where she might be
safe,' said Ada, 'and that way would lead to other problems.'

Isabel sniffed. 'It's true, a man is a man uphill or down. At least
here she is among God-fearing friends.'

'I have never seen the kirk so full,' said Ada.

'Fear makes saints of us all.'

A hissed argument behind them distracted Margaret. A woman
and a man Margaret took to be a soldier stood behind a second
man who knelt with head bowed, seemingly unaware of their
presence. The woman gesticulated dramatically and the soldier
appeared to ask whether she was certain.

'I've known him from a lad,' she spoke more loudly in exasper-
ation.

Now the kneeling man glanced behind him and with a
strangled cry scrambled to his feet, about to run. But the soldier
caught hold of his tunic and jerked him backwards. The man
went sprawling and those kneeling around him scattered. The
silence of the crowd and the malevolence in the accuser's eyes
chilled Margaret. She heard Ada ask Isabel for an explanation.

'It is the new game here – betray your neighbour. Accuse him before he accuses you. I do hope you had good cause to return, my friend, for you'll find no peace here.'

Margaret broke out in a cold sweat; James had warned them about the tension in the town, but she had imagined herself too insignificant to attract anyone's attention. That was quite obviously not true if neighbour was turning against neighbour.

The man's cries did not interrupt the Mass. In fact many of the townspeople kept their heads bowed through the entire drama, though there was a communal letting out of breath after the soldier departed. Ada and Isabel had fallen silent, and Margaret prayed that no one would make note of her or her conversation to come with Father Piers.

This proved impossible. After the Mass, several people called out to Ada, all of them elders of the town. Ada's friendly nods but determined stride made it plain she was on an errand, and none stopped her – no one was so self-involved that they were not reading such signals. How alert all were in this place on the edge of war. It was different from Margaret's experience in Edinburgh, where the threat had been less defined. Here the town sat above the most important bridge in this battle, and all knew that a confrontation must take place, and soon, whether or not they actually knew of the troops massing on the plain below the town.

Father Piers was a short, delicate man with dark, dramatically arching eyebrows that gave him a look as if surprised by life.

Upon recognising Ada he called out to her, 'My old friend, praise be to God for watching over you.' He embraced her. 'It is good to see you well.'

To Margaret's ears the greeting sounded forced, the priest's tone guarded. Indeed she wondered at a priest considering Ada, the never-married mother of five and former mistress of an English commander who was part of the occupying force in the town, a 'friend'. Though he might not be aware of all that.

'I rejoice to find you still here, Father.' Ada dropped her voice to a whisper. 'I feared for you.'

'God holds me in His protection,' the priest said quietly, and then, turning to Margaret, he asked rather sharply, 'Who is this?' No one listening would guess that she was the purpose of their meeting; indeed, they would think her unwelcome.

'My niece Maggie,' said Ada, snaking an arm around Margaret's waist and drawing her close, cheek to cheek. 'Do you not see the resemblance between me and James's friend from Edinburgh?'

Margaret held her breath as the priest looked from her to Ada and back. She thought he'd caught the code identifying who she was, for he looked closely, having a vested interest in their story being believable.

'You might be twins,' he said with a chuckle although his eyes did not smile. He seemed preoccupied. 'Let us withdraw to my quarters where we can tell our tales without an audience. I understand there was trouble in the nave this morning. A man who posed as a soldier to trespass and commandeer a woman's goods. Another neighbour recognised him and pointed him out this morning.'

'But you were at the altar – how do you know this?'

'I *must* know all this. Now, come with me.'

He swept them up and out of the kirk, across the kirk yard and into a cool, dark hall. Silence surrounded them as a servant brought in additional cups. As soon as he was gone, Father Piers sat down beside Margaret, leaning uncomfortably close to her. He smelled of incense and sour wine. Broken blood vessels on his nose bespoke a fondness for drink.

'You are so young,' he said, shaking his head as if in sympathy. 'Too young to be involved in all this.'

She thought it a feckless comment, implying that she had a choice in the matter. 'In what, Father? If you mean our struggle against King Edward, all in this land are involved, even babes in the womb.'

Piers tilted his head, studying her face for a moment. 'The resemblance is very, very good. Folk will not question whether you are a de la Haye,' he said, ignoring her comment. 'But that is the least of the danger.'

Margaret intended to stand her ground. 'I am here, Father, sent by James Comyn, and I require your assistance.'

Father Piers looked bored. 'You do indeed.'

Insulted, Margaret looked away, biting her tongue. Her attention was drawn to a jumble of clothing atop a chest near the door. A worn shoe, a blood-stained hat, a ripped, dun-coloured jerkin, a scrap of leather sticking out from beneath it that might be a scrip, a green tabard with a brown stain that might be either old blood or perhaps mud, much more of the same.

'Why would you wish to risk your life spying, Dame Margaret?' the priest asked.

'Call her Maggie,' Ada said. 'Maggie de la Haye. It sounds less – threatening.'

'So it does. But the question remains.'

'King Edward slew the citizens of Berwick and replaced them with Englishmen,' said Margaret. 'He won't stop there.' She moved closer to the pile on the chest, a sadness descending upon her.

'Indeed, he did not stop there. Just a few days past a young man of the town was hanged for treason. He was accused of taking weapons to Murray and Wallace, though he'd not yet crossed the river. Are you prepared for death, Dame Maggie?'

Margaret crossed herself.

Ada rapped the arm of her chair. 'Piers, my old friend, as you love me, quit your questions and tell Maggie what she needs to know. She *is* young – the Comyn believes that will stand her in good stead. I can vouch for her. I could not be more proud of her were she truly my niece.'

'What are these?' Margaret asked, reaching out, but not quite touching the items piled on the trunk.

'They are not our concern,' Ada said.

Father Piers had joined Margaret. 'When a body is found in the town it is brought to me. Kin might make use of the cloth or the leather.' He lifted a piece and let it drop.

'So many,' Margaret said quietly, not wishing to disturb the dead who she felt surrounding her. 'Do many kin come to claim the goods?'

Piers hesitated a moment. 'No,' he said, but nothing more.

Yet in that word Margaret heard his suffering. 'I would not think so,' she said softly. 'The fear of seeing proof of their loved one's suffering would give pause to all but the hardest of heart.'

'Yet I keep them, waiting for kin to claim the property,' Piers said, resignation dulling his voice.

'Yes.' Margaret turned her attention to him. 'You do not sleep well, do you?'

'Are you a seer?' He searched her face, as if setting eyes on her for the first time.

The question startled Margaret, determined as she was to hide her awakening Sight. 'I merely noticed that you feel so much for the people.'

'I'll give you some of my mandrake ointment for your wakefulness,' Ada offered.

Piers turned to her with a sigh. 'The apothecary has given me his best sleep potions, but nothing helps.' He lifted his hand, the tips of his fingers hovering over the dark circles beneath his eyes. 'It becomes more apparent by the day.'

Margaret was grateful for the change of topic.

'Applying mandrake to the skin is most effective,' said Ada. 'It is weakened when mixed with wine.'

'Wine, ale – most nights I drink myself into an uneasy slumber. But I thank you, it is a generous offer and I accept with pleasure.' Piers returned his attention to Margaret. 'Forgive me if I offended you. It is your youth – but you are right, youth are not spared. Let us sit in the light from the windows,' he said, motioning to a small trestle table surrounded by benches, 'and I shall tell you all I know that might be of value to you, and by my eyes you shall ken the truth.'

Margaret settled across from him so that she could watch his eyes, though she wondered at his implying that she might doubt him.

Piers moved with a grace that gave dignity to his small frame. His dress was impeccably clean, no small accomplishment when there were so many extra demands on the water supply at present. He pressed the tips of his slender fingers to his temples and stood before his chair with eyes closed for a moment, then settled down and, leaning forward with elbows on knees, began to talk.

'I am worried about the messenger – Archie. He's usually a reliable lad, but he's let me down of late. He says his mother has kept him busy. And now it is worse – he has not shown up for several weeks.'

'You do not believe his explanation?' Margaret asked.

Piers shook his head, a slight, precise motion. 'It is unlike his mother, Evota, to keep him away for she depends on the pay Archie receives for each trip out of town. She is a widow with a half dozen children to feed. She brews ale for the English – it is said she spits in it, and worse, but they pay well.'

'Are you worried that he has been taken for a spy?'

Piers nodded. 'Yet I have heard nothing of it, which would be unusual.' He gave Margaret directions to the widow's house. 'But I advise you to wait a day before you go to her, until folk have forgotten you.'

'They'll not forget me in a day.'

'You would not say that if you had spent any time here of late. Each day brings a new problem – there is little bread to be had, the soldiers boarding with a family are not always the most courteous guests, news of a family member's death or capture wipes out all other thoughts. In a day you will no longer be the subject of gossip.'

Impatient though she was, Margaret said, 'I'll wait a day, then, though no more. I understand that Archie is not the spy, merely a messenger.'

Had she not been studying Piers so closely Margaret would not have noticed his surreptitious glance at Ada, and a hesitation as he chose his words. 'No, Archie has been carrying information from a woman. She – entertained soldiers until she found one who was growing disaffected and careless, and she has been passing on to Archie the information he unwittingly provides.'

'Where might I find her?' Margaret asked.

'I'll tell you when the time comes. First you must find Archie.'

Margaret wondered whether the time he was waiting for was when Ada was not there to overhear.

Afterwards, as they walked back to the house, Ada wondered aloud at the priest's asking Margaret if she was a seer. 'Perhaps he has communicated with someone at Elcho and knows of Christiana's gift of Sight,' she said. 'You've not felt anything more since the owl's visitation, have you?'

'That was quite enough,' said Margaret, skirting the question. She had not told Ada of her vision at Elcho, not wishing to worry her. She was of course wondering about his question too, but not with Ada's idle curiosity. She had noticed the clothing because it emanated a sadness that was palpable for her. She'd felt the presence of the dead. The experience had been very clear despite her being in an unfamiliar place.

'I did think it odd how you picked out those rags in the corner,' said Ada.

Margaret was spared the need to respond as they had reached the house.

A fresh wind caught Celia's skirts as she walked along the curve that gave Bow Street its name, and she enjoyed the coolness for a moment before she smoothed them down in deference to Ada's butler John, who was a pious, pinched-face man. His tedious company did not bother her, though, for she was proud to be abroad on a mission for the Wallace. John was not aware that this errand to purchase a barrel of Evota's reputedly excellent ale would assist

Wallace's cause, but Celia had recognised the woman's name and volunteered to accompany him on the pretence of seeing the town. She might gather information for Margaret.

The house to which John led her was behind a modest two storey dwelling. It crouched in the backland, a small building of sticks and mud near the burn. Several very young children were playing in the yard, overseen by a girl who handled her drop spindle with a smooth efficiency that contrasted with her slatternly posture and dress.

'Is Evota selling ale today?' asked John.

The girl twisted her small mouth into an unpleasant scowl. 'You're too late.' She had to shout it to be heard above the cries of the younger children, who were fighting over a straw doll which was shedding its stuffing. 'An English soldier has just bought all we have.' She set aside the wool and stepped into the fray, yanking one of the children aside and slapping the other with a force that made Celia wince.

An older woman appeared at the door, a plaid wrapped about her and yet another small child in her arms, this one sickly. 'Are you watching them, Ellen?' She noticed the strangers and frowned.

Celia caught her breath as the soldier who had made her so uneasy at Ada's the previous day joined the woman in the doorway. The woman stepped forward to allow him room.

John repeated his question, adding, 'This young woman tells us we are too late?'

'You are a servant in the de la Haye household,' said the soldier.

John nodded. 'I am.'

'Let them have this barrel of ale, Dame Evota.'

Evota glanced back at the soldier. 'You're certain?'

He nodded.

She turned back, squinting almost as fiercely as Ellen. 'Pay now and you can bring a cart later to fetch it home.'

The English soldier had retreated into the house.

Evota stepped aside, nodding towards the door. 'Come within.'

The child on her hip had begun to whimper, and Evota bobbed him up and down as she followed them in.

The dark interior reeked of ale, urine and peat smoke, a combination that reminded Celia of Margaret's uncle's tavern in Edinburgh – it had nauseated her then, and it did so now. She wished she did not need to breathe.

Hitching the child on her hip, Evota stated a price and John agreed, but the Englishman chuckled.

'Dame Evota, you were given the corn to make the ale but you charge as if you grew it yourself.'

In the dim light Celia could not see the woman's expression, but she heard the resentment in her voice as she spit out a considerably lower price.

As they departed, Ellen openly stared at them, and Celia felt her fell eyes boring into her back as she and John made their way down the wynd. She wondered at the priest and Master James trusting Evota and her family. Celia did not. Having seen no young man, she was thinking that Margaret could not count on Archie's wary family to help her find him.

Ada had not expected to be so atwitter about the reunion. 'Once gowned in my finest silk I'll be more confident,' she'd assured Maggie, and she did calm a little once dressed. But the arrival of the soldier sent to escort them made her heart pound. It must be a dozen years since she had spoken with Simon – no, fourteen. In their brief meeting yesterday she'd found him changed, as of course was she. But this invitation had surely been made more from courtesy or suspicion than affection. Perhaps Simon hoped to learn something from her of the state of Perth or the country-side through which she had just passed. She prayed he did not so easily see through their ruse.

Climbing the hill to the castle, she stole glances at their escort, curious what he thought of his commander inviting two Scotswomen to sup. But the man was a cipher.

High atop the crag the wind blew fresh and slightly chilly for a summer afternoon – it had felt much warmer down below that morning. Their escort had slowed his pace as they entered the castle precinct. As it had been yesterday, the bailey was crowded with buildings, tents, carts, and people jostling for space in which to live and work. She was disappointed to see some townspeople there doing business, though in her heart she could not condemn them for the folk of Perth had been no more stalwart in their loyalty to King John Balliol.

'That is Isabel's husband Gordon, the goldsmith,' Ada said to Maggie, nodding towards the man sitting before a tent with a well-dressed Englishman, the pair deep in discussion. 'I wonder whether Isabel approves.'

Maggie had been unusually quiet, and even now simply nodded. Of course she was anxious, Ada was, and she at least knew Simon.

Their escort led them to the timber house in a corner of the south wall. This time a servant greeted them at the door, and as he stepped aside Ada saw Simon standing in the middle of the sparsely furnished hall, hands on his hips. She guessed from the pleasant expression fixed on his face that he had prepared himself for disappointment. But when he looked her up and down his eyes lit up, making her glad she'd chosen to wear the blue silk gown that gave her good colour and the gossamer veil – white hair she might have, but her face was young and the white became her. She'd kept her figure, which was more than she could say for Simon, whose thick neck and barrel-shaped trunk suggested that he now spent his time on diplomacy rather than arms. The fine wool tunic and surcoat he wore, long and elegant, was the attire of an adviser, not a commander in the field. She would have thought he would refuse such a passive part in any war, insisting on going down with his men – she wondered whether he'd perhaps been injured in such a way that he no longer trusted himself in battle.

Simon bowed courteously to Maggie, welcoming her, but as soon as possible he returned his gaze to Ada.

Ada felt herself blushing and bowed her head in confusion, having thought herself past such feelings.

'My beautiful Ada.' Simon caressed her with his eyes. 'I cannot tell you with what joy I beheld you yesterday.' His voice was husky with emotion.

A servant had brought a tray with three mazers of wine. After sending the young man away, Simon handed a mazer to Ada, and reached for another as he slipped an arm round her shoulders. 'I see that your niece favours you.'

Ada proposed a toast to this happy meeting, a little dizzy with relief that Simon did not question that Maggie was her niece. She was surprised by the intimacy of his arm round her and when he suddenly drew her even closer his kiss was as passionate as ever. So, much to her surprise, was her response. She drew away from him with reluctance, but she was uncomfortable with Maggie standing there, and glancing at her friend Ada saw that she was disturbed by their behaviour.

Simon must have also perceived Maggie's discomfort, for he left Ada's side and suggested that they sit by the fire circle and tell him what brought them to Stirling just ahead of Percy and Clifford's thousand cavalry and many thousand foot soldiers.

'Just ahead?' Ada whispered, pretending ignorance. She worried that the explanation she had rehearsed required Simon to find her much changed, a little forgetful – she would not have used such a ploy fourteen years past. She caught Maggie's eye and saw her doubt mirrored there, and her fear – so many thousands. But Ada had no time to think up something more appropriate, and so she focused on the fire, reaching out to it to warm her suddenly cold hands.

Maggie, too, was leaning towards the fire, her hands trembling. 'It is chillier up here than down below,' Maggie said. 'This fire is very welcome.'

'It is,' said Ada. 'I've come to a time of life when my hands are chilled by the slightest draught.'

Simon took her hands in his. 'Quite cold, indeed. That is a change. So, my love, why come you to Stirling?' he asked, and she saw how closely he regarded her.

'Well might you wonder,' she said, 'for I see I have chosen a most dangerous time for my return. God must have been watching over us.' She withdrew her hands and delicately pressed her temples. 'I do not like to admit it, but age must have addled my wits for I thought Stirling would be less astir than Perth, being protected by its position high above the bridge. We did see encampments, but we were permitted to cross the bridge.' She turned to gaze on Maggie. 'Still, those men who accosted us when we entered the town yesterday have made me very uneasy about my niece's safety.'

'Aunt Ada,' Maggie murmured in convincing embarrassment, 'I'm not a child.'

Ada took more than a sip of wine.

Simon grunted as he rose to pour more. 'That is the point, my dear. You are all too obviously no longer a child amidst a crowd of men long away from their women.'

Ada could not deny that Maggie was right in saying, 'That is little different from Perth.' But she knew that they'd been safer in Perth. Fortunately, Simon seemed willing to believe that Ada had made a mistake. She felt perversely irritated by that.

He resumed his seat. 'I am here to advise and keep the peace in the town, not to lead men into battle, and for that I am grateful – though I had resented that when it was first made known to me. I felt old and ridiculed. But King Edward has depleted our supply of men of fighting age with all of his wars and now he has gathered felons, rapists, rogues, and cut-throats, men who should not be serving in his name, men impossible to control. They fight amongst themselves, sometimes to the death, over petty issues. The captains are at wits' end to discipline them. And here in

Stirling they are short of food, of all supplies, and trapped on this great rock with only the townspeople to steal from. As happy as I am to see you, I am sad you are here. Yet I cannot in good conscience send you back to Perth. It is a miracle you made it here unscathed. Did you have an escort?'

'A friend escorted us to Elcho Nunnery. From there we joined various companies of farmers and tradesmen on the way, anyone journeying along our path.'

'No doubt most of them were spies,' Simon said wearily. 'You are fortunate to have arrived safely.'

❧ 6 ❧

Doubts

Maus's endless chatter about fabrics, fashions, beauty preparations had Celia seething with envy, and leaving the tittering maid she headed out to the privy in the backland to think how to lift her mood. She needed some occupation that would remind her that she was far more valuable to Margaret than a mere lady's maid. Despite the delicacy of her activity in the backland, she spied a neighbour peering at her as she emerged from the flimsy shed shaking out her skirts. The gawker was a woman, which was a relief, but the invasion of privacy put Celia in an even fouler mood than before.

'Have you never seen a woman relieve herself before?' she called out, angrily flouncing past the woman who had at least blushed quite vividly.

She needed occupation. Perhaps a walk would clear her mind. She had never experienced such a thing in Dunfermline or Perth, or even Edinburgh, where she'd been living in an inn where drunks were always tottering into the backlands for a piss. But as she walked she thought how the English occupation of the castle, the crowd of armed men, the battle everyone expected at the foot of the outcrop on which they lived had changed the lives of the townsfolk. No wonder they watched strangers so closely.

She discovered she had retraced her earlier steps to Evota the alewife's house. And who should be just stepping out into the lane but the English soldier who had been there yesterday. Fortunately he had not yet caught sight of her. Withdrawing into the shadows Celia watched him walk past. He was a handsome man, no doubt about it; studying him now she was reminded of someone – there was something in his eyes, and his colouring – pale hair and dark brows and lashes.

But this was no time for idle comparisons. She wondered why he'd returned to Evota's house. It was impossible for her to have replenished her stock of ale already. So the man had other truck with her. She supposed Evota might be selling sexual favours – or perhaps her daughter was – she had seen the suggestion of breasts in the young woman despite her small stature. Keeping close to house fronts and therefore in shadow, Celia followed the man.

Sir Simon's comment about spies made Margaret anxious for James. Had they been noted, then followed? Was one of Ada's servants too talkative? She was also very uneasy about Ada's behaviour. She was clearly still in love with Sir Simon – or at least sexually aroused by him. And the feeling was mutual. Margaret feared that Ada would forget herself and say something to compromise them, or worse she would decide she was better off supporting her English lover's king. She had never seen Ada exhibit such nervousness.

While they ate, the topic of their journey was revisited several times, Sir Simon disturbingly keen to learn more about their escorts. Ada was quite convincingly vague and disinterested, busy asking about her children. It seemed they were all well wed but for Peter.

'And that is my surprise for you,' said Simon.

'He is to be wed?' Ada asked.

Margaret silently applauded Ada's believable confusion.

'Wed?' Simon frowned, then caught her drift and nodded. 'I've confused you. No, he has no time to devote to courting at present, not while he is serving King Edward.' He smiled, obviously eager for her to guess.

'Peter is in Scotland?' Ada held a hand to her heart.

Simon nodded. 'I should like to introduce him to you.'

'He is here?' Her voice quavered.

'He is.' Simon looked quite satisfied with himself.

Tears and stammering expressed how overcome Ada was with the news that one of her children was so near.

But that was the last of the act to which Margaret was witness. For suddenly Sir Simon produced the soldier who had escorted them to the castle and suggested that Margaret return to the town while he and Ada enjoyed some time alone.

As she wound her way through the crowd in the castle yard Margaret tried to calm herself with memories of Ada's strength of character. She must not lose faith in her. Ada was merely playing her role and was not a silly young woman in the first flush of love. She had been quite convincingly surprised by the news of Peter's presence.

Once outside the castle gates Margaret looked round at the few people abroad despite the sunny afternoon. In this Stirling was much like Edinburgh, lives lived behind shuttered windows, folk hoping unseen was forgotten. In the marketplace on Broad Street she spied Celia hurrying towards Ada's house.

'There is my maidservant,' she told her escort. 'I'll join her.'

The soldier bowed to her and took his leave, and Margaret caught Celia before she'd reached the door. Her maid was flushed and out of breath.

'What have you been doing to be so exhausted?' Margaret asked.

'Following the soldier who seems to be wherever I am. He was at the alewife's again.'

Margaret felt as if her stomach had risen to her throat and she crossed herself. 'That does not bode well.'

'No.' Celia took a deep breath. 'But I learned nothing. He went straight to the castle gate.'

'Come. Father Piers might recognise him from your description.' As they walked she told Celia about the host of men forming down below. 'I fear for James.'

'I fear for us all,' said Celia.

As Margaret stood to one side of Castle Wynd waiting for a troop of foot soldiers to go past so that she and Celia might cross over to the kirk, she only partly listened to her companion's complaints about Maus and the nosey neighbour; she was going over all that Sir Simon had said in search of evidence that he'd had news from someone who'd followed them on their approach to Stirling, but she could find nothing specific except for his comment about all travellers being spies, and that was something he might have said quite innocently. Her fear left little room in her head for Celia's complaints, and she dismissed them as her maid's way of putting the massing army out of her head. However, when she realised what Celia was confessing she was alarmed by the risk she'd taken.

'Father Piers advised we leave Evota alone for a day. I thought I'd told you that,' Margaret said.

'I hadn't intended to go there,' Celia said in a peevish tone.

Margaret regretted her sharp response, appreciating Celia's help. She paused to apologise. 'I don't question your intentions, Celia, forgive my temper. I'm worried about Ada, and I confess I haven't been listening with care.'

Only now did she notice the chill of the late afternoon, the long shadows and how the streets had emptied. She wondered whether this late afternoon trip to the kirk was wise – they were the only women about. She resumed walking, quickening her pace.

'Why worry about Dame Ada?' Celia asked breathlessly as she hurried to catch up. 'She has a lover to protect her.'

'That *is* the matter,' said Margaret. Once they reached the relative safety of the kirk yard she expected to feel calmer, but a chilling flash of her vision of Roger's fall startled and frightened her. She squeezed her eyes shut and prayed for the spell to pass.

'Mistress?' Celia touched Margaret's arm. 'What is it?'

Waving off Celia's concern – she did not trust her voice – Margaret lifted her face to the sun and took several deep breaths. 'Just a spell of dizziness,' she said when she finally felt herself again. 'I hadn't realised how frightened I'd been up at the castle.' The kirk yard seemed peaceful once more, until she glimpsed the edge of a steep outcropping to one side of the graves, then glanced up to the castle on its height. She'd found the site of her visions of Roger's death. *Dear God, keep Roger from this place, I pray you.*

'I was frightened for you,' said Celia.

Margaret forced a smile. Celia need not know what she'd just realised. 'Ada is quite the player, God be thanked.' She described the tenor of Ada and Simon's reunion – quietly, for she felt exposed even in the kirk yard.

'They might become lovers again,' Celia said. 'That is unwelcome.' With her dark brows knit together, she looked as if she were ready to take on the worry for both of them. 'Do you think she knew she still held him in her heart?'

'You put it so prettily,' said Margaret, amused despite the eerie silence. 'I doubt she knew she still lusted after him.' She recalled her own unexpectedly passionate reunion with Roger and felt herself blush.

Celia took no notice, already knocking on the door of the priest's house. But they both jumped as a shriek broke the silence. It seemed to have come from a house in the market square.

'Where is that clerk?' Celia said with worried impatience when the door was not opened at once.

'We are not expected,' Margaret reminded her, though she, too, was anxious to move inside.

At last the clerk appeared, looking harried as usual, and asked them to follow him to the kirk, where Father Piers would see them in the sacristy after he'd completed some business.

'The sacristy?' Margaret asked. 'Behind the high altar?'

'The soldiers will not go there,' explained the clerk.

'What do you think that shriek was?' Celia asked in a low voice as they hurried across the yard.

Margaret shook her head. 'I think I'd rather not know.'

She wished she had returned to the kirk to announce that she'd found Archie. She had to remind herself how unlikely it had been that they would find him straightaway; had it been so simple James would not have needed her here. But she felt adrift and a little frightened. She tried to think what James would do next. For all their careful planning, they'd been unable to see to details because they hadn't known what she'd find. With the English army gathering below, she wondered how Archie would have avoided being caught down there. To distract herself from unwelcome doubts, she asked Celia about her movement about town.

'What did you note about Evota and the daughter – was her name Ellen?'

Celia nodded. 'Yes, Ellen.'

'Anything that might help us find Archie?'

'You might find this of no consequence, but they are tiny women – I felt almost tall,' she grimaced comically.

'I believe that is the first time you've mentioned your size to me.'

Celia shrugged. 'It's seldom to the point, is it? But it might be this time.'

Margaret smiled a little at Celia's earnest expression.

'I thought Ellen a child,' she said, 'but when she stood to rebuke the children – well, she has a mature figure. Do we know how old Archie is?'

Margaret realised she did not. 'Father Piers calls him a lad, but that is of little help. I wonder whether Evota kens her son's whereabouts.'

The priest's clerk reappeared, bobbing his head. 'Father Piers is at leisure to talk with you now. If you will follow me.' He led them down the north aisle and into the sacristy.

Father Piers rose from a table strewn with parchment and came forward with an expression of concern. 'Has something happened that you return so soon?'

Margaret introduced Celia, who explained her concern about the English soldier, describing him with care.

Piers dropped his gaze and thought for a while, fingering the prayer beads hanging from his girdle. Margaret was disappointed when he looked up, shaking his head.

'I do not think I know him.'

He moved back to his table and settled in his chair, scanning the documents with his eyes as if ready to return to them.

'Forgive us for taking up your time,' said Margaret, stung and ready to depart.

But the priest glanced up, shaking his head. 'No, do stay.'

'But you are busy.'

He glanced back at the desk. 'So I am. But I've sent my clerk for the woman you wished to meet – the one who provides Archie with information.'

'Does she live within the castle walls?' Margaret asked.

'No, without, on St Mary's Wynd.' He glanced at Celia. 'Your maid can be privy to this?'

'Yes, Celia is in my confidence.' Margaret grew a little bolder. 'This morning you did not wish to speak of the woman – was it because Dame Ada was present?'

Father Piers looked uncomfortable. 'There is no such thing as too cautious at present. Everyone's loyalties can be challenged. I pray you, heed what I say, Dame Maggie.'

She nodded.

'Dame Ada's liaison,' he averted his eyes at the word, 'with Sir Simon is of great concern to me.'

Now there were three of them concerned – four if she counted James, who would have been quite disturbed had he witnessed Ada's reunion with Simon. Margaret prayed that Ada might remain strong.

'Now please, sit down,' said Piers. He told his clerk to serve some watered wine. 'Forgive me, but it is scarce, and is truly almost gone.'

Margaret had been surprised to be served any in the town, though not at the castle. The English kept themselves supplied. 'Of course,' she said as she took a seat.

He picked up some of the documents, then dropped them and came around the table. 'The matter is out of my hands; I don't know why I am worrying over it.'

'Can you speak of it?'

'It is no secret. The Lord Steward and the Earl of Lennox met with Longshanks's royal lieutenant – Warenne, Earl of Surrey, the pompous b—' he covered his mouth, embarrassed. 'Forgive me, but it has raised my choler that our nobles should try negotiating with Warenne. I fear they are now hesitant to engage the enemy, a sudden timidity on seeing the expanse of the English camps. Wallace and Murray may not have the support they are counting on.' He raked his long fingers through his thin hair, making it stand up, an uncharacteristic gesture for the fastidious Piers.

Margaret took it as a sign of his distress.

'I understand that our party made it through the valley with little time to spare before the English troops began massing below,' said Margaret. 'But I didn't know Warenne is already here.'

'Whatever is to happen will happen soon,' said Piers. He looked a little relieved at her knowledge of the situation. 'I wonder whether James knew how close they were on his heels. Perhaps messages from the castle are no longer of much importance.' He paused, considering it. 'But we cannot assume that.' He smoothed his hair and turned his attention to Celia. 'Tell me what you noticed at Evota's home.'

He expressed what seemed sincere concern about the English soldier, which Margaret thought odd after seeming disinterested a few minutes earlier.

It was not long before Dame Johanna was announced.

Demurely dressed in a simple gown and white wimple, the woman looked more like a nun than a soldier's mistress. Sensing her hesitate on seeing strangers, Margaret rose to greet her, introducing herself and Celia.

'James sent me.'

Johanna visibly relaxed upon hearing that. 'I am so grateful that you have come to Stirling.'

Margaret guessed that Johanna was a little older than herself. Her smile was the sort that could light up a room, which it was doing at the moment. She was buxom and graceful, with dark brows, blue eyes, and milky white skin with just a sprinkling of scars from some pox – it was small wonder she had the pick of the soldiers.

But the smile was short-lived as Johanna continued, 'Have you heard? Gordon Cowie the goldsmith has been murdered in his shop. Stabbed in the heart and neck.'

'The scream we heard,' said Celia to Margaret.

'God have mercy on his soul,' said Father Piers.

Margaret crossed herself and said a silent prayer for the man's wife, the fine Isabel. She remembered Ada pointing out the goldsmith in the castle yard. 'Why?'

It was Piers who answered. 'In faith, I am not surprised by this news. Gordon has angered many in the town by buying favoured treatment from the English at the castle. But when did it happen, Johanna?'

'Not long ago. I heard of it as I came here – they are crying it out in the marketplace.'

'In daylight?' Celia whispered. 'How frightening that a murder could happen in daylight.'

Piers shrugged. 'I suspect that with the garrison on the move someone must have felt the castle would not bother with a townsman's death.' He seemed quite unmoved by the news.

Margaret thought perhaps he approved, but as a priest he would never say so.

'Let us talk of something else,' said Johanna. 'Have you found Archie, Dame Maggie?'

'No.'

'I'd advised Dame Maggie to wait a day before going to his home,' Father Piers explained, 'although Celia had cause to go there today.'

'I did not see him,' said Celia.

Johanna sank down on to a bench, shaking her head slowly. 'It is so unlike him to stay away for so long, and now, with this murder, I fear for him – or us.'

'Tell Dame Maggie what you fear, Johanna,' said Piers.

She glanced round at the waiting faces. Margaret could see that the strain of her work for Balliol had etched lines on Johanna's forehead that belonged to an older woman.

'Archie has mentioned many things of late that he's seen within the castle walls. One day he bragged that they have all our meat there and he'd managed to steal a few bites. Once I forgot myself when he mentioned the soldiers' quarters – I try not to seem too curious – and I asked him how he managed to see them. He said he had been delivering ale for his ma, which I already knew, and I asked no more, although I can't believe he would deliver to their quarters. Mostly it was the way he said it, as if he had something to hide. He answered too quickly, too sharply. Do you see?'

Margaret found it disturbing to look into Johanna's eyes as if her anxiety could be contagious. 'I understand what you mean. Do you think he has betrayed you?'

Johanna fidgeted on the stool, uncomfortable with the question. 'I cannot tell. His mother brews for both the English *and* folk in the town who are loyal to our King John, but I cannot condemn her for I ken how desperate she is, a widow with all the children to feed. In faith, the English have eased her burden, providing her with the corn for the ale.'

'How did she attract the English custom?' asked Margaret.

'Anyone would have advised them that Evota is the best alewife in the town,' said Piers. 'She has a gift for it, no mistake.'

Margaret noticed that the priest was sweating, which was surprising on such a fastidious man, on a day not so hot as of late. 'None of this encourages me about the wisdom of your choice of messenger.'

'Until now there was no question of his trustworthiness, Dame Maggie,' Piers said with a defensive lift of his chin.

'None at all,' Johanna agreed. 'But it was as if Archie knew he had endangered me in some way, or Rob, my lover.' She blushed.

Margaret shivered at her words and for a moment the room seemed to darken. She realised she was not breathing; once she took a deep breath the feeling eased. Regarding Piers, she understood he was defensive about his choice of Archie, but to break out in a sweat – it seemed extreme for him. Perhaps she had read too much into his careful dress. She reminded herself that James trusted him. And when Ada had learned who Margaret was to contact in Stirling she had been surprised because she had thought he'd be one of the first clerics to antagonise the English – he was Norman and shared the French disdain for the English. Still, he *looked* guilty.

'What do you ken of Archie's sister Ellen?' Celia asked Johanna.

'My lover believes he has seen her at the castle, but whether it was her choice he could not tell.' Johanna nervously picked at her skirt. 'Rob does not trust anyone in Archie's family.'

'I pray you, reassure me that Rob and Archie have not met!' Piers exclaimed.

Johanna shook her head. 'No, or not as you fear. The lad is known by the soldiers – he *does* deliver ale. And he's willing to act as a guide. In truth, that is how he can carry messages down the hill to the Scots camp without raising suspicion. Of course he is up at the castle almost daily – it's how he speaks of it that has me worried. And that he has disappeared.'

'Celia, tell Johanna about the soldier who seems to haunt Evota's house,' said Margaret.

Celia looked pleased to be called upon once more.

Johanna nodded at the description. 'I believe I saw this man today. His eyes sought mine and there was such a look of knowing I felt weak with fear.'

'God help us,' Margaret whispered, crossing herself.

'I pray Archie has not betrayed us to this man you speak of,' said Piers. 'I've thought him a good lad, if a little simple. But hearing all this, I'm uneasy.' He squared a few of the documents on the table as if hoping a bit of tidying might calm him. 'It is Archie's way to commit to a job and stop at naught to finish it. If someone has coaxed him into shifting his loyalty, he might now be working for the English – with equal determination.'

Johanna had shaken her head as Piers spoke. Now she said, 'That might be true if the English have offered him more coin, but I do not agree about his being simple. There is something about him – a cunning beyond his years.'

'How easily they turn against Archie,' Celia whispered to Margaret.

'Though I, too, am uneasy, I'll not condemn Archie until I've proof he's no longer worthy of our trust,' said Margaret. 'Meanwhile, we need another messenger.'

Father Piers spoke up. 'I propose that Johanna tell you what she has been saving for Archie, in case someone should sneak *up* the hill in desperation. I shall see to finding another messenger.'

'Are you so certain you will find another to take the messages?' Margaret asked.

'If I cannot, and I deem it still necessary, I'll go myself.'

She had been about to ask him why he had not found a messenger to replace Archie earlier, but if he was to be the replacement she understood. His absence would be noticed. But seeing the determination in Piers's face, Margaret did not argue.

She turned to Johanna. 'I want to hear all that you were to tell

Archie. Celia will also listen so that nothing is forgotten.'

The precaution proved invaluable, for as Johanna spoke a veil seemed to form around her, as if Margaret were seeing her through a piece of the sheerest silk, of a smoky colour. A feeling of such intense doom fell on Margaret that she broke out in a cold sweat; no one else in the room seemed aware of either the veil or the fear in the air. After a while, the smoky veil moved, gathering and reshaping itself into a figure standing over Johanna with what looked like a club in their hands.

'Dame Johanna, you are in grave danger.' Margaret's voice came out as a mere whisper, her throat being so constricted by fear.

Johanna crossed herself. 'I have understood the danger from the beginning. Like you, I could not stand aside and let Longshanks take our land from us.' She bowed her head. 'But my lover has gone with the other soldiers down to the camps near the river today, and I'll hear no more from the castle.' For a moment she rested her head in her hand, then looked up with a forced smile. 'I'll no longer be a threat to anyone.'

Margaret could not see what good it would do to describe her vision to Johanna, for she could not provide any practical advice. In fact she wanted to escape the vision. She rose to take her leave, grateful that Celia had known to be her eyes and ears.

In the nave, Margaret asked Celia what Johanna had told her. 'You had a vision?'

'Yes, while Johanna was talking. She is in mortal danger.'

Celia crossed herself, her face pinched. 'She described the hanging of Huchon Allan, the son of our neighbours to the north.'

'For carrying weapons to the river?'

Celia nodded. 'The soldier I've spoken of – the one at Dame Ada's yesterday – he presided, and Dame Lilias, the mother, suddenly attacked him. The townsfolk are frightened, everyone suspecting everyone else of betraying Huchon. She also spoke of the poisoning of a soldier by the family he'd boarded with – they have disappeared, and it's believed they are at the castle. Someone has been watching the castle from the outcrop in the kirk yard, though Father Piers swore that wasn't so.'

Margaret crossed herself. 'That is where Roger dies in my vision,' she whispered.

They both knelt to pray.

Before leaving the kirk, Celia told Margaret the most important piece of information Johanna had provided: Rob had told her of a path up the side of Stirling rock that was no longer guarded because of a rock slide. This was something James must be told.

As Sir Francis's company rode through Lothian, Andrew wondered at the eerie quiet. In such dry, pleasant weather there should be folk working in the fields, but he'd seen none so far. The crops must still be tended, the animals herded. He prayed that the English had not stripped the land, for then it mattered little who won the coming battle, for the people would die of famine.

As they neared Edinburgh Andrew caught sight of the saddle-shaped outcrop known as Arthur's Seat and shivered, thinking of his abbot in the monastery on the far side. Abbot Adam would be furious to know his fallen angel was unshackled and so close at hand. As they grew closer and Edinburgh Castle became visible on the horizon, flashes of memory assailed Andrew, particularly scenes with his sister Maggie, whose strength in adversity had taken him by surprise. He prayed that she was safe with her Uncle Murdoch in Edinburgh. Better that she never be reunited with Roger Sinclair; he'd never been worthy of her.

Summer it might be, but Ada's light cape did nothing to block the wind that buffeted her as she followed her son through the castle ward. Son. She did not feel anything for him. In fact she found him almost lacking in personality. He moved like a well-trained fighter and his face, what little she could see of it in the lantern light with her aging eyes, lacked all expression. She found him as chilling as the wind that slipped beneath her cape and up her skirt.

That was not all that had been up her skirt this evening. Heaven, what a reunion this had been. She had never dreamed that she would share Simon's bed again, never, in all the years since she left him. Not that she had not wished to, nor could she refuse him without endangering everyone, but she knew that what she had done was nothing he would easily forgive. And she was not at all contrite. He'd had a wife, and heaven only knew how many other women he'd dangled on his knee. Why should she not have had a lover of her choice? In faith, she knew why, so that he might know that his bastards were truly his bastards. But she had not lied to him; when she knew she was pregnant with Godric's child she had told Simon. He had flown into a rage and insisted that she go to the midwife to be rid of it, and to swear she would never speak to, let alone touch, Godric again. In love with both the father and the child growing in her womb, she had refused, and with her lover she had fled back to Scotland, foolishly expecting this child to be born, if not conceived, in wedlock. In the end Godric had deserted her.

'Too fast, young Peter,' she breathed, her night vision not what it once had been. How ridiculous to be filled with her lover's seed at such an age, and even more ludicrous to be escorted back to her house by a son she had not seen since an infant. Her life was a farce. She wondered how much Peter knew about her, whether he knew of her rebellion, his father's unbending nature.

Once past the castle gate it was much quieter, and Ada thought she might have some conversation with her son.

'Have you served before with Sir Simon?'

'I am not serving with him. I am with the governor of the castle.'

'Ah. You are merely in the same place at the same time.'

Peter nodded.

She had thought she detected a less than cordial relationship between father and son, but thought perhaps she was the thorn between them, the mother who was merely a mistress. But perhaps not.

'I pray that the situation of your birth has not caused you suffering.'

'Madame, I was brought up in a household of noble bastards.'

He was a charming conversationalist. She thought it might be quite easy to hate this particular bastard of hers.

'Had you arrived earlier you would have met your cousin Maggie.'

'I wonder – is she not my half-sister, about my age, I think, perhaps several years younger?'

So he had been told the tale of her leaving with Godric. 'No, Maggie is not your sister.' She wondered who had told this unfeeling young man, but did not care to ask. He was ruining what had otherwise been a quite wonderful evening. She wondered how a de la Haye offspring had gone so far astray.

Home at last, as she slipped into bed beside Maggie, Ada was suddenly overwhelmed by a memory of Peter's half-sister, five years his junior. She had suffered so much in her brief life. But had Simon been less unbending she would have lived in far more congenial circumstances, and with her health intact. Ada should have loathed bedding with Simon after what he'd done, but pleasures had been scarce of late.

Waking early and impatient to begin the day, Celia slipped out of the curtained bed she shared with Maus and found John stirring the fire in the kitchen. He was grumbling about the short supply of ale.

'We cannot have already drained the barrel of Evota's ale,' said Celia. She'd thought her portion meagre last night.

'No. I've not had anyone to spare, so it's not been fetched.'

'I would not mind a walk.'

John gave her a searching look. 'You would return there? What is your interest in that family?'

'My portion of ale was so small last night. I thought perhaps you would be more generous if I did you a favour.'

John grunted. 'You are too small to roll a barrel up the hill.'

'Send the groom from the stable with me.'

'So that is your plot.'

Celia blushed, realising what he thought.

With a nod, John agreed. 'In a little while. There is little enough pleasure in our lives at present.'

It was difficult, but Celia bit her tongue and let him think what he liked. It served her purpose.

As the household began to waken, cook stirring from his pallet in the corner, Maus sleepily reaching out towards the heat of the fire, Celia grew impatient with John.

'Someone as needy as Evota will have been up with the dawn, or earlier,' she argued.

'Not if she is entertaining soldiers to help with the expense of raising her children,' said John.

It irritated Celia that she could not flatly reject that idea. But going out for some fresh air, she soon cleared her head enough to admit to herself that her impatience stemmed from her concern about Margaret's behaviour the previous evening – as they'd left the kirk her mistress had fallen into a grim silence that Celia could not penetrate. She felt as if Margaret had slammed a door in her face. She could not remember a time, even when first in Edinburgh they had argued over every bit of work, that Margaret had so ignored her. That she knew it had to do with the Sight made it all the worse. Once back at the house Margaret had climbed the steps for bed quite early, without supper. It was very troubling to Celia.

She'd had only Maus to keep her company for the evening, who kept moaning about how the household was in terrible danger because of the mistress's invitations to the castle. When she could

no longer bear the woman's fear, for it echoed her own, Celia left
her waiting up for Dame Ada.

According to John, Dame Ada was not likely to rise until
midday, so Maus would probably sleep late, too.

'She woke me to help her stay awake after you had gone to
bed,' he explained, 'but the fire was warm and we were both
frighted from sleep when Dame Ada arrived with the sombre
young man she calls her son.'

'What does he look like? Is he as handsome as Dame Ada is
fair?' Celia was very curious about Dame Ada's past.

'He has the cold eye of a born soldier,' said John. 'He's like his
father.'

'So you've met him?'

John said nothing.

'Do you think we're in danger because of Sir Simon and Dame
Ada? The goldsmith was friendly with the English, too.' Celia
hoped the butler would laugh at her fear.

'It does seem that what I'd considered to be our protection
might be our undoing,' said John. He nodded as the groom came
in for his meal. 'Soon as Sandy's eaten, the two of you might fetch
the ale.'

The prospect would have cheered Celia had John dismissed
her fears. But it was best to be busy, so she tidied herself and
pushed the groom out the door the moment he set down his
morning tankard. The market square was alive with folk criss-
crossing it on their way to the day's business, or standing about
trading theories about the goldsmith's demise. It seemed that
commerce had been allowed to continue here far more than in
Edinburgh. Yet she'd already heard many complaints about the
lack of meat and fresh vegetables, that everything went straight to
the castle. Her heart went out to a man being led up towards the
castle in chains. He looked innocent as the day was young, and his
expression was one of utter despair. Crossing herself, Celia urged
Sandy to walk faster with the handcart. Once they'd crossed over

the burn and turned down Bow Street they encountered fewer folk. Sandy the groom was one of the servants hired in Stirling for their stay. Celia thought she might learn something of the town from him. She asked about the damaged homes.

'They're mostly where spies have been caught,' he said with an uncomfortable expression. 'It's best not to talk about them.'

Particularly when pulling the noisy cart – he was practically shouting. Celia waited until he paused to rest his hands before asking her next question.

'Is this the poorer part of the town?'

Sandy glanced around. 'Might say so, but most of it isn't nice like the de la Haye house. Fortune brought me to the attention of the tenants who recommended me to Dame Ada's butler. Just a bit farther now.'

They turned into the wynd leading to Evota's small house.

The yard was quiet this time, and Celia was about to knock on the door when a young man came round the side, a hand up the front of his tunic, scratching at his groin. He flushed with embarrassment, then nodded and hurried on down the wynd in the direction of Bow Street. Celia thought it likely to be Archie.

'Sandy, knock on the door and collect the barrel – we already paid good coin for it. I must have a word with that boy.'

'Man, more like,' said Sandy. 'And a troublesome one, I warn you.'

There was no time to ask the groom what he knew of Archie. Celia hurried down the wynd, glad that she had worn her soft-soled shoes which were much easier to run in than her boots – quieter, too. In Bow Street she was momentarily turned in the wrong direction, following a dark-haired lad who she suddenly realised was too small, and then corrected herself in time to see Archie slipping down St Mary's Wynd. She gathered her skirts and hurried after him, glad that the streets were still quiet. But at the crossing of Broad Street she slowed, not wanting to call attention to herself from the busier market square. Unfortunately, the delay cost her the quarry, for she saw him not, though she peered down all the wynds and closes.

Breathing hard, she retraced her steps and met Sandy in the wynd that led to Evota's. He paused.

'Did she give you any trouble?' Celia asked quietly.

Sandy shook his head. 'But the other wanted to know why you hurried away.'

'What other?'

'A tall Englishman. Soldier.' He kept his voice low and nervously glanced back towards the house.

Celia, heart pounding, moved towards Evota's in the shadows and was almost caught in her spying by the man she so feared. Now he knew she was aware of him. Perhaps it meant nothing. But she was very much afraid.

Back on Bow Street, as they paused to let some people past, she asked Sandy what he had said to the soldier's question.

'That you were not to be hanging about me so you'd hoped to run off before they saw you,' he said, blushing.

Celia almost hugged him, but restrained herself and merely thanked him.

'Do you know the lad I followed?'

Sandy nodded as he looked at her with curiosity. 'You don't? But you followed him.'

'We have not been introduced,' she said, for it was unwise to let the groom know she knew of him. 'What is his name?'

'Archie. So that is why you called him a 'boy'? He is small, but so are they all in that family.'

'You said he is trouble?'

'Trouble for ladies is what I meant. I never thought, but mayhap they all think him a lad and no trouble in that way, you see, and then – well, there are many short children born to the poor wenches of these parts.' Sandy was blushing furiously by now.

'You don't think I would–' She stopped herself.

'Forgive me. I just thought to warn you.'

Celia was irked that he thought her in danger of being lured into sin by Archie. She was older than her mistress, for pity's sake. But he meant well, and the information might prove useful in some way, though she didn't see quite how at present.

'We should have a care when we're abroad,' said Celia hoping to lure Sandy to gossip. 'I would not wish to meet up with the goldsmith's murderer.'

'If as some say his wife killed him you've nothing to fear.'

'His wife?'

'Others say it was a neighbour whose son was killed by the English in a skirmish last summer, or the one whose son was hanged for a traitor. But all say it was punishment for giving so much money to the English.'

God help us, Celia silently prayed. 'Who is looking into the matter?'

'I doubt that anyone is. The English are too busy and the townsfolk don't care. We must get this to the house. I've work to do.'

Celia couldn't believe that no one cared – she certainly did. But she knew it was not safe for either her or her mistress to begin asking questions about the goldsmith's death.

7

BETWEEN CAMPS AND CASTLE

Celia's concerns about Margaret's uneasy silence the previous evening had not fallen on deaf ears. Margaret had heard her, but she had not the strength to respond. Now she understood her mother's lethargy after a vision, for she was experiencing just such a draining of strength. She wanted silence and darkness, and that is what she sought in the curtained bed.

But in all the hours of lying there she had not slept, seeing the kirk yard and the castle crowning the hill. When Ada came so late to bed, Margaret was awake and aware of every movement, as well as the scent of sex on her companion. Even that additional evidence that Ada might be so in love with Simon that he might succeed in persuading her to change sides stirred no emotion but a little jealousy. At last that turned her thoughts to James, and as the early morning noise of the household comforted her with the sense of an ordinary day, she fell asleep wondering how he would be as a lover.

She woke with Celia shaking her and reminding her that she had wished to attend Mass. Margaret could smell fresh air in her maid's clothing.

'You've been outside?'

'Yes,' said Celia, averting her eyes. 'We need to hurry.'

As Margaret swung her legs off the side of the high bed, Celia asked, 'Are you certain you wish to go out? You do not look well.'

'I did not sleep well, but I wish to attend Mass all the same.'

'You went up so early in the evening. I should have checked to see if you needed something–'

Margaret had managed to straighten and reach for her gown. 'Peace, Celia, just dress me now.' While Celia helped her with her sleeves Margaret caught the scent of fresh air again. 'You have been out for quite a while this morning.'

'I accompanied the groom to Evota's.'

'Again?' Margaret exclaimed. 'Thrice now you've disobeyed me.'

'I pray you, Mistress, speak softly, or you'll wake Dame Ada,' Celia said, glancing at their hostess's still form, no part of her visible beneath the bedclothes. 'I went to fetch the barrel of ale John purchased yesterday.'

'Something happened,' Margaret said more quietly. 'I see it in your face. You were frightened.'

'I followed Archie.'

When Celia told her of chasing the lad and then seeing the English soldier back at Evota's, Margaret despaired at the risks she had taken.

'Celia, what have you done?' She held her breath for a moment as Ada stirred in the bed, but she did not waken. Still, only heavy drapes closed off the solar from the hall below. She did not want the household joining the argument.

'I pray I caused no mischief,' said Celia, 'but I fear that I might have.'

Margaret did, too, but what was done could not now be undone with words of remorse. 'Let us pray all the harder at Mass.' She led the way to the steps down to the hall.

They walked out in silence, for which Margaret was grateful. She greedily breathed in the fresh air and tried to force the memory of the veil around Johanna from her thoughts. She'd yet to find any use in the Sight – it seemed only to stir her feelings and provoke frightened prayer. In the kirk the Kyrie was already being sung, and Margaret and Celia dropped to their knees near the back of the nave. God would hear their prayers here as well as closer to the altar.

After Mass they waited behind, nodding to people who greeted them, and when it grew quiet Margaret suggested that they go to the choir screen to see whether Father Piers was still at the door. She hoped he might have discovered the identity of the English soldier or might give them some counsel about Celia's encounter with him this morning.

The look of relief on Piers's face when he saw them worried Margaret. Had he cause to think they might not appear, or had something happened to Johanna? He motioned for them to follow him down the aisle, then led them to the sacristy.

'What is it? What has happened?' Margaret asked.

'Archie came last night,' said Piers.

'God be thanked,' she said, though she wondered at the priest's solemn expression – he should be relieved.

But Piers was shaking his head. 'He says he can no longer carry messages because someone is watching him.'

'Celia's English soldier.'

'He would not say, though I'm sure it was an Englishman.'

'Do you think it might have something to do with Gordon Cowie's murder?'

'Would that I had an answer for you,' Piers said.

'If someone is watching him, they might also be watching Johanna.'

Piers was nodding. 'We must be quiet for a few days, convince whoever it is that there is nothing to watch.'

'We have no time to wait,' said Margaret, exasperated by the man. 'The armies are gathering, Father. What little information we have must get to James.'

'Everything has changed, don't you see that?'

'We have some details that might be of use to Wallace and Murray. If you are saying that you won't take it, I must.' Though she would need his help in finding the contact down below.

Father Piers looked distraught. 'If something should happen to you James Comyn would have my life, without hesitation. In faith, I would guess that Sir Simon is having you watched. I have told you that if necessary I shall go myself.'

'Surely you're watched as well,' said Margaret.

'There might yet be someone else–' said the priest.

'Who else might there be? All the men who can be trusted are gone, except for some servants.'

'Among them there are possibilities. I must think.'

'Don't think too long,' Margaret said, taking her leave.

Celia followed silently, but when they were back at the house she asked to speak to Margaret up in the solar.

'What is it?' Margaret asked, expecting a question about her behaviour. But Celia surprised her.

'What you said to Father Piers, that made me wonder how Archie has escaped service. Sandy the groom says that he is a man, not a boy, and has fathered many bastards off serving girls who think him harmless in that way, looking so young.'

'Yet Father Piers calls him a lad.' *If only James were here.* 'I am uneasy about Piers,' said Margaret. 'With a murder in the town we need James. Perhaps it's time I donned men's clothing and tried to leave as we came, quite out in the open.'

'And what happens to Dame Ada when her niece has disappeared?' asked Celia. 'I'm the one to go, Mistress. No one would miss me. And I'm as small as Archie. I have his colouring, too. I could pass for him, name and all.'

'I hardly think that is true, Celia.' But Margaret was moved by the offer, and the love with which it was made. 'I am ever in your debt. I know you offer this from your heart. But I am the one who accepted this mission, not you. I cannot risk your life for this. Yet you are right about my disappearing, I cannot do that to Ada.'

There seemed no responsible way to proceed. 'I wish I knew whether I could really trust Father Piers.'

When Dame Ada had at last risen and gone below to break her fast, Celia took the opportunity to tidy Margaret's trunk. It was a warm morning and the solar was hotter than the hall below, so Celia worked more slowly than usual. She regretted that when Ada caught her up there.

'John tells me that you were out early this morning following a young man.'

Sandy must have told John. 'John sent me to fetch the ale.' How dare Sandy betray her?

'You left Sandy to the task and chased after the young man. Is that not so?'

'I did it for my mistress,' Celia said with as much dignity as she could muster, her anger making her want to spit.

'You call attention to yourself, running through the streets. You will have everyone watching us and with my friend Isabel's loss – haven't you heard of the goldsmith's murder?'

'Might we talk more quietly?'

Both women turned in surprise to discover Margaret had joined them. Celia was relieved to have her mistress put a steadying hand on her shoulder, which she interpreted as a sign of support. But Margaret's expression was grim.

'You heard about Gordon's death, then?' asked Margaret.

'Yes,' whispered Ada. As her composure crumbled she hid her face in her hands.

'I am so sorry, Ada,' Margaret said.

Ada lifted her face, her expression one of determined calm. 'I should go to Isabel.'

'I won't keep you long,' said Margaret. 'I just wanted you to know that I have asked Celia to assist me. I am not happy that she openly pursued someone today, but we have little choice.'

Ada nodded. 'I am only thinking of your safety, Celia,' she said.

'I know, Dame Ada.'

'Good,' said Margaret. 'We must work together. That is our strength.'

Sir Francis dropped back to ride by Andrew as they reached the eastern boundary of the troop encampments – King Edward's troops. He seemed to enjoy conversing with Andrew, trying out his philosophy of life, of leadership, of faith. Andrew found him a man of honour with a strong sense of responsibility for his men – those who were not felons.

'There is some news,' said Francis. 'James Stewart and the Earl of Lennox met with Surrey several days ago to request a week's grace in which to persuade Wallace and Murray to put down their arms. He granted it.'

With a glance at Andrew, Francis paused, obviously awaiting a comment.

'An unexpected development.'

'What do you think is the likelihood of a peaceful settlement?'

'I know none of these men, Sir Francis,' Andrew said.

'You must have an opinion.'

He'd grown comfortable with Sir Francis, but not so that he forgot the danger of his intention. 'I pray for peace, but do not expect it.'

'John Balliol has made no attempt to escape back to his people here. Nor is there any evidence of his communicating with his subordinates to rally the people against King Edward. Why are your people so stubbornly supportive of a man who does not seem to miss being their king?'

Andrew looked out over the sea of men. 'It is possible that Balliol is not necessarily what they are fighting for, but simply rule by their own king, so that they retain their sovereignty rather than become a little-loved part of Edward's kingdom.' They – it was so simple as long as he used 'they' instead of 'we'.

Sir Francis did not respond at once, and Andrew wondered

whether he'd gone too far. But perhaps he was simply distracted by the army among which they rode.

Despite the fairly steady stream of soldiers passing through the spital at Soutra, Andrew had not been prepared for the size of the camps stretching along the water meadows, or pows, to the south of the River Forth and into the dry land south of Stirling. In sheer numbers his countrymen could not hope to compete against such a host. He wondered whether it was possible for them to make up in strength, courage, and the passion they felt for defending their own land and people what they lacked in numbers. He was not sanguine.

'You might be right, Father Andrew,' said Sir Francis at last. 'It would explain much that I have heard. What do you think of the rumours that the younger Robert Bruce, now Earl, has turned against his benefactor and long-time friend, King Edward?'

Andrew smiled – an easy, quite natural smile. 'I think it laughable that anyone would give any credit to such a rumour.'

'I think it quite possible,' said Francis, 'but doomed to failure. Balliol's Comyn relatives would never support him. Who do you think they would put forward?'

'Though of course I know of them I know little about them, Sir Francis.' It was true, and he was glad of it. 'Abbot Adam is able to expound at length upon such matters, but I have never moved in such circles.'

Sir Francis nodded, then excused himself to ride to the head of his men as they neared the base of Stirling rock. Andrew wondered whether he'd inadvertently given away any information.

In the evening, after Ada had been escorted once more to the castle, Margaret turned her attention to her growing sense of urgency about Johanna. She argued with herself about whether to go to her and warn her of the vision, not entirely certain whether it had been the Sight or her own intuition. She must keep her head about this, for surely she was still capable of perception and judgment. In Father Piers's chamber she might have been drawn to the clothing of the dead by the Sight, but it was by her own powers of observation that she had understood his distress and noticed the signs of his drinking and lack of sleep.

Dame Bethag believed Margaret's vision and Christiana's visions were from God; if she was right, they must have a purpose. But beyond a general warning for Johanna, Margaret could think of no other way to help her. She had no one who might stand guard at the woman's home, and an attack might happen anywhere. Yet she felt she owed it to Johanna to give her the choice whether or not to heed the warning and seek sanctuary.

She sought out Celia, who was sitting with Maus in the doorway to the backlands, enjoying the evening breeze. Drawing Celia aside, Margaret told her she was going out for a little while, not far, and did not need an escort.

'But it's dark, Mistress, or nearly,' Celia said, glancing up at the dusky sky. 'The men will have been drinking.'

'I doubt there is enough ale left in the town to make them dangerous,' Margaret said. She was not as sanguine about that as she tried to sound, but she was not ready to discuss the Sight at length with Celia. 'This I shall do alone.'

Dusk was darkening the backlands, though the sky was shot with eerily lit clouds. Margaret wondered whether the colours were caused by the armies' cook fires down in the valley. The smoke of the cook fires in the town gave texture to the air. From the surrounding houses came the murmur of voices, punctuated now and then by shouts, snatches of arguments, or a child's cry, but Stirling seemed subdued this night. She imagined that Huchon Allan's hanging and more recently Gordon Cowie's murder had frightened many – particularly those who supported the English. She had been disappointed that Ada had learned nothing from Isabel – except that the widow was weak with grief and terrified that she would be next. 'A wife is judged by her husband, as a husband his wife,' she'd repeated over and over again to Ada.

But besides her concern for Johanna, what was oddly uppermost in Margaret's mind this evening was the coming battle for the bridge across the River Forth. She'd not given much thought to the fighting before, focused as she was on reopening the line of communication between Johanna and James, but despite her irritation with Father Piers's hesitation to proceed she, too, worried whether it was now too late for James to relay any message to Murray and Wallace. She did not know how he would make his way through the English camps and across the River Forth to the Scots on Abbey Craig. James had told her so little, and having never been in battle she could not imagine what might be happening down in the valley.

Awakening to the danger, she realised that she and the rest of the townsfolk were precariously balanced over a deadly precipice with little information about what lay below them, or even whether the fighting would be contained in the valley. She had assumed that any battles would occur down below, but considering the charred houses farther down the hill, the bloodstains on walls near the Grassmarket in Edinburgh, the rubble left along the route of a siege, she realised that these were such chilling scars because they were evidence that the fighting often encroached on or even moved through the towns. Here on Stirling Rock they would be overrun if Wallace and Murray sent a raiding party to the castle. Margaret's heart pounded in her ears. There was no way out. She and everyone in Stirling were trapped here, between the battling armies and the castle. Perhaps it was this tension that was behind Gordon Cowie's death, an anger fanned by fear.

'God help us,' she whispered. And what was it for, but that they might have a slightly less English, slightly more Scots king to rule them. Suddenly it all seemed like a pathetically misguided child's game.

She'd picked her way out to the midden as if headed to relieve herself, and then slipped into what had been a carpentry shop until the English had confiscated the wood and tools. Idle now, it was dark and deserted, lacking both door and shutters, merely a wattle and daub shell, truly only twigs and mud, which was made apparent by a chilly draught on her feet. It had been stiflingly hot in the house, but out here a breeze cooled the day's heat. She'd intended to wait in the shelter for a while to see whether anyone followed her. Now it seemed less important. Perhaps she and Celia would be safer slipping down the hill in men's clothing than waiting here for what was to come.

This was panic, she told herself, not clear thinking. Longshanks had ordered the men of Berwick slaughtered the previous summer, their bodies left to decay in the streets, to be eaten by scavenger birds. He was a murderer, not fit to be king, and that was why they fought him. She had never heard what became of the women and children of Berwick. Had they been taken away, sent out of the town? Had they died of the disease brought by the putrefying corpses? Had they tried to bury their men? Although she'd prayed for the victims often, she whispered a prayer for those she'd forgotten until now, now that she feared she might have something in common with them. She wondered whether there was enough earth in Stirling for all the corpses that the army might leave behind.

But Wallace and Murray knew that Scots were still in the town; they would not slaughter their own people, else they would have little left to defend and rule. And Father Piers had mentioned an attempt at negotiations, about which he disapproved but which might save many lives. Waiting to give the negotiations a chance might give James time to carry a message across the river.

The usually quiet Allans were loudly arguing – Margaret assumed it was them and not their servants.

Lilias Allan shouted, 'How could you stand there and say nothing? He had no right to wear the garnet.'

'God's wounds, will naught satisfy you?' a man cried.

Margaret tried not to listen to their argument. She thought she might still do some good by warning Johanna. That is what she'd set out to do, and with God's grace she would accomplish that this evening, and afterwards she would see Father Piers and insist that either he personally deliver the information to the contact or tell her where to go herself.

What had seemed a quiet night was alive with sound once she gave it her full attention, with the high-pitched buzz of insects seeming to own the air and the low murmur of voices providing an almost rhythmic drone in the background interrupted by occasional shouts that startled her. She had grown accustomed to the noise of an occupying army in Edinburgh; Perth had fortunately been quieter. Except for the sense of a collective waiting it might be an ordinary night in Stirling. By now Margaret felt assured that she had not been followed. Leaving her shelter, she made her way to St Mary's Wynd through the backlands rather than going out into Broad Street. The murmur of voices grew louder as she approached St Mary's Wynd. It sounded as if folk were out on the street and talking rather loudly, in anxious tones, as she imagined they'd done with news of the goldsmith's death. She prayed his murder had not been the beginning of anarchy while the soldiers were occupied elsewhere, particularly caught as they were between the army's camps and the castle, with no easy escape. Fear created a terrible energy.

In the alley she paused to collect her thoughts, planning how she would approach the subject of having Second Sight, how little she understood it, and how it was possible it had not been a vision, but that she believed it was for Johanna to choose whether or not to heed it and seek sanctuary. Margaret was flustered by how foolish it all seemed when laid out so. God help her if she mentioned the owl's warning – Johanna would laugh so loudly the entire town would soon ken that Margaret was mad. She must take action now before she lost her courage.

After tidying her wimple and shaking out her skirts – she'd no doubt that her hems had collected dust and debris in the backlands – she continued down the alley and emerged into a tableau of a half-dozen townsfolk, several carrying lanterns that darted light here and there, seemingly silenced in mid-sentences to stare at her in alarm. She regretted her stealthy approach. As she distinguished faces and expressions she saw that they all looked either angry or frightened.

'Has something happened?' Margaret asked. Into the resounding silence she added, 'I'm the niece of Ada de la Haye,' hoping that might reassure them.

'The de la Haye house is on Broad Street,' a man said. 'Why'd you come through the backlands?'

'What is wrong with that? I came to see Dame Johanna.'

One of the women began to weep, leaning on her companion who was faring better with fighting tears.

Crossing himself, another man asked, 'Did you hear her scream all the way over in the market square?' He'd poked his lantern so close to Margaret's face that she took a few steps backward, frightened by the emotions swirling around her.

'Scream?' Margaret cried. 'Holy Mother of God, what monster has been unleashed on this town?'

'Did you come upon anyone in the backlands?' asked another man from behind her.

It was like a nightmare, the crazy lights, the angry strangers questioning her, when all she wanted was to see Johanna.

'I saw no one,' said Margaret. 'Has Johanna been hurt?'

'She's been murdered,' sobbed the weeping woman, 'beaten about the head, her beautiful face, God help us!'

'One of the English guards is in there now,' said the first man, nodding towardss a small house.

That sweet, beautiful woman beaten to death. Margaret's vision blurred; she felt sick to her stomach. It had happened. She'd been too late. What was the use of the vision she'd had if she could not save Johanna from the threat? She wanted to scream.

'Who is doing this?' one of the women cried. 'First Gordon, now Johanna. Are they going to kill us all?'

'Friends of the castle, those are the ones dying,' said one of the men in her ear. 'Like Dame Ada.'

The hatred and fear in their voices woke Margaret to her own danger. 'I must go to Johanna,' she said as she ducked past one of the lantern-carrying questioners, pushing past her own fear and doubt. She felt drawn to bear witness.

'There's naught you can do,' said a woman. 'The guard has warned us to stay out.'

Margaret turned at the door and faced the frightened neighbours. 'What right has he to keep us from her?' she exclaimed, conjuring anger to give her the energy to cross the threshold. 'Has anyone gone for a priest?'

No one moved forward to join her, but one man said that another had gone for a priest from Holy Rude. She hoped that Father Piers came, for he knew how worthy Johanna was of God's grace despite her sinful life.

The door to Johanna's house stood ajar. As Margaret stepped within she felt an almost suffocating wave of fear, not her own, and for an instant clearly saw Johanna's lovely smile, how it had lit up Father Piers's parlour the previous day. Beaten, they'd said. That was a personally passionate act, not a dispassionate action of war like she assumed the goldsmith's stabbing had been. Margaret took a deep breath and moved farther in.

A portly soldier was crouched down beside Johanna, the light from his lantern illuminating her still form on the floor. She was surrounded by signs of the violence that had occurred: benches and a stool were on their sides, crockery from a shelf lay shattered beneath it, and meal had spilled from an overturned jar, which had already attracted rats. Johanna lay face down; her veil was dark with blood, as was the ground round her head. Margaret choked back a sob; she fought to see, not to react, for this was all she could do for Johanna now, find out what had happened, who had done this. She forced herself to look at Johanna's clothing – it was bloodstained and torn near the waist on one side.

Margaret closed her eyes and prayed that the Sight might help her. When she looked again, she was focused on Johanna's hands, which were stretched over her head, not bent as they would be if she'd tried to break her fall.

'Have you moved her, or tidied her clothes?' she asked.

'What?' the man, startled, almost dropped the lantern as he straightened. 'Who are you? What are you doing in here? No, I've not touched her.'

'Have you checked whether she's breathing?' Margaret asked.

'I have, and she's not,' he said with impatience. His accent was that of the north – he might be a Scot.

Besides the sickening sweet scent of blood there was another smell, of charred, damp straw. 'Did something burn?' Margaret asked.

'Lamp was turned over. That's what raised the neighbour, smoke in the doorway. We put out the fire. Who *are* you?' He came closer, shining the lantern in Margaret's face. She smelled his fear.

'Maggie de la Haye – Sir Simon Montagu will vouch for me. The folk without asked whether I'd seen anyone in the backlands. So the murderer escaped?'

The man snorted. 'Do you think anyone came out when she screamed? They say she screamed, and looking at her, you *know* she screamed.' He shook his head, disgusted.

'How did you come to be here?' Margaret asked, although her heart pounded so in her ears that she feared she wouldn't hear his response.

'I should ask the questions,' he barked quite clearly.

'Is that the weapon?' With the toe of her shoe Margaret pointed to a log the width of a woman's forearm, with knobs where branches had been cut off. It lay near Johanna.

'Aye, it's bloody. Why are you here?' His face was very close to hers now and she could smell that he'd been drinking.

'She was my friend. I had come to see her. We must find who did this. She was a good person–' Margaret covered her mouth. She was babbling, though it would not matter to him.

'She was a whore. Slept with half the soldiers in the castle.'

Margaret slapped him in the face. 'I'll not have you speak about her with disrespect, God rest her soul.'

He grabbed her by the wrist and the vice-like grip made her cry out in pain. But she was too angry to desist. His lantern tilted so far sideways that it was dripping oil.

'You'll burn us all if you don't see to your lantern,' she said, a little breathless. She did not know what had gotten into her, to refuse to withdraw.

'You'll pay for that, lass,' he growled, but let go of her hand. He put the lantern on the ground and with his heels tried to scuff the oil into the packed earth floor. Much good that would do.

Margaret rubbed her burning wrist. 'Respect the dead. God knows you don't the living.'

'I've not touched her!'

'I expected you to stand guard at the door.' The voice came from a man who stood at the threshold, so tall that he filled the doorway. The lamp lit his face from beneath, rendering its chiselled features sinister.

'I stepped within for a moment and this woman fell upon me,' whined the guard. 'She accused me of not respecting the dead.'

Margaret had picked up the lantern and now held it up to the newcomer's face to assure herself he was human. She thought him familiar, and as he wore the livery of the castle guard she was reassured that he was the sort of devil to which she'd become accustomed, one of Longshanks's soldiers.

'How was he disrespectful?' the man asked.

'The woman lying there in her own blood was my friend, and this man called her a whore,' said Margaret.

'Walter, guard the door – from without,' said the man.

When the portly guard had pushed past them, the tall man closed the door behind him. Margaret still held the lantern.

'I would like to turn her over so that you could assure me this is Johanna.' He glanced at Margaret over his shoulder. 'Are you willing?'

Willing she was, but she did not know how well she would stand up to it. Still, she nodded and stepped closer.

'Turn that bench upright,' he said, indicating a long one. 'I'll lay her there.'

Margaret set the lantern on the shelf, shaking so hard that she knew she needed both arms to turn over the bench without fumbling with it. She was fighting a surge of fear and regret for having stood her ground by staying in the room. She wished someone else were facing this terrible task. The room was hot and the odour of blood nauseated her.

With considerate care the man lifted the body from the floor and managed to turn her as he lay her down on the bench.

Margaret cried out. Johanna's jaw had been broken with a blow, and she yawned crookedly, the visible gums bloody. Her eyes were open. Margaret knelt to close them.

'It is your friend?' asked the man.

In touching Johanna Margaret felt a surge of terror that propelled her up and away from the body. She could not speak at once.

The man stepped towards her. 'I must be certain.'

'Yes, it is Johanna,' Margaret managed to say. *Forgive me for coming too late.* She had been badly frightened by the touch and wanted to escape, but she felt she should not, at least until the priest arrived.

'I'll have the women who stand without take care of her. Your household will be worrying about your absence on such a night.'

'Who could have done this? She was a gentle woman.'

'I have seen you with Ada de la Haye. I will have Walter escort you home,' said the man, ignoring her question.

'I'll wait for the priest, and then I'll take myself home.'

'Walter is a foul-mouthed villain, but there is someone abroad who has killed once tonight, and a prisoner escaped to sanctuary, quite the slippery one. In thanks for identifying this poor woman I must have you seen safely home.'

'Who are you?'

'A captain, a soldier intent on my duty.'

Margaret did not move. 'I said I'll wait for the priest.'

'I'll wait here for him,' he said. 'There is no need for you to stay.'

She sensed in the man a strength of will that she decided it was best not to cross. Without a word she departed, nodding to Walter as the other ordered him to escort her. She did not speak all the way, nor did her escort, and as soon as John opened Ada's door she hurried in without looking back.

Celia ran to her and Margaret asked for some strong drink and a basin of water in which to wash.

'Dame Johanna has been murdered,' said Margaret, crossing herself. 'Beaten about the head.'

'Dear God,' Celia cried.

Margaret gathered her skirts and was about to climb up to the solar.

'Father Piers's clerk came for you a while ago.' Celia's voice shook. 'He said Master James was taken by the English and escaped to sanctuary in the kirk. What a night, Mistress, what a terrible night.'

Margaret crossed herself and prayed for strength as she turned away from the steps. 'I still need to wash and have a good strong drink.'

8

REVELATIONS

Frightened by the events of the evening, which had strengthened his terror of being found out by the English, Father Piers began to fuss to avoid facing his demons. He considered the room, trying to determine how he might best receive Margaret, how best to tell her of James's misadventure and his sad news, as well as the summons that had come for a priest to administer the last rites to Johanna. He'd sent his elderly assistant, Father John, for Piers was needed here, to stand his ground against soldiers demanding James. He'd had a terrible feeling that Gordon Cowie's murder had set off a wave of fighting to mirror that going on down below, and now he feared he'd been right. *God have mercy on all their souls*, he prayed, crossing himself.

He wondered how he, called to a contemplative life, had become so involved in treachery. It was frightening to be in the middle of all of it. He was within his rights to grant James sanctuary, but he was uneasy about how the English would judge his doing so. He had assured the captain who'd pursued James that despite his wish to cooperate with the castle it was his duty to respect the sanctity of sanctuary.

'Do you know who he is?' the captain had demanded.

'It matters not a whit who he is,' said Piers, 'he has claimed sanctuary and it is his right.' He would lie outright if necessary – he had before, despite his fear of becoming mired in a quicksand of lies. The captain had hesitated, as if about to tell him of James's connection with King John Balliol, but then decided against it.

'I'll return in the morning,' he'd said, and departed.

Just as worrisome was Margaret's being abroad in the town, and without an escort, not even her maid. He did not know what she could be thinking, to take no precautions after the death of the goldsmith. Most felt that Gordon had been murdered because of his support of the English. For all others knew Margaret, too, was on the side of the invaders – they didn't know of her work for King John.

'Dame Maggie is here,' the clerk said.

Praised be God.

The first thing Piers noticed was that despite the summery night Margaret had a plaid wrapped around her. He also noted that her hem was filthy. As she stepped into the room she stumbled despite having her hand resting on the arm of her small maid.

'Dame Margaret?' Piers looked closely at her.

She raised her eyes to his, fixing on him with exaggerated attention though it made her blink. Her face was flushed and slack.

God help us, she's been drinking.

He pulled the chair slightly out of the light – her eyes must be sensitive to it – and appreciated Celia's coaxing her to take the seat so proffered.

Margaret did not move at once. 'I was too late,' she said.

The clerk caught Piers's eye – *Water? Wine? Neither?*

But Celia asked for some watered wine for her mistress.

'Forgive me, but Dame Maggie appears to have already drunk overmuch,' said Piers.

'And so would you had you been asked to look closely at a woman beaten beyond –'

'You were there?' Piers said, horrified.

'Celia, quiet.' Margaret kept her hand raised just a little too long, then dropped it as she gingerly sat down. 'Yes, I've had a mazer full of Evota's fine ale.' She said nothing more for a moment, but emotion welled in her eyes. 'Her face did not take the brunt of the blows – it was the back of her head. But her jaw – the teeth–' Margaret had reached out, sculpting the air with her hand as if drawing the horror.

Thank the Lord she could not actually make him see what she'd seen, thought Piers, for in her dazed eyes he saw enough. 'Who made you look, Dame Maggie?'

'He had to know whether it was Johanna,' Margaret said.

'Christ have mercy,' said the clerk.

'What were you doing there?' Piers asked.

'I'd gone to see her,' Margaret said. 'But too late.' Her voice broke, yet she sat rigidly staring towardss him.

'You describe such terrible injuries,' said Piers. 'You arrived after she'd been attacked?'

Margaret nodded. 'May the Blessed Mother hold her to her breast and comfort her,' she whispered as she took the cup from the clerk's hands, her own hands trembling so that she needed both to bring the cup to her lips.

Piers left her in peace for a moment, but he was bursting with questions and finally asked, 'Who did it?'

Margaret shook her head. 'I know not, but the people think she was murdered for her English lover, as Gordon Cowie had been murdered for doing so much business with the castle.'

'We must tell James of this. He awaits you in the kirk. Who was it who had you look upon her?' Piers asked once more.

Margaret took a breath, visibly shivering as she exhaled. 'An English soldier, very tall, slender, sharp-featured. He spoke like a noble.' She pulled the plaid higher round her neck.

'Why were you there this evening?'

She lifted her eyes to his and seemed about to speak, but pressed her lips together and dropped her gaze again. It was a few seconds before she said, 'I heard shouts in St Mary's Wynd and was curious. It was my undoing.'

'Was she touched?' Piers asked. 'Or robbed?'

Margaret shook her head. 'Neither.' She struggled to her feet. 'Let us go to James.' She looked pale and terribly fragile.

'Do you think you should, Mistress?' asked the maid, rising to support her.

She'd been so still that Piers had forgotten her presence. He had a sense that there was much the two were not telling him. God help him if he'd been mistaken in trusting them.

'I wish to talk to James, to tell him what I saw,' said Margaret.

She was steadier on her feet now, but Piers was having second thoughts about her seeing James tonight.

'There is no need for you to tell him, I shall,' Piers offered. 'You have witnessed such violence. You should rest. Come to him in the morning.'

Margaret kept walking towards the door. 'I'll not sleep tonight, so I'd as lief have someone to talk to,' she said.

She was a very stubborn woman.

'It is out of my hands,' Piers murmured as he crossed himself. 'Stay a moment. There's bound to be someone watching. We'll carry bedding to him.'

When all three were so burdened, they moved out into the kirk yard. Torchlight illuminated a guard at the side door of the kirk, and another apparently stood by the nave door, where his torch danced wildly in the breeze.

'God have mercy.' Piers said it as if a curse. He had not thought that they would set up sentinels so soon. Thank God he'd prepared.

Margaret covered her head with her plaid.

'I'll not tell them who you are,' Piers promised. 'They ken they haven't the right to deny the faithful access to the kirk.' Perhaps it was best that Margaret go to James now, in the dark, before the gossips fed on the night's deeds.

*

The market square had been almost deserted when Ada stepped out of her house with her escort to the castle.

'How it has changed in a day,' she said.

'All are fearful since the stabbing of the goldsmith,' said the young man. 'There will be little law in the town when most of the soldiers have gone down to the camps.'

Ada prayed that those loyal to King John would not take it as an opportunity to punish those who had courted the English. She hesitated, wondering whether she should warn John to be extra vigilant. But he was, as a rule.

In the castle bailey she sensed that here, too, was a heightened tension, and looking around she noticed only martial activity, no townsfolk doing business, no idle hands. The men were cleaning and sharpening weapons, training, packing, dismantling tents, talking in hushed tones. The eyes that followed her passage were already haunted. Just yesterday Gordon Cowie had been here, doing business. She picked out the spot where he'd sat. Not since she had defied Simon and then almost died birthing Godric's child had she felt so close to death, for she understood there was little, perhaps nothing to prevent anyone from murdering anyone when the captains and commanders were fixed on the enemy across the river. Who would punish a murderer? What difference was it to them whether someone was murdered, killed in battle, or merely in the wrong place at the wrong time? She hurried after the escort, uneasy about being so exposed in the castle yard.

Simon, too, was different this evening, repeating himself and sometimes forgetting his train of thought. She tried to bring him back to subjects that bonded them because she felt so vulnerable tonight.

'Where was I?' he'd just muttered for at least the eighth time when the servant announced Peter. They were at table, talking about the children, making plans for Ada to travel south to see them, although she doubted it would happen and knew full well that she would not be welcomed by any of them. Still, she yearned to know her children. Except for Peter – she was not eager to renew acquaintance with him. He'd shown up in her dreams last night as a chilly-eyed executioner.

And here he was now, standing over them, a sheen of sweat bringing a welcome imperfection to his handsome face. Perhaps that was part of what disturbed her – such a beautiful man should be angelic, all things good.

'What's amiss?' Simon asked, rising slightly as he gestured to his son – their son – to join them at the table.

Peter took a seat and helped himself to some wine, adding almost as much again of water. Apparently he meant to keep his wits about him this evening.

'The Welshman led us right to our quarry,' Peter said to Simon. 'But the prisoner escaped us and has claimed sanctuary in Holy Rude Church.'

'What? How could he escape?' His face reddening, Simon inexplicably looked at Ada as if she might answer that.

But of course she had no idea of whom they spoke. She returned to her study of Peter, watching his jaw muscles flex. He held himself so tightly it was plain to her how humiliated he was to have lost a captive, and thus that he was human after all, which was good in a sense. Beneath this motherly observation she realised with great unease that Simon had looked at her as if he thought she knew something of the prisoner's escape. But she'd known all along that they would find her presence at this time suspicious.

'The men are too excitable tonight,' said Peter. 'They jump at the slightest movement or sound. My prisoner must have noticed and watched for his chance. When the men were distracted by a pair of brawling drunkards he rushed straight to the church and claimed sanctuary before we could recapture him.'

'The priest will not hand him over?' asked Simon.

Peter shook his head. 'Father Piers insists that he must honour sanctuary.' Now he took a drink, avoiding his father's eyes.

'The Comyn is in sanctuary.' Simon wearily pressed his brow. 'What a sad end to a good day's work.'

Ada's stomach fluttered to hear the name. The Comyn was almost certainly James, for he'd complained that few of his kinsmen were yet rising for either side. James a prisoner. God help them if it was so. She tried to recall whether anything she'd done since she'd arrived in Stirling had connected her with him. But of course there had always been the risk that spies had seen them riding here together.

'And there is more,' said Peter. 'A woman of the town has been brutally beaten.'

'Dead?' Simon asked.

Peter nodded, more at ease with this news, Ada noticed with disgust. 'Johanna of St Mary's Wynd – the one who bedded with a dozen soldiers or more before choosing someone unhappy with his lot.'

'She wanted a man willing to talk?' asked Simon.

Peter nodded.

'She was spying for Wallace and Murray?'

'I believe so.'

'And you've spied on her.'

'I have a certain skill,' said Peter.

Ada fought to hide her fear that they spoke of the woman who had been sending messages to James. 'No matter what she had done, to be beaten to death is a horrible end,' she said, looking first to Peter, then to Simon. 'It is not an honourable means of execution.'

'I agree,' said Peter, 'although "beaten to death" makes it sound as if she were repeatedly hit. I believe she was hit but twice, once in the back of the head, once on one jaw.' He delivered this assessment in a cool voice, his expression one of mild impatience.

'That is still horrible,' said Ada, crossing herself and saying a prayer for her son's soul as well as for the victim's.

'But I doubt it was an execution.' Peter tore off the corner of his father's trencher and chewed on the bread as if he'd completed what he'd had to say.

'By saying you doubt it was an execution you imply you have an idea what the motive was,' said Simon, adjusting his heft on the bench so that he might observe his son.

Peter, poking at a slice of cold meat with his dagger, shook his head. 'No. But execution would imply a soldier's deed, and soldiers carry weapons, they don't pick up logs to beat a woman and risk her surviving such an uncertain attack.' He took a bite of the meat, only now meeting his father's eyes. 'There had been two, perhaps three blows.'

Simon grunted. 'The wisdom of Solomon, presented with a bold confidence.' He shook his head at Ada's expression of dismay. 'He has none of your fine feelings, eh?'

'How could I?' asked Peter, the meat on the knife poised before his mouth. 'She did not raise me.'

'That was not my choice, if you care to know,' said Ada.

Peter was too busy eating to bother to answer with more than a shrug. Ada had never imagined a warm reception from her children, but Peter's discourtesy was uncalled for. The more she saw of him the less she thought of the family who had fostered him. He would have grown up with far better character if she'd brought him up.

'How did your commander receive the news that Comyn escaped?' Simon asked.

Peter had finished eating and was wiping down his knife. 'How do you think?' He rose, sheathing his knife. 'I must decide who takes the next watch at the kirk.' He came to stand behind Ada, lightly resting his hands on her shoulders, then bending to say, as if conspiratorially, 'Cousin Maggie was a good friend to Johanna. On your recommendation, Ma?'

She must have guessed correctly that the woman had been James's connection. Ada did not dare breathe, though she longed to slap Peter for his insolence.

'How do you know that?' Simon angrily demanded.

'She was at the woman's house.' Peter straightened. 'I had her look closely to make certain that the woman was Johanna.'

'How cruel,' Ada cried. She had not expected Maggie to be so incautious. She might have been killed.

'I had need,' said Peter. 'It was my opportunity to discover whether Maggie knew Johanna or was merely over curious. And then one of my men escorted her home.'

With his every act Ada disliked him more.

Simon looked at Ada. 'Had your niece any cause to murder Johanna?'

Ada stood up abruptly. 'My niece is not a murderer, Simon. How dare you–'

'I did not mean to suggest that,' Peter cut in. 'She arrived after I'd set a guard on the house. Ill fortune on her part to choose tonight to seek out her friend.'

'Yes,' said Ada, uncertain whether her outrage had compromised anything. She thought not. It was natural for her to react so. She allowed herself to breathe, though she remained standing.

Moving to the head of the table Peter bowed to both. 'I must leave you now. Forgive me for casting a pall on your merrymaking.' The ghost of a smile played around his mouth. 'You should advise the lovely Maggie to choose her friends with more care, Ma.'

Ada controlled herself and merely wished him a good evening. Once he was out of sight she and Simon silently stared at one another for a long while, her standing, him sitting, like a pair of cats challenging one another to be the first to look away.

She was thinking a great deal, and had no doubt that Simon was, too. It worried her that she did not know what he was thinking. Both he and Peter acted as if they trusted her less than on the previous evening, despite her having had no opportunity since arriving in Stirling to do anything behind their backs. Yet why then were they confiding in her?

And now Maggie had been to Johanna's house. Ill fortune indeed to have gone there, especially on the night of James Comyn's capture. Ada wondered whether his capture and Johanna's death were connected. She felt sick at heart for Maggie, that she'd been forced to look at the body.

'Our son is a cold, unfeeling creature,' she said, easing back down.

'As a small boy he suffered night terrors,' said Simon. 'His foster parents were at a loss what to do.'

She thought his mind was wandering again.

'But on his own Peter decided that he wished to train in the arts of war,' continued Simon, proving her wrong, 'a rigorous, unrelenting training through which he honed his skills until he felt–'

'Invincible,' Ada said, finishing for him.

'I was going to say "confident".'

'Safe,' Ada added. 'He no longer had cause to fear anything.'

'Any*one*,' Simon corrected. 'He's helpless against a storm at sea, as are we all. But you make a good point.'

'If the dead woman was a spy, God must have been watching over Maggie that she did not come to harm,' said Ada.

'Hm.' Simon rose to pour them both more wine. 'Most unwelcome news. I had looked forward to another happy evening in your company.' He gazed down at her with a half smile, his eyes affectionate.

'It is still early, My Lord,' she said, taking his hand and kissing his palm. How dry and rough it was.

He lifted the hand to her face, tracing her features. 'I sorely need distraction this night, Ada. I want you to stay.'

She would much prefer to go home and see how Maggie fared, but she did not dare disappoint Simon when the evening had put her friends' mission in jeopardy. So be it. She prided herself on being a consummate player. He would have no cause to suspect her of wishing to be elsewhere this night.

As she began to flirt with Simon, Ada experienced a familiar sense of having left her body and taken up a position across the room from which she might clearly observe their play. It often happened when she was purposefully manipulating her companion. She believed God caused this, to frighten her from her duplicity, and she blasphemously ignored Him, thinking that in time He would see it was for the best. Although, since He was omniscient and all powerful, all was in the moment to Him and He knew the outcome before she came up with the plan. Perhaps this was how He tested the strength of her convictions.

After a while she allowed her smile to fade into a fretful expression and averted her eyes as she leaned forward to take up the goblet of wine.

'What is it?' Simon asked. 'Have I offended you in some way?'

She could see by the movement of his eyes that he was reviewing his recent comments. 'No, not you, Simon.'

'Then what?' He caught her hand, cradling it in his, and gently uncurled her fingers to kiss the centre of her palm, as she had his.

A delicious warmth spread upward. He took hold of her arm and pulled her towards him. She did not resist, but came to rest in his lap, vulnerable and willing. He kissed her ears, her neck, the rise of her breasts. One hand slipped up her skirts.

'What is bothering you, my love?' he whispered into her hair.

She groaned. 'You, my love,' she chuckled. 'Our dour son would be horrified.' She shivered as his fingers found her wetness. 'Oh sweet Simon,' she moaned, holding tight round his shoulders as he rose and carried her to the bed. God help her but she found this such sweet, fulfilling work. She enjoyed how he slowly undressed her, his eyes sleepy with desire, his member rising beneath his shift.

'How are you still so slender, so beautiful, mother of my children?' he wondered.

Passion played with his vision, she thought, but she enjoyed the deliciously wicked excitement of being stripped naked. One was never too old for that.

She must guard her tongue, though; Peter's news had been fraught with traps for her.

Their lovemaking was not so wild as in their youth, but hot enough that their bodies were slippery and must be covered from the draughts as they lay together smiling.

'Have you forgotten your worries now, my Ada?'

She heard the grin in his words and hated to disappoint him, but timing was all.

'Oh, sweet, why have you reminded me?' She sighed and snuggled closer to him.

He propped himself up on one elbow, idly caressing one of her breasts. 'Tell me. Do you want for anything?'

'I hesitate to mention it here, in our bower—' She turned on her side, ran a hand from his temple to his jaw, then down his neck, and under the covers down the centre of his chest, to his stomach, his flaccid member, which felt as if it trembled at her touch.

'Ada,' Simon caught her hand, laughed. 'We'll solve nothing with such idle hands.'

She felt mischievous and gave the throaty chuckle he loved. 'You are right. The sooner I make my moan, the sooner I might devour you again.'

'Wanton woman.' He pressed her hand, released it, and pushed himself upright, leaning back against the pillows.

Ada sat up as well, pulling the blanket up to her neck for warmth. 'Will you do anything to bring this Johanna's murderer to justice?'

Simon pulled up the covers a little, too, she thought to hide the scars she'd just noticed on one shoulder. 'It was a terrible act, to be sure, but Peter may be right, a soldier has weapons.' He shook his head.

'Would he carry them to see his mistress?'

'In this town? I should hope he would.'

'So nothing is to be done? Have you not taken over the governing of this town? Is it not your responsibility to see that the people are safe?'

He shifted and she saw that she had broken the spell. 'Why trouble yourself about it?' he asked.

'It sounds as if Johanna and I had much in common, being the mistresses of soldiers. I would hope that my murder would be avenged.'

His eyes softened a little. 'Do not speak such things, Ada. She was quite another matter.'

'Her murderer must be brought to justice. Will you question her lover?'

'I might suggest it. Particularly if Peter is right that he's a traitor.'

She risked pushing a little further. 'Might I talk to him? He might talk more readily to a woman.'

Simon made an impatient sound deep in his throat. 'Things are tense in the garrison. The man may already be in the valley. In faith, we have no time for such things.'

'I do, Simon. A war is no excuse for slack justice. Do you want a dishonourable soldier fighting under you?'

'You choose a poor argument. Edward has granted us an army of felons and miscreants. The English soldiers blame the Welsh for their own misdeeds, the Welsh desert ingloriously. It is a shambles. Only our number overwhelms Murray and Wallace.'

'And some honourable and excellent commanders,' she whispered.

He grunted, then surprised her with a bemused smile. 'You have a knight's courage. I'll consider your request that we look into it.'

'Thank you, Simon.'

'I promise only to consider it.'

It was enough for now. Ada was tired, and she sensed Simon's weariness. But she must keep up the lovemaking a little longer so that he did not suspect how important Johanna was to her.

*

Shivering in the breeze despite her plaid, Margaret was sorry the strong ale no longer dulled her senses. The guard's torch snapped and sputtered loudly in the quiet night.

'Let us pass,' demanded Father Piers in a strong voice.

'Who are these women?'

'Maidservants come to fix a place for the man to sleep,' said Piers, holding up the blankets he carried.

Margaret appreciated the priest's sensible approach.

Apparently the guard believed Piers, although he made a few snide comments about fussing over a man as good as dead.

Ignoring him, Piers fitted the key into the kirk door and stood aside to let Margaret and Celia hurry within.

The cavernous nave engulfed Margaret, the darkness huge beyond the meagre light from a small lamp beside the door. When Father Piers closed the door and locked it, the sound echoed and expanded through the vastness. Margaret felt dizzy, as if her spirit were spreading wide and high to fill the inhuman space. She moved into the light for reassurance.

'Maggie, is it you?' James's voice came from behind her.

She turned around slowly, not trusting her balance. James caught her up in his arms, kissing her with a passion that she did not return at once, unable to push away the memory of Johanna's battered head so quickly. But the warmth of his embrace and the tenderness of his kisses drew her back to the present, to the world of the living, and in a few moments she responded with passion equal to his.

Father Piers's voice reminded them that their companions could see all despite the darkness of the nave, and they stepped back from one another, reluctantly withdrawing their hands.

'I had not realised how it was between you,' said the priest.

'I do not think we did either,' said James, sounding a little breathless.

Margaret marvelled at how easily James could play to the situation, pretending that he had not professed his love for her just a few days earlier. She had not known how she would feel when she saw him again, but his presence had made the nave a far less frightening expanse despite his need to seek sanctuary there. Tenderly grateful, she wanted to see to the scratches on his face and the wound that was staining his tunic at the shoulder, as if by tending his wounds she might save both of them from danger.

'We have much to talk about,' said Father Piers. 'Let us withdraw to the chapel we are preparing for you, James.'

The priest motioned to Celia and Margaret to follow him, but James caught Margaret's arm.

'What I must tell you will be easier without the others,' he said, and in his voice she heard weariness and pain.

Although the shadows obscured his expression, Margaret could feel his eyes fixed on hers. She glanced back at their companions.

Piers bowed his head slightly. 'As you will,' he said, and picked up the bedding that Margaret had set aside. 'Come, Celia. We will await them in the chapel.'

As they withdrew, the echo of their footsteps reminded Margaret of the vast stone structure around her and once again she felt like a mote in the draughts of the dark nave, at the mercy of an inhuman force. She stepped closer to James.

'I feel too small in this great nave.' She forced a little laugh that eerily echoed.

'It was not built for our ease,' said James, 'but to put us in awe of the Almighty. I'm sorry to keep you here. We will join the others as soon as I've told you–'

'I have troubling news for you as well,' she whispered.

'Troubling? I said nothing of that.' James took her hands. 'Do you feel what I am feeling? Are we already so bound?'

Margaret realised that in his hesitation she'd known what he was about to tell her. Both of her frightening visions had now been realised, with her powerless to have prevented them. The Sight was a thing of madness, a curse.

'Something has happened to Roger,' she said.

He pulled her closer, stooping to look into her eyes. 'How do you know?'

Surely it was a sign of madness to have forgotten to wait for him to tell her. Think, she screamed in her head as he stood waiting for her explanation. If she revealed her madness he would want to know more, he would expect her to see into the future, and she could not do it. She had no control over this affliction. *Think*. She'd already been worried about Roger before the vision. Because of Christiana. 'My mother was worried about him, and it seemed one with her concern about my coming to Stirling. What is it, Jamie, what are you thinking?'

He relaxed his grip on her hands a little. 'I feared that Dame Christiana has passed you the Sight. I don't know how I would feel about that regarding our mission.'

Margaret did not dare respond for that's why she'd said nothing of it.

'He is dead, Maggie. Roger is dead.'

The power of the words startled Margaret. She had relived Roger's fall in the visions and dreams many times, and yet she had not been ready for the finality of James's words. Dead. No more. There would never be a reconciliation. She would never know the truth of Roger's feelings for her. Feeling light-headed, she leaned against James not because she thought his embrace would ease her pain but because she feared falling in this place, disappearing through the stones to the ancient power that lay beneath.

James put his arms around her and held her close.

'How did he die?' she whispered.

'He'd fallen from an outcrop behind this kirk. His head hit another great stone.'

'In the kirk yard,' she said. 'So close.' She should have searched out there.

'One of my men found him. The brush and the rocks shielded him from sight.'

Her vision had been accurate – and utterly useless.

'God grant him peace,' she prayed. 'Did you see him?'

'Yes.'

'Do you think he suffered?'

'His neck was broken, Maggie. I don't think he would have lingered.'

He held her tight and she turned her head to one side to take a few deep breaths, hoping to ease the lump in her throat. Roger would have counted his death by a fall ignoble. He had once predicted that he would die defending the goods on one of his ships. He would have preferred that.

'I think he'd been robbed, for there was nothing of value on him,' said James, 'not even his personal knife.'

Margaret straightened a little, needing more air. 'Do you think he was pushed?'

'That I cannot guess, Maggie. He might have given chase if he'd discovered he'd been robbed.' James tucked a stray lock into her wimple. 'I saw no knife wounds, nor did I see any marks on his neck, so he wasn't strangled before falling.'

Margaret stepped back and turned away, into the lamplight beside them. 'You so closely examined him?' She did not like the idea, his being examined by – what was James to her? Not yet a lover, so he was not a rival, though regarding Balliol and the Bruce he and Roger had been in separate camps.

'I wanted to give you as full an account as I might, for I knew we could not wait to bury him. I thought it a miracle he'd fallen where he was not noticed by the English – he'd been dead at least several days.'

She might have found him herself. Yet what would that have changed but that the English might then be certain of their connection. 'Did you find his companion Aylmer, the Bruce's watchdog?' Margaret distrusted the man, a distrust validated by a letter she'd found in his belongings when he'd stayed in their home in Perth. He and Roger had been on a mission to coax her father into supporting Robert Bruce, and Aylmer had carried orders from the Bruce to kill Roger or her father if either proved false in any way.

'No. We found only Roger.'

She cursed Aylmer for not helping Roger – he might even have pushed him. The lump in her throat seemed to have travelled to her stomach and now burned like a coal, yet her hands were aching with cold. 'Where did you bury him?'

'My men took him to Cambuskenneth Abbey.' James moved behind her and put his hands on her shoulders.

'With all those camping down below? How could your men carry a body across the river without being caught?'

'We respect each others' dead.'

'They did not respect the dead in Berwick.'

'It is always possible that my men did not make it, but it would not be for want of trying. I have done all I could to honour him, Maggie.'

She moved back into James's arms and let the tears come, a brief outpouring that eased the fire in her stomach. But in its place an iciness spread from her hands up her arms and encased her heart. She'd been cursed with the Sight and no man might undo that.

Celia had been surprised to find a straw pallet already tucked into a corner behind the chapel's altar, and some dishes sitting on a small table.

'What is to prevent the English from taking Master James when the kirk is open during the day?' she asked.

'Fear of eternal damnation,' said Father Piers.

Celia did not have his faith that such fear would protect James.

'But I'll not risk it,' said Piers. 'I'll lock the gate to this chapel. The chaplain has long been gone and it is now merely the burial place of the ancestors of a family gone from Stirling for many a year.'

It was no place she would care to sleep, but Celia knelt to

arrange the bedding. Father Piers crouched down to assist her, his second act this evening that proved wrong her early impression of him as self-centred – the first had been when he upheld James Comyn's request for sanctuary.

She was glad to have a chore because the depth of feeling evident between her mistress and James Comyn in those first moments in the nave had shaken Celia. She felt as if she'd missed a crucial development in the motivation behind their coming to Stirling. Her confidence had already been shaken by Johanna's murder and James's capture. She felt as if the English soldier knew everything that they'd done since they arrived; she would not be at all surprised to hear that he was the one who had captured James.

'What did the captain look like? The one who came for Master Comyn?'

The priest's description fitted her English soldier. When she told Father Piers, he looked frightened. 'It had not occurred to me that he was the one of which you and Johanna had spoken.' He knelt at the small altar to pray.

'You said you had sad news for me,' James reminded Margaret.

She'd withdrawn from his embrace and held her hands over the lamp, trying to thaw them, but as soon as she took them from the heat they were cold as the stones beneath her feet. And now she must tell James of her other vision become reality.

'When did your men find Roger's body?' she asked instead. An uncomfortable sensation had begun, as if she wanted to run from James, as if he were dangerous to her.

'Yesterday.'

James stepped closer; Margaret moved to the far side of the lamp, as if meaning to share it with him.

'Do you think your finding him had anything to do with your being found by the English today?'

'It might, though I think it more likely it had to do with the

Welsh archer. Do you remember him? The one who brought news of Andrew?'

'The one you didn't trust.'

James nodded. 'He showed up at our camp with a tale of escape from his guard because he had gone through hell to be part of the battle that is about to take place for the River Forth. My men believed him – before I arrived he'd insinuated himself into their ranks. This morning he disappeared.' He pressed his palms to his face for a moment and looked so dejected that Margaret felt cruel for avoiding his touch.

'You were right to distrust him,' she said. 'I doubted him a little, too.'

'I wish we'd been wrong.'

'How did you *know* to distrust him?' As he began to reiterate his reasoning Margaret interrupted him. 'I remember your reasoning, but how did it *feel*? Did you sense it the moment you met him?'

'Are you asking me now whether *I* have the Sight?'

'No, no, I'm wondering how to know whom I can trust in such times.'

James gave a little laugh. 'Would that we *could* know. Why do you think both Roger and I wanted to talk to your mother? We wanted to learn more about her prediction that you'd watch the true King of Scotland ride into Edinburgh. We wanted to learn what she knows with her gift of kenning.'

Both had been disappointed, for Christiana swore she'd seen only Margaret's features in the vision. She'd refused to see Roger at first, which was why her befriending him when he returned to the nunnery wounded had surprised Margaret. But it might have meant little – he might have spent time with her hoping to learn more about the prediction. It had been Margaret's lifelong experience that few people wanted anything to do with her mother except to learn something through her Second Sight, and they often blamed her if they were unhappy with what she had to tell them. Never did they ask about her as they would a woman without that gift. Margaret did not want that to be her own fate.

James reached out for Margaret's right hand. 'Maggie, what is this bad news?'

She almost recoiled from his touch. Perhaps because he had touched Roger after death. It was a moment before she could draw herself from that thought.

'Johanna was murdered this evening.'

'Our spy?'

Margaret nodded.

'God's blood, how?'

'She was hit in the back of the head with a thick branch, at least once, and once in the jaw. She was lying on the floor of her home when I arrived.'

James caught Margaret's arm. 'You went to her home? Why? You were to communicate through Father Piers and Archie.'

'Father Piers introduced us. And I've yet to meet Archie,' said Margaret. 'He's a slippery young man. He's told Father Piers he cannot help us any more.' She did not want to tell James about her fear for Johanna; he'd want to know who was next. 'I was in the backlands and heard a scream. It was foolish, I know, but I ran to see who it was. Her neighbours told me. There was an English soldier in the house.' She was talking too fast, hoping he would not stop her for details. 'And then his captain came and asked me to look on her, tell him if it was Johanna. He told me that he'd lost a prisoner, that the man had claimed sanctuary here.'

'Do you know his name?'

'No.'

'Pale hair and dark brows?'

'Taller than you, lean and well-spoken?' Margaret finished for James as he nodded. 'Your captor?'

'Aye, Maggie, and his name is Peter Fitzsimon – Ada's son by Simon Montagu.'

She began to shake her head in disbelief, but in her mind's eye she now saw how much he favoured his mother. Even so, she asked, 'Are you certain?'

'I am.'

'God help us.' She wondered whether the night was yet finished with them, twisting all their fates about. 'If the archer has met with Peter, he might have mentioned me.'

'I don't believe he's met with Simon yet. We can only pray that the archer does not see you.'

'I still might be Ada's niece.' But that did not matter, she realised that. 'They'll act on suspicions, whether or not they are certain. Ada and all in her home are threatened by the archer's knowledge.'

'I should have killed him,' said James. 'I felt in my gut that I should.'

'What if I claimed sanctuary with you?'

'You would condemn Ada.'

'What can we do?'

'For now, withdraw into Ada's home. Call no attention to yourself.'

❧ 9 ❧

EVERYTHING CHANGED

Perhaps it was the quiet in the kirk, or perhaps it was the ordinary motions of preparing a bed, but Celia could sense for the first time in a long while the presence of God. She felt confident that if she prayed with all her heart He would hear, which she'd doubted since leaving her comfortable life in Katherine Sinclair's home in Dunfermline with Margaret. She'd been unable to reconcile the cruelty and suffering she witnessed in Edinburgh, Perth, and Stirling with the welcoming Lord she'd always imagined. But at this moment she felt invited to pray. Kneeling, she bowed her head and told God all that was in her heart: her fears, her angers, her wishes for those she loved, her wishes for herself. A surprise awaited her. She had not been aware that her wish for herself had changed since the last time she'd opened her heart to Him. No longer did she yearn to be a lady's maid and travel to castles and manor houses; now her heart's desire was to find a kind man and to bear his children, to create a home filled with love – a tidy home over which she ruled with joy and peace of mind. She felt God smile on her and almost wept for the hope it gave her.

'At last they join us,' Father Piers mumbled behind her.

Celia raised her head and in an instant her happy mood dulled as she saw the tension in her mistress's face and the set of James Comyn's jaw.

Margaret joined her on the wide prie-dieu before the altar and bowed her head.

'Have you had darksome news, Mistress?' Celia whispered.

Margaret took a deep, shuddering breath. 'I am widowed.' Her voice caught on the sorrow-laden word.

Celia's first thought was of Roger's mother Katherine Sinclair, anxiously waiting in Dunfermline for news of her son. Tears filled her eyes as Celia remembered the love between mother and son. She also recalled Margaret's shy, happy face on her wedding day. Roger Sinclair had proved a disappointing husband, but even so Celia knew that his death would weigh heavily on her mistress's heart. As she put a comforting arm round Margaret she felt how tense she was, how shallowly she breathed.

'I am so sorry,' Celia whispered. 'How can I help?'

Margaret covered Celia's hand with hers, pressing it in thanks, but she said nothing, jumping when Father Piers spoke to James in a loud whisper.

'In the kirk yard? *Deus juva me*. That is too close.'

Celia glanced round as the priest crossed himself. His arched eyebrows almost disappeared in creases his frown made in his forehead as he regarded James.

'They found Roger below the large rock in the kirk yard,' Margaret said softly, for Celia's ears only. 'He'd fallen. His neck was broken.'

'Holy Mother of God,' Celia whispered, trying not to imagine the scene and realising with a shiver that another of Margaret's visions had come to pass.

'How do you know the English had not found him there and set a watch to see who would claim him?' Father Piers asked James.

'Roger had been dead for at least several days when James's men found him,' Margaret said to Celia.

'Don't think I haven't wondered that,' said James. He was so tired his voice was failing.

'Where is he now?' Celia asked, glancing out into the nave.

'James's men are taking him to Cambuskenneth Abbey.' Margaret's tone was flat.

'God watch over them,' Celia said.

Margaret pressed her fingertips to her temples.

Selfishly, Celia wished to leave before so much was said in here that its peace would be lost to her for good. She still had a warm memory of God's welcoming ear. 'You need rest, Mistress. There is no need for you to stay here.'

Margaret rose, but instead of the door she turned to the bench against the wall where Father Piers and James were sitting. 'Will Johanna be buried tomorrow?' she asked.

Piers seemed to remember himself and relaxed his forehead. 'Johanna? Yes, God willing and the English permitting, we shall honour her tomorrow,' he said. Pressing palms to knees he rose, wincing as he straightened. 'I grow older by leaps and bounds of late. May your husband's soul rest in peace, Dame Maggie. I grieve for you in your sorrow.' He blessed her.

Bowing her head, Margaret crossed herself. 'I shall attend Johanna's funeral Mass.'

'I do not think that wise,' James said gently.

Hearing the affection and concern in his voice, Celia considered the possibility that he truly loved her mistress. She wondered how that might colour his judgment – and Margaret's, for that matter, for to be loved by a man must surely be as heady as brandywine.

'Are you worried about Peter Fitzsimon?' Margaret asked, still speaking in a voice so devoid of emotion that Celia thought she might be feeling faint.

She was about to coax her mistress into departing when she remembered who Peter Fitzsimon was. 'What does Dame Ada's son have to do with all this?'

'He was my captor,' said James.

Celia glanced at Father Piers. He, too, was listening with growing concern.

'He is also the captain who had me identify Johanna,' said Margaret.

'He cannot be.' Celia realised her words came out like a whine. She realised that all had grown quiet and all three were staring at her. 'Forgive me.'

'Tell me about Peter Fitzsimon,' James said. 'Tell me where you've seen him, what you've observed about him.'

Knowing that this would dispel any lingering calm, Celia hesitated, but of course she must share with them all that had occurred. She gathered her thoughts and related her encounters with the man as completely as possible.

James's expression was grave as he thanked her.

'I pray that Roger is safely buried in Cambuskenneth by now,' Margaret said with a catch in her voice.

Father Piers said nothing.

'We should go home, Mistress,' said Celia. 'Can someone escort us?' she asked the priest.

He nodded. 'Come. We will fetch my clerk.'

James reached out to Margaret, but she did not go to him.

'Sleep if you can,' she said.

In a few strides he reached Margaret and embraced her. 'I am sorrier than I can say that I involved you in this. I failed you, I failed my king.'

Celia averted her eyes, but she couldn't help but hear his words.

'It has been my choice, and I have no regrets. You have not failed your king. We shall find a way to disappoint Peter Fitzsimon.'

'Have you already forgotten what I told you? Stay hidden. It's too dangerous.'

Father Piers stepped back into the chapel. 'Are you coming?'

'Yes,' said Margaret. 'Do not worry about me.' She moved away from James. 'Come, Celia.'

Celia was startled by James's shattered expression. She almost wished her mistress were in love with him.

A soft rain fell outside their bower, lulling Ada and Simon to sleep for a while after their lovemaking. When Ada woke, Simon was no longer beside her and had apparently taken the lamp away with him. The twilight in the chamber felt ominous and disorienting, for Ada could not tell whether it was evening or morning. Lying quietly, she heard Simon's voice outside the door, and another voice that she guessed to be Peter's. That did nothing to calm her. As she sat up her pounding head informed her that it was evening, for she'd not yet slept off the wine.

Knowing from experience that a mouthful of wine would ease the headache, Ada wrapped a blanket round her and searched for the flask of wine they'd brought with them. Simon had moved it to another table and taken one of the mazers, but there was enough wine left in the flask for her purpose. She'd drunk little wine and almost no ale since the English had taken Perth, finding the lengths one needed to go to for such luxuries too much bother. Relative abstinence meant the wine affected her more quickly, and she should have known better than to drink so much this evening. She knew why she had – the murder of the soldier's mistress, James's capture and the uncertainty about how much Simon and Peter knew of her activities as well as Maggie's had frightened her; but dulling her fear with drink was irresponsible in the circumstances.

She dressed, braiding and winding her hair about her head as best she could with her shaking hands and in the half light that provided only a ghostly shade in the silvered glass. The voices rose and fell, and now she detected more then two; perhaps she should not join Simon. He seemed determined not to introduce her to others at the castle, which she imagined meant he was unsure how they would react to his dallying with a Scotswoman.

But it grew darker by the moment and she felt as if she would suffocate in the room despite the small window. The scent of their lovemaking sickened her now. It was unfortunate that she'd awakened and found herself alone, for without the need to play-act for Simon she had too much time to judge herself for playing the whore. There was no longer any love between them; their mating was lust, nothing else. *God forgive me.* Yet she could not stop now without risking everything.

It had grown quiet in the next room. Ada put her ear to the flimsy door in case it masked sound more than she imagined, but all was quiet. Just as she began to move away, she caught the sound of footsteps. Pressing back to the door she recognised the sound of someone pacing in a rhythm that echoed the rain, and she knew it to be Simon. She'd forgotten how he fell into a rhythm with the sounds around him. She'd often teased him about it.

She was relieved to have some activity to dispel her self-loathing. Easing open the door, she watched him for a moment. He held his hands behind his back and thrust forward his pudgy middle as if proud of it, which might be true if he enjoyed playing the wise older man to the soldiers. The light was behind him so she could not make out his expression, but by the downward angle of his head she doubted he was smiling.

Taking a deep breath, she stepped through the door and called softly to him.

'How kind of you to let me sleep, my dear Simon.'

He started, and then averted his face for a few breaths as if framing the expression and words to use with her. He then came forward with an odd smile. 'Are you rested?' It was an uncharacteristic response, which did not bode well.

'In truth I have a headache. Too much wine. I am old enough to know better.'

'A little more will mend that,' he said.

'I'd as lief go home to rest, Simon. I'm sorry if I'm disappointing you, but I would be so grateful if you fetched a servant to escort me.'

'Not yet, Ada,' he said with nary a scrap of sympathy in either his tone or expression. Taking her firmly by the arm he led her to the table, assisted her in taking a seat, and then busied himself lighting more lamps until the room was quite cheerful.

Ada's heart was racing. His mood was all wrong.

At last Simon sat down across from her and poured wine for both of them, handing her a mazer with a smile that looked false to her. 'I have good news, Ada. There may be no battle for the Forth Bridge.'

Using both hands, Ada had taken a sip of the wine. She took time to set the mazer down before replying. 'But that *is* good news, Simon.' She used her smooth, calmly happy voice. 'Have Wallace and Murray retreated?'

He grunted. 'I should not trust it if they did. No, we are at last dealing with those who might be considered to have a right to their interest in this matter – James Stewart and Earl Malcolm of Lennox. They have asked Surrey to give them some time to bring Wallace and Murray round to peace.'

'And he has agreed?'

'Of course. Robert Bruce was defeated but a few weeks past, his daughter demanded as hostage – they do not wish to risk so much. He says it was clear to him that Stewart and Lennox are now determined to rid the country of the rebels, which might require them to take arms against their own countrymen.' Simon sat back in his chair. 'So much the better for us, eh? Now aren't you glad you stayed to hear this?'

The wine had soured in Ada's throat and her stomach burned. Such a promising beginning, now to be aborted. Her countrymen did not know how to unite against their common foe – their pride tripped them every time they began to succeed.

'Ada?' Simon had leaned forward to look into her eyes. 'What is this frown on your face? You are not disappointed?'

She was frightened that she'd forgotten herself and allowed her feelings to show at the worst possible time. 'I am worried, that is all. So much depends on their ability to unite my countrymen in peace.'

'It is only now that you begin to worry?'

'Peace seemed impossible before. What you've told me gives me hope.' She shook her head, feeling the wine, the fear, the lovemaking pulling her down into such a weariness she could not clearly form her explanation. 'I am so tired, Simon. I would leave now, if it please you.'

'It doesn't please me, Ada. I have more to tell you.'

His tone chilled her with the sudden memory of when she'd encountered this mood in him before – when he presented to her the evidence he'd gathered about her and Godric. He'd played with her that night, given her just enough information to make her fearful, then changed the subject, letting her stew in the juices of her fear, and then returned with more information, attacking and falling back until she'd shouted for him to tell her all, unable to bear the tension, needing to know the worst of it.

'We spoke of the Comyn earlier, Peter's escaped quarry,' Simon began. 'He was betrayed by a Welsh archer, a cunning archer, it turns out. I'm uncertain whether to reward him or kill him when he's completed his mission. Traitors don't make trustworthy allies.'

'Simon, why are you telling me this?' She was nauseated by the wine and his mention of James – still assuming that it was he.

'On orders from his English commander the Welshman pretended to escape from the spital on Soutra Hill, taking a route that sickened him, and then headed for Perth to beg admission to the army of William Wallace – from James Comyn of Edinburgh, who was known by his commanders to be in Perth, near one of Wallace's camps. Are you following me, my love?'

Holy Mary, Mother of God, pray for this sinner, Ada prayed silently. It *was* James. And now they'd connected him to Perth, and of course Maggie – this must be the Welshman who had brought her news of Andrew.

'Ada?'

Simon's eyes taunted her and in that moment she knew that he now understood her treachery; she hated him as she'd done on that other night long ago. Hated and feared him. She knew that in this he would not be ruled by his heart – if he had one. She realised now how like his father Peter was.

'The archer was sick yet managed to journey from Soutra to Perth?' she asked in what she hoped was a steady, slightly bored tone.

'You *have* been listening,' Simon said. 'Yes. He managed to make the journey in good time, which is perhaps what made the Comyn wary of his sincerity, for Peter says the Welshman – David, by name – talks too much. A smart man, this James Comyn, for David had of course been advised of a safe route and had a mount for some of the time while his fever weakened him. The Comyn found a woman to nurse him in a small house quite isolated. More a prison than a house.'

'How did his escape bring on a fever?'

When Simon described the man's escape route, Ada made quite a fuss, hoping to annoy him enough that he would end the discussion for the night. But she was disappointed.

'You grow tiresome, Ada.'

Simon was studying her closely. With all the lamps lit she could find no shadow and felt frighteningly vulnerable.

'Do you know James Comyn of Edinburgh, lately in Perth?'

'The Comyns are a large family, Simon. It's likely I've met him on some occasion. I doubt that I can be of help to you, but what does he look like?' She forced herself to breathe quietly, not gulp air.

Simon shrugged. 'I've no idea – haven't seen him yet as he's in sanctuary.'

'Of course. I *am* very tired, Simon.'

'There seem to be many spies in Stirling at the moment – I should not be surprised, but I thought we'd secured it better than this. We've even found a dead one in the kirk yard.' He sighed as if impatient. 'We've allowed his friends to take him away to bury him. Comyn's friends, actually, which is odd for the man was known to be working for Robert Bruce. Isn't that odd, Ada?'

God grant him peace, Ada silently prayed. 'The families are not on friendly terms, it is true.' Robert Bruce's man, James taking an interest in his burial – she prayed it was not Roger Sinclair. She must get to Maggie.

Simon suddenly pushed back his chair and rose. 'You'll stay here tonight.'

'But Simon, your men . . .'

He stood behind her and rested a hand on her shoulder. 'I don't care if they see you leaving my lodging.' He reached beneath her veil with the other hand and pulled her hair loose. 'It might be the last night we have together.'

She rose and found herself wrapped in his arms, pinned to him so tightly it was difficult to breathe. It was not inconceivable that he might kill her; she had loved his dangerous nature and she did not think he'd mellowed with age. But the thought of dying at his hands infuriated her and she pushed against him with all her strength.

He released her with a laugh. 'Forgive me, my delicate Ada.'

'Why might it be our last night together, Simon? Have you found someone who pleases you more? A younger woman, perhaps?'

'Would you still care? I am glad.' He held out his hand to her. 'But no, you have my heart while I am here in Stirling. But should peace be declared I'll no longer have cause to be here in the north and I'd not hesitate to depart. I weary of the company of soldiers.'

Had she still loved him his indifference would have broken her heart; now it just frightened her. 'Do you weary of our son?'

'I despair of his manners. He needs a wife, a woman who will teach him the gentle arts. What think you of a Comyn or a Bruce if we make peace with these people? He *is* half Scot.'

Ada wanted to scream at the suddenly inane conversation. 'It is late, Simon. Let's to bed.'

For Celia it seemed like old times, her mistress crying herself to sleep over Roger Sinclair. Only now there was no longer any hope of reconciliation.

She'd asked Margaret how they might get word to Dame Katherine.

'We must deliver this terrible news ourselves, Celia, when the fighting is over. If the fighting is ever over. We will reach her somehow. I cannot let her hear it from a stranger.'

It comforted Celia to think of such a journey. 'Would you leave me with her?'

Margaret had not replied at once. 'It will be your choice.'

That had given Celia something to ponder.

After a frighteningly brutal lovemaking Ada lay awake, aching and fearing what Simon would do with her and Maggie now that he held her in such low regard. How far they had come. She wondered whether it would have been different had they been wed. But of course, she would yet live in England and be respected as the mother of his legitimate children. Peter would look forward to being a wealthy landowner, perhaps a knight.

As she began to drowse she imagined Simon ordering Johanna's lover to murder her in such a way that no one would guess a soldier had done it. And then what? Had Simon had the lover executed?

She wondered what method of murder Simon would choose for her – strangling, poisoning, beating to make it look as if someone was murdering the English soldiers' whores, a knife to the heart and neck to mimic Gordon Cowie's murder. She was oddly calm as she considered the various methods, and then fell to wondering who might have murdered Gordon.

Once among his fellow commanders Sir Francis seemed to forget about Andrew and Matthew. They were left to their own devices and wandered a bit away from their company without causing any stir. Andrew kept his direction towards the river. The pows, this marshy land cut through with many rivers and burns on the south bank of the Forth, was not easily navigated. Andrew had reluctantly hunted here with Abbot Adam on occasion, a preferred companion because of his experience with water meadows along the Tay. Matthew, too, had walked this area. They moved cautiously but steadily northeast, in the general direction of Cambuskenneth Abbey, which was on the far bank of the Forth. When at last Andrew paused, Matthew pointed to an empty area in the shelter of a rocky outcrop and suggested he lay out their plaids there. Andrew absentmindedly agreed.

He was thinking about summer in his childhood, how he'd learned to swim in the Tay so that he could assist with small repairs on the outer hulls of his father's ships. It was an uncommon skill and the mates had found him useful. He'd enjoyed listening to their tales of far-off places.

'Can you swim?' he asked Matthew, almost hoping he could not, for Andrew had just made a pact with himself that if his servant could swim he'd take it as a sign that God approved of his plan.

'What?' said Matthew. 'Swim? Were we going to need to swim out that drain at the spital?'

'I don't believe so,' said Andrew. But it might have been necessary, and he'd never thought to ask Matthew then. 'Can you?'

'Why?' When Andrew didn't answer, Matthew said, 'I can. I suppose I still can.'

God willed it, then. Andrew moved close to where the young

man was working on a small fire. 'Would you rather stay here or try to swim across the Forth to Cambuskenneth Abbey?'

Matthew paused, but didn't raise his head. 'Escape?'

'At night. You would be risking your life.'

'Where you go, I go, Father.'

'You might be safer here.'

Matthew shook his head, still not looking up. The fire liquefied the shadows so that the young man's flesh looked by turns haggard and mysterious. Andrew had one qualm – Matthew was clean, pleasant-looking, young, which appealed to some of the soldiers. The lad might feel he had no choice but to follow Andrew. He owed it to Matthew to give him a true choice.

'Perhaps I'm being a fool. The abbey might be full of English soldiers by now, and here we are safe. In truth, it isn't fair to leave the soldiers without a confessor.'

'They would think nothing of leaving you behind to die if they might save themselves, Father. You ken that as well as I do. We owe them nothing.'

He spoke with more passion than Andrew had ever witnessed in him. Looking round he saw that they were as yet isolated from the others, too far from the nearest campfires to be noticed once theirs died down later on.

'Keep the fire small and let it die out,' he whispered.

Matthew nodded.

Late in the evening, as Andrew prayed by the dying fire, he glimpsed two of Sir Francis's men at the nearest campfire and tried to withdraw completely from the light without so much movement that he'd attract their attention. But it was too late, one of the men at the fire gestured in their direction, and the searchers approached.

'Damn,' Andrew muttered. 'Matthew, pretend to be asleep.'

Matthew snored softly.

'Who goes there?' Andrew demanded in a hushed tone, as if not wishing to wake Matthew.

'Father Andrew, forgive me for waking you.'

One of the men stepped into the meagre light and Andrew recognised him as Will, an unexpectedly pious man considering his large repertoire of profane expressions in French and English. He was one of the felons in the company.

'I was not asleep, Will. Did you want me to hear your confessions?'

He now recognised Will's companion, a scrappy young man, Pete, who was missing an ear and a finger though he swore he'd never committed a crime.

'Bless you, Father,' said Will. 'I feared you'd been relieved of your duty to such as us, gone to the knights and such. They're sinners, too, some worse than me, but I'm the one who will be dangled first as bait, eh? And Pete, here.'

Sir Francis did plan to place the felons in the most vulnerable positions. Andrew wondered whether he had already announced his plan or whether Will was prescient. Perhaps it did not take much intelligence to guess that would be a commander's strategy.

'I'll move away so I can't hear,' said Pete, dipping into the shadows.

Andrew made the sign of the cross over Will and bowed his head to listen. As the man laid bare his soul, Andrew could not help thinking of the others in the company who might be comforted by his presence. He was forgetting his vows. He must minister to them, safeguard their souls. If the day was won and the company safe, God would surely allow Andrew another chance to escape. He pronounced Will's penance and called softly to Pete.

When he had given Pete his penance, Andrew asked the two if they would escort him and Matthew back to the camp. 'I sought some peace in which to think. But I see now I was selfish.'

The men glanced at one another questioningly, and Andrew realised they'd meant to desert. He waited, wondering what they would do.

'Aye, we owe it to you to see you back safely,' said Pete with forced cheer.

Andrew gently shook Matthew awake – it seemed he had actually fallen asleep – and explained his change in plan. Without a word the young man rose and draped his plaid round him. Andrew did likewise. They collected their small hoard of food and their lantern and followed Pete and Will into the darkness, heading away from the river.

'Forgive me, Matthew, but I could not desert them.'

'There is nothing to forgive, Father.'

'We will escape when the time is right.'

'I am bound to you, Father. It does not matter where we go.'

Never before had Andrew felt so keenly what a burden he had accepted in taking his vows. Escape had been within his reach. And now he carried the added burden of Matthew's devotion. He prayed for the strength to live up to all that was expected of him.

Towards dawn Margaret fell into a light sleep, but wakened at the first birdsong and knew her rest was over for the night. She lay there trying to be quiet so that Celia would not hear her through the flimsy divider and come to fuss over her. She found her thoughts turning to Gordon Cowie's murder. She was grateful for the preoccupation for it was better than dwelling on Roger's suffering or her own danger, but she also found it frustrating, as if she had some knowledge that might reveal the murderer but could not recall it. She had seen the goldsmith in the castle yard, but she had seen other townsfolk as well. Evota and her family apparently frequented the castle precinct, and she'd heard of no organised resistance to the soldiers in the town, though there had been the poisoning. Celia had reported a rumour that Isabel had murdered her husband, but it did not seem founded on any evidence, merely the fact that Isabel was well-liked and her late husband had been generally resented for his fustian speech and superior manner.

Stabbed in the heart and the neck meant to Margaret that the murderer wanted to ensure the man died, and quickly. She wondered whether a pair of murderers were responsible, each wanting to strike the death blow. Might it be possible that both Johanna and Gordon had been murdered by the same person, or persons, or at the bidding of the same person or group, the purpose being to punish those who seemed too friendly with the occupiers? She had a feeling there was a connection between Gordon's murder and Huchon Allan's execution. Perhaps Huchon's fellows believed Gordon had betrayed his neighbour. She remembered the suffering in his parents' voices in the night.

Slowly she turned onto her left side to quiet a throbbing behind one of her shoulder blades. Once settled again she put her mind to alternative motives. Johanna might simply have been silenced by the English. Gordon might have cheated someone – his death need not necessarily be related to the occupation. But Johanna's brutal beating – what motivation could there be that had nothing to do with the struggle against Longshanks? She was a beautiful woman and promiscuous. No doubt she'd broken a few hearts. Margaret considered the possibility that a jealous former lover had waited until her English protector was away and then avenged his pride. A man's pride was so different from a woman's. Only recently had she begun to understand Roger's anger about her behaviour, how he'd felt it reflected on him because he considered her his property, his responsibility. If his wife misbehaved, he was at fault. Just as God banished Adam as well as Eve when she managed to tempt Adam with the forbidden fruit. She had certainly heard of men beating their wives for less than she had done. Thinking it through, she could believe that one of Johanna's former lovers had murdered her.

Lovers – she'd never made love with anyone but Roger. Often of late she'd wondered about James, what he would be like. She sensed there was some part of him that he shared with no one, or at least not her.

A sound down below startled her for it came from the street side rather than the rear of the house where the servants slept. She recognised the creak of the street door, its muffled groan as it swung back into its jamb, and then the thud of the bolt in its socket. Light footsteps crossed to the steps leading up to the solar, and now the steps creaked. She prayed it was Ada returned at last, but in case it was not she drew out the knife she kept beneath her pillow and sat up, ready to defend herself.

'Sweet Jesus,' she breathed as Ada's head appeared.

Ada started when she grew aware of Margaret sitting up.

'Oh, Maggie, it has been a most horrible night,' she said as she sank down on to the bed.

'For all of us, Ada,' Margaret said.

As Ada unfastened her shoes, Margaret lit a cruisie from the embers of the small brazier in the room.

'So you know about James and Johanna,' Margaret said.

The light did not compliment Ada. For once she looked her age, haggard and puffy-eyed.

'You are in danger, my friend,' Ada said.

'I know.'

'I feel unclean,' Ada said, her voice trembling. She tugged at her veil and wimple with such impatience that she tore the silk. 'Damned silk.' Leaning over to toss the head dress on a chest, she suddenly slumped, and face in hands began to weep.

Margaret knelt to her and drew her head to her shoulder, smoothing out Ada's long white hair. Her own heart was pounding, wondering whether Ada knew of an immediate danger and what her friend had suffered.

After she had been quiet for a while, Ada raised her head 'It is all my fault. I should not have insisted you play my niece, for it has brought you to his attention. He would not have given you a second thought otherwise.'

Margaret sat back on her heels. 'Do you mean Peter?'

'Peter?' Ada shivered and held out her hands to the warm brazier. 'No, Simon. But I forgot – you met Peter tonight.'

'He told you?'

Ada seemed to take on the weight of the world in her nod. 'He said he asked you to look at the murdered woman and tell him if it was Johanna. Was he unkind?'

'It was not a gentle moment, though he played the role of a considerate man.'

'I can imagine,' Ada said in a bitter tone.

'He is a busy man, your son Peter. He has spent much time at Evota's house, he seized James, he showed up at Johanna's soon after she was found murdered; why, Celia says he was here in the hall the day we arrived. Wherever we turn, Peter Fitzsimon is there. I am almost certain that it was he who silenced Archie.' *And perhaps Johanna*, Margaret thought, but did not say it.

Ada crossed herself. 'He and Simon are so much alike. I had not seen it until tonight.' She rose and began to fuss with her sleeves.

While Margaret untied them for her, Ada said, 'So you have solved your mystery.'

How pointless it seemed to Margaret now. 'With James in Holy Rude, Archie's situation is no longer of any consequence to me – unless it was he who murdered Johanna.'

Ada shrugged. 'At least James is safe for now.'

'Are you so certain the English will honour the sanctuary?'

'I often wonder at the niceties of war,' Ada said. 'But in this case yes, they have no cause to risk excommunication because Simon is satisfied that James can do no harm while hiding in the kirk. I should think that the keeper of the castle feels the same.'

'I am glad of it,' said Margaret, though she felt little relief. 'Ada, before we talk of anything else you must know – Roger is dead.'

Ada caught her breath and bowed her head for a moment, then met Margaret's eyes. 'How do you know this?' she asked, but she was not surprised.

'You already knew.'

'I guessed. Simon spoke of a dead spy in the kirk yard. He knows that James's men took him away for burial, which he thought strange since the dead man was believed to be a spy for Robert Bruce. A Comyn caring for a Bruce's soul is unexpected. It's plain to me that they had left him there as bait.'

Margaret could not speak for her anger.

Ada let her be for a while, then said, 'Would you tell me about it, Maggie?'

Margaret swallowed bile and nodded, though she waited a while before trying her voice. 'James's men found Roger in the backlands of the kirk. He'd fallen from a height and broken his neck. He'd been dead for several days when they found him hidden in the underbrush.' She'd begun to shake and hugged herself tightly. 'I hate the thought of him lying there, exposed – How could the English be so unchristian as to leave him there unburied?'

'As in Berwick,' Ada whispered.

Margaret moved closer to the brazier, hoping the heat would dispel the trembling. 'I am a widow before I ever felt truly a wife.'

'Maggie, oh my dear child, I am so sorry. Here I sat weeping like a baby in a fit and you had such a heavy heart.'

'I'd already spent my tears.'

Ada reached for one of Margaret's hands and held it, palm up, tracing the lines. 'There are some who believe our lives are written in these lines. I've never wanted to hear what they would say about mine. But how could anyone have guessed what has happened? If they had, we would have fled. Our country would be empty.'

Ada had never sounded so despondent.

'What will happen to us?' Margaret asked, expecting no reply.

Ada shook her head. 'There is more you must know. David, the Welshman who came to you with news of Andrew, is here in Stirling. If he sees you and tells Simon who you are there will no longer be any doubt. I don't know what Simon will do.'

'We are found out, and all we can hope is that the battle comes soon.'

Ada lay back on the bed. Margaret lay down beside her.

'I hate him now,' said Ada.

She did not need to explain whom she meant.

'I just pray you have a chance to marry again and have children,' said Ada. 'The child Christiana saw in your arms.'

'Do you still believe her vision will come to pass?'

'I cling to it for hope, Maggie. Don't you?'

'But who is the husband? Not Roger – it's too late for that.'

'I wonder whether Christiana knew it was not Roger and spared you the knowledge of his death.'

Margaret considered the possibility, fighting a sudden drowsiness. 'I doubt it.' The Sight was deceptive, cunning in its opacity. She could believe that her mother truly had no idea who the man was. 'I intend to find out who murdered Johanna,' she said, preferring to think of a practical matter. 'And Gordon Cowie. He has been on my mind, too. Perhaps I am tricking myself into believing there is a future, that I have time to accomplish something, to solve a murder. He was Huchon Allan's neighbour. Might their deaths be connected?'

Ada made worried sounds. 'You must not leave the house for a day or two, Maggie. I beg you.'

'James gave me the same advice. Will you go to Johanna's funeral?'

'I will. For you. And for myself.'

Margaret wondered at Ada's last words, but she was too close to sleep to make the effort to speak.

⤐§ 10 ₰⤏

A Funeral and a Ring

Will and Pete, true to their words, escorted Father Andrew and Matthew back among the small camps, but their progress was slowed by penitents begging for confession. At first Andrew thought that word of the possible truce had not spread through the ranks, but it became clear that few believed peace would come without a battle, and the lower the rank the greater they believed their risk of death. It saddened him to witness the fear and resignation of these men, and he could not refuse them absolution despite being sleep-deprived and very hungry.

By the time the four entered their own camp the air was heavy with early morning dew and a light rain that beaded in Andrew's curly hair and then coursed down his face in rivulets. He had not slept, but his belly was empty and his mind too full, so he went straight to the cook fire. After oatcakes and a mongrel potage that tasted like heavenly manna as it warmed his empty, anxious stomach, he moved away from the bustle and bowed to his prayers while Matthew dozed beside him. Andrew wondered whether Pete and Will, who had left them at the cook fire, would now disappear.

Ada had Sandy the groom accompany her and Celia to Johanna's service. She thought she would feel better with a muscular young man along to protect them, though she wondered whether he would feel any obligation to defend a woman for whom he had worked so briefly. She admitted to herself that he was essentially a charm against attack.

A fine rain had arrived with the dawn, and though now it was but a drizzle it had refreshed the air and brought out the scents of earth and stone, which reminded Ada that life went on, nature taking no notice of the affairs of men. She wondered how her garden in Perth fared; the plums and apples had been close to ripening when she'd departed. She hoped the couple she'd left in charge would not let the rats have too much of the fruit.

Few parishioners attended the service – none of Ada's neighbours. She noticed a young man sitting in the shadow of a pillar as if trying to hide the intensity of his grief and wondered whether he'd been one of Johanna's lovers.

Once out in the kirk yard Ada felt she'd done her duty and was about to suggest to Celia that they should depart. But she noticed that the bereft young man shifted his gaze to someone behind her and his bearing shifted as if he were trying to make himself so small as to be invisible, letting his shoulders sag and curl inward, his head droop. The hackles rose on Ada's neck at the sound of her son's voice.

'I had expected to see your niece Maggie here, Ma,' Peter said. 'She claimed to be the woman's friend. I should have thought she would attend her burial. Was she too upset after her ordeal last night?'

'Seeing her friend's body so violated? You ken full well she was.'

'Were you also a friend to the woman?'

'She had a name, Peter. Johanna.' Ada wondered whether he had always been so irritating. 'And no, I did not know Johanna; I am here in Maggie's stead. But I also felt a kinship to her, and I want her murderer found and punished.'

'A kinship. I see.' He did not try to mask his amusement.

At the opposite side of the grave the young man had now withdrawn behind some of the mourners yet he kept shifting so that he might keep his eyes on Peter, as if reassuring himself that he was keeping his distance. His damp hair was wavy and long, greasy where it fell over his eyes; he repeatedly pushed it aside. He had dark, heavy-lidded eyes and the cheekbones and chin of a handsome man. Though small he was well-formed. He was not in livery, so she doubted he was a soldier. Yet he knew Peter.

'Who is that young man across the way?' she asked Peter.

'The pretty lad, you mean?'

Ada nodded.

'Archie, the son of Evota the alewife. Are you in the market for younger flesh?'

Ada jabbed her elbow backwards into her son's taut gut and found satisfaction in his gasp. 'Respect your mother, dear,' she hissed. The mild humour was for her benefit, not his. It was a base sin to hate one's own child. She prayed God to show her some better part of him, something more than Simon's feeble explanation that he had perfected his fighting skills because of his innate fear, a product of his parentage. But God had so far left her ignorant of her son's virtues.

Celia could not help but eavesdrop on mother and son, and was glad she had, for now she knew for certain that the man across the way was Archie. She'd been moved by his expression of abject sorrow in the kirk, breaking down into softly audible sobs as Johanna's shroud-wrapped body was carried past. Now he was quiet, and definitely distracted by Peter Fitzsimon's presence, but the depth of his mourning had been unmistakable.

Sandy's warning came to mind. Archie had a way with women, had *his* way with women. If he'd been Johanna's lover, and loved her deeply, Celia imagined that her taking an English soldier for a lover would have deeply wounded Archie, perhaps enough to beat her to death, and now he could not bear the guilt. But she could equally well imagine that he was not guilty, but missed Johanna, knowing that there was now no possibility of ever winning her back.

His reaction to Peter Fitzsimon was not surprising, for the man had certainly been watching Evota's house. But when Archie had caught sight of him his expression had subtly changed, and she'd read a flash of anger – not merely resentment – before he'd drawn himself in with fear. Perhaps Peter had murdered Johanna, or at least Archie believed he had.

Celia's observations intrigued Margaret, who'd spent the morning sitting in the solar with some spinning while she tortured herself with a review of her sad marriage, wondering whether she was in some way responsible for Roger's death.

Earlier she'd sat beneath the eaves of the house facing the backlands watching the light rain, letting the cool air refresh her. But the Allans had begun quarrelling loudly again.

'The ring had been in your family for generations,' Lilias cried.

'You'll not be alone, wife, I assure you. We'll both suffer the torments of hell, and the soldier will most likely be there with us. I pray you are satisfied.'

'We are talking of our son!' she screeched.

Margaret had withdrawn, not wanting to witness their private agony.

'Ada has wondered about Archie and Johanna,' she told Celia. 'But he needn't have attended the funeral – why would he if he is guilty?'

Celia sighed as she settled beside Margaret. 'I wish we'd never come here.' Her delicate features framed by the dark brows were pinched with worry.

Margaret thought Celia might more honestly extend that wish to never having left the home of Dame Katherine Sinclair.

'I confess I wonder what good we've done here,' Margaret said.

'We still don't know why Archie stopped delivering the messages to James's men. I failed to prevent either Roger's or Johanna's deaths. Simon Montagu knows who I am, knows what Roger was about, knows of my connection to James–' She caught her breath and could not face Celia's frightened expression. Bowing her head, Margaret fussed with the spindle and wool though her hands were trembling so much she was creating a tangle.

'God help us,' Celia said. 'What do you think Sir Simon will do?'

Margaret did not want to think about that. 'I pray the battle begins soon or a truce is struck so that he has more important things to think about.'

'We are harmless with Master Comyn in the kirk,' Celia said.

Margaret raised her head. 'Sir Simon doesn't know that, does he?' She tugged at the wool. 'I would that I could sneak James away.'

Ada knocked on the wall, announcing her presence. 'May I join you?'

Margaret welcomed her.

Ada waved to someone behind her, and Maus appeared carrying a tray of cups and a wine flagon.

'I hoard brandywine for days such as this.' Ada took a seat on the bed near where Margaret and Celia perched on the bench. 'Leave us, Maus. We will bore you with our dull conversation.'

The maid set down the tray and departed, looking pleased to be excused from the glum company.

For glum was the only word Margaret could think to describe both her companions, Celia with her pinched expression and Ada looking the part of a mourner even to her exhausted posture.

'Celia has told you about my son's presence in the kirk yard?' Ada asked.

Margaret nodded. 'Why would he attend Johanna's burial?'

'To frighten us,' said Ada. 'I've been thinking that you would be safer in sanctuary with James.'

'I've thought of that,' Margaret admitted, 'but I'd rather find a way to release him. I can't bear just sitting here spinning while my country is being crushed beneath the boots of Longshanks . . .' She shook her head as Ada seemed about to respond. 'I am hardly a threat to Peter while I sit here. Would that I were!'

Celia poured a little brandywine in each cup.

'People are executed for past deeds as well as present threat,' Ada said softly, her expression solemn as she worked the tablets. 'I regret the night I conceived that young man.'

So did Margaret. Ada's words were disturbing, to say the least. 'I wonder about the fate of Johanna's lover,' she said. 'From the way Peter and the other soldier spoke of her that night, as she lay there, I believe they know who he was. She does not seem to have been as careful about her liaisons as she should have been, considering her purpose.'

'Many loved ones will never know the fates of the young men who have come here to fight,' said Ada. 'Someone will be broken-hearted when he doesn't return.'

Celia choked back a sob. Her face was flushed and her eyes red. Margaret reached out to her, but she shook her head. 'Don't mind me. I hadn't thought about all the mothers and wives worrying and praying. And men like your son, Dame Ada, they act like it's a game. As if after death the victims rise again and come back for another round. But they're gone for ever.'

Margaret crossed herself. 'I'm not going to join James in sanctuary. I prefer to remain free to do whatever I might to help our cause.'

'I pray that my other children are more like you, Maggie, and not at all like Peter. It seems a cruel penance to meet one of my children only to be ashamed of him.'

'It is the times,' said Celia.

Ada broke down. 'He is my son, flesh of my flesh, and for that I do love him. God save me. I love him and hate him both.'

Eventually the three bent silently, nervously, to their spinning and tablet weaving.

In the night, Margaret dreamt that an owl-woman sat beside her bed listening attentively to her narration of all that had happened to her since Roger left their home in Perth a year earlier. Now and then the owl-woman would ask Margaret to explain her feelings, or to expand on a detail, and by this method all became clear to both of them. Margaret embraced the downy yet strong woman and understood that she need never fear again. She clearly saw her purpose and her path.

But when Margaret woke at dawn the clarity was gone. Rising, she dressed in a simple gown, picked up her shoes and slipped down to the hall, where she opened the door to the backlands and breathed in the fresh morning air.

An owl-woman. She tried to recall her features but could remember only white and grey feathers, dark eyes, and how she had completely trusted the woman and through her had known her own strength. What was much more vivid in memory was the setting, a lushly green glen studded with mounds and stone circles, seemingly alive with music and old memories. The owl-woman had not controlled it but had instead been an integral part of it, as was Margaret. It was powerfully seductive, even in the morning light. She wished she might return to it and explore not only the place but the change in herself that it engendered.

She laughed at herself when she realised she was yearning for Kilmartin Glen as her mother had described it, a place she'd never seen. This was madness. To pull herself more firmly into the world she inhabited, Margaret began to walk. She wandered towards the house next door, remembering the argument she'd overheard. A ring, damnation. She had heard such suffering in both their voices.

As she crossed the narrow wynd between the two houses something tickled her awareness. She paused, straining her eyes and ears to catch whatever it had been, and then took a few steps down the wynd. On the ground near the street she thought she saw movement, then nothing. She felt as if something or someone were tricking her into coming closer, but tried not to let her imagination get the best of her. It might be nothing more threatening than a rat, a cat chasing a mouse, or a hardy weed catching a draught. Lifting her skirts she moved down the wynd with caution, for the morning sun had not yet dipped between the houses and it was quite dark. As she drew nearer to where she'd thought she'd detected movement a shape resolved, a body stretched on the ground, a child, she thought by the size.

'Have mercy.' The voice was so weak Margaret could just hear it.

Taking no chances, she crouched down more than an arm's length away and asked, 'Are you injured?'

'He beat me and broke my leg.'

Margaret saw that one leg lay at a peculiar angle. She could not make out the lad's features, for his face was covered with blood.

'How long have you lain here?'

'All the night. I pulled myself out of the square.'

'I'll fetch someone to carry you into the house.'

As she turned away, he cried out, 'Don't leave me!' There was terror in his voice. 'I can stand with your help.'

His fear was catching. 'Surely your attacker won't return in the short while I'd be away.'

'I pray you, take my arm and help me rise.'

He did seem small enough for her to support. Margaret moved closer, crouched, and took him by the elbow. He clutched her shoulder with the opposite hand and managed to pull himself upright by sliding along the wall behind him. When he was balanced on his good leg, Margaret realised he was not a lad, but a young man, though of small stature. She guessed who he was.

'Who attacked you, Archie?'

He almost lost his balance, but caught himself. 'How do you know me?'

That he had fallen so near her lodging was unsettling. 'I'll explain once we're within,' she said, wanting to be safely inside as soon as possible.

They both turned at the sound of footsteps coming towards them from the backlands. Margaret frantically considered what to do, whether to cry out or to leave Archie and run for the door. She was about to shout for help when she recognised Sandy the groom.

'Thank God,' she breathed. 'Help me get Archie into the house, Sandy.'

The groom hesitated. 'I thought I heard something in the night. It woke John, too, but we saw nothing and did not wish to go too far–'

'What are you doing here now?' Margaret asked.

'I thought I heard voices again. This time I was right.'

'Help me now,' Margaret said, sharply interrupting him.

With both arms supported, Archie was able to hop the short distance to the street door of Ada's house. Fortunately John was already in the hall and Archie was inside before the small procession caused a stir in the square. Now Margaret could better see the young man's condition. On his forehead was a bleeding gash, the eye beneath it swollen shut, and his nose was a pulpy mess. His clothes were bloody and torn as if he'd been in a brawl.

Once they'd seated him by the fire, she asked, 'Who attacked you?'

'I attacked *him*, the devil. I'm the greatest fool.' He talked with difficulty through swollen lips, but his anger was quite clear.

'Who, Archie?'

He looked away.

'Are you in trouble?'

'Not so long as you tell no one I'm here.'

'Not even your family?'

'Especially not them.'

'I'll clean him up, Dame Maggie,' said Sandy. 'I see to the animals when they're injured.'

She could see by Sandy's humbled manner that he wished to make amends for not venturing far enough to find Archie in the night, and grateful for his offer she thanked him, and then said to Archie, 'We'll talk when Sandy has seen to your injuries.'

'How do you know me?' Archie asked again.

She had no intention of confiding in him in the presence of others. 'Servants talk, and I listen.'

'I don't believe you.'

'I have no cause to lie to you, Archie. I've taken you in, remember?'

Sandy had returned with water and rags. Margaret withdrew to the kitchen, the butler on her heels. John had kept his distance while she was with Archie, but she could see in the way he held himself that he was bursting with questions.

So was she. 'Sandy told me that both you and he heard something in the night. Did you see anything at all?'

John angrily glanced back towards the hall as if resolving to have a word with the groom, then shook his head as he met Margaret's eye. 'No. We hear more of the night out here in the kitchen than you do in the hall. Whatever it was, it woke both of us, and we both looked without. He thought he saw something by the garden shed next to us, but then nothing. Cat after a mouse, rat after some dung, the backlands are not still at night.'

Margaret began to pour herself a mazer of ale, but John jumped to serve her. She was settling down near the fire when Celia entered the kitchen.

'I saw the injured man in the hall. That is Archie, Mistress,' Celia said. 'What has happened?'

John moved closer, and Margaret explained to both of them how she'd found Archie in the wynd. At her request John then related how he and Sandy woke to a sound – John thought it a cry, Sandy a moan – but had seen nothing unusual astir.

'I don't yet know who beat him,' Margaret said. 'He needed tending before I questioned him. It was plain to me that he was frightened to be left alone again.'

'May God watch over this household,' said John as he crossed himself. 'His clothes are old and filthy. He is no stranger to trouble.'

'Perhaps not,' said Margaret, 'but he had been brawling. I've no doubt those clothes looked better yesterday.'

In a little while Sandy entered the kitchen with a bowl of bloody rags.

'Are his injuries serious?' Margaret asked.

'We need Dame Bridget, the midwife,' said Sandy. 'His leg is swollen and hot and I'm afraid to set the bones – I've done only a dog and a goat. Do you want me to fetch her?'

Margaret nodded. 'Yes, fetch her. What about his head wound?'

'It bled a lot but he's not confused. If you want to talk to him, you might do so – he'll sleep soon, now that he's warm and safe.'

Archie lay on one of the servants' pallet beds near the hall fire, staring at the ceiling. As Margaret brought a stool near she saw that his eyes were filled with tears.

'Are you in much pain?' she asked, thinking about giving him some of Ada's brandywine. They had not finished it.

'No,' he said, brusquely wiping his eyes on one of his sleeves. 'The fire is smoking.'

It wasn't, but Margaret let him have his pride. 'You say you picked the fight?'

'I did.' He glanced at her, then quickly away. 'With Captain Fitzsimon, the bastard who wouldn't let me see her that night. He shouldn't have come to her funeral, the bastard. Murderer.'

Dear God, the small young man before her had picked a fight with Ada's well-trained son. It was a wonder Archie was alive. 'You call him a murderer. Do you know that he is?'

'Ask the soldiers – they'll tell you.'

'But do you know of any murder he's committed in Stirling?'

Archie looked away. 'Maybe.'

'Johanna?' Margaret asked.

'Who else would have done it, eh? For weeks he watched me and watched me but when it came to–' Archie's voice broke. 'Why her?' he moaned through the lump in his throat. 'Why not me, damn him? Damn him to hell.' He turned away to hide his emotion.

Margaret sat back and gave him time to compose himself as his words sank in. He'd loved Johanna, and believed that Peter had murdered her. It was quite plausible that Peter had if he'd discovered Johanna spying.

'Do you have any proof of this, Archie?'

'Just my gut when he's near. I followed him from the kirk,' Archie said through clenched teeth, 'but he went straight to the castle, so I had to wait until he came back out into the town, alone, away from his friends. Then I stepped out and challenged him. Like David taking on Goliath.' He groaned.

'What did you mean he wouldn't let you see her that night? Were you speaking of the night of her death?'

Archie let out a long, sob-like sigh. 'I went to her house, but he'd blocked the door and wouldn't let me past. I just wanted to see her. Say goodbye. What right had he?' He was clenching his fists and his colour was high.

Margaret regretted having started the conversation for his ordeal had weakened him, and yet she needed to know what he knew. 'This was while she was alive?'

'After. Fitzsimon is everywhere. I can't breathe – he's taking up all the air in the town. He's no mortal. He's the devil.'

Archie's words echoed between them while Margaret collected her thoughts. She knew she could not count on his talking for long. 'Were you and Johanna lovers?'

He flinched and dropped his gaze. 'She could have anyone at the castle. Why would she take me?'

He's no boy, Johanna had said. 'You loved her, didn't you?' Margaret asked, though she was quite sure she already knew the answer.

'I told you I'm the greatest fool.'

'Is that why you stopped going to her for the messages?'

'He was always there, Rob, her English lover.'

'Did you tell her how you felt?'

He shrugged.

'Was Peter Fitzsimon also her lover?'

Archie turned away from Margaret. 'I don't know.' He looked so small lying there on the pallet, so young and heartbroken.

'She wouldn't have you?'

He caught his breath. 'She laughed.'

'So it wasn't that Peter Fitzsimon's interest frightened you from helping James Comyn any more, it was your love for Johanna.'

'Fitzsimon couldn't catch me at spying. He worried Ma, but I told her I was too good to be caught by an Englishman.'

'Why did you challenge him last night?'

'God knows. I wanted to kill someone. He was the best I could do.'

Margaret didn't think it would serve much purpose to ask why he wanted to kill someone. She already believed that he hadn't killed Johanna.

'Was Peter injured last night?'

'I doubt it.' He glanced around. 'Where are my things?'

'I'll ask Sandy.'

'He grabbed my knife. Da gave me that knife.'

'We'll find your knife, Archie. Why don't you want your family to know that you're here?'

'It's best that way,' he mumbled, his voice beginning to fade.

She had a look around the hall for his clothes, but did not find them. Before heading for the kitchen she checked on him. His eyes were closed and his mouth had gone slack.

In a short while a strongly built woman of indeterminate age strode into the hall with Sandy. Her gown was a simple russet, but very clean, as was her undyed wimple.

'Dame Maggie, I've brought Dame Bridget to see to Archie's leg,' said Sandy.

'God bless you for coming so quickly,' said Margaret.

The woman nodded as she reached Archie's side and crouched to examine him. 'He's picked on a better fighter than himself this time, I see. I'll attend him, Dame Maggie. He's in good hands. I'm familiar with most of the bones in his young body.'

The midwife made Margaret feel for a moment as if everything would be fine. How reassuring she must be to women in labour.

'I'm glad to see his eyelids fluttering,' said Bridget. 'He should be propped up more – we don't want the blood pooling in his brain.' She gently ran a hand down his leg, her fingers seeming to float, pausing here and there. Sitting back on her heels, she glanced up at Margaret. 'I believe it's a simple break.'

'Will you need someone to help you straighten the bone?' Margaret asked.

'Sandy will do. Come on, lad, a good pull and Archie will be walking out of here soon enough.' She shook her head at Archie and glanced back at Margaret. 'Not enough babies since the English marched up the hill. I need the work, and I need some pay.'

'You'll be paid,' said Margaret. 'Sandy, did you find a knife on him?'

Sandy shook his head.

'Who is this?' said Ada as she descended from the solar. Smoothing down her clothes she studied the midwife and patient for a moment. 'I don't recognise the injured lad, but you are young Bridget, Dame Alice's daughter, are you not?'

The midwife's eyes brightened. Hands on hips she wagged her head. '*Dame* Bridget now, but just Bridget to you, my dear friend.'

The women embraced, and Margaret smiled to see the years

fall off Ada as she and the midwife exchanged news for a while. Even the story of Alice's death the previous summer seemed to cheer Ada.

'She pushed away the potion saying she was warm, in no pain, and at peace with the Lord, so it was a good time to die. She closed her eyes, and in a little while stopped breathing. I've never witnessed a happier death,' said Bridget with a wistful expression on her pleasant face. 'I thank God that she died before the English came.'

At last Ada remembered the others in the hall. 'Who is he?' she asked Margaret, nodding towards Archie, who had wakened. When Margaret explained, Ada shook her head in wonder that she'd slept through it. 'And once again Peter is involved.'

'Archie attacked him,' Margaret said. She started as Bridget and Sandy snapped the bone into place. Archie was stoically silent, except for his shallow breathing.

'We aren't needed here,' said Ada.

She passed through the hall to the kitchen with Margaret following, hungry at last. After breaking their fast Ada suggested that they take their spinning and weaving up to the solar.

'And you can tell me all about that little man down below. We seem to have so few peaceful moments like this.'

They settled near the window in Ada's chamber. Margaret with her spinning and Ada a border she was weaving on tablets. After Margaret related the morning's events, they worked for a while in silence, interrupted only by Bridget taking her leave, promising to return the following morning to see how Archie fared the night. Ada's generosity pleased her.

After she departed, Ada sighed. 'I suppose we should be thankful that my son hasn't made a habit of paying me visits here, else I would worry about brawling in my hall. What was he thinking, accepting a challenge from that slip of a man? I should think his honour would prevent him from taking such an unfair advantage.'

'He might have been taken by surprise, Ada. He was attacked, and he defended himself. A small dog can do much damage to one twice his size if he's fierce and quick.'

Ada looked doubtful, but nodded. 'You may be right.'

While she worked it was not Johanna's murder but that of Gordon Cowie over which Margaret kept puzzling. She did not fight this preoccupation for if it was the Sight teasing her she'd not win the fight. Perhaps she was about to put the pieces together. A goldsmith came into contact with the highest and the lowest of the town's society, she imagined, customers and thieves. What could she make of that, she wondered. The Allans had mentioned a ring in the family. But it was old.

'How well do you know Isabel?' she asked Ada after a while.

'We were children together here,' said Ada.

That had not occurred to Margaret. She'd thought Ada had been born in Perth. 'I should have guessed, though I had not realised until I overheard you with Bridget that you'd grown up in Stirling.'

Ada looked around the room, then nodded. 'This was my parents' home. I was probably born in this bed – delivered by Dame Alice. What do you want to know about Isabel?'

'It was actually her late husband I was wondering about. Was Gordon also from Stirling?'

'Oh yes. His family have been goldsmiths here for several generations.'

A ring in the family for generations. Margaret wondered. 'What was Gordon like?'

'Do you mean was he likely to be murdered in his shop in midday?'

'I do not mean to disrespect the dead.'

'I know.' Ada straightened and gazed out the window for a few breaths, the lines in her face starkly visible again. 'Gordon. In his youth he played the fiddle and was light on his feet. He was also grasping and selfish, and those are the traits he cherished to his death. It was quite like him to trade with the English, to ensure that they would consider him to be on their side. Isabel devoted herself to raising their children and enjoying as much of Gordon's wealth as she could squeeze from him.'

Margaret remembered Isabel's elegance at Mass. 'I would say that she'd been successful.'

'And yet her mourning is sincere, she is not play-acting. She remembers his youth, his music, how they danced–' Ada's hands lay idle in her lap, her weaving forgotten, her gaze unfocused. 'We forgive much in the men we love.'

Margaret left her in peace with her memories until she bent once more to her work.

'Did Isabel notice whether anything had been stolen when Gordon was attacked?' Margaret asked.

Ada wagged her head. 'You are quite focused on Gordon's murder today. Isabel was not often in the shop. She asked his apprentices and her son whether they were missing anything and they'd noticed nothing out of place.'

'I find that most strange,' said Margaret. 'I should think few would be able to resist taking a small token of gold.'

'Quite restrained. You're right.'

'Don't you wonder how the murderer knew that Gordon was alone in the shop?'

'There had been little work of late, so he was often alone.'

'It sounds as if you've asked her quite a few questions.'

Ada glanced up. 'I suppose I have. I hope I haven't been too obvious.'

'Do you know the Allans in the house between theirs and yours?'

Ada frowned down at her work. 'It is terrible about their son. Ranald and – I don't recall his wife's name.'

'Lilias.'

'Oh yes. He trades – I believe wine was his chief trade, though with the English interfering I imagine he now trades whatever he can. The house belonged to Dunfermline Abbey. It may still, and they are tenants. I haven't introduced you to the neighbours because I thought it might be dangerous. On the other side is a saddler who has made a fortune from the castle. I should have thought he was as likely to be resented by the townsfolk as Gordon.'

Later, when Margaret could sit still no longer, she excused herself and went down to the hall. Celia sat quietly watching Archie, who moaned in his sleep.

'He is feverish,' she said when Margaret asked about his condition. 'I have made him something to cool him, but his mouth is so swollen he does not want to drink. So I drip a little into his mouth now and then.'

'You are very kind to him.'

'The worst I know of him is that he fought with Peter Fitzsimon,' said Celia. 'I cannot fault him for that.'

Margaret yawned.

'You could do with a rest, Mistress.'

'Or some air.'

Seeing that Archie was being well looked after, Margaret felt free to do what she pleased, as long as she didn't wander out into the town. She headed out into the backlands and settled on a seat beneath a pear tree on the edge of the property near the Allans's house. The sense that she was about to understand something grew stronger and she had an uneasy feeling that the Sight was playing with her. So be it. She welcomed it if it showed her what to do next.

After what seemed a long while a man came out of the next house. She felt a shiver of anticipation, and silently proposed a bargain with the Sight, that she would honour the gift and seek out Great-Aunt Euphemia in Kilmartin Glen so that she might learn to use it for good if it proved now that it could be used for good. She prayed that it was God's gift and not that of the Devil. She almost laughed at herself for bargaining with a mere string of thoughts, but she reminded herself of its power, how it ruled her mother's life. Ready now, she turned her attention to the man.

He wore a wide-brimmed hat and carried a bundle of clothing. Because of the hat, she could not tell the colour of his hair, but his shape and posture were those of an older man, perhaps like Roger in his early forties, so she guessed it was Ranald Allan. He picked up a long-handled spade from a small gardening shed – she noted that his right hand was bandaged and he held the spade awkwardly. He continued a few paces past the tidy kitchen garden and there crouched down, setting the bundle to one side, and with his hands cleared an area of weeds and debris. Rising, he stabbed the spade into the dry earth and drove it into the soil with one foot on the blade, then suddenly abandoned the project, walking away, farther into the backlands. Behind him the handle stuck out of the ground like a feeble marker. Margaret noticed his shoulders heaving as he fell to his knees, his head in his hands.

She was uncomfortable about observing his sorrow. But he need only have glanced her way to see her sitting there. She had not hidden from him.

When at last he rose, never glancing in Margaret's direction, he attacked the digging with a grim determination. His behaviour intrigued her. As the mound of earth grew she wondered how deep a hole he needed. Perhaps she'd been wrong about what he'd carried out with him. Although it looked like a small bundle of clothes, it might actually be something wrapped in a piece of clothing. She watched closely as he jabbed the spade into the pile and then bent to pick up the clothes. When he tossed the bundle into the hole it flowed in; if there was something other than clothing it was small and light. He made short work of filling in the hole, tamped down the earth with his feet, and propped the spade by the shed as he passed it, headed back towards the house.

Just opposite the spot where Margaret sat he paused, took off his hat and rubbed a sleeve over his sweaty grey hair, then fanned his face with the hat as he glanced around, as if considering what to do next. Margaret wished she could sink into the bench. When he noticed her, which had been inevitable, he strode over to her.

Hands on hips, he demanded, 'What are you gawping at?' His face flushed crimson.

Margaret reminded herself that it was perfectly reasonable for her to sit beneath a tree on a warm early autumn day behind the house in which she was staying. 'I came out to enjoy the garden,' she said. 'You look hot. Would you care to sit here in the shade with me?'

'You're biding here with Ada de la Haye?'

Margaret nodded. 'I'm her niece, Maggie.'

To her surprise, he sank down beside her, the bench creaking under his weight. 'Ranald Allan,' he said. 'I should not have shouted so.'

'I understood. I startled you. But there's no harm done.'

'You've chosen a darksome time to bide in Stirling.' Pain resonated in his words. Margaret sensed the mourning in his posture and his voice and her heart went out to him.

'I know, and I regret it. I pray my aunt does not suffer because of my selfishness in wanting to come here.'

'Your choice? Why did you wish to travel at such a time?' He spoke with a delicacy, as if he anticipated a sad tale.

'My husband died recently and I could not bear to be in the house we'd shared. I hoped that if I were away for a little while . . .' She let her voice trail off. It was not really a lie. She *had* wished to escape the house she'd gone to with such hope when first married, and she *was* a widow. It was not a story she'd planned to tell anyone, but she had a sense that Ranald would respond with his own tale of grief. She was following her impulse, still challenging the Sight to prove itself worthwhile.

'You are so young to be a widow,' Ranald said. 'Did your husband die a soldier?'

She hoped not to shut him up with her nod.

'It is a terrible time.' Ranald's voice broke and he turned away from her.

She waited, feeling horrible for causing him to recall his sorrow.

'My son was hanged by the English,' he said, catching his breath at the end as if biting off a sob.

'God grant him peace,' Margaret whispered, crossing herself.

'They made an example of him, hanging him in front of the townspeople. He'd been caught with a cache of weapons in his pack, down in the pows.'

'How horrible for you to see that.'

'My wife knew she could not bear to watch, but they forced us out to the market square to stand at the head of the crowd. I'd meant to be there all along; I believed that my son would know I was there, and find some comfort in that.' Ranald's voice broke again and he shakily dabbed his forehead with his bandaged hand. 'My wife has not recovered.'

'I'm sure he died bravely, and in God's grace. His brothers and sisters must be proud of him.'

'He was our only child,' said Ranald. 'He was soon to be wed, and Lilias, my wife, looked forward to having a daughter, and grandchildren.' He opened his hands on his lap, as if letting go a dream. 'All lost now.' His palm was wrapped, the bandage bloody. His digging must have opened a wound.

'I hope his betrothed is a comfort to you in your grief,' she said.

'Her? A comfort? Do you know what she–' He stopped himself. 'Her parents sent her away. To kin up north.'

With the sharpness of his anger, she realised she'd touched on the source of his deep bitterness.

'You hadn't heard about my son's execution?' Ranald asked.

'I think people are too frightened to gossip. Death surrounds us.' Something in his mood shifted as she spoke. She tried not to think, but to let words come as they would. 'You must also mourn your neighbour Gordon Cowie.'

'Gordon?' Ranald seemed startled, but then hurriedly murmured, 'God grant him rest.'

'Were you burying your son's clothes just now?' Her heart pounded at the boldness of the question.

'What? Oh,' he flushed and nodded. 'My son's. Yes.'

'What of his ring?' she asked, though she had not meant to.

He turned and grabbed her by the wrist, his face livid. 'What do you know of that? Who are you? Has she talked to you?'

It felt as if he might break the bones in her wrist, he held her so tightly with the bandaged hand. But Margaret could not stop the flow of words. 'What happened to your son's ring?'

'God, help me. Dear God, help me,' Ranald moaned, and letting go her wrist he hurried away, disappearing into his house.

Margaret could not breathe for a moment; she thought her pounding heart would break through her ribs. She cursed herself for mentioning the ring. If this was what she must suffer with the Sight she wanted none of it. She fled into the house.

'What is it, Maggie?' Ada said, stepping in front of her and grabbing her by the shoulders. 'You look terrified. Was that Ranald you were talking to? Did he say something to frighten you?'

Finding her voice, Margaret said, 'We spoke of his son's hanging.'

'Poor man,' Ada murmured. 'No wonder you are upset.'

Margaret was grateful that Ada queried her no further, but allowed her to escape up to the solar where Celia was soon beside her, helping her remove her wimple and shoes.

'You are shivering, Mistress,' Celia murmured as she helped Margaret into bed and pulled the covers up over her.

By the expression on her maid's face Margaret knew she looked as strange as she felt. Her mind was agitated and she thought that the last thing she wanted was to lie down, and yet her body felt drained of life. How she was going to quiet her mind while lying with the covers pulled up over her head she did not know. Sleep was impossible, yet motion was equally impossible.

Dear God, teach me how to contain these thoughts, this knowing. I can do no good if I go mad.

ᨋ 11 ᨌ

WOUNDS

Ada had just taken a soothing tisane to Margaret, having hoped to talk to her some more about their neighbour. She had been alarmed by Margaret's state after speaking with him. That his son was hanged as a spy was horrible, but Margaret had already heard of the execution. Ada sensed that something else had deeply unsettled her. She was disappointed to find Margaret asleep.

Celia was sitting beside the bed. 'After tossing so that I worried she'd never rest, she's finally calmed,' said the faithful maid.

Although glad that Margaret was resting, Ada was frustrated to be left in the dark about what had so disturbed her – yet not so much that she considered waking her. Leaving the cup with Celia, Ada had reached the head of the solar steps when she heard voices outside the hall door, and then a knock. John hurried to open the door, saying as he did so, 'Sir Simon.' He bowed his head with respect.

Simon gave the butler a curt nod and stepped past him into the hall. He was dressed as a soldier today and looked like one, straight-backed and grim. A stranger followed him in; he wore an unfamiliar livery, and was clearly a commoner.

Anxious to know why Simon was breaking his rule about being

seen outside the castle precinct with her, Ada hurriedly descended to greet them.

'Good day to you, Dame Ada,' said Simon with an uncharacteristic formality. He glanced towards the fire, noticing Archie on the pallet. 'An injured servant?' Simon asked, walking over to see him more clearly. 'This young man is often at the castle. Is he a member of your household?'

'No, Simon. We found him lying in the wynd this morning,' said Ada, grateful that Peter had not accompanied him. 'As you can see, he was in no condition to be moved far.'

Simon grunted, 'Drunken brawling,' and moved away from the fire. 'Has Peter been here – last night or this morning?' he asked.

Ada's heart raced. 'No. He has not graced me with his company. Did he say he was coming to see me?'

'No. No matter.' Nodding to his companion, who waited by the door, Simon motioned for him to join them.

'Can I offer you something? A cup of wine?' Ada asked.

'I'll not be here so long as that. I want a word with your niece.'

'With Maggie?'

Simon gave a curt nod.

'Who is this man with you?' Ada did not like the stranger's slightly amused expression.

'He's a soldier in King Edward's army,' said Simon.

'I guessed that. Why is he here with you? Why have you brought him here?'

The stranger glanced away, as if realising he'd offended her.

'Fetch your niece,' said Simon.

'She's been taken ill. She's lying down and should not be disturbed.'

'I won't keep her long.'

'But–'

'Shall we go up to her?' he asked, eyeing the steps.

'No. I'll ask her to join us.'

As she climbed to the solar Ada wondered what mischief Simon was about. The stranger irritated her, but Simon's formality frightened her. It was a bad sign that he was distancing himself from her.

In the solar she found Margaret sitting up, her loosened hair tucked into a neat cap, sipping the tisane as Celia helped her into her shoes.

'I heard,' Margaret said. She was pale and her hand trembled as she lifted the cup to her lips. 'What can he want?'

'I don't know. There's a soldier with him in a livery I haven't seen before. Can you walk?'

Margaret set down the cup and rose. 'We'd better find out what he wants.' She shook her head as Celia moved to assist. 'Stay here. I'll go with Ada.'

Ada could not help but admire how her young friend lifted her chin and walked over to the steps though she still lacked colour and energy. Margaret paused at the steps and motioned for Ada to go first.

'In case I stumble,' she said.

Dear girl, Ada thought, and said a prayer as she descended that this was some foolish whim on Simon's part.

When Margaret had joined them, Simon glanced over at his companion. 'Do you know this woman?'

The man nodded. 'Dame Margaret Kerr,' he said in a Welsh accent, 'we meet again.'

Ada's heart skipped a beat at the use of Margaret's name, and she heard her companion gasp. She took Margaret's arm to steady her and angrily demanded, 'Simon, who is this man?'

But Simon was looking at his companion. 'Kerr. So this is the woman you met in Perth, David?'

'It is, My Lord.'

Simon turned back to Margaret. 'Do you recognise this man?'

To Ada's despair Margaret nodded. 'He brought me news of my brother. He claimed to have escaped from the English camp at Soutra. Your sores have healed well,' she said to the stranger.

'I am grateful to James Comyn for his care,' said the obnoxious David.

One of his hands was wrapped in a stained bandage. 'I see you are not completely healed,' said Ada. She wanted to say more, call him a liar, but that would be hypocritical in the situation, for she'd done her share of lying and did not want to chance angering God.

'Wait without, David,' said Simon.

The Welshman withdrew at once.

While Simon stood regarding Ada, she remained silent, unable to think of anything she might say to improve the situation.

'Of course you knew Dame Margaret was a spy for James Comyn, Ada. You are too smart to be fooled by her.' His voice was cool though she had no doubt of the anger he suppressed.

'You know me well, Simon. Who was that Welshman?'

'A spy,' Margaret said. 'James was right not to trust him.'

'What I don't understand, Dame Margaret,' said Simon, 'is how it came to be that you serve the Comyns while your husband was in service with the Bruces. The families are enemies. But I'm certain you know that.'

'She knows her own mind,' said Ada.

'It's almost amusing. Peter and I thought you were the spy, Ada, until the Welshman arrived and opened our eyes to your niece's activities. She isn't your niece at all, is she?'

'It matters little now.' Ada did not know whether Margaret was safer as her kin or as a friend. 'What do you mean to do now, Simon?'

'I should have killed you when you chose Godric.' He said it as if he was at last coming to some decision.

Ada had no doubt he knew she'd lost her daughter shortly after birth and that Godric had left her to fend for herself. 'You almost did. And in the end I lost everything I loved. Everything.'

'You need not have suffered. It was your choice.'

Bastard. 'Can you be so cold? Surely what we've shared in the past week has meant something to you.' As soon as she spoke she wished she could take it back, annoyed with herself for sounding as if she were pleading with him.

'I thought I was keeping you from spying,' said Simon.

She could not believe his arrogance. 'Liar.'

'Dame Margaret Kerr.' Ada felt Margaret stand straighter as Simon studied her. 'I believe I know where my son has gone. He's searching for your late husband's friend.'

'What friend?' Margaret asked.

'I am sure you know of whom I speak. Did you know that Aylmer is English? My men wanted to kill him at once, but I'd hoped to learn more about his kinsman, Robert Bruce. Curious man, Bruce, one season fighting for King Edward and amusing himself at the English court, the next season turning against his sovereign.'

'I don't trust him,' said Margaret.

Ada wished she'd keep her tongue. Simon needn't know any more about her.

'I certainly think you're right in not trusting the Bruce.'

'I meant Aylmer,' said Margaret.

'Ah? Neither do I. Unfortunately, with most of our soldiers headed to the battlefield Aylmer managed to escape the castle. At least we think so. And I have a feeling Peter is tracking him.'

'May they have joy of one another,' said Margaret.

'As I said, she is not well,' said Ada. 'Is that why you asked whether he'd been here – because she might have spoken with this Aylmer?'

'I had no idea he was at the castle,' said Margaret.

Simon regarded Margaret as if deciding whether or not to believe her. 'Well, then,' he said at last, 'I shall trouble you ladies no longer.' He bowed to Margaret, then to Ada. 'This is, I believe, farewell, Ada.'

'What will happen to us?' she demanded.

'I don't know.' He said it as if he'd not given it any thought. 'At present I am needed in negotiations with the Scots. I have some hope that your nobles are about to turn on Wallace and Murray and their rabble. Then – I don't know.' He bobbed his head again and headed towards the door.

'Remember me to our children,' Ada said, hoping that would make him turn, that she might read something in his eyes.

But he did not pause.

'Bastard,' she hissed as the door closed behind him. 'Lying bastard.' Her face burned with anger and shame and she wanted to both cry and scream. 'Forgive me, Maggie,' she said, pushing past her, heading out to the backlands. Once outside she gulped the air. Hugging herself to try to stop the trembling, she stepped out into the sunshine and stood with head bowed, letting the sun's warmth soak into her. She cursed herself for coming to Stirling. In Perth she had at last found peace with herself and a contentment in her life, participating again in the lives of her family by taking in various members when their lives over-whelmed them. But coming here had opened wide all the wounds she had worked so hard to heal. Damn Simon, damn him for dallying with her and then shoving her aside. He might at least have kept up the pretence of affection. All the power was in his hands, he had nothing to fear from her.

Margaret touched her on the shoulder, then held out a cup of brandywine. 'Are you all right?' she asked.

Ada shook her head, and then drank the wine down in one gulp. As it warmed her she noticed that Margaret looked more herself.

'*Have* you seen aught of Aylmer?'

Margaret shook her head. 'I'd imagined him long gone. I am going to the kirk to tell James all that has happened.'

Ada felt she should protest, being responsible for Margaret's welfare while her young, impetuous friend was a guest in her house. 'He does not want you going about.'

'It is over, Ada. Whatever Simon means to do is already decided. Nothing I do will change that. I might as well go about my business.'

'But why risk yourself?' Ada was not ready to give up all hope of reaching Simon.

'James might be able to advise us. I've had John pack food and drink for him.'

For a moment, Margaret looked so like her mother that Ada caught her breath. Perhaps it was the wimple and the signs of exhaustion on her face, but she had never so reminded Ada of Christiana before. Yet she saw a stillness in Margaret that she'd never seen in Christiana. Thinking of what Margaret had gone through with her mother's Sight and the havoc it had caused her home life, as well as all she had suffered with her ill-suited husband, and now her widowhood, Ada felt horrible for causing yet more strife in her young life.

'I should have turned around when James told me Simon and Peter were here,' Ada said.

'Should you?' asked Margaret. 'I don't know that I agree.'

'What did Ranald Allan say that frightened you so?'

Margaret glanced over in the direction of Ranald's house. 'Isn't the tale of his son's being hanged for a spy enough?'

'And now Simon knows you came here as a spy.'

Margaret closed her eyes and nodded.

Ada still sensed there was more, but she was too drained to press her. 'You are right, James may have some advice for us. Heaven knows we need some. Reason tells me Simon will do nothing now that he considers us exposed and thus powerless. He would gain nothing. But Peter–'

'Simon was cruel to you,' Margaret said, touching Ada's shoulder. 'I am sorry.'

Ada shrugged. 'Go along. I'll take care of myself. Be careful.'

She watched Margaret cross the yard to the back door. Beautiful, intelligent, courageous, and at nineteen already a widow. She wondered what would become of her dear young friend.

*

A strange hush had descended upon the town. Margaret sensed even more than she had the night of Johanna's death the collectively held breath of the townsfolk as the armies massed below. She noticed Celia's hesitation when they stepped out into the quiet market square.

'We are not the only ones who have stayed within, out of harm's way,' said Margaret. 'But today the harm came calling. It doesn't matter whether we stay within.'

'Where do you think Aylmer has gone?' Celia asked.

Margaret wished she knew. Not that she had forgotten how she loathed him, but if he'd witnessed how Roger had fallen she wanted to hear it.

'I would imagine he's trying to escape Stirling and the battle-field below,' she said in belated answer to Celia.

They both halted as a cry broke the silence.

Margaret laughed with relief when it resolved into a cat fight. 'It's so quiet they must think it's night,' she said.

But Celia was not about to be sidetracked with levity. 'What did happen in the garden?' she asked.

'I spoke to Ranald Allan, our neighbour. I'd heard him and his wife arguing about a ring last night – one that had been long in the family. I mentioned it today – I'd watched him bury some clothes and – it was the Sight working through me – I asked whether he had also buried his son's ring. He became furious. He was so *angry*.'

'What does it mean?'

Margaret shook her head. 'I wish I knew. Huchon was betrothed. Ranald spoke as if she'd abandoned them.'

They crossed over towards the kirk and sought out Father Piers.

'He is already in the kirk,' said the clerk.

They crossed the yard again, to the north door, where the guard searched the basket for weapons before allowing them past.

'They hope James comes out, but unarmed,' Margaret muttered, trying to distract herself from the fear the nave's enormity had caused her the night James had sought sanctuary. But the sun had broken through the clouds and the light of early afternoon softened the great expanse. Across the nave, in the south aisle, Father Piers stood over someone who knelt on the stones with head bowed. Margaret and Celia nodded to the priest and then sought out the chapel in which James was biding.

Fully dressed even to his boots, James lay dozing on his pallet. Celia gently set the basket down, but the slight noise brought him to his feet, his eyes wild, his fists ready.

'St Columba!' Margaret cried. 'You startled me.'

Celia laughed nervously. 'Master James,' she bobbed her head.

He recognised them and relaxed his hands. 'I dreamt I was to be hanged.'

Margaret caught Celia's eye and knew she, too, was thinking of Huchon Allan.

'What's the news?' James asked, now fully awake and seem-ingly glad to have company. The cleft in his chin seemed deeper and his hair was longer than his wont, swept back from his high forehead and lying softly on his collar. Margaret thought it suited him. 'You've brought food?' He'd noticed the basket.

Celia nodded, holding it out to him.

'Have they buried Johanna?' he asked Margaret.

'They have,' she said. 'And there is more news.'

'Not a truce, I hope?'

Margaret shook her head, smiling at his energy. 'Come, sit and eat while I tell you all I know.' She told him nothing of the Sight, although she did mention Huchon Allan.

'I'd heard of his fate,' said James. When she told him of Aylmer's escape from the castle he shook his head at the news. 'I'd imagined him long gone.'

What most disturbed James was Simon's visit; he suggested that both Margaret and Ada take sanctuary with him. But Margaret reasoned once more that they had been rendered ineffectual by

Archie's injury, Johanna's death, James's being stuck in sanctuary, and Simon's knowledge of their purpose.

'How can we be of any threat to him?' she asked. 'We've nowhere to go, no one to pass messages to with the troops all around us.'

He touched her cheek. 'True. But I should like you to stay here with me.'

Apparently taking that as a cue, Celia stood up. 'If you have no need of me, I would like to spend some time in prayer, Mistress. I'll be in the nave when you are ready to return to Dame Ada's house.'

Margaret nodded. 'I'll find you there.'

As soon as they were alone, James leaned close to Margaret and kissed her on her forehead. 'It could be quite innocent, your seeking sanctuary here. With me.'

He looked deep into her eyes and she could not resist moving closer. After all, she was now a widow, and James was not married. What a happy temptation amidst all the gloom.

'Say you will stay, Maggie.' He cupped her chin in his hand and drew her closer still, kissing her lightly on the lips. He put his arms around her and tilted her back.

He kissed her as if he'd been starving for her, and she found herself responding with delight. What else was there to do than to take what joy they might in this dark time? But as he began to fuss with the bodice of her dress she pushed his hand away, unwilling to commit a sacrilege in the kirk.

'We are in the kirk, Jamie. Father Piers is just out in the nave.'

He desisted, but not before some final kisses. 'My love, you must stay here with me.'

'It will still be a kirk,' said Margaret.

He sat up, raking back his hair. 'You're right, and I'm forgetting why I'm here. You must help me escape, Maggie.'

Watching him so quickly shift to his usual preoccupations, Margaret thought what a stranger he still was, and she to him, she was certain. They had shared much, but not about their hearts.

'Jamie, do you know how Roger fell?'

James stared at her for a moment, then slowly shook his head. 'My men found him – do you suspect them?'

'No! By the tears of the Virgin I never considered such a thing, Jamie. I just wish – I should have looked out in the kirk yard . . .' She stopped, realising how strange that might sound. She would not have had any idea that he was out there without the visions.

James rose and walked over to the window, standing silently, hands on hips, for a long while. Margaret could not know what he was thinking, but she could tell by the tension in his neck that he was angry. She joined him, not presuming to touch him.

'Were he alive I'd curse him, but I'll not curse the dead,' said James in a voice tight with frustration. 'Even from the grave he stands between us.'

'That is not so, Jamie.' She reached out to him. 'If I find a way to free you, where will you go? Not to Ada's and safety, I think.'

Now he faced her, looking into her eyes. 'If there is time before I am needed by my kin, I would come to Ada's.' He pulled her into his arms.

She pressed her head against his shoulder, kissed his cheek. 'I cannot ask more than that.'

As she and Celia were leaving the kirk, Father Piers joined them at the door. He looked drawn and sad. She recalled the man kneeling before him. Once on their way to the house, she asked Celia if she'd noticed who the man had been while she was by herself in the nave.

'Ranald Allan. You must have stirred something in him today, for he was sobbing while he spoke to Father Piers. Perhaps he was speaking of his son.'

'That would explain how sad Father looked.'

'Poor man,' said Celia.

*

Later, as the long early September dusk filled the hall with a soft twilight, Margaret and Celia sat by Archie, talking quietly while he slept. He'd awakened and taken some food, but his leg was causing him much pain, so Margaret did not ask questions, and soon he had slept again. It was warm by the fire, but Celia considered it unsafe to leave the injured man unattended, and John claimed he had spent enough time watching over Archie while they'd been at the kirk.

'Head wounds are slippery things,' said Celia. 'It could turn against him at any time. He might slip into a deeper faint.'

'What would we do then?' Margaret wondered aloud.

'Wake him, and make him move about a little,' said Celia.

When they'd returned from the kirk they'd learned from Maus that Ada had gone out to see Dame Isabel. Margaret wished that she'd been invited to accompany her. She was considering whether to go along when John answered a timid knock.

A young woman stood in the doorway, her stance that of someone unsure of her welcome. Her head looked too large for her slender body, the effect of having her hair tucked in a white cap while her much-mended gown reached only to the top of her collar bone, thus exposing a thin, delicate neck.

'My neighbours heard that my brother Archie has taken shelter here. Is it true?' she asked John.

Margaret was intrigued as Celia said, 'That is Ellen, Archie's sister.'

As John turned for instructions, Margaret beckoned Ellen over to the fire. The young woman opened her mouth to speak, but appeared to change her mind and instead silently approached. She gave Margaret a little bow and then knelt to look at Archie, who still slept. Margaret explained how she'd found him and what his injuries had been.

'You aren't surprised that he picked a fight with Peter Fitzsimon?' Margaret asked when Ellen did not respond.

'I don't know all my brother's friends,' she said.

'But Peter has been to your house,' said Margaret. 'While you were there.'

Keeping her head low, Ellen glanced over at Celia. Margaret had wondered whether she would remember her. 'We don't fuss about who buys the ale,' Ellen said. 'Archie,' she called softly to her brother. His eyelids fluttered and opened for a moment, but his eyes were unfocused and he was soon asleep again – if he'd ever actually awakened. 'Will he wake?' she asked, lifting one of his hands to kiss it. 'I would have come sooner but the soldiers were all about today.'

As she leaned towards her brother, a trinket that had been tucked into her neckline slid out, shining in the lamplight. It hung on a short cord around her neck. Margaret shifted to see it better. It was a garnet ring, of a size and shape suiting a man's fingers. Margaret kenned it was Huchon Allan's, the one long in his family. How had Ellen come by it? For surely she was not his betrothed.

Archie's sister's eyes were brimming with tears when she left her brother's side. 'You are so kind,' she said, averting her eyes. From Celia's description of their earlier encounter, Ellen had not been shy, so her averted gaze intrigued Margaret.

'We could hardly do otherwise,' she said. 'You are welcome to sit with him for a while.'

'I should go. Ma needs me to watch the little ones. Will you want us to fetch him home?'

'He can bide here as long as he needs to,' said Margaret. 'Has he had trouble with Peter Fitzsimon before?'

'I don't know. Why would he?' Her voice was not sullen; Margaret sensed she was frightened.

'Peter Fitzsimon didn't worry your mother?'

Ellen edged towards the door. 'Is there anything you would have us do? The corn's run out so we have no coin to spare.'

But you have that ring, Margaret thought. 'At this point he is not eating or drinking much, so you need not pay us. You are welcome to return.' She accompanied Ellen to the door. 'I could not help but notice the ring you wear around your neck. It's a man's ring. Was it your da's?'

Ellen lifted small, work-hardened hands to her neck and tucked in the ring. 'It's naught but a trinket, too big for my finger.' She shrugged. 'God bless you, Dame Maggie,' she murmured. John opened the door for her and she fled into the blue-tinged twilight.

Margaret turned from the door, her mind churning over all that had been said as she searched for what, if anything, she had just learned. If she could trust the Sight, that was Huchon Allan's ring. Ellen was worried about her brother, and did not wish to acknowledge knowing Peter Fitzsimon. What else? Margaret could find nothing else in it. She would like to ask Ranald whether his son had known Ellen, but she imagined Ranald was not ready to talk to her again. Perhaps she could learn something from Isabel Cowie.

'I'm going to join Dame Ada,' she told Celia.

'I shouldn't leave Archie,' said Celia.

'There's no need. I don't need a companion for such a short distance, and I'll return with Ada.'

It was an evening of delicate colours, although the woodsmoke from below was beginning to tinge the air. Margaret wished a good evening to a woman who was sweeping just outside the door downhill from Ada's.

'It will be a good evening now, with the soldiers gone down to the camps,' said the woman. 'I thought we'd never be rid of them.'

'You had some biding with you?'

The woman nodded. 'And I ken who told them up at the castle that we had room to spare. I've been too trusting.' With an energetic nod the woman withdrew, broom in hand.

Margaret wondered how many small feuds would linger among the townspeople after the army was gone. Turning uphill, she was just passing the Allans's house when Maus came running up behind her from the wynd.

'Dame Margaret!' She caught Margaret's arm. Her face was white, despite her exertion. 'In the gardening shed – a body – we think it's Dame Ada's son!'

'God help us!' Margaret gathered her skirts and rushed down the wynd.

At the shed Sandy and Alec stood in the doorway, and John was within, crouching down over something on the ground. He rose and stepped back to let Margaret see what they had found.

He'd wrapped himself in some ragged, filthy bags, perhaps trying to get warm, but the amount of blood pooled round him – Margaret looked away. How would she tell Ada?

'The knife is still in his chest,' John said softly. 'The young man in the hall was asking about his knife.'

'Could he have killed Peter without knowing it?' Margaret wondered aloud.

'Stabbed him as he fell, in a struggle,' John nodded. 'It is possible.'

'It must have been him I saw last night,' said Sandy, 'that bit of movement. He might have been alive if I'd gone to see. Just next door.'

'What do we do with him?' cried Maus. 'If they find him here, we'll be blamed and they'll hang us all.'

'Keep your wits about you,' Margaret said, looking round the backlands. Thank God the neighbours appeared to be tucked inside their homes. 'Leave him here while I think what to do. Close the door and secure it.'

She moved away from them, staring out into the fading light seeking a spark of the Sight, a sense of something leading her, but she felt nothing but her raw fear. Why hadn't she seen this was coming? Why hadn't she sensed that Archie had murdered Peter? Or that Peter was dead? She'd felt not the least shiver of knowing. She crossed herself and prayed for strength for all the household, especially Ada. Despite her disappointment in Peter, he was her son. The sight of him – Margaret turned back. Something was not right. She almost ran into John.

'Why would he not pull out the knife?' she asked.

'Could he?' The butler wiped his forehead. 'I've never had a knife in me. My mistress, who is to tell her? This is a terrible, terrible thing.'

'Bring a lamp out to the shed,' said Margaret.

'But we will call attention to ourselves,' John protested.

'God knows we've already risked that. Do as I say. Get Sandy if you're too frightened to do it.'

John was obviously too frightened to care about his pride, because Sandy appeared in a moment carrying a lantern, the shutters closed. Without a word, the two returned to the shed, Margaret holding the lantern while Sandy unfastened the door and pulled it open. The odour was stronger than it had been, but she noticed it only for a moment.

'Shine the light on his chest,' she whispered to Sandy, then crouched down. He did as ordered and she saw now that the knife went through one of the bags. She also noted that Peter's left hand was badly cut up. She motioned for Sandy to move the light up to Peter's face. His eyes were closed. She looked more closely. Blood was caked on his eyelids, but she saw no wounds above his neck, so he must have touched his eyes with his bloody hands. Taking a deep breath and holding it, she pulled one of the blood-soaked bags away from his middle and found a gaping wound. The bag above it was not torn.

Feeling queasy, she struggled to her feet, grateful for Sandy's helping hand beneath her elbow, for she quit the shed just in time to vomit without it. Afterward, she leaned her head against the wall and let the night air cool what it could. Had Sandy not been hovering about her she would have torn off her wimple to feel the breeze in her hair. Death was horrible enough, but violent death was a vision of hell. Peter's fellow men had torn his body like that.

He'd been a difficult man, hard, but she'd thought that of James before she'd joined his cause. Had Peter been fighting for the return of King John Balliol she would have thought him a brave man, committed to a righteous cause.

'Do you want to see any more?' Sandy asked. 'I've pulled aside the bags and see no more wounds.'

They both started as faint shouts rode the night breeze. 'Would that he were down in the camps with the others,' Margaret said.

'Aye.'

'Take a good look at the knife's hilt, so that you can describe it to me,' she said. 'Then we'll leave him in peace for now.'

Ada might wish to see him. Margaret must tell her, but the thought of going to Isabel's house filled her with a strange weariness.

'I must clean myself,' she told Sandy. 'Ask Celia to come to the kitchen.'

The servants shrank from Margaret as she stepped into the kitchen. She hadn't realised she was cold until the warmth enveloped her.

'I need hot water to wash in,' she told Alec. 'And an old cloth.'

Celia gasped when she saw her mistress.

'I am unharmed, Celia, but you'll have some work washing this from me.' In the light Margaret now saw that she had blood on her sleeves and on her skirt, as well as on her hands. She could just imagine the state of her wimple.

'I'll fetch some clothes,' said Celia.

'I'll come into the hall.'

Celia shook her head. 'No, don't. Ellen has returned. With Evota. I'll bring your clothes here.'

Margaret was dismayed that they had visitors in the hall, with the servants overwrought, as well they should be. Surely even in their concern for Archie, Evota and Ellen would notice something odd. 'How long have they been here? What do they want?'

'They've not been here long,' said Celia. 'Evota came to see her son, but Ellen took me aside and said she must talk to you. I'd thought to fetch you from Isabel's if you didn't return soon.'

'We must hurry then. At least they are there to sit with Archie.' Celia hurried out.

When at last Margaret entered the hall, she was touched by the tender scene beside the fire. Evota sat on the pallet, Archie's head on her lap, and as she rocked him gently she sang a wordless song, a lovely tune. Ellen glanced over and nodded a greeting, but Evota caught the movement and paused in her song, though still she rocked her son. Margaret took a deep breath, willing herself to forget the dead man in the shed for a while, and crossed the room to the three.

'God bless you for saving my son,' said Evota.

'I pray that he is soon as he was,' said Margaret. She took a seat on a stool between the two women. The firelight shadowed Evota's face, but Margaret could see that Ellen favoured her mother with her delicate features, although in the mother's worn face they were puffy and embedded in wrinkles. Yet the woman must be younger than Ada.

'Always fighting, like his da.' Evota shook her head and traced the bandage on her son's forehead with a finger.

'I would speak with you, Dame Maggie,' Ellen said. 'Alone. Ma will sit with my brother.'

Where in this house might they talk alone, Margaret wondered. She did not dare take Ellen into the backland.

'I know that my daughter wishes to talk to you,' said Evota, making it clear by her tone that she didn't approve, but had resigned herself to it.

'Let's retire to the corner,' Margaret suggested.

'It's about your husband's death,' said Ellen, at last looking squarely at Margaret.

Aylmer, Margaret thought, *she's spoken to him*. She led the way to the corner, out of the light.

⤜§ 12 ⧽⤚

THE DYKE BREAKS

'Have you heard the soldiers' shouts from below, down by the river?' Ellen asked.

Margaret nodded. 'We can only pray that God is with us.'

The young woman sat with her hands clutching the bench on either side of her. Margaret felt Ellen's anguish and wished she could just run away. How was it that after all the pent-up tension of the past week – months for the people in this town – everything was bursting apart now? All those troops massing below them. The town floated on a sea of armed men that would soon turn to blood; they would all drown in the hatred. God must have a reason for this, but Margaret could not fathom it.

She was trying to catch her breath and calm herself. She wanted a cup of wine but did not trust her legs to carry her across the room, so she judged it best to just get this over with. 'What is on your mind, Ellen?'

'What I have to say, Dame Maggie–' Ellen paused. 'I'm telling you because he wants you to know that he didn't kill your husband.'

'Who?'

'Aylmer.'

Margaret was taken aback. 'How do you know my husband's

comrade? Have you seen Aylmer since he escaped from the castle?'

'He came to see me last night. I wish I didn't know him.' Ellen's voice caught and she bowed her head for a moment. 'I was with Aylmer that night. Your husband was on the great rock behind the kirk and they were to take turns watching the castle. It's dark up on the rock and the torches up at the castle make the movement up there like a play. I was with Aylmer down below the rock, in its shadow.' She paused, biting her lip.

'Go on, go on.' Margaret's heart was racing.

'He went after Fitzsimon last night because of what happened.'

'Aylmer did?'

Ellen nodded.

Aylmer had struck the second, mortal blow? 'What *did* happen the night my husband died?'

'Peter knew I'd been with Aylmer before, and he made me lead him to where your husband and Aylmer were watching that night – or he'd take Archie – he knew Archie was carrying messages. After Aylmer fell asleep, I was sneaking away when your husband cried out. I wish I hadn't moved.' She took a breath. 'He tumbled off the rock and landed right next to me. He'd come down with the most awful speed and his head – Oh, Dame Maggie, I *heard* it hit the rock.' Ellen moaned.

Margaret stifled a sob, remembering the vision.

'When I looked up, I saw Peter standing at the edge of the rock, looking down on your husband. Aylmer grabbed me and I thought he was going to kill me, but Peter came running down with his men and I ran away. I ran and ran.'

'Peter Fitzsimon killed my husband?' Margaret asked, trying to grasp what Ellen was telling her. 'Peter *pushed* Roger off the rock?'

'Yes, I'm sure of it. He likes to tell me that I am responsible for your husband's death because your husband saw me running away and then lost his balance, but I saw Peter up there. He gave me this ring for my reward.' Ellen snapped the thong from her neck and pressed the ring into Margaret's hand. 'I don't want this. It's blood pay. I never thought– I'm so sorry.' She began to sob. 'I never meant any harm. I helped my family, sleeping with men. Peter would have taken my brother from us.'

Margaret stared at the floor, the ring heavy in her hand. 'How did Peter get this ring?' She repeated the question several times before Ellen calmed enough to respond.

'He said he bought it fair, from the goldsmith. It's Peter's.'

'It wasn't,' Margaret said. But she'd forgotten that Ellen did not know Peter was dead. 'I'm confused, don't mind what I say,' she muttered, pressing the ring back into Ellen's hand.

'Keep it!' the young woman wept.

Margaret did not want it, but she agreed. 'I shall keep it for you until–' *Until what?* She found it difficult to think clearly. 'Until I find the owner. Bless you for telling me how my husband died, Ellen. I am grateful, and I know that you are not to blame.'

The young woman looked over at her mother. 'There is more I would tell you, but not now. Archie might hear.' She rose. 'We should go now. Ma wants to bring him home tomorrow.'

Considering the corpse in the shed, Margaret thought it a good idea to send the young man home to heal. 'We'll talk of that tomorrow,' she said.

Evota and Ellen had not long been gone when Ada returned, and Margaret faced the moment she'd been dreading since seeing Peter in the shed.

The marketplace was very quiet but for a few small clusters of folk as Ada hurried back to her home. The few there were talking softly among themselves, wondering how the Scots could gather enough men to stand against all the troops they could see camping down below.

'Torches and fires as far as the eye can see,' one man said.

Ada had enjoyed the evening with Isabel. Her old friend was already coming to terms with being a widow, planning to join her daughter who was away in the north if that became possible, determined to go on with her life. Without revealing that Peter was here in Stirling, Ada had talked about having at last met one of her adult children only to find him an unpleasant young man, someone of whom she was not very proud – although he was quite handsome and skilled in the arts of war. Isabel had listened with sympathy and confided some of her own disappointments. All in all it had cheered Ada and she felt much better about her life.

But the moment she entered her house she knew something was wrong. Maus sat by the fire with Archie, but the moment she noticed her mistress in the room she put her hand to her mouth and hurried out to the kitchen.

It was nothing unusual for Maus to abandon her post. Ada had considered replacing her many times – she was the youngest daughter of a couple whom Ada had taken under her wing many years ago, the husband a man who seemed unable to thrive in any occupation and the wife a long-suffering saint who would have done better for her family by losing her temper now and then. Maus seemed to have inherited the most useless traits from each parent. Muttering a curse, Ada headed for the kitchen after checking that Archie was resting peacefully.

Margaret and Celia sat near the fire talking quietly with John, Sandy, Alec, and cook. Ned was scrubbing something in a tub, Maus whispering some direction. The water seemed pink in the firelight. As they individually became aware of Ada's presence, not one smiled or greeted her, but rather whispered her name. *Dame Ada. The Mistress. Ada.*

'What has happened here? Why are you all so upset to see me?' she demanded with a frisson of fear that perhaps she would regret asking.

Only Margaret rose and moved towards her. All the others seemed frozen where they were.

'This is a pretty greeting,' Ada said. As Margaret put an arm around her Ada noticed that her friend was so pale her freckles were visible in the firelight. 'What has frightened you, Maggie?'

'Come into the hall.'

Margaret urged her forward, but Ada walked over to the tub. 'Those are the sleeves of the dress you wore today.' She glanced back at Margaret's gown. She wore her better one, for no apparent reason – except that the sleeves to the grey one were bloody. 'What happened? Are you wearing bandages beneath your sleeves?'

'Come into the hall with me,' said Margaret. Her mouth was grimly fixed and her eyes anxious, but she did not appear to be in pain.

'It's someone else's blood. Archie's?'

Margaret pulled her out of the kitchen with more strength than Ada could resist.

After the kitchen the evening air felt cool and clean. 'The air is so soft out here – let's go into the backland,' Ada suggested.

Margaret stopped and faced Ada, a hand on either shoulder.

Suddenly, Ada was frightened. 'What is it, Maggie?'

'Peter has been killed, Ada.'

Her first reaction – God forgive her – was relief, but that was short-lived. 'My son? How?'

Margaret took a breath, and Ada knew that this was the part that her friend most dreaded telling her.

'He was stabbed. First, I think, by Archie. Then he–' Margaret pressed her forehead to Ada's for a moment, then looked up again. 'Sandy and I have tried to put it all together. We think that Archie managed to stab Peter in his left side and he sought shelter in the garden shed. He pulled some old bags around him for warmth.' Her voice was gruff and it was plain she was holding back tears.

'Dear God,' Ada moaned. He would be grievously wounded to do that.

Margaret nodded. 'I know. As much as I feared him, I think of his pain–' She shook her head. 'Someone else came upon him and stabbed him in the heart – through one of the bags – that's how we know it was later.' Margaret began to sob. 'I don't know where to begin, Ada. I don't know where to begin.'

'Begin what? No, shush now. He was heading down a road that could lead only to his death, Maggie. Archie should be grateful his wasn't the fatal wound.' *I'm rambling on*, thought Ada, *trying to fill in the silence. The one child I knew is dead. He suffered. So near here. So recently.* She stepped away from Margaret and began to heave. She felt Margaret behind her, steadying her, holding her forehead. When her stomach was empty, her knees threatened to buckle beneath her.

'Come,' Margaret said, supporting Ada as she straightened. 'Brandywine and bed, that is what you need. Plans can wait until morning.'

In the early morning, as Ada dully stared out the solar window trying not to think about how little love she'd felt for her now dead son, she noticed Simon departing the castle on horseback, leading a group of foot soldiers. *God be praised*, she murmured when he continued on Castle Wynd to St John Street. He would feel far less ambivalent about their son's murder than she did. *Now* she mourned Peter, *now* that he was dead she considered his courage and wished she had offered him affection. Surely she might have found a way to his heart. If she'd only tried.

She wanted to strangle the young man who slept so peacefully down in the hall. Had he not injured Peter, her son would not have sought shelter in such an exposed place. Aylmer she'd hated from the moment she met him in Perth. Shortly after he'd arrived with Roger Sinclair, Margaret had found documents on him that revealed he was not quite who he claimed to be. He was Robert Bruce's kinsman, and was making certain that Roger fulfilled his mission and proved his loyalty to the Bruce; if Roger had failed, Aylmer was to kill him. It was not just Ada's loyalty to Margaret and therefore her husband that had tainted her impression of Aylmer – he had seemed an arrogant man of no courtesy.

Margaret had explained Peter's part in Roger's death, so Ada understood why Aylmer might have gone after Peter. Yet hadn't Christ told mankind to turn the other cheek? And how could the man who had carried an order to deal with Roger as needed consider it his right to avenge the man's death?

Margaret knocked on the flimsy dividing wall of the solar. She'd slept with Celia and Maus to give Ada some privacy in her grief. 'Did you sleep at all?' Margaret asked.

Ada shook her head. 'Come, sit with me a while.' She patted the bench beside her. Margaret looked refreshed; so much better than she had the previous night. 'You slept.'

Winding her red-gold, wavy fall of hair round one hand, Margaret fastened it with two polished wood sticks as she took the seat. She was a beautiful woman, Ada thought.

'John has gone to Father Piers,' she told Margaret. 'I hope he will agree to bury Peter in the kirk yard.'

'Will you tell Simon?'

'He's just headed down the hill, leading foot soldiers.'

Margaret closed her eyes and bowed her head. 'We have a respite. Thank God. But Ada, you cannot attend your son's funeral.'

Ada nodded. 'But he'll have a proper burial. And later . . .' Whether she would tell Simon was something she was not yet ready to consider. One thing at a time. They must make safe the house by ridding it of her son's corpse. 'I wonder what Simon's departure means,' she said, 'whether he's to negotiate a truce or lead those men into battle.' She pressed her hands to her face. 'This town reeks of blood.'

They sat silently for a time.

'I'd thought to join you at Isabel's last evening. How did you find her?' Margaret asked.

'Glad to be alive,' said Ada. 'She hopes to join her daughter in the north if the truce comes to pass. She sent her there when–' she remembered that Margaret would be most interested in a piece of information that had surprised her. 'Maggie, her daughter was betrothed to Huchon Allan. When he was to be hanged, Gordon and Isabel sent her to kin in the north. Poor Isabel – she has suffered so much of late.'

Margaret suddenly brought her face so close that Ada could see shots of gold in the irises.

'Her daughter and Huchon Allan?' Margaret said, her voice high with excitement. She sat back so suddenly the bench rocked. 'If it was his ring, then Peter – I must go out.' She was off the bench before Ada could ask where she was going. 'Celia, dress me. Hurry!' Margaret called.

Margaret struggled not to jump to conclusions, though she kept thinking of her bargain with the Sight, that if it proved helpful she would go to her great-aunt in Kilmartin to learn more – she wondered whether the Sight was making sure she would. She wanted to ask Isabel about the whereabouts of Huchon's ring when Gordon was killed, but first she needed to make sure that it *was* his ring that Peter had given Ellen, which meant she must show it to Lilias and Ranald Allan. It was not an encounter she looked forward to.

As Celia dressed Margaret, she listened quietly. When she was finished, she touched the ring in Margaret's hand. 'So this was Peter Fitzsimon's ring? He gave it to Ellen?'

Margaret belatedly realised that she hadn't explained any of this to Celia – she hadn't expected her to be involved.

'You know enough now. Don't worry whether you understand it. All you need to do is be sure to not contradict me.'

Celia's dark brows were knit in concern. 'Where are we going?'

'To the Allans's house.'

'Next door? You hardly need a companion to walk across the wynd.'

One could count on Celia to get right to the telling detail, thought Margaret. 'I don't want to go alone.'

'Oh.' Celia pressed her lips together and was quiet a moment.

'Maggie, come quickly,' Ada called from below, 'James is here!'
Margaret's and Celia's eyes met.

'He's escaped?' Celia whispered.

'God help him,' Margaret said. 'We'll go to the Allans soon.'

Celia crossed herself. 'May God watch over him. Perhaps he will be able to join the others.'

As Margaret hurried down to the hall she felt a knot forming inside. She'd not thought about James fighting in the battle with the others.

He stood by the back doorway, dressed for travel, listening to Ada's recounting of the conversations in the market square the previous night.

'I've not had the courage to look down at the camps,' she said, 'but I can imagine. How can we possibly prevail against them?'

'We cannot fail, else things will be far worse than they are now. We must carry the day.' He glanced up, and seeing that Margaret had come, bowed to Ada. 'The guards are gone,' he said, taking a step towards Margaret.

'Sir Simon Montagu left early this morning, leading some foot soldiers,' said Margaret, guiding him to the far end of the hall, away from Archie.

James looked tired. 'What of Peter? Is he still lurking about?'

Margaret's stomach clenched, instantly back in the shed with Peter's blood on her. She drew James down on to a bench beside her, taking his hands. 'No, Jamie. Peter is dead.' She told him how they'd found him, and explained how the fatal stabbing had occurred after he'd taken refuge in the shed, and that Ellen had said Aylmer had gone looking for Peter.

'Aylmer. God's blood. How did he find him there?' James glanced towards the fire circle.

'I don't know. Archie admitted that the knife was his. Peter had grabbed it by the blade and Archie had not the strength to retrieve it.' She remembered Peter's cut-up hand and shivered at the thought of the pain he must have experienced.

James pulled her close. 'I am so sorry you've seen the bodies of people you knew so viciously injured, Maggie.'

She clung to him, trying not to see the blood, the battered flesh, the gaping wounds, but her mind was full of Johanna's and Peter's suffering – and Roger's, though she had witnessed it through the Sight, not her fleshly eyes. She could not help but think that souls so violently wrenched from the body were never entirely freed.

'Maggie, Maggie,' James whispered, 'you are so young to be seeing all of this. I wish I could protect you.'

She turned her face towards his, and their kiss was long and sweet. This was a cruel courtship indeed.

When they moved apart, Margaret asked, 'What will you do now that you are free?' She did not for a moment expect him to stay here with her, knowing that his first loyalty was to John Balliol, his kinsman, and she respected him for that.

'Free? I hardly feel that. I must return to my men below. This battle will decide whether we go on to fight another day, Maggie. I cannot bide here while they fight for my kinsman.'

'I did not expect you to.'

'I wonder whether Aylmer has run off to Robert Bruce? We could use all the men we can find.'

Margaret shrugged. 'Will you try to reach Wallace and Murray on Abbey Craig?'

'Yes, God help me.'

'May God watch over you, Jamie,' she whispered.

He kissed her forehead, her cheeks, her lips and held her tight for a moment. 'I'll come back to the house if I can't get through. And in time I *will* return for you, Maggie, no matter what happens.' She knew by the fullness of his voice that he meant it, and that he regretted that he could not simply stay with her. 'It is possible that the English will use the townspeople of Stirling as hostages, Maggie. If you begin to see patrols on the streets, seek sanctuary in the kirk. Promise me you will.'

'I promise. May God watch over you, Jamie. I'll be here, praying for you.'

'May God keep and protect you.' He kissed her forehead again, and then her hands. 'I wish I'd never brought you here.'

'I regret nothing, Jamie, except that we've had so little time together.' She knew so little about him, and he her.

'I'll leave you now.'

They rose. Margaret kissed his cheek and then crossed to the solar steps, feeling his eyes on her.

'Maggie!' he cried as she climbed.

Already feeling the heat of her emotion in her cheeks, she knelt down by the bed and prayed for strength. This was not a day on which she could give over to weeping for James.

A hint of autumn was in the air in the mornings, chilling toes and stiffening joints, and making everyone in the camps eager for something to happen so that they might turn towardss home. This enforced rest was no rest at all, but rather fuel for anxiety, fear, anger, resentment – Andrew feared that the pressure would make someone snap.

'What sins have they still to confess?' Matthew asked Andrew after yet another impromptu confession had taken him away from his prayers.

'They begin over again, fearful lest they have forgotten a detail, as if God doesn't already know all, as if He forgives only what has been thoroughly described.' Andrew leaned back against a sun-warmed stone. 'My neck hurts from bowing my head to listen so that they cannot see how I fight to keep my eyes open.' He stretched out his legs and pressed his palms to his thighs, stretching into his lower back. 'They need activities to occupy them. This waiting gives them time to worry. For some of them it is the first chance they've had to review their lives since leaving home. Some have killed their fellow men for the first time. Some ache for home. They tell me they don't feel like themselves. They are frightened that God has misplaced them.' Andrew understood, but all he could do was listen and assign penances. 'I have no wisdom to offer them.'

'They are fortunate to have a chaplain to care as you do, Father,' said Matthew. He nodded towards a page picking his way through the camp. 'I think Sir Francis wants to consult with you again.'

Ever since Andrew had returned to the camp Sir Francis had kept him near. At first Andrew thought he suspected that he'd almost lost his chaplain, but gradually it became clear that he wanted a companion, someone with whom he could mull over what was happening – or not happening. Andrew had little to add, but it seemed his listening was sufficient for Sir Francis.

'I hope and fear that it is news of Stewart and Lennox; today is the day they were to return.'

'What will Sir Francis do with us if there is to be peace?' Matthew asked. 'The men would no longer be desperate for a chaplain.'

Andrew also wondered what they might intend for him. Send him back to Holyrood? To Soutra? He belonged nowhere at the moment. Abbot Adam wanted him safely trapped in Soutra, but if the English were victorious the spital would no longer be so dangerous for him. He glanced at Matthew and saw by his earnest gaze that he awaited a response.

'May God watch over us, Matthew. I fear peace almost as much as an English victory. I pray you never have cause to regret your loyalty to me.'

Matthew crossed himself, then forced a smile. 'If God suddenly allowed me to understand the written word I might desert you for a monastery, but save that I am content serving you.'

The page escorted Andrew through the clutches of men idly passing the time – some played dice, many obsessively polished their weapons, some dozed, others talked in small groups. Many glanced up and greeted Andrew. As they passed the small tent in which Sir Francis slept and took his meals a man hurried towards them.

'Father Andrew, I would talk to you.'

'He is wanted by Sir Francis,' said the page.

'I doubt I'll be long,' said Andrew. 'Come to me later.'

The man bobbed his head and turned away.

'They give you no peace, Father. How can you bear it?' asked the page.

'It is my calling,' said Andrew.

A half dozen men stood beside a young willow, its branches arched but still too buoyant to reach down to the water though one root seemed to wave freely in the stream, its land side crowded by a mature birch. Something about the juxtaposition of the men and the struggling willow calmed Andrew with a thought of how men follow the same paths as nature. His countrymen's struggle was young and uncoordinated as yet, but the blood and the effort were strengthening it day by day.

Sir Francis broke from the others to greet Andrew and draw him back to the group.

'This is Father Andrew, my chaplain and counsellor,' he said.

Most of the men were familiar, peers of Sir Francis or experienced soldiers he respected. Their expressions were universally grim.

'We could use a blessing, Father,' said Holm, a huge man whose left cheek carried an old puckered scar that pulled down the outer corner of the eye and his mouth. 'A truce is not to be.'

'Truce,' spat Sir Marmaduke. 'They never intended it, riding in here empty-handed after all this time.'

'They did promise to return tomorrow with forty barded horses,' Sir Francis reminded him.

'I don't believe it. Not after one of Lennox's men killed one of ours,' said Holm.

Andrew could not keep up with them, though he caught the fact that someone had finally snapped. 'Would one of you help me understand what you're so angry about?'

'Treachery,' said Sir Marmaduke. 'Stewart and Lennox still claim to support us. They told Surrey today that although they've been unable to convince Murray and Wallace to throw down their arms they would return tomorrow with forty barded horses. Caparisoned horses, but no men to ride them.' He cursed. 'And then, as they departed, Lennox's men found some of ours foraging, began to argue, and killed one of our men. That is not the behaviour of an ally.'

'What does Surrey say?' Andrew asked.

'He is trying to calm everyone, assure us that it is worth waiting to see whether they return with the horses tomorrow,' said Sir Francis.

'And if they don't?' Andrew asked, though he could see the answer in the faces around him. Tired and angry men have little patience.

'If the horses are not brought tomorrow, tomorrow we cross the Forth,' said Sir Francis, 'and slaughter the lot of them. They can't possibly stand against our numbers.'

'We should strike before then,' said Sir Marmaduke, 'while we have the advantage.'

'What do you fear, My Lord?' asked Holm. 'That Robert Bruce is going to escape our watch in Ayr and appear leading his dead men?'

Sir Francis laughed nervously. Sir Marmaduke cursed again. Andrew crossed himself.

John returned with word that all the English still in town were lying low in the castle, so Father Piers had agreed to bury Peter the following day – if Dame Ada was certain that she did not wish to give Sir Simon the opportunity to pay his respects to their son.

Ada felt a twinge of guilt, but she would jeopardise lives by revealing to Simon how Peter had died – and where. It would not surprise her if he were to accuse her of the fatal strike. She wished Margaret and Celia were there to help, but she and Maus were quite capable of preparing her son's body for burial.

The men had fashioned a table from planks and benches in the corner of the kitchen and laid Peter there. Maus had gathered as many lamps as she could fill to light him, as well as rags and several bowls of water with which to bathe him. Ada hesitated in the kitchen doorway, reluctant to see her son. Noticing that Maus had wrapped cloths around her gown and sleeves to protect them from the blood, Ada realised that she was not dressed appropriately and turned round to change into a simpler gown.

'I'm not thinking clearly this morning,' she muttered as Maus hurried to her.

'I'll help you, Mistress,' said Maus, and she impulsively hugged Ada. Her kind gesture brought on tears, but Ada reassured her maid that she was grateful for the affection.

'I don't know that I can do this,' she whispered, fearing that for once her courage was failing her.

'Come, I'll find something old for you to wear, and then you can decide,' said Maus, the adult for now.

Ada put herself into her maid's hands, allowing her to fuss and console, and gradually she convinced herself that she would always regret having walked away from this final opportunity to see to her son's needs. Though he was dead, his spirit perhaps already departed, she told herself that in some way this moment might still have meaning for both of them.

This time when she entered the kitchen she went straight over to where Peter lay on the table. It was terrible to see her handsome son bloody and torn, and at first she could only stand over him and weep. But in a little while she took a rag, wet it, and began to clean his face. Softly she spoke to him, telling him the story of his beginning, what she could remember about carrying him, birthing him, her dreams for him, her heartbreak when she had to let him go. Her hands were bloodied as she cut the bags and then his clothes from his cold body, but it was her son's blood, her blood, and she thanked God she had been given this chance to ease her son to rest.

*

The Allans's hall was sparsely furnished, but tidy and made pleasant by a beautiful tapestry depicting scenes from the life of the Blessed Mother. Lilias Allan noticed Margaret's interest and explained, 'That is not ours. It belongs to the Abbot of Dunfermline – we are his tenants. My husband does much trading with the abbey.' She kept glancing at Celia, as if wondering why Margaret had felt the need to be accompanied by her maid-servant. 'I am sorry that I did not welcome you when you first came to Stirling, but I am sure you know about my son.' She averted her eyes on the last words.

It brought to mind Margaret's embarrassment whenever her mother had made a scene in the town. 'You are in mourning, I know, and I apologise for disturbing your peace.'

Lilias invited them to sit by the door to a small garden that Margaret had not seen from the backland because it was surrounded by a low fence. Herbs and berry bushes attracted small birds to the wide, shallow bowl of water atop a stone in the centre.

'This is a beautiful spot,' said Margaret.

Lilias smiled, her long, thin face almost pretty for a moment. She was cadaverously thin, as if she had been fasting for a long, long while.

'I have something to show you, Dame Lilias.' Margaret drew out the ring.

'Holy Mother Mary!' Lilias gasped, staring at it. 'Where did you get this? I never thought to see it again.'

'Is this your son's ring?' Margaret wanted to be certain that she understood.

Lilias timidly reached out to it, stopping before she touched it, and met Margaret's eyes. 'How did you get this?' Her lips trembled.

'From Peter Fitzsimon, a soldier at the castle.'

'A soldier. An Englishman. That would be the man I saw

wearing it the day they hanged my son. He watched coldly. I flew at him when I saw he wore Huchon's ring.' Lilias pulled her hand back and stood up so quickly she stumbled against a small table. Margaret caught her and held the woman as she began to sob.

'What is going on in here?' Ranald Allan's voice thundered even before Margaret saw him.

Lilias pushed away from Margaret, wiping her eyes and shaking her head at her husband. 'Go away, Ranald, go away.'

'I will not. What has this woman done to upset you?' he demanded, staring at Margaret.

'Tell him nothing,' Lilias whispered.

But of course her husband heard her.

Margaret closed her hand over the ring. Celia looked to her for direction, uncertain how to handle this explosive scene. Ranald's face was contorted with anger and fear – Margaret could not tell which was strongest. Lilias was terrified and heartbroken.

Standing behind Celia, Margaret said, 'We meant only good, but I can see this is not the time, it is too soon. Come, Celia.'

The maid slipped towards the door and Margaret followed.

'No!' Lilias cried, slapping Ranald hard across the face.

He clutched his nose and stumbled backward.

'You will *not* silence these women. I won't live like this.'

Celia had grabbed Margaret's hand. 'What shall we do?' she whispered.

Margaret was watching the couple. 'Stay a moment,' she told her frightened companion. She, too had been frightened, but Ranald's fierce attack had been halted by the woman he was trying to protect, and Margaret sensed that he was no longer dangerous to them.

Lilias took Ranald by the arm and drew him away, speaking to him in a quiet voice. She seemed suddenly calm, and Margaret believed that in her refusal to let her husband command the moment Lilias had found her strength.

'He'll be all right now,' Margaret told Celia. 'We'll stay.'

Ranald left the room, and when Lilias was sure of that she invited Margaret and Celia to sit again.

'My husband does not have a violent nature. It is the times – they make beasts of us all, defending our cubs, our homes.'

'There was no harm done,' said Margaret.

'He thinks to protect us, but he has imprisoned us,' said Lilias. 'Father Piers was not nearly so harsh with Ranald as he is with himself.'

'What has Ranald done?' Margaret asked.

Lilias looked from one to the other. 'Don't you know? Didn't Dame Isabel send you to hear it?'

'Do you think Father Piers told us something?'

'How else did you know that was my son's ring?' Lilias asked. 'Oh dear.'

'Dame Lilias, my mother is a seer, she has the Sight. Of late, I have seen things, too.' Celia made a small sound and Margaret felt her maid's eyes on her. 'I was drawn to you and your husband, I believe to bring some comfort to you.' Margaret opened her hand, letting the ring on her palm speak for itself.

Lilias stared down at it.

'Take it,' said Margaret. 'It is yours by right.'

'Even though Ranald – God still would comfort us?' Lilias shook her head, her eyes a little wild.

'Tell me what happened,' Margaret said softly, 'and I'll tell Dame Isabel.'

Lilias still did not reach out for the ring, but she kept her gaze on it as she sat in silence. Margaret almost wept with disappointment, having been certain she was following the Sight, and that this was why she had been touched by it.

'Huchon gave it to Agnes Cowie when he left home,' Lilias finally began in a strained, hoarse voice, 'for her to keep until he returned. And when he was captured, and to be hanged, Isabel and Gordon sent her north. I thought she'd taken the ring, but when–' she looked away, catching her breath.

Margaret was afraid to breathe.

'No parent should ever witness such a deed.' Lilias's face was so pale as she spoke her veins might be traced beneath her skin. 'They ordered us to watch, along with what townsfolk they could find. I think many hid.' She nodded to herself, her long, thin face drawn with pain. 'The soldier in charge spoke to us. I can't remember what he said, I was watching my son. But I noticed his hand, the ring on it. I reached for it, and Ranald held me back.' She hugged herself. 'An anger grew in me, from a seed it grew and I watered it, I nurtured it, until one day I could contain it no longer; it had grown so wide and tall and it would root me to the ground and destroy me. I went to Gordon and accused him of selling the ring to the Englishman, of benefiting from our grief, and he admitted it. He defended himself, the greedy snake, he said his daughter had suffered, too, and it had cost them to send her north. Cost them! I flew at him, grabbed at his hateful eyes and he slapped me so hard I fell.' Lilias rose and turned away from them, towards the garden. 'I didn't know Ranald had followed me. When he saw me hurt he attacked Gordon. He spent all his grief and anger on Gordon.' Her voice shook. 'He has confessed to Father Piers, and he is truly remorseful.' She looked back at Margaret and said with a defiance that chilled, 'I am not. I regret nothing but that Ranald drew the knife instead of me.'

'May Gordon Cowie rest in peace,' Margaret whispered, crossing herself.

Celia did so, too. As she glanced at Margaret it was clear that she was overwhelmed by what she'd heard. 'What now?' she mouthed the question.

Margaret shook her head.

Suddenly Lilias sank down on to her chair and put her head in her hands. 'Why has God done this? Why did He return the ring?' Her voice was muffled, but Margaret could tell that she was weeping.

Margaret rose and searched the hall for something strong to

drink, finding a little stale ale in a mug on a small table. Sitting down beside Lilias, she gently took her hands and placed the mug in it. The woman's face was shattered with grief. She gulped the drink, then glanced up almost shyly at Margaret.

'Perhaps God meant to melt the ice that held your heart imprisoned, Dame Lilias.' Margaret said as she rose, placing the ring on Lilias's lap. 'Be at peace.'

Crossing the hall, Margaret called to Ranald to comfort his wife and departed with Celia, hurrying before the trembling overcame her and made it impossible to walk. She fled into Ada's house, somehow managing the steps, and collapsed on the bed.

◆§ 1 ﴾◆

STIRLING BRIDGE AND AFTER

Still hoping he might escape in time to provide information to the Scots, Andrew stayed with Sir Francis and the others into the early evening, listening to developments when they were still fresh, before being contorted by being passed from man to man, adding opinions to the facts. The commanders planned to send troops across the Stirling bridge at dawn; Surrey had at last agreed. Sir Francis was to lead a later crossing. So far Andrew had heard nothing of battles around either Edinburgh or Perth. He prayed that meant Fergus and Margaret were truly safe.

The men were quietly discussing the plans when someone joined the group by the fire. Holm glanced over at him and asked Sir Francis who it was.

'Sir Simon Montagu,' said Francis. 'We conferred at Soutra. He's been biding at the castle. Let's hear what he has to say of the situation up there.'

Andrew wanted to slip away, not eager to meet Ada de la Haye's former lover again. The fewer Englishmen who knew him and where he'd been posted the better; especially now that his hope for escape was stirring.

But he ducked too late.

'Father Andrew? Well, I'd not thought to meet you again so

soon,' said Sir Simon. He crouched down by Andrew, the firelight adding menacing shadows to his face.

'He agreed to come as chaplain for my men, a sudden change in plan,' said Sir Francis. 'I thank God for him. He's kept my men from despair.'

'That's more than the priests of Holy Rude have managed in Stirling,' said Simon, studying Andrew's face. 'Murders abound in the town. The townspeople have all gone mad. Your sister is there, Father, did you know? Margaret. She's a beautiful widow – my son Peter might be a good match for her.'

Knowing full well that Simon was trying to goad him into responding inappropriately for his post, Andrew asked merely, 'Margaret is widowed? What happened to Roger Sinclair?' while his mind was frantic with concern. What was she doing in Stirling of all places, and being courted by Sir Simon's son?

'He met an unfortunate accident while spying on Stirling Castle for the traitor Robert Bruce. Fell from a rock, hit his head, broke his neck.'

'May he rest in peace,' Andrew murmured, crossing himself and keeping his eyes lowered. It was not good that Simon Montagu knew of Roger's alliance.

'Your sister is here with an old friend of mine, Ada de la Haye. Peter is our son.'

Andrew ignored the scenarios vying for attention, needing a clear head. 'I pray I have the opportunity to see her after the battle,' he said. *I pray for her*, he silently added.

With that Simon seemed to become bored with the sport and withdrew.

'I am sorry to hear of your sister's loss,' said Francis. 'No matter how ill-advised her husband's loyalties, it is sad news for you, too.'

'I should pray for her,' said Andrew.

'I understand.'

Rising, Andrew made a show of yawning and excused himself. 'If there is to be battle tomorrow, all the sinners in the camp will find their way to me tonight. I must catch sleep when I can.'

All but Sir Simon bade him a good night.

Ada had never witnessed Celia so withdrawn. She could not get a word out of her regarding Margaret's collapse. Maus thought she'd seen them coming from the neighbour's house, but Celia would not even verify that, going about her tasks pinched-faced and pale. It had been late morning when Margaret rushed through the hall and up to her bed; it was now mid afternoon and Celia was a cipher, though she had assisted Ada in sewing Peter into his shroud. Only then had she spoken, and only to say, 'This minds me of the night my mistress opened Master Jack's shroud.'

'Roger's cousin?' He'd been murdered in Edinburgh while searching for Roger and his body had been taken home to Dame Katherine in Dunfermline for burial. 'Maggie opened his shroud?'

Celia nodded. 'She knew something wasn't right. That was the beginning, I think.'

'Of what?' Ada had asked.

Celia had shrugged and gone silent. Maddening woman. Ada knew the moment she'd seen the dark, tiny maid that she would be difficult. Small people often made up for their lack of size in the strength of their will, and she'd seen that strength in Celia's strong brows and clear, dark eyes. But she had proven her worth, standing by Maggie in some harrowing times, so Ada kept her mouth shut and let the woman be. Perhaps Maggie was simply that worried about James's joining the battle.

It was to be a day of aggravating servants, Ada thought, when John asked if Archie would be departing soon.

'Is that a request?' Ada snapped.

'As he gains strength he's eating more and more,' said John. 'We have food for a week, perhaps a fortnight if we can barter for some oats that cook could grind into cakes. They'll not let us off this cursed rock to seek out fresh supplies – we've tried. We're trapped here. I hadn't planned for a siege.'

'We've food only for a week despite my eating every evening at the castle?' Ada did not believe it. 'You just want him gone.'

John denied it.

Ada knew the English had commandeered all the food for miles around, and she'd begun to feel they were as trapped as if under siege, but she wasn't going to concede to a servant's demands.

It was late afternoon when Margaret at last wandered into the hall looking like a wraith, her curly red hair loose like a caplet over her shoulders, her shift sleeves lacking their outer covering. Her appearance was not inappropriate when there were no guests, but it was very unlike Maggie. Celia hurried after her with sleeves in hand.

'I'll not wear Peter's blood,' said Maggie, pushing the sleeves away.

Ada shook her head when Celia appealed to her. 'Let her be. Archie won't mind her without decorative sleeves.' Noticing that Margaret seemed confused by her surroundings, Ada put an arm around her and guided her to a chair a little away from the fire, out of Archie's sight – the young man was sitting up today and quite curious about the household.

'What happened, Maggie?' Ada asked under her breath. 'You are behaving – well, I almost think Christiana has taken your form.'

Margaret sank back in the chair, eyes fixed on the ceiling, and breathed deeply.

'Can I bring you something?' Ada asked.

'A sip of brandywine, if you can spare it, and then I'll be myself again, I promise.' Margaret glanced down at the hair spilling across her shoulder. Pulling on a tress, she said, 'Sweet heaven, Celia will have a fit about my unbound hair and no sleeves.' Apparently she'd not noticed her maid shadowing her.

'What happened this morning?' Ada asked. 'You looked even worse than when you spoke to Ranald.'

Taking Ada's hand, Margaret affectionately squeezed it. 'I'll tell you all in exchange for some brandywine.'

Ada did not know what to make of Margaret's behaviour.

Gradually Margaret felt coherent enough to look outward and trust that she was seeing with her own eyes. By the expression on the face of her good and loyal friend, she knew that she must at last explain her behaviour to Ada. She needed to know that the Sight had come to Margaret, and that she was struggling to learn how to use it and how to live with it. It was plain that she'd frightened both of them, for Celia had heard quite a lot at the Allans's house.

They sat up in the solar, just the three of them, talking softly. At first it was mostly Margaret who spoke, telling them of the beginnings before they left Perth, Dame Bethag's advice, how frightened and lost she'd been as she rode towards Stirling.

'I have wondered what was bothering you ever since you told me of the owl,' said Ada. 'Roger's death – how horrible to dream of it. I wish you had told me.'

'There is nothing you could have done for me, my friend, just as I've never been able to help Ma.'

'Father Piers guessed that you had the Sight that day when you asked about the clothing in his parlour,' Ada remembered. 'I've been so blind.'

'I wanted you to be,' Margaret assured her.

She told them of her fear for Johanna, and how it had brought her to Johanna's house, but too late.

'Why have you seen nothing about her murderer?' Ada asked, sounding as frustrated as Margaret felt. 'Have you no idea who beat that poor woman?'

Margaret shook her head. 'I know it's difficult to understand, but the Sight seems to choose what it reveals – or God chooses.'

She told them of her growing obsession with the Allans, and the question about Huchon's ring that she'd asked Ranald without knowing why.

'Poor Lilias Allan. What was Peter thinking, to insist they watch? And to wear that damned ring!' Ada growled.

'He might not have known whose it was,' Margaret said. 'In truth I doubt he could have. Why would Gordon tell him? But it is returned to the Allans now.' She bowed her head. 'I have prayed and prayed that the Sight is God's gift, and not a curse.'

Celia looked up from her work. 'I am sure it is God's work, Mistress.' She had been quiet until now, delicately scraping the last traces of blood from Margaret's sleeves. 'What you did for Lilias Allan was a blessing for her. You drew her out of the despair that threatened her soul's salvation.'

'Perhaps God has yet some information about Johanna to give us,' said Ada. 'It is not right that such a murder go unpunished.'

'The English don't care about her death,' said Margaret. 'She was unimportant.'

'I know. But I do. My situation with Simon was not so different from hers with Rob.'

'He hurt you deeply.' Margaret took Ada's hand.

'Perhaps his punishment will be to never know Peter's fate,' said Ada. 'That will give him pain, I know it will.'

'If he returns, will you not tell him?' Celia asked. 'Someone will surely notice the burial.'

'If Simon returns to Stirling we'll have far more serious concerns,' said Ada, 'for that will mean our people have lost the battle.' She shook her head. 'As for telling Simon about Peter, I shall know what to say when he asks. I always do.'

'I wonder about Johanna's English lover,' said Celia, 'what Rob's fate will be – or has been.'

'I've wondered that, too' said Ada. 'I should have thought they'd make an example of him.'

'Like poor Huchon Allan,' said Celia. 'Only her lover Rob did not know he was committing treason.'

'Then he was a fool,' said Ada.

Margaret wondered at the turn in the conversation. Her friends seemed to have accepted the change in her and gone on to other concerns. But then she hadn't told them of her bargain with the Sight. By following it, she had done some good, so she intended to keep her vow to seek out Euphemia when she was free to do so. That would not be received without argument. She expected Ada and Celia to try to persuade her not to take such a radical step. For now she was relieved that they knew, and grateful that they accepted her as she was.

At dawn the noise of men arming and gathering to march woke Andrew and Matthew, though it was not their camp on the move. Word passed through the camps that some infantry had been sent over the bridge. The battle had begun. Andrew soon found himself surrounded by soldiers wanting his blessing. It was not only Sir Francis's men, but many of those who had stopped him as he moved through the camps a few days earlier with Pete and Will.

'Do they think your blessing will make the arrows and axes glance off them?' Matthew asked.

'For a man who cannot learn his letters, you are a canny one, Matthew,' Andrew said.

'I pray they don't come after us when their comrades are killed,' said Matthew.

Andrew was finally eating some hard bread soaked in watered ale when Holm arrived, cursing and kicking at anything in his path. The infantry that had been sent over Stirling Bridge had been called back because Surrey had overslept and was furious that someone else had ordered the battle begun. Andrew feared Holm would end up killing one of his own men, but he eventually gained control of himself, though he was anything but calm.

The news was enough to sow panic in the camp. Andrew had never seen men so agitated as the soldiers were now. Rumours abounded – that Wallace had fierce highlanders waiting to pick them off from beneath the bridge, that sea monsters were heading upriver from the firth – and fights broke out as fear frayed tempers.

'If King Edward were here he'd have Surrey's head, and ride with it into battle,' said Sir Francis, already looking spent and anxious. 'I've never known such incompetence. I have a bad feeling about this day, Andrew. Pray for us.' They had been ordered to the bridge once more, and this time troops seemed to be crossing.

Andrew blessed him, and was choked with sorrow as he watched Sir Francis ride off, leading his men into the chaos. Andrew might be free now, but he respected Sir Francis and had grown fond of many of the men who had come to him for absolution and guidance. He wished he were ministering to the army of his own cause, but that did not make him hate these men. This was a war begun by a king who had sucked the heart out of Wales and now intended to do so here in Scotland. It angered Andrew that a king's lust for power had forced men to take sides against their fellows with whom they had no personal argument. He prayed that Sir Francis, his men, and all the men he had met here might pass this day unharmed, but he did not have much hope. There was a witless feel to the movement of the troops.

When they were alone except for servants and camp followers, Andrew and Matthew packed their few belongings, adding some of the dwindling provisions, and headed up the hill to Stirling. He might be surer of escape by heading into the countryside, but he was worried about Maggie. His heart lifted a little with the thought of seeing her. But Matthew was muttering prayers beneath his breath as they climbed.

Andrew tried to distract him with talk about what they'd missed most since leaving Holyrood Abbey.

'The bed I thought so hard,' said Matthew.

'I miss the quiet work of copying out a letter in my best hand,' said Andrew, surprising himself with fond memories of the cloister.

'The singing,' said Matthew. 'And the food.'

They had eaten well at Holyrood.

'How will we find Dame Margaret?' asked Matthew as houses began to appear.

'Quiet, Matthew,' said Andrew, catching sight of guards ahead. 'We're headed for the kirk. We know no one in the town.'

'Halt! What do you want in the town?' one of the men demanded. He looked more frightened than fierce.

'I am Father Andrew, late of the Hospital of the Trinity on Soutra Hill. My servant and I have been travelling long with the troops and our supplies are gone. We would take communion wafers from the kirk here to the men below, for their blessings before the battle.'

'How goes it below, Father?' the other asked.

'Our men have begun crossing the river. Wallace and Murray will be only now seeing how great a host comes after them.'

The frightened one made a noise that might have been a chuckle. 'You may go on through,' he said, 'but without weapons.'

The other moved forward to search them.

'We have nothing but our small knives for the table, I assure you.'

The guards stepped aside, letting them pass.

'Just two of them?' Matthew whispered as they moved on.

Andrew shook his head. 'Behind the house there were more, ready to ambush us at a signal. God is watching over us.'

The streets were almost deserted, and the few folk they encountered averted their eyes when they saw strangers. Andrew headed for the kirk.

An elderly priest greeted them in the nave.

'We had no word of a priest visiting,' said Father John. He seemed to be supervising the cleaning of a chantry chapel; it looked as though someone had been living there.

'Sanctuary?' Andrew guessed.

The old priest looked uncomfortable.

275

Andrew quickly explained who he was.

With a sigh of relief, Father John relaxed. 'Dame Maggie, yes, she is biding with Ada de la Haye.' He nodded. 'I can direct you there. But tell me, how did you find your way here? The English surround us.'

'With care,' said Andrew, softening the curt answer with a smile. 'Is there a place my servant and I might stay tonight?'

'You'll want to ask Father Piers,' said John. 'I am his assistant; I make no decisions.' He led them across the kirk yard to the rectory where a clerk said that Father Piers was at prayer.

'I know that,' said John. 'Tell him that Father Andrew, Dame Maggie's brother, is here. He's made it through the English down below and deserves a welcome.'

Andrew thanked the elderly priest.

The clerk looked interested. 'You've been down there, Father?'

Andrew nodded. 'And if I lodge here tonight I'll have a tale or two for you.'

He and Matthew were soon invited to lodge with the priests; once relieved of their things they headed to Ada's house. Andrew was not yet saying prayers of thanks for deliverance. Not until he was safely beneath Ada's roof and knew his sister safe.

'Andrew!' Maggie cried, running to him as the butler showed him in to the hall. 'I can't believe it's you. I've prayed and prayed for you.' Her hug was fierce, as if she intended never to let him go.

'I've heard about Roger,' he whispered before they parted. 'I am sorry, Maggie.'

She stepped away, wiping her eyes, but remembering her duty she welcomed Matthew. 'Let us sit.' She led them to some benches away from the fire, where a young man lay on a pallet, but they had little time alone. Indeed, he learned only that their father had returned from Bruges and was lodging at Elcho Nunnery, hoping to win their mother back to the marriage bed.

He was still puzzling over that when Ada entered, and then her maid. Gradually the entire household joined them, wanting to hear of the battle below. They were all disappointed that he'd left the camps before there was any news to tell. Andrew reclaimed a little of their interest by describing the confusion before the battle and the guards halfway down the hill.

'Do you think our men have a chance?' Ada asked.

'More than a chance,' said Andrew. 'Surrey behaves as if he is fighting against idiots, and that his mere presence will send terror through the ranks of his opponents. We all know that isn't true – and so do the other English commanders.'

'Then why are you not smiling, Father?' asked Sandy.

'Because I have come to know the men I served, and most are good men who will be much mourned, just as those who may be lost to us this day.'

On that dour note the servants dispersed, making excuses about work that needed doing.

'I should leave you two in peace,' said Ada to Andrew and Maggie. 'Matthew, why don't you come out to the kitchen?'

Suddenly Andrew and Maggie were alone in the hall except for the young man by the fire.

'Who is he?' Andrew asked.

'Archie,' said Maggie. 'I'll explain about him later, after you've told me about your time at Soutra and the English camps. You've had such an adventure.'

'I might call it many things, but not adventure, Maggie. Still, it wasn't so horrible at Soutra.' He told her about his friendship with Father Obert, and how he had arranged for Andrew's release. 'Now it's your turn, Maggie. How did you come to be here, in the centre of the fighting?'

'I came as a spy for James Comyn. To find out why his messenger had faltered.' She nodded towards the young man by the fire.

'Damn him! Why didn't Comyn send his own kinswoman into danger – why you?'

Andrew realised he'd said the wrong thing even before Maggie snapped, 'I chose to come, Andrew.'

What a stubborn lass she was still. 'Aye, for you didn't understand what you'd risk.'

'I'm no one's fool.' She said it with a quiet authority.

Andrew, remembering their arguments in Edinburgh, saw how much she had matured. 'At least you've had Ada,' he said. 'She's a one for keeping misfortune at bay.'

But he was playing his old role with her. In truth he was feeling oddly numbed. It seemed as if he'd been moving through a dream since he'd left the camp, and he half believed that he was in the battle down below and was cruelly teasing himself with thoughts of freedom.

'What is it, Andrew? What's wrong?'

He tried to describe what he was feeling.

'I should have guessed,' said Maggie, 'after what you said earlier, about them being good men. This is the sort of thing I want to understand, Andrew. This struggle has taken over our lives. I want to understand it.'

'For that you'd need to talk to Balliol, Bruce and Longshanks.' All at once Andrew was overcome by the thought of the lives that might be lost by twilight. 'God help us.'

'What can I bring you? We have a little ale left, and cheese and–'

Andrew held up his hands to stop her litany. 'My body is fine, Maggie. We brought some provisions from the camp, and I shall dine with Fathers Piers and John tonight. I understand that food is in short supply in town.'

Maggie smiled at herself, and in that moment she was lovelier than ever. 'I'm forgetting that you're no longer the skinny boy who had to be coaxed into sitting still and completing a meal. I'm just so happy you are here. I feared so for you.'

Despite her smile Andrew saw a great sadness in her eyes, and taking her hand he told her again how sorry he was about Roger.

She took a deep breath and bowed her head. 'I was unkind to him when last I saw him. It's difficult to forgive myself.'

'God would have reunited you if that was meant to be, Maggie. You risked your life to find Roger – that required more love than most wives are ever asked to give. Remember that.' He kissed her hand and pulled her to him, kissing her forehead and holding her tightly for a while as she silently wept.

The moment was interrupted by knocking at the door. The butler emerged from somewhere in the hall – Andrew wondered how he had managed to be so invisible – and opened the door to a tiny woman.

'I would sit with my son for a while,' she said.

Maggie nodded to the butler, 'Evota is welcome, John.'

As the woman entered the room she noticed Andrew and almost stumbled. While she gazed on him he was struck by the hardness of her eyes, as if she had closed them against intruders. He wondered what had made her so fearful of others.

Ada joined them. 'Maggie will tell me all you've told her, I know, but I must ask how you knew we were here, Andrew.'

'Sir Simon Montagu had a word with me last night.'

Ada winced at the mention of his name.

'Simon,' said Maggie. 'I hadn't thought to ask how you knew.'

'It was he who told me of Roger's death, suggesting that your son Peter might find Maggie a good match. I don't mean to insult you, but he made it seem a threat.'

Ada crossed herself. 'My son.' She glanced at Maggie questioningly.

'We've not yet spoken of him,' said Maggie.

Something had both women holding their breath.

'Has he tried to force the match?' asked Andrew.

'Let's go without, get some air,' Maggie suggested, nodding

towards Evota and Archie, who were quietly pretending not to listen.

'Yes,' said Ada. 'I have a favour to ask of you, Andrew.'

By now it was early afternoon, and shouts and a steady roar came from down below. The battle must be engaged. Andrew crossed himself and prayed for the souls of those who were falling. Ada and Maggie had paused at the sounds and crossed themselves as well, both bowing to pray. They were all one in this moment, shocked by the nearness of death.

The women set two benches in the shade beneath the eaves, away from the door and the one tiny window that looked out on to the kitchen and beyond to the backlands.

In daylight Andrew noticed with some surprise that Ada had at last begun to age beyond the whitening of her hair. Fine lines encircled her mouth and eyes, and her flesh had sagged a little. He wondered if his mother, too, was showing her age.

It was Ada who began. 'I bore five children, four to Simon Montagu. Peter is the only one of my adult children I've met, and I will always regret that I did. He might yet be alive had I not come to Stirling.'

'That is not true,' Maggie interjected, and Andrew could see by the way she sat forward that she was impatient for Ada to come to the point.

But Andrew thought she had. 'Your son is dead?' he asked.

Ada dropped her gaze to her lap, where she was clasping her hands together so tightly that her fingernails were white. 'Murdered. Just without this house. The boy inside fought with him, Peter withdrew to the garden shed, and while he lay there he was stabbed in the heart.'

Andrew was caught off guard by her bluntness. 'God grant him peace,' he whispered, and then looked up at the sky, trying to think of something comforting to say to her, but he could only wonder at their kindness to the man's murderer. 'Archie followed and killed him?'

'No,' said Maggie. 'I don't think Archie killed him.'

'Have you asked?'

'Archie's leg was broken, Andrew. He could not have been near the shed after that.'

'Would you say Peter's requiem, Andrew? It would mean so much to me if you would.' Ada was looking at him, her face composed. 'Please don't feel that you need to comfort me, for I did not like him. He caused much grief here in Stirling and no doubt elsewhere as well.'

'But Sir Simon spoke as if Peter were alive,' said Andrew.

'He does not know. I feared what he would do, whom he would blame.'

'Where is your son now?'

'At the kirk.'

'Why did Archie attack your son?'

'Peter controlled Archie's family with fear,' said Maggie. 'And Archie suspected him of murdering the woman he loved.'

Andrew looked from one to the other. 'You've witnessed more horror here than I have while travelling with an army.'

Neither woman responded.

'Well if Archie didn't strike the mortal blow, who did?' Andrew asked.

'Archie's sister told me that Roger's partner was looking for Peter that night,' said Maggie.

'Roger's partner?'

As Maggie explained who Aylmer was, Andrew thought that he did not know half of what his sister had suffered since she'd seen him off to Soutra.

He turned to Ada. 'Certainly I will say Peter's requiem.'

'God bless you, Andrew,' said Ada.

Maggie leaned over and kissed him on the cheek.

They talked a little more about family matters, Maggie telling Andrew how Fergus had carried a message to Murray. 'James says he is fighting with Wallace this day, and Hal as well.'

'Uncle Murdoch's groom?' Andrew asked.

Maggie nodded. 'He's gifted with animals.'

'Uncle must have been furious when he left.'

'Only because he'll worry,' said Maggie. 'He thinks of Hal as his son.'

'What will you do now, Maggie? If we don't win the day, if the English release the guard on the town, will you stay here?'

'We'll talk of that by and by,' she said.

James Comyn had plans for her, Andrew imagined.

'What will *you* do, Andrew?' Ada asked. 'Will you return to Sir Francis?'

'He'll have no need of me. I don't know what I'll do. I thought I'd seek Bishop Wishart's advice.' The bishop of Glasgow made no effort to hide his animosity towards Edward Longshanks. 'I believe he'll sympathise with my estrangement from my abbot.'

'I still fear Abbot Adam,' said Maggie. 'Is the bishop—'

She was interrupted by a shriek. It came from the house. The servants went running towards it from the kitchen. Maggie was the first to follow. Andrew and Ada were right behind her.

The scene in the hall was very confused by the time they reached it. John knelt beside the shrieking Evota, who appeared to be bleeding from her shoulder. Archie was on the floor near her, moaning and kneading his injured leg with one hand, while in the other, which was held in the air by Sandy, he clutched a knife.

'He's gone mad,' Evota sobbed. 'My poor boy, the head wound has addled his wits. He tried to kill me!'

'Murderer!' Archie shouted. 'Show her no pity, the murdering whore. She killed Johanna. Ask her. Ask her, Father! She'll not lie to a priest.'

'God help us,' Maggie whispered. 'Can it be true?'

Celia had knelt down by Evota to examine the wound. 'It is not deep. You are in no danger,' she told the woman.

Andrew crouched down beside her. 'What is your son talking about?'

The woman looked up at Celia. 'But the blood!'

'It is the sort of wound that bleeds freely, Evota, but it is far from mortal,' Celia assured her.

'Celia, come away,' Maggie said. 'Let Andrew talk to her.'

The maid left with a sigh of frustration. 'I'll fetch a rag to staunch the flow.'

'I tell you he's confused,' Evota said.

'Why would your son call you a murderer?' Andrew asked. 'Who was Johanna?'

Sandy had taken the knife from Archie and let him go. Maggie now knelt by him.

'My leg,' he moaned, 'I think it's broken again.'

She and Sandy helped him back to the pallet.

'Why do you think your mother killed Johanna?' Maggie asked him.

'She told me. Just now. She was trying to make me understand what she'd done, how it was for our family, but you saw what she'd done, you *saw* Johanna. They said her head was beaten in. *She* did that, the bitch who calls herself my mother.'

'We've got to live, you stupid boy,' Evota cried. 'You were paid good money by Father Piers. We depended on that. Your sister had to go whoring because Johanna rejected you and then you'd have naught to do with her. You good-for-nothing lovesick ass!'

Andrew looked up at Maggie. 'Do you understand what they're talking about?'

'Yes.' She closed her eyes. 'Poor Johanna.'

Andrew took the wounded woman by the chin and held her so that she must look at him. 'Did you beat a woman to death?'

Evota whimpered. 'All I asked her was to favour Archie, sleep with him – she'd slept with all the soldiers at the castle, why not my son? Then he would go back to work as a messenger.'

'Selfish cow,' Archie shouted. 'Johanna wasn't like that.'

'She wouldn't agree?' Andrew asked quietly.

'She hit me. Hard. On the mouth. And she said she'd tell Father Piers and wouldn't use Archie any more. They'd find another messenger. My son wasn't good enough for her, the whore. He wasn't English, that's what she meant.'

Andrew let her go and drew away from her, sickened by the hatred in her eyes, her voice. The young man was sobbing. When Maggie looked up, her face was wet with tears, too.

'What should we do with them?' Ada wondered aloud. 'I don't want them here. Who is the law in the town now?'

Andrew shook his head. 'There is none.'

Celia had brought a bowl of water and some rags, and now knelt to Evota, who stared at the ceiling wide-eyed, breathing in a laboured wheeze.

'Go for Dame Bridget,' said Maggie to Sandy. 'I don't know what to do for Archie's leg.' She rose and joined Andrew and Ada.

'Had you any sense of her guilt, Maggie?' Ada asked.

'When she was startled to see a priest here in the hall, I wondered, but anyone might have,' said Maggie.

'Was this Johanna the woman over whom Peter and Archie fought?' Andrew asked.

Ada nodded. She looked spent.

'Was she a friend of yours, Maggie?' Andrew was still trying to grasp all the implications of what had just transpired.

'She was the source for the messages Archie carried to James's men, which is why we met.' She explained about Johanna's English lover. 'When she met me, I knew she was in danger, but I didn't know whence came the threat, and I didn't know what to do.'

'Of course she was in danger,' Andrew said. 'But if anyone was responsible for that it's James Comyn, using her as he did.'

'He's forced no one to fight for his kinsman, Andrew. Johanna wanted to do something for the cause.'

'So why do you feel guilty?'

'I told you, I kenned she was in danger, but I didn't know what to do with the knowledge.' Her voice had risen and she pressed a hand to either side of her wimple as if trying to close her ears to some noise. 'I don't understand how to use the Sight.'

'My God, Maggie.' Andrew reached her in two steps and laid his hands gently on hers. 'The Sight? Tell me you're not accursed with it.' But he knew by the suffering he sensed in her and the fear in her eyes that she was.

'I pray it's God's gift,' she said. 'I pray He'll show me how I might use it for good.'

Ada had gone over to the wounded woman. 'Take her home, John. Let her daughter tend to her. We'll get no justice for Johanna by hanging this woman. Dame Bridget will advise us where Archie might go. I'm sick of them.'

Maggie broke away from Andrew. 'The war has done this to them, Ada. They would have done none of this if Longshanks hadn't torn apart their lives.'

'You don't know that, Maggie.'

Maggie turned back to Andrew. 'You must feel you've walked into a house of madness.'

'How could this town be otherwise, trapped between the castle and the camps?' He put his arm around her. 'How long have you known about the Sight, Maggie?'

'Not long. Only you, Ada and Celia know. And Ma, I think. I'm going to Great-Aunt Euphemia, if I can. I want to learn about it, not let it destroy me like it has Ma. Let's not talk of it any more today.'

Thank God. Andrew did not think he could bear more.

~§ 14 ₹~

RESOLUTIONS

Far off shouts and shrieks rendered the late September day the tinge of horror, as Margaret sat in the backland with Ada and Andrew. The delicate brandywine did little to ease the tension and chill that lingered after John led Evota away and Archie was moved out of the house to the kitchen. Celia was supervising the removal of the bloodstains in the hall, but no one could ever erase Margaret's memory of Johanna's suffering. She doubted Archie would ever forgive his mother; at least he had been spared the sight of what she'd done to his beloved.

Andrew's encounter with the guards below had frightened Margaret. She prayed that James had managed to outwit them. She prayed for him, Fergus and Hal, and William Wallace, whom she'd found a kind, noble man. She wondered what the future held, what defeat might mean to all of them.

What had begun as a happy reunion was now not ruined, but subdued. The town was very quiet, though now and then she and her companions lifted their heads as folk who'd been watching the battle from the heights wandered home loudly sharing the hopeful, yet horrible news that the English were being slaughtered and being left to die in the carse, and their survivors retreating.

'Is it possible?' Margaret asked Andrew.

He looked drained by the confrontation between mother and son. 'Nothing is impossible, Maggie. It is God's to choose the outcome, though it is mankind's sorry way to play it out by killing their own.'

'I know that this is an important battle,' said Ada, 'but Longshanks has never been a man to accept defeat. I fear for us even if we win the day.'

Margaret looked to Andrew, who looked away.

'Tell us about the journey from Soutra Hill,' Ada suggested. 'Are the fields ready for harvest?'

'It was a ghost land,' Andrew began, but the clatter of horses out in the square distracted them, and all three hastened out to the street, fearing trouble. Most of the household were already there. In fact, townsfolk lined the square.

Andrew craned his head to see the approaching troop. 'That's Sir Marmaduke Twenge,' he said, pointing out a man who was clad in armour and riding a destrier.

The soldiers riding and walking behind him were bloodied and wore expressions that were a mixture of exhaustion and defeat. One dismounted in the market square, looking around at the houses as if uncertain where to go, and then approached Margaret.

'I bear a message for Ada de la Haye.'

Ada stepped forward. 'I am Dame Ada.'

The soldier bobbed his head to her. 'Sir Simon Montagu sends greetings. He requests that if his son returns to Stirling you tell him that his father has ridden south and will not be returning.'

'Simon survived,' said Ada, crossing herself. 'Is the battle over? Did– Who won?'

The messenger looked around, and seeing none of his fellows within hearing, said, 'We are routed. The Earl of Surrey has raced south. Sir Marmaduke says the day went badly because some men are fools. Sir Hugh Cressingham, the Treasurer, was torn to pieces and many, many Englishmen lie dead in the swampy ground across the bridge. Pray for us.' He bowed to her again and turned his horse towards the castle.

'May God grant them eternal peace,' Andrew said.

'God speed,' said Ada.

Margaret did not think she meant the messenger.

'Why have the English gone to the castle?' Celia asked.

'If the bridge is lost to them, they can at least hold the castle as before,' said Andrew. 'This is one battle won by our side, not the war.'

He sounded so very weary. 'Perhaps you should rest, Andrew,' Margaret suggested.

'No, I can't rest yet. I'm as eager to hear more as anyone. I'm better here with you.'

The townsfolk lingered in the square for a long while afterwards, waiting for more troops to arrive, sharing gossip. Suddenly cries rang out and the pounding of men running up the steep street from below echoed against the buildings.

'It's a rout!' a man down towards Bow Street shouted.

As the panting, sweat-soaked men appeared Andrew crossed himself. 'The guards from below,' he said.

'Praise God,' Ada cried.

A cheer went up as the runners began to collapse and their pursuers arrived, wielding swords. Margaret cried out at the first blow and buried her face in her brother's shoulder.

'We'd do more good in prayer,' he said.

'Come, all of you,' Ada commanded.

The women retreated into the house, and without a word Celia and Maus fetched the paternoster beads. By the time they knelt near the fire Matthew, Sandy, John and cook joined them. Soon Alec appeared, ashen faced.

'They murdered them all,' he said, 'right there where they lay.' Pressing his hand to his mouth, he hurried out the rear door.

'The killing is hard to stop once it begins,' said Sandy. 'I've seen it before. We're no better than them, once it starts.'

They all bowed their heads.

Images of terrible suffering and death filled Margaret's head. She prayed that it was her imagination and not the Sight. A marsh awash in blood, arms reaching out, imploring, weapons caked in blood and worse, a terrible stench, flies thick on the bodies. Suddenly she straightened with a kenning that drew her to her feet. She was already walking towardss the door when the knock came, heavy and insistent. Crossing herself, she took a deep breath and opened the door.

All she saw at first was Fergus, her brother, his head lolling to one side, his eyes unfocused. 'Dear God in heaven!' she cried, reaching for him, stroking his bloody cheek. 'Fergus,' she moaned, 'not you. Dear God.'

'Maggie, step aside. We'll carry Fergus in,' someone said.

Behind her, Ada cried out for a pallet by the fire, water and rags.

Andrew gently drew Margaret aside. Two muddy, bloodied men carried Fergus upright towards the fire.

'His feet are moving,' Margaret whispered, realising that Fergus was trying to walk. Celia put a cup to her lips. A mouthful of brandywine steadied Margaret.

Moving closer her heart leapt as she recognised James beneath the grime. Free now of Fergus, who had been eased down on to the pallet and was already being tended by Maus and Ada, James approached Margaret, but stopped short of her.

'I am filthy. Hal found me and together we pulled Fergus from the marsh. If Hal had not seen him fall beneath the English knight's warhorse–' James glanced back at the group before the fire.

Andrew was now kneeling beside his brother, making the sign of the cross on his forehead with oil.

Margaret reached for James's hands and waited until he looked her in the eyes. 'How serious are his wounds?' she asked.

He shook his head. 'I don't know, Maggie. He's lost much blood. I think some ribs are broken. He's not spoken, nor can he

walk on his own. But I don't know the extent of his injuries. All
Hal and I thought was to bring him here. I pray we did the right
thing.'

He kissed Margaret's hands. 'I must sit down.'

'Of course. I'll fetch something to drink.'

But Celia was already there with Ada's flask and cups. Hal had
taken a cup and withdrawn to one side of the fire, looking on with
dead eyes.

Margaret went to him. 'Your hair,' she said, 'you've cut it away
from your eyes.' His straight, fair hair had always fallen down over
his eyes. He'd had a habit of speaking down to his shoes, never
making eye contact.

He reached to push back what wasn't there. 'James said the
Wallace wanted to see the eyes of his men.'

Margaret took his hand. 'God bless you for watching over my
brother.'

'He'd've done the same for me, Dame Margaret.'

'Maggie, call me Maggie,' she said. 'And you? Are you injured?'

He shook his head. 'Bruises, scratches, naught else. I am sorry
about your husband.'

'Much has happened in the month since we parted, Hal. It's as
if a lifetime has gone by.'

'I know.'

Although it seemed a silly concern when so many men had
died, Margaret asked: 'Where is Mungo?' He was Fergus's dog,
who'd accompanied him to Aberdeen.

Hal's eyes warmed. 'I've no doubt that Mungo is eating well
down at Cambuskenneth Abbey. We asked the monks if he might
stay there during the battle and they were happy to have him. I'll
bring him here if Fergus–' he dropped his gaze.

'You'll feel better if you wash off some of the marsh,' she
suggested, and went to see about hot water for Hal and James,
who had nodded off on a bench. It felt better to be in motion.

In the late afternoon Ada drew Margaret aside. 'I'm not as

young as I once was,' she said. 'I'll leave you for a while. Fergus will stay here, of course. Hal and James are welcome.'

'I'll attend Peter's requiem with you in the morning.'

Ada kissed her cheek. 'Bless you.'

Margaret sought out Maus and sent her up to Ada; then she went to sit with Fergus. Celia quietly reviewed his condition.

'His head is bruised on the right side. He bled from the ear.'

Margaret gently touched the bandage, then the one on his right side. 'And this?'

'The ribs feel broken and the bruise beneath the skin is so dark we think he's bleeding – there was also some blood from his mouth, but his teeth are all there. His right hip also feels different from the left, and he cried out when Maus cleaned it. We've sent for Dame Bridget. She must have Archer settled by now.'

Margaret sat down beside Fergus, drawing out her beads.

Much later, after Andrew and Matthew had left for the kirk and James had disappeared, promising to return by dawn, Dame Bridget arrived. Celia took the opportunity to coax Margaret to the backlands for some air, and sat with her beneath the starlit sky, listening to the eerie silence. The air was very welcome.

'Fergus has always been so full of life,' Margaret said after a long while. 'It's so hard to see him lying there.'

'He will mend, Mistress,' Celia said. 'He is young, strong, and too full of life to let go so easily.'

'God grant you're right,' Margaret said, rising to return to the hall. She found Hal sitting with Fergus, who had begun to snore. Dame Bridget was mixing something over the fire.

'I've never heard a snore from a dying man,' said Hal. 'It's a good sign.'

He made Margaret smile. 'I miss sitting with you in the stable,' she said. 'I did my best thinking there.'

'I miss Bonny and Agrippa,' said Hal. They were her uncle's donkey and cat. 'But most of all I've missed you, Maggie.'

She found him watching her with such intensity she looked away.

'I know you're with James Comyn now, but I swore to myself that I'd tell you if I saw you again. I love you, Maggie. Just so you ken that – well, if you– *Jesu*, I'm a bloody fool.'

Moved by his unexpected declaration, Margaret couldn't immediately think of a response except, 'You're as far from a fool as anyone I've ever known.'

He was a good man. He'd always been willing to do whatever she asked, with no reward but a thanks, if that, for he'd been her uncle's groom, and when she'd taken charge of the inn he'd become her servant. He'd been resourceful, wise and loyal, and she had counted on him time and again. But she'd never considered falling in love with him. He was her age – young, inexperienced. Of course now they had both been forced to mature quickly.

'Let's go without,' said Margaret. 'Dame Bridget is attending Fergus, and the fire is too hot.'

She watched how wearily Hal moved and hoped some air would calm him enough to sleep.

'You don't know me well, Hal,' she began when they were out beneath the eaves.

'Did Roger?'

The question caught Margaret off guard and she laughed, not a happy laugh. 'No. You probably know more about what I like, what I fear, what I want than Roger ever did.'

Hal stopped, his head tilted, listening. 'It's even quieter now.' He sniffed. 'They're lighting fires down in the valley.'

Margaret closed her eyes. 'I don't want to know what's going on down there. Not right now.'

'Maggie?' a voice came from the wynd.

'James,' Hal said, disappointment clear in his voice.

Two men appeared around the corner of the house, stepping into the pool of light from the lanterns. James had brought Aylmer.

'Dame Margaret,' Aylmer said with a nod of his head.

Margaret rose and forced herself to look into his eyes. 'I heard you'd been kept at the castle.'

James joined her.

Aylmer nodded once. He looked thin and haggard, and instead of cockily meeting her gaze and holding it, he lowered his eyes. This was a changed man.

'Why are you here?' she asked, slipping her arm around James for support.

'I wanted to tell you how sorry Roger was that he'd hurt you, how determined he was to find a way to win you back to him. I was honoured to be his friend, and I made certain that Peter Fitzsimon died knowing it was for Roger's life.'

'Tell me what happened to my husband, Aylmer.'

'Didn't Ellen come to you and explain?'

'I want to hear it from you.'

He described the incident much as Ellen had. 'I have cursed her over and over for choosing to leave just then, but in my heart I know that Fitzsimon would have found another opportunity to kill Roger – he merely took advantage of the moment.'

'So you did kill Peter. How did you find him?'

'I was watching for him, but that lad was faster – Ellen's brother, mad as a hatter to take on a fighter of Fitzsimon's skill, I thought. But he gave it his all and managed to badly injure him. I let Fitzsimon crawl to the shed and get some rest. I wanted him quite clear in the head when I killed him. I wanted him to hear me when I told him why he was dying.'

Margaret bowed her head. 'I suppose I should thank you,' she said when she'd recovered her voice. 'For Peter, and for sending Ellen to me.'

Now Aylmer looked up. 'He disgusted me, how he preyed on her family.'

She nodded. 'What will you do now?'

'Return to the Bruce, tell him how the battle went, what a fool

Surrey proved to be, how worthy Wallace and Murray are.'

'I hesitate to invite you into the hall,' said Margaret. 'Because of Ada . . .'

Aylmer nodded. 'James told me that Fitzsimon was the son of the mistress of the house. I'll not disturb her. I've done what I came to do.'

She stepped out of James's arms and took one of Aylmer's hands in both of hers. 'God go with you, Aylmer. Thank you.'

He bowed to her and withdrew. When he'd disappeared down the wynd, James said, 'He's a good man.'

Margaret nodded. 'You will fight together.'

'What?' James looked baffled.

She had not intended to tell him so soon, but her heart was so full she had no room for lies.

'The moment you said he was a good man, I saw you with him. As if I'd moved forward in time. You will fight alongside him.'

James glanced back to the wynd, then stepped closer to Margaret, putting a hand on each shoulder and looking into her eyes. 'You have the Sight.'

'I do.'

'How long have you known?' His tone was almost accusing.

'I'm not sure – I did not want it. But I saw Roger's death long before you told me of it.'

James shook his head as he stepped back. 'God's blood, Maggie.' He sank down on one of the benches beneath the eaves and put his head in his hands.

Margaret remembered Hal and looked around, but he had vanished. She sat down beside James.

'Murray is badly wounded,' said James, lifting his head. 'Things will fall heavily on William's shoulders now. But Lennox and Stewart hid in the woods near the pows and followed the English as they retreated. So the nobles are openly supporting William now.'

'Then there is hope.'

James nodded. 'And much to do. Are you– Will you still work with me?'

'When I am ready, I will, Jamie.' Margaret turned to look at him. 'This is a power that must be guided. I must learn how to do that.'

'Your mother never did.'

'No. But I shall. I'll seek out Great-Aunt Euphemia. Ma fought learning from her, but I intend to learn. I'll not let it ruin my life, make me a shade of what I might be, a pawn for someone to manipulate.'

'You'll go off to the west? Now?'

'When Fergus is recovered.'

'I must stay with William,' James said.

'I know, Jamie.'

'What of Dame Katherine, Roger's Ma? Will you not go to her?'

'Yes, Celia and I will go there together, and then I'll leave Celia with her.'

'You'll go alone to – where is Euphemia?'

'Kilmartin.'

'You can't go alone!'

'I won't. I'll find an escort.'

James rose. 'We'll talk of this later.' He leaned down, tilted her chin and kissed her. 'I love you, Maggie. We'll find a way through all this.'

'I pray that we do.'

He sighed. 'But there is work to be done. I understand Andrew is at the kirk. I want to know what he's seen.'

'Go. I'll sit here a while longer.'

He drew her up to him and held her tightly. 'We *will* find a way to be together, Maggie.'

For the first time, Margaret believed that might be true. 'God watch over you, my Jamie,' she whispered.

When he was gone, Margaret sat down, leaning her head against the wall of the house and closed her eyes, waiting for her head to stop spinning.

Someone sat down beside her and took her hand.

'Oh, Hal, it's all a muddle,' she moaned, falling into her old easiness with him. 'Did I ever tell you that my ma has the Sight?'

'Murdoch talked of it. He thought she was mad.'

'I wonder what he'd say if he heard I have it?'

'He'd tell you to make use of it.'

'You're right. That's just what he'd say.'

They sat quietly for a while, hand in hand.

'I mean to go to my great-aunt in the west and learn about the Sight.'

'You cannot go alone.'

'I know.'

'Would you let me escort you?'

It was a possibility. And yet his declaration had changed things between them. 'I could use a good friend and companion. We'll talk when Fergus is better.'

She rose, and so did Hal. Without a word, he gently kissed her on the cheek, and then retreated to the kitchen. Margaret stepped into the hall, uncertain whether she should sleep or watch over her brother.

Dame Bridget sat snoring in a chair near him.

'She says he'll make it through the night, you can be sure of it.' said Celia as she rose from her stool beside Fergus.

'God be thanked,' said Margaret, crouching down to kiss her brother's forehead. She needed help rising.

'It's bed for you, Mistress,' said Celia, holding her firmly. 'You're worn to the bone.'

'Bless you, Celia, you are a blessing to me.'

Author's Note

My novels and lectures are often inspired by tantalising pieces of the past. In this series set in Scotland the pieces are often small fragments, or mere wisps of memory.

A braw wind blows across Soutra summit, and the view is spectacular. At the top is a small car park abutting a farmer's field. From there it's a short walk to a small stone building no larger than a garage. Called Soutra Aisle, it is believed to have been cobbled together with the remaining stones of the great Hospital of the Trinity at Soutra, an Augustinian establishment that once straddled the highway leading from the border north into Lothian and then west to Edinburgh. Beside it is an area posted with biological hazard warnings where a great drain was excavated packed with biological waste centuries old; it's possible that it was the sewer carrying waste from the infirmary. It provided the seed idea for Father Andrew's plan for escape from Soutra.

There is nothing left of the small, narrow bridge that crossed the Forth River below the town and castle of Stirling in 1297; archaeologists and historians are not even certain of its location. But the boggy ground is easily imagined along the old river as it almost curves back upon itself. When my husband was working on the maps for this book he commented that the pows and the carse were as good as siege engines for the Scots. This wasn't the only battle in which the wet lowlands just south of the Forth River benefited the Scots – Bannockburn was also won with help from this geographical phenomenon.

Standing atop Kinnoull Hill one can see a faint square scar in a farmer's field if one knows where to look – that's what is left of Elcho Nunnery. But the ruins of the Cistercian nunnery on Iona, hints from various archaeological digs, and educated guesses formulated with the assistance of my friend Kimm Perkins helped me recreate the small but lovely nunnery on the Tay. Stirling Castle and town are also mostly conjured from maps, contemporary accounts, and geological aspects that remain beneath newer buildings.

There are also people whose names and positions we know but who are never fleshed out in the narratives – I've included a few here: Abbot Adam, Sir Simon Montagu, Master Thomas of Soutra, Sir Marmaduke Twenge, and prioress Agnes de Arroch.

Even the phenomenon of Second Sight has proved tantalisingly elusive. I've listed Michael Hunter's book below, but even in that one book the record of Second Sight is contradictory. We have far better records of the Church mystics than we do of the lay seers. I've depicted them as parallel points on a continuum, not so different from one another.

We know more about the Battle of Stirling Bridge than the bridge itself. With their victory at Stirling Bridge the Scots proved themselves a force to be reckoned with, proving to King Edward that his progress around the country the previous summer had not subdued the resistance. Warenne, his lieutenant and thus chief commander in Scotland, and his treasurer, Cressingham, also underestimated the determination of the Scots. The treasurer had sent reinforcements back to England claiming they were too expensive. Andrew Murray and William Wallace had won back many of the northern castles and towns taken by the English, and in early September had gathered an army to the north of the River

Forth; the English seemed confident that they could win by virtue of their greater numbers alone. The following description is taken from Barrow (see Further Reading).

When Warenne reached Stirling he granted James Stewart and Earl Malcolm of Lennox a week to try to pacify the Scots. They returned on schedule to admit failure, but promised to appear with forty barded, or caparisoned, horses the following day – if they couldn't provide more men, they'd at least help equip the English. But as they rode off one of Lennox's men killed an English soldier. Warenne had difficulty calming his army. What I find amazing is that he overslept the next morning. Someone had already sent many of the infantry across the bridge over the Forth River, which was the only route across from where they had encamped, but they were recalled. Once Warenne rose, he sent them across again, but again they were recalled when Stewart and Lennox appeared. The two Scots nobles claimed they'd been unable to detach any of their own troops from Wallace and Murray. Warenne postponed the charge yet again to allow two Dominican friars to ask Wallace if he would yield. Wallace reportedly responded, 'Tell your commander that we are not here to make peace but to do battle to defend ourselves and liberate our kingdom. Let them come on, and we shall prove this in their very beards.'

When the Dominicans reported Wallace's reply, Cressingham rejected a knight's proposal to go with a detachment of horse upriver to the wide Fords of Drip where sixty men might cross the river at once and take up a position behind the Scots. Instead, Warenne gave the order to cross Stirling Bridge. Wallace and Murray swooped down on them when half of the English army had crossed, surrounding them while the other half were unable to cross the river to their aid. On the north side the carse was too soft on either side of the causeway for heavy horse. The result was a slaughter. Warenne, who had not crossed, escaped south; but Cressingham had ridden across and was torn to pieces by the

Scots. The Scots army also suffered casualties, including the mortal wounding of Murray, who never fully recovered and died that winter. (A more detailed description of the Battle is available on the website: www.bbc.co.uk/history/scottishhistory/independence/trails_independence_stirlingbridge.shtml)

Further Reading

Geoffrey W. S. Barrow, *Robert Bruce and the Community of the Realm of Scotland*. (Edinburgh University Press, 1988)

Elizabeth Ewan, *Townlife in Fourteenth-Century Scotland* (Edinburgh University Press, 1990)

Andrew Fisher, *William Wallace* (John Donald Publishers Ltd, 1986)

Michael Hunter, *The Occult Laboratory: Magic, Science and Second Sight in Late 17th-Century Scotland. A New Edition of Robert Kirk's The Secret Commonwealth and Other Texts* (The Boydell Press, 2001)

Perthshire Society of Natural Science, *Pitmiddle Village and Elcho Nunnery: Research and Excavation on Tayside*, undated.

Fiona Watson, *Under the Hammer: Edward I and Scotland 1286–1307* (Tuckwell Press, 1998)

An expanded list for the Margaret Kerr and Owen Archer mysteries is available on my website: www.candacerobb.com